Demon on the Down-Low

SUPERNATURAL SELECTION

E.J. Russell

Cover art: L.C. Chase https://lcchase.com
Editors: Carole-Ann Galloway, Rachel Haimowitz, Kelly Miller

ISBN: 978-1-947033-78-8

Second edition
March 2024

Contact information:
ejr@ejrussell.com

Demon on the Down-Low

SUPERNATURAL
SELECTION

E.J. Russell

For Mom.

GDM WLTM NS IRL no PDA

(Gay demon male would like to meet
non-smoker in real life; no public displays
of affection.)

Discretion a must (or there'll be hell to pay)

Supernatural
Selection

Chapter One

With every step down the dim corridor toward the rehearsal studio, Hamish's stomach knotted tighter. *Gods, I hate this.*

He used to be so chuffed for every rehearsal, for every concert, even for the miles on the road when Hunter's Moon couldn't cut through Faerie to their next gig. Because every minute was one more he could spend with *her*. Any minute might be the one when Tiff finally paused between one bass progression and the next, and glanced back at Hamish with love instead of annoyance.

Now? All those moments he used to cherish were nothing but torture, because Tiff was glancing with love, all right—at her wife. Or her boyfriend. Or both at once.

Bollocks.

But when he peeked in the studio door, the room was empty except for a tall, dark-haired fae stretched out on the studio's ratty orange sofa—and he wasn't even part of the band.

Hamish heaved a relieved sigh and sauntered into the room. "Oi, Niall. You looked better after you got pulled out of hell."

Niall McTierney, the band leader's boyfriend, didn't even flinch at Hamish's greeting. "It wasn't hell. It was the underworld. In Govannon's forge, to be exact. There's a difference."

Hamish tossed his backpack behind his drum kit. "Govannon's forge. Hades's joint beyond the Styx. Sheol. All of 'em sound like hell to me, so why muck about with different names?"

Niall didn't bother to open his eyes. "Try visiting each of them, and you won't ask that question. From what I've been told, compared to Sheol, the forge is a bloody picnic, and Hades's gloomy court is a four-star resort."

"Remind me to stay out of all of 'em." Hamish grabbed his drumsticks off the snare, then sat on the sofa arm, nudging Niall's legs out of the way so he could plant his feet on the threadbare cushion. "You didn't answer my question."

"You asked about underworld names. I answered."

"The question was implied. Why—" Hamish started to beat a double paradiddle against the sofa back "—do you look like shite?"

"Working on a case. It's kicking my arse. Now stop pounding on the furniture so I can sleep."

Niall's command was ridiculous, so Hamish ignored it. "A rehearsal studio's the wrong place for a nap, mate. Doesn't your brother"—he added the sole of Niall's boot into the beat—"the Faerie *Kiiinnng* have a spare room in that bloody great Keep of his? For that matter, what's wrong with your own house?"

"I'd like nothing better than my own house, but I haven't been home in thirty-six hours, and I've got approximately fifty-eight minutes before I have to meet an informant. I thought I'd use at least a few of those minutes to kiss my boyfriend before you lot start rehearsal. Unfortunately—" he cracked an eyelid and peered up at Hamish "—he's late. And so is everybody else. Except you." He closed his eyes again. "Imagine my joy."

"You know you love me. Who else would you get to go bungee jumping or cliff diving with you?" Hamish switched to a nine-stroke roll. "PI business is booming, eh?"

Niall grunted.

"Last I checked, you had a business partner. Isn't Mal pulling his weight, or does he look like five miles of bad road too?"

"I wouldn't know." Grimacing, Niall shifted his shoulders as if he were trying to find a more comfortable spot on the sofa. *Pointless, mate. You ought to know that by now.* "I told him I'd handle this one so he can get ready for his wedding."

Hamish missed a beat. *Weddings. Gah!* He gathered his sticks in one hand and forced a smirk that he hoped looked superior and not constipated. "Did you volunteer, or did Mal's fiancé threaten to put a druid curse on you if you made him work leading up to the ceremony?"

"It was my idea. But there might have been a druid curse looming on the horizon." Niall groaned, pressing the heels of his hands against his eyes. "If I'd known how much paperwork was involved in being a PI, I'd have turned the job down flat."

"Nah. You'd have taken it. When it comes to duty to the supernatural community, you're a goner. And Mal's just as bad or worse. Crusaders, the both of you." Hamish flipped a stick in the air. "Seeing you like this makes me glad I'm a care-for-nobody."

Niall snorted. "You care, all right. You just pretend otherwise."

Hamish fumbled the next stick toss, and it clattered to the floor. *Not talking about that. Not now. Not ever.* He retrieved his fallen stick, then got up and set the pair of them back on the snare on his way to the mini-fridge. "I thought you had that human photographer working for you? What's his name? Matt? Isn't *he* pulling his weight?"

"He's tied up on surveillance for this case, but he couldn't handle the paperwork anyway. He doesn't have the clearance."

"Then hire some bloody office help." Hamish grabbed a couple of waters out of the fridge. "Or is the supe council so stingy you can't afford it?"

"The council pays just fine, not that either of us need it. But Mal has unrealistic expectations of what office help should be. If he can't find someone who meets his sky-high standards, he says he'd rather go without."

"Easy for him to say." He dropped one bottle on Niall's belly, causing Niall to flinch—although he caught the bottle before it rolled onto the floor. "He's off gallivanting with his fiancé."

Niall pushed himself up and swung his feet to the floor. "If it was me getting married, I'd want the same." He cracked open the water and downed half of it in one go.

"Speaking of that . . . why *aren't* you and Gareth getting married? Isn't waiting two hundred years long enough?"

"I'm waiting for the right moment." Niall leaned his head against the sofa back, holding the water bottle upright on his belly. "Somehow, when the band is still touring and I'm barely conscious half the time and chasing an impossible target the rest, the ideal moment hasn't exactly presented itself. Besides"— he closed his bloodshot eyes—"I wouldn't want to steal the spotlight from Bryce and Mal, and neither would Gareth. When you spent two hundred years being a dick to your brothers, you've got a lot of arrears to make up."

When Niall had first shown up again after a couple centuries of being MIA, Hamish hadn't trusted him. What kind of idiot bloke would abandon the love of his life—who actually loved him back—and do a runner? If Tiff had ever given Hamish the least hint that she was interested, he'd have been her slave for life.

He still was, worse luck. But at least he and Niall were mates now.

"Hmmm. Seems to me you need a break. How about we head out after rehearsal and do some bungee jumping?"

"Are you mental? It's February." He peered at Hamish through slitted lids. "Not that you'd know by your outfit."

Hamish waved the comment away. "Shifters run hot. Come on, Niall. It's winter in Portland, but you're fae. You can gate us through Faerie in the twinkling of a kelpie's eye and we could be in midsummer in Cairns."

"You do realize," Niall said, tapping one finger against his water bottle in a non-rhythm that set Hamish's teeth on edge, "that someday Gareth is going to find out about those trips and he'll go ballistic on our asses?"

Hamish shrugged and took a swig of his own water. "You were tied up in hell for a couple centuries. Can you blame him for wanting you to be safe?"

Niall cocked an eyebrow at him. "It's not me he's worried about, boyo. He knows *I* do that daredevil shite. He just doesn't know I do it with you."

"Me? Why would it matter whether I—"

"Aside from the fact that you're his friend, and have had his back in some of his worst times—" Niall winced "—including ones that I caused myself, you're the drummer in his band. It'd be a little hard for Hunter's Moon to hit their tour stops if your arms—or other bits—were broken."

Hamish's fist tightened on the water. "My other bits are nobody's business." Literally. Nobody was interested in his other bits, least of all the person he really wanted to be interested in them. "They could fall off from atrophy and nobody would care."

Niall scrunched his face. "I'm not talking about *those* bits, you wanker. I mean your legs, your head, your back. Although . . ." He tossed his empty water bottle into the recycling bin. "Maybe we should talk about them."

"How about we don't?" Hamish put a little don't-fuck-with-me into his tone while he ditched his water and grabbed his drumsticks off the snare. "Gotta warm up."

He should have known Niall wouldn't listen. The mad bloke had spent two hundred years resisting torture to keep Gareth safe. He knew how to persist, damn it.

"She's worried about you, you know."

"Tiff? Yeah. So worried she can't help but glow with bleeding happiness. Do you know how weird that is? She's always been nearly as surly as Gareth was gloomy."

"Trust me. I'm aware. I thought she might remove my spleen when I first showed up here. But some people are capable of being happy and worried simultaneously. Tiff's not exactly shallow."

Hamish counted off on the snare rim, but couldn't make himself go any further. He laid the sticks on one of the toms.

"She's always there, Niall, just like she always was. I always had hope before, you know? That maybe one day she'd turn around and say, 'There he is.'" Hamish ran a finger along the snare rim. "Except every time she turned around it was to tell me to sod off for something. And now when she turns, she never gets more than halfway because her wife is standing in the wings." He flicked the hi-hat with a fingernail. "Her wife or her boyfriend. Her wife's *brother*. I mean, come on—twins? How the bleeding fuck could I ever compete with that?"

"I heard"—Niall's tone turned tentative—"that Vitor asked you out."

Hamish snorted. "No. Not just no. *Hell* no."

"Not into blokes? Or not into the poly thing?"

"It's not that. I mean, I'm not picky." *Except I've been in love with the same person for decades.* "But if you're in love with somebody, the last thing you should do is hook up with their friend. Or worse, their boyfriend. You're too close and not close enough at the same time."

"Ah. That makes sense, I guess."

"Don't get me wrong. I like Luci. Who wouldn't? I mean she's probably the nicest person—certainly the nicest jaguar shifter—on the planet. And Vitor is fucking hot, not to mention a little bit nuts, which would be attractive on anybody who *wasn't* Tiff's boyfriend. But I can't."

Niall stood up and strolled over to stand in front of the bass drum. "So date somebody else."

"You got somebody in your back pocket? Because I haven't found anybody else who'd—"

"You haven't found anybody else because you haven't looked. You've been focused on Tiff." Niall lifted a hand, as if he'd pat Hamish on the shoulder if the kit weren't in the way.

But then he let it drop. "And she's out of reach, boyo. She always was."

Hamish sighed. "I know. But I need time to process."

"I get it. But you may not have the time."

"What do you mean?"

"The wedding's next week. You planning to be the only unattached member of Hunter's Moon at the festivities?"

Hamish felt the blood leaving his head. "Bollocks."

Niall pulled a business card from his pocket and held it out. "Here."

Hamish took the card between a thumb and forefinger. "What's this?"

"Supernatural Selection. Matchmaking agency for supes."

Hamish scowled at the card. "Why do you have something like that? Planning to ditch Gareth, are you?"

Niall chuckled, completely unperturbed. "Not hardly. I've only just gotten him back. No, this case is connected to them. It's run by a witches' collective, and the matches are facilitated by spells—guaranteed perfect. As I understand it, they've got a range of services, including short-term casual contracts. They can find you a date for the wedding. Somebody you can have a good time with, even if you say 'so long' after the last bite of cake."

Hamish studied the logo—a stylized frontward and backward S, forming a heart. "Perfect you say?"

"That's their brand. Although they've had a bit of a scare recently."

"Related to your case? What's the deal?"

Niall shrugged apologetically. "Can't say."

"Right. Snoop-client privilege."

"We're investigators. Not snoops."

"You're supe snoops. Own it, mate."

A laugh echoed in the hall outside the practice room. *Tiff.* Tiff laughing. The sound curled in Hamish's chest and squeezed his heart until he gasped.

He tucked the card into his back pocket. "Guaranteed perfect matches?"

"That's what they say."

Tiff strolled into the room with her arm around Luci's waist, Vitor grinning down at her. Vitor caught Hamish's eye and winked.

Strewth. "Good." The fates knew Hamish hadn't had any luck finding his own match. If he couldn't have Tiff, it didn't much matter who it was.

As soon as Vitor cleared the door, Spence and Josh entered together, although it must have been one of Josh's days where he didn't want to be touched, because Spence was close but not in actual contact. But the way they looked at each other—as if they didn't need anybody else to be happy . . .

Then Gareth walked in, frowning down at the sheet music in his hands. But the instant he glanced up and saw Niall, his face lit up like the sun, and he walked straight into Niall's arms.

All this love. It's enough to make me hurl.

Hamish didn't need love. Love did nothing but kick you in the bollocks. But a match? A partner? A mate?

Yeah. He could go for that. Because he was done being alone.

Chapter Two

I wonder what it's like to be able to go wherever you want.

Zeke parted the curtains of his apartment's living room and peered at the humans on the street five floors below. Sure, some of them were striding down the sidewalk as they scowled at their phones, or were huddled in their jackets against the wind that flipped their hair, but far more of them were laughing, smiling, chatting with friends, or peering into the windows of the Pearl District's eclectic storefronts.

As a demon on the pilot Sheol work-release program, Zeke wasn't allowed abroad in the Upper World. Although he could use the translocation door on the fourth floor of the building that housed Supernatural Selection's office to access other supernatural realms, he was forbidden to walk out the front door.

Even being allowed down on the first floor would be nice. On peril of his work visa, he couldn't go below the second floor where his office was located, but the aromas wafting from the street-level falafel restaurant regularly tempted him to the edge of his endurance. And sometimes the distant laughter of the people in the street was so joyful that it lifted his heart—something he could never confess.

After all, demons weren't supposed to have hearts, any more than they were supposed to have souls. *At least not our own.*

Zeke sighed and rested his palm against the window pane, the glass chilly against his warmer-than-human skin. It was nearly time for his Supernatural Selection shift, and it was bound to be boring as, well, hell. He had no client appointments, and hadn't for weeks, not since the Johnson/Moreau . . . thing.

He still wasn't sure how that had happened. There was no way a shifter, however inactive, should have been the perfect match for a vampire—and Zeke could have sworn that they had nothing in common whatsoever, had never even *met*. Yet the spell had not only allowed their contract when Rusty Johnson had waltzed in and proposed the match, it also refused to return any other alternatives for either one of them. In the resultant uproar from both the vampire and shifter communities—none of which seemed to bother Mr. Johnson or Mr. Moreau in the least—the witches' collective who owned the agency had bowed to the pressure and taken the spells offline for "evaluation."

None of the other counselors had had such peculiar results. Of course, none of the other counselors were still in training. *None of them are demons either.* And *they'd* all been granted indefinite paid leave—the vampire-shifter boycott had seriously reduced Supernatural Selection's client pool.

But Zeke didn't have the option of leaving. Unless he wanted to admit defeat and return to Sheol, he was stuck in this building, on effective house arrest, not to mention double probation: Magistra Lenore, the director of the collective, was conducting her own evaluation, both of Zeke's general performance, and of how he'd managed to subvert the spell.

I didn't mean to subvert it. It just happened.

He doubted Magistra Lenore would accept that particular excuse, despite how eloquently Quentin Bertrand-Harrington, the incubus whose match had been the first to implode, had argued that the spell was merely correcting itself.

Even self-correction didn't explain how Rusty Johnson, the inactive beaver shifter who was supposed to be mated with bear shifter Ted Farnsworth, had finagled a match with vampire Casimir Moreau.

Everyone knew that vampires and shifters were inimical. How on earth had the spell not rejected *that* particular pairing, regardless of the clients' wishes?

And that was the question, wasn't it? If the spell could misfire so wildly, yet result in two apparently mismatched couples who were both deliriously happy, how on *earth* had it been accomplished? Since it *shouldn't* have been possible for it to be accomplished on earth, the witches' hypothesis was that other forces must be at work.

Forces like the alleged insidious evil agenda of the first demon allowed out of Sheol since a succubus and her dragon shifter mate defied the high presidents of Sheol and founded the first Upper World 'cubi dynasty eons ago.

Yeah, the Sheol C-suite demons were still pissed about that. And since time didn't mean much when you were immortal, they really knew how to carry a grudge.

A yellow glow shimmered on the window in front of Zeke, blurring his view of the street. Letting the curtains fall shut, he turned to face his mandated monitor: an angel interface, manifesting as a pillar of supercilious light, that was his constant shadow. Assuming light could be a shadow.

Whatever.

"What is it now?" The AI flared magenta at Zeke's wrist level. "I am not late. My appointment with Magistra Lenore isn't until six." Green edged the magenta in a double pulse. *Not a good color combination.* "Why? There's no point in going down early. She won't see me until six, and there's nothing to do in the office. I've already notified all the clients that their matches are on hold." The green crept outward in amoeba-like tendrils. "Just because you're bored up here—"

"Haven't you learned by now that arguing with one of the angelic host is pointless for someone like you?"

Zeke whirled to see Melchom, his Sheol supervisor, standing in the kitchen doorway, wearing a black cutaway morning coat, white shirt, and gray trousers, his chin-length hair slicked back under a top hat. *Channeling the Edwardian era today.* You never knew with Melchom. He monitored the time stream from the turn of the last century forward, and complained bitterly that it was boring at the same time he complained that no other supervisor was responsible for more than a single century and he was approaching a century and a quarter.

"Supervisor. To what do I owe the p-pleasure? It's not time for a check-in."

Melchom stepped out of a circle of brimstone dust. *I'll have to vacuum again.* "Demons live for chaos. Such paltry things as schedules are for the lower orders." He glanced dismissively at the AI. "Or for priggish *rule followers.*" The AI pulsed gold. "Oh shut up, you self-righteous git. You can't hope to win a curse war with an upper-echelon demon, no matter how successfully you've managed to neuter Ozul-y—"

"Zeke. Please." Zeke glanced around furtively, never sure what kind of surveillance spells might be in effect in the apartment. It was owned by the witches' collective, after all. "Here in the Upper World, I'm Zeke Oz."

"Don't be so skittish, boy." Melchom settled in the wingback chair in the corner, crossing his legs and folding his hands in his lap. "No demon has been summoned by name since 1999. Practitioners can get anything they want now from Amazon without resorting to blood sacrifice."

"That doesn't mean we should be careless with our names. If anyone should—"

Melchom's eyes flared red. He might dress like a British MP from 1906, but he was still a demon—even if he was only in charge of Sheol's civil service. "Don't question me." His voice reverberated in the cramped room. "Regardless of this ridiculous program, you are still my minion."

Zeke bowed his head. "Of course, Supervisor. Forgive me. I meant no disrespect."

"That's better." Melchom's voice returned to normal, and Zeke dared look up. "Now. You." He made a shooing motion at the AI. "Go away." The AI sparked like a downed power line. "Nonsense. You're not required to monitor him when *I'm* here. Get out." Melchom narrowed his eyes. "Unless you want me to report you to *your* supervisor. Regardless of your pompous attitude, the only difference between the demonic and angelic hosts is one of relative address."

The AI slunk toward its own bedroom, with a final flash of indigo before it slammed the door.

"I saw that," Melchom called. "Don't flip off a demon lord unless you're ready to face the consequences." He shook his head. "Really. If it weren't so irritating—and therefore a perfect sort of torture—I'd lodge a protest against that creature for insubordination."

Zeke twisted his fingers together, uncertain of whether he was allowed to sit in Melchom's presence this time. "It doesn't consider itself under our jurisdiction, you know."

"Yes. Isn't it amusing?" Melchom steepled his fingers, tapping them against his thin lips. "I'm extremely disappointed in you."

Zeke hung his head. "I'm sorry, Supervisor. As I told the magistra, I don't know what happened to cause the spell to misfire. I did everything according to protocol, but—"

"Not *that*, you fool, although that's part of the problem. Have you learned *nothing* from me in the last centuries about the lovely stultifying effects of bureaucracy? You're not supposed to be *efficient*. And you're definitely not supposed to exceed their expectations. Those disasters were the only things you actually did *right*, and then you had to ruin everything by *fixing* them."

Zeke blinked. "You can't mean . . . Surely you didn't *want* me to fail?"

"Your personal failure or success is irrelevant." Melchom's mouth pinched. "But you're a demon. We make people *miserable*, not happy."

Zeke was well aware of that, but he'd never enjoyed tormenting humans, supes, or other demons, for that matter.

That was one of the reasons he'd jumped at the chance for the work-release program. He'd been surprised that so few other volunteers had stepped forward. He'd expected to have to fight for the opportunity, but instead he'd had no opposition whatsoever. Even the AI had had to be recruited. *Maybe that's why it's such a jerk all the time.*

"But then why place me here?"

"Don't be naive." Melchom's contemptuous gaze nearly cut Zeke to the bone. "Nothing makes people more miserable than love." He folded his hands on his knee. "Since I'm here anyway, I'll accept my tribute now."

"But—"

"Don't make me scourge you, boy."

Zeke sighed and shuffled to the bookshelf to take down a wooden box with a protection sigil carved on the lid. "I wasn't expecting you until next payday, Supervisor, so I don't have much left. I had to buy groceries."

Melchom tutted. "You see how ridiculous this is? If you were still in Sheol—your *proper* place, need I remind you—you wouldn't need to eat."

Not true. Well, he might not *need* to eat, but he'd still be hungry. All low-level demons like Zeke were. It was one of the ways the upper echelon demons controlled them. Occasionally feeling almost full was an unexpected bonus of living in the Upper World.

"Mainstreaming demons into the Upper World supe community is important. The council said—"

"The council. Pfaugh!" Melchom snorted, smoke curling out his nostrils, and held out his hand with its perfectly manicured claws. "Why would we want to be mainstreamed? Hedged in with rules, regulations, and ridiculous secrecy constraints. Homogenized like the dynastic 'cubi. Virtually castrated like the vampires. Even that annoying AI has its wings clipped when it's here. And why? Because the *council* is too fainthearted to exercise their true power and put humans squarely where they belong." He grinned, displaying his pointed teeth and equally pointed tongue. "At the bottom of the food chain."

Zeke's fist closed around the small handful of bills and coins. "You don't really, um, *eat* them. Do you?"

"Not their flesh. That would be . . ." His snout wrinkled in distaste. "Unappetizing. But the brush of their anguish? The sweetness of their guilt? The tang of their despair? Delicious." He waggled his fingers. "Hurry up. I don't have all day. The inhuman resources department is undergoing an audit today, and there'll undoubtedly be lashes to hand out."

Zeke offered the money. "I'm sorry there's not more, Supervisor."

Melchom rolled his eyes. "Don't be an idiot. You know I can't accept that currency."

"If you'll wait a moment, I'll ask the AI to convert it."

Melchom waved one hand as if trying to dissipate a bad smell. "Not now. My stomach couldn't stand it. Have it ready for me next time." He lifted his lip, exposing a fang. "And I expect you to have the full measure by then. Perhaps fashioned into a tasteful golden calf. I'm in the mood for a little gratuitous idolatry."

"But the witches don't pay me that much. And the conversion rate is—"

"Then you'd best find a way to supplement your income." Melchom bared his teeth fully. "The only reason the overlords agreed to this ridiculous arrangement is because they thought it would benefit them. If it doesn't . . ." He shrugged. "We'll shut it down and put you back where you belong—firmly under my hoof."

Before Zeke could properly abase himself, Melchom vanished in a puff of smoke reeking of sulfur. Zeke coughed, staggering to the window to open it and clear the air.

When he turned around, the AI was looming in the middle of the room in a sullen swirl of turquoise and ochre, still flashing random sparks.

Zeke scowled as he set the box back on the shelf. "He sends you out of the room because he doesn't like you." A bolt of pink shot through the light pillar. "Yes, I'm aware the feeling is mutual." He slapped his money into the obsidian crucible on the coffee table. "Could you convert that for me, please?"

Green infused the AI as it drifted over the table.

"Yeah, yeah. I know. Take your cut." When the pillar retreated, the crucible held a gold nugget no bigger than Zeke's pinkie fingernail. He peered at it, then fixed the AI with a narrow-eyed glare. "That's not—" The AI flared white on one side, illuminating the clock. *Five minutes to six? Shit.* "You know what? Never mind."

He grabbed his tie off the back of the barstool and raced out the door. Some days he'd almost prefer Sheol to being saddled with an angel.

Chapter Three

Hamish eyed Niall, who was sauntering along the sidewalk next to him, hands in his pockets, glancing around with a half smile on his face. "You know, mate, you don't need to escort me. I always keep my appointments. I'm not about to skive off the Supernatural Selection *orientation*—" Hamish made air quotes with his fingers, even though he hated people who did that. "Not after filling out that bloody questionnaire online. I thought you said the whole thing was handled with spells."

Niall blinked at Hamish as if he'd just noticed he was there. "What? Oh. They are. Usually. But they've had a couple of—" Niall squinted into the air, head tilted to one side as if he were listening to something, then smothered a laugh. "Let's say irregularities."

Hamish cocked an eyebrow. "That's not what you were about to say. Come on. Spill."

"It's not me. It's—" Niall rubbed the back of his neck with a grimace. "Gareth ever mention the *ethera* to you?"

"If it's something you two get up to in bed— Ow!" Hamish rubbed his arm where Niall had punched it.

"Nothing close, arsehole. Show some respect. No, they're . . . spirits for lack of a better word. Sort of a supernatural interface between realms. Since I was out of pocket for so long, they try to be helpful. Kind of like supplying subtitles for popular culture."

"So you hear voices?"

He sighed. "I do. Whether I want to or not."

"Yeah? So what'd they say about the Supernatural Selection situation?"

Niall's mouth quirked in a crooked smile. "They very obligingly referred to it as a fuckup."

Hamish barked a laugh. "Oh that's grand. You recommended me to a shite matchmaking agency? What, I don't rate one that does a decent job?"

"Oh, they did a decent job despite the *irregularity*." Niall emphasized the word to the air at large, which was just weird. "Two of the most successful matches in recent years, even though nobody—including the men involved—would have believed it to begin with."

Huh. Maybe if this place could snatch success out of the maw of fuckup, they could do something to fix his sorry-ass social life. "So why are you visiting? If you're thinking of cheating on Gareth—"

"Don't be an idiot. I'm interviewing the collective's director for the case." His brow puckered. "There's something dodgy going on, and the witches want Quest Investigations to prove it wasn't a problem with their spellcraft." Niall stopped in front of a glass door between a Mediterranean restaurant and a new age-y bookstore.

"Think you can do it?"

Niall shrugged and opened the door. "Not if the problem really *was* with the spellcraft."

Hamish followed Niall into the building and up a staircase. "You're not filling me with confidence here, mate."

"Can't help that." He gestured to a door with the Supernatural Selection logo on it. "This is your stop. Good luck." Niall continued up another flight of stairs.

"Luck," Hamish muttered. "Shite. I don't need luck. I need a bloody miracle."

He pushed the door open, the slight tingle as he passed the threshold a tip-off that the place was secured by perimeter spells. The empty reception area wasn't particularly big—*guess they're not hosting speed dating for trolls*—and the decor screamed *Pleasant! Tranquil! Intimate!* in a way that set Hamish's teeth on edge. He was a drummer, sod it. He didn't do pleasant or tranquil or gods-help-him intimate.

The reception desk at the end of the room was vacant. *No clients and no staff.* Not exactly a ringing endorsement for the Supernatural Selection brand.

"Oi! Anybody home?"

A weird golden light spilled from an archway behind the desk, and a moment later, a man with a mop of dark curls hurried into the room. He blinked big dark eyes behind wire-framed spectacles that glinted with some kind of obvious spell, and Hamish didn't need to be the Oracle of Delphi to tell the guy was frazzled to within an inch of his pert little arse.

"I'm so sorry no one was here to greet you." His smile was clearly forced. "I was waiting to meet with Magistra Lenore, our director."

Hamish grinned. The guy was just so cute. "Yeah? About anything interesting?"

"Yes. No. I mean, well, you, I suppose."

"You're saying I'm not interesting?" Hamish slapped a hand over his heart. "I'm crushed. Although impressed by your instant insight. I mean, we've barely met. Usually folks wait until they've known me at least an hour before they figure that out."

The guy's lips twitched, as if he were about to smile for real, but then a pillar of dingy yellow light as big around as Hamish's bass drum oozed out the door behind him.

The hairs lifted on Hamish's arms and the nape of his neck. *Settle down. It's a pillar of light.* Hamish was used to lighting effects—he was a bloody rock musician, and Hunter's Moon demanded state-of-the-art tech—but that much wattage without an instrument to generate it kicked his kangaroo instincts into fight mode.

The guy must have felt it too, because as soon as the light cast his shadow onto the desk, his almost-smile disappeared and he seemed to shrink at least two inches. "I beg your pardon. I meant no disrespect."

"Hey. It was a joke, mate. No worries." Hamish extended his hand. "Hamish Mulherne."

The guy shot a sidelong glance at the light, and reached across the desk. "Welcome to Supernatural Selection, Mr. Mulherne." He took Hamish's hand, and a prickle of some kind of power raised Hamish's hair a little more—but not in a bad way. "I'm Zeke. Zeke Oz."

"Oz, eh? Then we'll get along fine."

Zeke blinked. "We will? Why?"

"Oz. You know. That's a nickname for Australia."

"Oh. Of course." Zeke's tongue flicked out to lick his lower lip. "Mr. Mulherne, I'm afraid—"

"Hamish."

"What?"

"Call me Hamish. I don't stand on ceremony. Ever."

"A-all right. Hamish, I'm afraid there's been a misunderstanding. Well, not a misunderstanding so much as an oversight. Or rather, not an oversight, but a . . . a scheduling difficulty?"

Hamish grinned. "You trying to say somebody bollixed something up?"

Zeke blew out a breath. "Yes." The light turned greenish, like it had been hit with a vomit-colored filter. "I mean no. But Supernatural Selection is not currently accepting new clients, nor arranging matches for our current clientele. I'm not sure how your intake appointment slipped by. I've been contacting all our clients personally over the last few days, and I deactivated the intake website myself. How— If I may ask, how did you arrange this appointment?"

"Me? The usual way, I reckon. I got your card from a mate of mine who's doing a spot of work for your witches. Hit the website. Filled out the form. Got an email with the appointment time."

Zeke's eyes widened. "You— The website— But that's impossible." He turned to his computer and typed something, his fingers moving almost too fast to see. *What kind of supe is this guy anyway?* He pointed to the webpage on the monitor. "You see?"

The screen read *Our sincere apologies, but our site is down for maintenance.*

Hamish shrugged. "Don't know what to tell you, mate. That's what happened, and here I am. Can we move forward?"

"But that's just the thing. We *can't* move forward because the matchmaking spells have all been dismantled." He waved a hand at the screen. "For . . . for maintenance."

"Need a bit of dusting and vacuuming, do they? A little spit and polish?"

Zeke's eyebrows drew together. "Of course not. There were a few incidents that—" Dark-blue sparks flashed inside the bilious light, and Zeke flinched. "The reasons are immaterial. Suffice it to say that Supernatural Selection is committed to finding the perfect match for each of our clients. When our spellcasters discover ways to enhance the process—"

"Make the matches more perfect? How does that work out?"

"Not more perfect. Of course not. But to streamline the process. To—to—"

"To not bollix it up?"

Zeke's nostrils flared, and red glowed in the depths of his eyes for an instant. "That's not what I said."

"Relax, mate. I know you lot had some . . . what did Niall call it? Oh yeah. *Irregularities.*"

Zeke's already pale skin drained of all color, and he sank into his chair. "You know? Does everyone know? Is it public?"

Hamish sat down on the other side of the desk and held up his hands, palms out. "He didn't spill any details. In fact, he kept it close to his vest, so don't get your knickers in a twist. But since he's the one who recommended I sign up with you, he can't think it's too bad, eh?"

Zeke glanced over his shoulder at the light before meeting Hamish's gaze as if he were facing the guillotine. "No. I suppose not."

Hamish tilted his head, squinting at the turquoise tendrils snaking through the light. If a column of light could look smug, this one did. What the hell was that thing? "If you don't mind my asking, what's up with the lighting effects?" Hamish flicked a finger at the effect in question.

"Lighting eff—" Zeke glanced over his shoulder. "Oh. That's the AI."

"AI. Artificial intelligence?"

"No. Angel interface."

Hamish snorted. "Right."

"No. Seriously. The angelic host can't interact directly with beings on this plane of existence without risking contamination."

"Contamination of who? Us or them?"

The AI pulsed red, and splotches bloomed on Zeke's cheeks to match. "Um . . ."

Hamish chuckled. "It just said something rude, didn't it?" Zeke's expression turned bland, which was a dead giveaway as far as Hamish was concerned. "Don't worry. I won't ask for a translation. But why were you inflicted with a sentient follow spot anyway?"

Zeke tugged on his shirt collar. "It's required."

"Why? A safety measure in case the lights go out? Couple of flashlights could handle that."

"No. I— I'm a demon. As part of the pilot Sheol work-release program, I'm required to have an AI observer at all times."

"Fuck me dead." Hamish leaned forward in his chair, his foot searching vainly for his bass pedal, because if ever he needed to pound on something . . . "You're joking, right?"

Zeke half rose from his seat. "If you'd rather not work with a demon, I understand. I can—"

Hamish lunged across the desk and caught his wrist. "That's not the fucked-up part, mate. Hells, I've played on the same bill as Death Metal Porcupines. Nothing could be worse than that. I mean they're treating you like a prisoner, and this thing is your bloody guard."

Zeke sank back in his chair, his gaze focused on Hamish's hand. "It's for everyone's safety and comfort."

"That's what the bloody Victorians said about the poor blighters they shipped off to Botany Bay." He released Zeke's wrist. "And if you don't mind my saying, you don't look all that comfortable."

Zeke's lips twitched again. "Compared to Sheol, *anything* is more comfortable. Now, back to the issue at hand. Without the matchmaking spells, we're not able to provide you with our normal services, so—"

"So provide me with different ones."

Zeke's mouth dropped open. "We—we don't have any different ones. Our brand is to provide your perfect match."

Hamish leaned an elbow on the desk. "Look. I don't need perfect. In fact, I don't believe in perfect." *Rather, I know who my perfect would have been, but she's permanently unavailable.* "I just want someone who'll do. You know what I'm saying?"

"That's not really what—"

"Look, mate. You said you've been calling people for days telling them to put their dreams on hold. Aren't you tired of that?"

Zeke rolled his eyes. "You have no idea."

"Then look at this as a treat. I'm not picky. You know something about your clients, am I right?"

"Yeeesss." Zeke couldn't have sounded any more uncertain if he'd tried.

"Then find me a partner." Hamish leaned back in his chair, rested one ankle on the opposite knee, and laid down a single stroke roll on his thigh with his fingers. "There's absolutely no way you can screw this up, because I know going in that perfect is a giant load of shite."

Zeke goggled at the big kangaroo shifter across from him, whose grin caused a dimple to crease one cheek under his golden scruff. Supernatural Selection forbade him from contradicting a client outright, but . . .

"You . . . you don't think love is real?" Zeke wanted to demand that Hamish hold still and stop that driving rhythm that set up an odd resonance in Zeke's chest. Sheol was all about the chaotic and unexpected. Zeke wasn't used to organized, structured rhythms, and the sound made it hard for him to think.

"I didn't say that. Love's obviously real. But it's not perfect. And it's not symmetrical. One bloke can be in love up to his eyeballs, but the one he's arse over teakettle for?" Hamish shrugged, but didn't stop hammering on his thigh. "Maybe up to their ankles. Or worse, maybe up to their eyeballs over some other person." He scowled. "Or persons."

Clearly there's a story there. If the spells were still active, Zeke was certain Hamish's mind would be changed regardless of his backstory, because Supernatural Selection could absolutely find him the perfect mate. Not that the perfect mate guaranteed love necessarily, but ever since Zeke had been a counselor-in-training here, it had happened every single time.

Even when it shouldn't have. The Johnson/Moreau pairing was inexplicable, yes, but he still got hot behind his eyes when he thought of the Farnsworth/Bertrand-Harrington disaster. Yet that had turned into one of the most successful marriages in the supe community, judging by the way the two men doted on one another.

But Zeke's past mistakes were immaterial right now. The main thing at this moment was to convince Hamish Mulherne to postpone his search for a match until after the spell was back online—and until Zeke could figure out not only how Hamish had accessed the website in the first place, but how he'd been able to opt out of entering any match preferences. It was almost as if the spell had still been in effect.

If only he'd stop that distracting *sound*.

"Mr. Mulherne—"

"Hamish."

Zeke took a breath. *"Mr. Mulherne, I'm* not entirely certain why, if you don't believe in . . . in symmetrical love, or in the possibility of a perfect match, you've chosen to seek out our services."

"That's obvious, innit? You lot are in the business of pairing people up. I'm unpaired."

"Just to be clear—you don't believe in love or in a perfect match, yet you still want to be paired?"

"That's it. Shouldn't be too hard, right? Like I said, I'm not picky."

"Don't you think you ought to be?" Zeke couldn't help the edge of annoyance in his tone. *If you're not picky, go hit the Bullpen.* Surely the shifter bar could provide plenty of choices for the non-discriminating.

Hamish's brows snapped down and—thank Lucifer—his fingers stilled. "What's that supposed to mean?"

"Don't you think you should at least *consider* what—or rather who—would make you happy long-term? And how you'll make your partner happy as well? The match involves at least two people. You can't expect the other party to do all the work and make all the sacrifices simply because you're lazy."

The AI jerked forward, its nimbus enveloping Zeke's shoulder, and a shock passed through his body. Zeke's eyes clenched shut, his muscles seizing. *Pain!* Then it vanished as the AI backed away—although not as far as it had been before— while Zeke panted in the aftermath. *Yeah, yeah. I get it. No being rude to the client, even if we want him to leave.*

When he opened his eyes, Hamish was half out of his chair, reaching across the desk. "You okay, mate? Need a bit of a lie-down? Should I call someone? Get you some water?"

"No. No, I'm fine. Just a . . . momentary, er, glitch."

"A glitch, eh? You sure? You're still looking a tad rocky."

"I'll be all right. But could you excuse me for a moment?"

"No worries, mate. Take your time." Hamish sat back down and began that distracting drumming again as Zeke stood up and escaped the lobby.

The AI, of course, followed.

Zeke refused to look at it as he nearly ran toward the private staircase to Magistra Lenore's office. "I know I shouldn't have been cheeky, but you heard him. He doesn't want perfect. There's no way we can make him happy." The AI pulsed a sullen, faded indigo. "That's easy for you to say. Do you know the problem with somebody who doesn't know how to ask for what they want?" He pointed a finger at where the AI's chest would be if it were an actual person. "They'll *never* get it. Because they wouldn't recognize it if it bit them in the ass."

He turned and ran the rest of the way up the stairs. Magistra Lenore's door was open and he didn't hear voices. The fae who'd appropriated Zeke's scheduled meeting time with her must have left. Zeke took his courage in his hands, ignoring the AI's snarky magenta flashes, and peered inside. She was standing at the window, her back to the door.

"Magistra? Could I have a moment?"

"This is not a good time." She didn't turn. "Tomorrow."

"I'm sorry, but this can't really wait."

She sighed heavily and turned, her face morphing from Crone to Maiden without passing through Mother. But then, Magistra Lenore wasn't the Mother type. "Then be quick."

"There's a prospective client downstairs. Somehow he was able to register and obtain an appointment even though—"

"You informed me that you had disabled the registration software." Her face slipped toward Crone again.

"Yes. I did. However—"

"And took the appointment scheduler offline."

"Of course. But—"

"Then the problem is yours to resolve."

Zeke's palms grew damp, something that never happened outside the deepest recesses of Sheol—demons were very heat resistant. *But not panic resistant, apparently.* "Magistra, how can we—" She shot him a look. "I mean how can *I* find his perfect match without the spells? If we— If *I* don't succeed, it will reflect poorly on the Supernatural Selection brand."

"No, Mr. Oz. It will reflect poorly on the success of the Sheol work-release program. This is your last opportunity to prove you shouldn't be sent packing and the entire experiment shut down as a failure. You've made error after error, and I have to ask whether those errors were intentional."

Zeke's stomach plummeted. "Wh-wh-what?"

"Demons are well-known to thrive on chaos and strife, to seek it out, to engender it in others in an attempt to ensnare souls since they own none of their own. What better way to cause strife than by interfering with love?"

Has she been talking to Melchom? "I swear to you, Magistra, that I never—"

"Do not swear." Her face was fully Crone again, and pitiless. "Vows taken in this place hold a power you, as someone who is unused to our magic, can never comprehend. You have one chance to save the program." She raised one grizzled eyebrow. "To save yourself. Make Hamish Mulherne happy, whatever it takes." She turned back to the window. "Now leave me."

"But—"

"Are you stupid as well as incompetent? Go!"

Zeke went, the AI bouncing along at his side as if it were skipping, glowing a smug electric pink. "Shut up. Nobody likes hearing 'I told you so.'"

Although Zeke kept his tone sharp, inside he was quaking like a gelatinous mound. Thank Darkness that the AI couldn't read minds, because if it knew how terrified Zeke was, he'd never hear the end of it.

The AI flashed yellow.

"I'm coming. Keep your shirt on." Zeke trudged down the stairs. "Assuming you have a shirt," he muttered. "Or a chest to put it on." Turquoise bloomed inside the yellow. "Yeah, yeah. I'm sure you're a paragon of angelic beauty. Pardon me if I don't believe it until I see it. The angelic host's benchmarks don't exactly align with the demonic, you know." Silver joined the turquoise. "Well, that suits me too, so don't gloat."

He forced one foot in front of the other. *This is a disaster.* The entire fate of the work-release program lay on his shoulders, on his ability to find a perfect match for a man who wouldn't articulate his definition of perfect, who didn't believe in perfect, who didn't even know what perfect *meant.*

No pressure. I just need to find what Hamish Mulherne is looking for and when I can't, it'll bite me in the ass. In other words, he'd have his old life back and he'd do anything to avoid that. If he couldn't make Hamish happy—

Wait a minute . . .

Zeke froze, the AI bouncing past him. Magistra Lenore hadn't said Zeke had to make Hamish a perfect match—only to make him happy. That was splitting hairs perhaps, but she was right about the power of words within the confines of the Supernatural Selection building.

She's given me an out.

Now all he had to do was figure out how to take it without jeopardizing his job, his life in the Upper World, and his nonexistent soul.

Chapter Four

Judging by Zeke's stiff gait and the way he was gritting his teeth as he sat in his chair, someone must have inserted a steel pipe up his arse. "I'm sorry for the delay. I had to check on a few things with the management."

"Like I said, no worries." Hamish took his leg-drumming in another direction, switching to a Swiss Army triplet. "Moving on?"

"Yes. Of course." Zeke turned to his computer, his fingers poised over his keyboard. "Perhaps you can tell me why you've decided to contact Supernatural Selection at this time."

"Told you. I'm unpaired. I want to fix that."

"And the reason you've chosen to use a matchmaking service rather than seeking your own partner?"

Hamish frowned. "Getting kind of personal, aren't you, mate?"

Zeke stared at him, a flicker of red in his eyes, but then his gaze cut to the AI and the flame died. "I'm sorry, Mr. Mulherne —"

"Hamish, for crying out loud."

"—but without the spell's assistance, the only way we can find a match for you is if you tell me everything about who you are and what you need." His gaze flicked to his monitor. "When you filled out the online registration form, you elected to bypass entering any profile data in favor of letting the spell do all the work. Without the spell, we have to go back and fill in the data."

Hamish's beat faltered. He could see Zeke's point, but his stomach curdled at the notion of telling a stranger about his pathetic love life. Bad enough that he'd fallen for Niall's suggestion—which was admitting that he was incapable of scoring on his own. "I told you. I'm not picky."

"I'm afraid our search parameters don't include an option for 'all of the above.' Do you have a gender-identity preference?"

"Nah. I'm open."

Zeke's eyebrows dipped, and he inhaled as if he were praying for strength. Did demons pray? Hamish knew zip about them. For that matter, everybody knew zip about them because they'd been stuck in Sheol since the beginning of forever.

"You left the sexual orientation selection empty. Shall I enter Bi? Pan? Omni?"

"Enter whatever you like. Like I said—"

"You're not picky. However, computer software—without magical assistance—is extremely picky." Zeke peered at the screen, clicking his mouse a few times. "You've also left the preferred-species selection blank. What type of supe are you interested in?"

"I'm not—

"Stop. You must have *some* preference. We're talking about your life partner here."

Hamish shrugged. "I'm not much into tentacles. But anything else is fair game."

Zeke's eyes flashed red again. "Fair *game*? This isn't a safari. Our clients are not *prey* to be—"

"Hey hey hey." Hamish held up his hands in surrender. "Bad choice of words. I apologize. I'll try to be more cooperative." After all, it wasn't Zeke's fault that the love of Hamish's life didn't want anything to do with him. *Hmmm.* Maybe he should call out some specifics after all. The last thing he needed was to be reminded of Tiff. "Shifters are fine, although I guess I'd rather keep away from the big cats." He tapped his nose. "Allergies."

"Okay." Zeke gnawed on his lower lip and clicked his mouse. "But since we're between the solstice and the equinox, a lot of shifter types are still in hibernation season. They don't feel much like socializing. They just want to nap."

Hamish shrugged. "Doesn't have to be a shifter. I'm good with fae—at least the ones that don't eat people. Vampires are out because of the whole shifter-blood-is-poison-to-them thing. Plus I'd prefer to date someone who doesn't wrinkle his nose in disgust if I get too close."

"Noted. We have no vampires on our rosters now in any case. The last one was recently matched. To a shifter, as a matter of fact." Zeke's brow knotted in confusion. "I'm still not entirely sure how that happened."

Hamish grinned. "That one of the *irregularities* you're bothered with?"

Zeke's cheeks turned blotchy red again. *Guess demons don't blush gracefully.* For some reason, that was rather endearing.

"So." Zeke cleared his throat. "Species isn't a deal breaker for the most part. Is there anything that *is* a deal breaker?"

"No groupies. That's my only hard line. Last thing I need is somebody who's only into me because I'm in the band."

"So you want someone who hates music?"

"Nah. They've gotta like music. You can add that to the deal breakers, I guess. They can even like the band. They just can't like the band first and me second."

Zeke typed a few notes. "What kind of music should they like?"

"Rock. Blues. Soul." When Zeke winced, Hamish realized his misstep. "Balls. Sorry. I mean if you're sensitive about the whole demon-soul thing—"

"It's all right." His grin was a little wobbly. "I'm used to it."

But why should you have to be? "So what kind of music do *you* like?"

"Me?" Zeke blinked. "I don't know."

"What do you mean you don't know? You mean you like all music, so nothing's a favorite?" Hamish grinned. "That's pretty bloody eclectic, mate. Your playlists must be a trip. What's your favorite song?"

"I don't have one."

"Everyone has a favorite. Or maybe you're the type of bloke who has a dozen favorites. Come on. Name one."

"I—I can't."

"Is it against the bloody rules or something?" Hamish scooted forward in his chair. "I won't tell."

"No, you don't understand. I can't name one because I have nothing to choose from. There's no music in Sheol."

Hamish's jaw sagged. "No music? You're shitting me."

Zeke shrugged. "I'm afraid not. Now—"

"Wait wait wait. I want to unpack this a little. No music *at all*?"

"Really, Mr. Mul— Hamish. This is not about me. Since you've entered 'musician' as your profession, we can filter on —"

"I still want to know—"

"What about sex?"

Hamish blinked. "Sex? You want to—"

There was that splotchy blush again. "Not *me*. You. You left the consummation box unchecked, but since you left everything else unchecked as well, I need to ask. Are you expecting sexual consummation of some description as part of your relationship?"

"Well. Yeah. Doesn't everybody? I figured that was a trick question."

"No, Mr. Mulherne. It was not." Zeke's tone was positively arctic—and he'd reverted to *Mr. Mulherne*.

Just grand, Hamish. You've bollixed it up again. And he didn't have an excuse, either. Hells, two of his bandmates were on the ace spectrum. Thanks to an ill-timed visit to the rehearsal hall restroom, he knew Niall and Gareth, er, consummated, but

Gareth was gray ace. Hamish had no idea what Josh got up to with Spence—nor was it any of his business—although most of the time Josh didn't shy away from Spence's touch.

"Sorry." Hamish hung his head and scrubbed his hands through his hair. "I've got a bad habit of being too flippant. Defense mechanism, I guess. But I should have known better." He raised his head and met Zeke's gaze. "I *do* know better. I'd like consummation, but it's not a deal breaker."

"Very well. You can choose optional. Will that do?"

"I reckon."

Zeke frowned at him, and Hamish got the impression that if the AI weren't looming like a giant Taser at Zeke's back, Zeke would have popped off another zinger. *Wonder what it would take to get rid of that thing?*

"If you're not willing to engage in the process, Mr. Mulherne, I'm not sure we can help— Augh!" He rubbed his shoulder where the AI had bumped him.

Hamish surged out of his chair and pointed at the AI. "Look, you. I'm not much into watching some arsehole who hides behind a light screen torture a bloke who's only trying to do his job. So back the hell off." The AI brightened, swirling red and orange and gold, as if it were about to supernova. It didn't move, though, and its nimbus brushed Zeke, who winced. "I mean it. Now. I've got friends on the supe council"—*not that I want to bother them with my pathetic love life*—"and I'm pretty sure they'd feel the same."

The AI's glow turned muddy yellow, and it didn't subside all the way to its pre-tantrum level, but at least it moved away from Zeke.

Zeke rubbed his shoulder, his dark eyes shiny behind his glasses. "Th-thank you." He cleared his throat. "I hope you know I'm only trying to find the best way to serve you, Mr. Mul — Hamish, but you have to realize that the feelings of your prospective partner are equally important. I want to match you with someone you'll find compatible, someone who has similar interests and expectations. If you don't tell me what those interests and expectations are . . ." He held out his hands, palms up. "Well, you see my difficulty?"

Hamish didn't sit down again. He wasn't used to being stationary for so long. Even when he was drumming, he spent more time off his stool than on it. He paced in front of Zeke's desk. "Yeah. I get it. I'm sorry. But I never thought I'd be at this point, you know? I thought that someday, she'd—" His throat closed up.

Zeke's lips parted, and he let out a barely voiced *Oh.*

Damn it. Hamish paced to the window and looked down at the street. "Never mind."

"I don't mean to be intrusive, since I can tell this is a sensitive area for you, but why have you decided to seek a partner at this particular moment?" Zeke's voice was soft and apologetic. It raised Hamish's hackles and made him grind his teeth together. "If you've suffered a recent disappointment or trauma, making another major life change might not be the best option."

Hamish whirled and glared at Zeke. "If you must know, I need a wedding date and I really, *really* don't want to hook up with the bloke who's the twin brother of the wife of the love of my life—who's never looked twice at me except to tell me to sod off."

Zeke blinked at him. "If the, er, bloke tells you to sod off, why would you think he wants to hook up with you?"

"Nah, *he* didn't tell me to sod off. *She* did."

"His sister?"

"No," Hamish said through clenched teeth.

Understanding dawned on Zeke's face. "*Ooohhh.*"

"Yeah, now you get it. The last thing I need is to hook up with her boyfriend."

"Wait. What? Whose boyfriend?" Zeke pulled on one of his curls. "I'm so confused."

"Can we just put that aside? My bandmate's brother is getting married next week, and I don't want to be the only one there without a partner."

Zeke's brow knotted. "But you're seeking a permanent contract?"

"Yep. One and done, that's me."

"Forgive me if I'm stepping out of line, but don't you think selecting a permanent mate so precipitously, and simply because you need a wedding date, is a bit extreme?"

"Nah. I've been alone long enough. It's time." He plopped in the chair again. "Now, can you help me or not?"

Lucifer's balls, if anyone finds out I did a desire evaluation on Hamish . . . Reading a client's desire was against his employment agreement with Supernatural Selection. The spells were supposed to sift through inappropriate or superficial *wants* to address the underlying *need*.

But it's what demons do. All of them, Zeke included, could assess a target's weakness, their deepest longing—although only those who'd achieved collector rank could use that knowledge to start negotiations for a victim's soul. Zeke wasn't a collector, nor was he ever likely to be, so he'd trained himself not to delve into hungers and weaknesses that didn't concern him.

When he'd re-entered the room, Zeke had steeled himself not to peek, even though it would have made his job easier. If he hadn't caught the edge of real loneliness and despair in Hamish's voice, Zeke could have resisted, just as he'd done with every other Supernatural Selection client.

But he did catch it, so strongly that a vision of a woman sprang fully formed in Zeke's mind. She was sturdily built, on the short side, with two full tattoo sleeves. She was hunched over a stringed instrument, and when she looked up, he could tell she was a jaguar shifter.

So Hamish would be happy if she *loved him.* But tangled up with the desire was regret and resignation, because more than wanting her, he wanted her to be happy too.

Not an option then, even if Zeke *did* have the power to make it happen on his own.

But someone who likes music. Someone who may or may not be interested in sex. Gender identity irrelevant.

Oh.

"You know, I think I may have someone in mind for you. But you'll need to engage."

"I thought that's what we were doing here?"

Zeke smiled. "I meant in forging the connection with your prospective partner. Without the help of the spell, you'll have to, well, date."

"Date? I don't date. I don't think I ever have."

Zeke blinked. "What? Never?"

Hamish shrugged. "Never had the time or inclination. Hooked up here and there of course. Who hasn't?"

That would be me. Zeke hoped he wasn't blushing again, but the heat in his cheeks probably meant that hope was in vain. "Yes. Well. I'm afraid you'll have to do so now. I can arrange a date for you with a prospective partner, but you'll have to meet them. Get to know them. Learn if you think you'll both be happy with one another."

"You mean woo them? On my own?" Hamish looked horrified.

"I'm afraid so. I can facilitate the introduction, but without the spell?" He spread his hands again. "Most of the burden will fall on you. Just as if you had met at a party or a bar or through friends. In fact, if it helps, you can think of this person as a friend of a friend."

Hamish grinned crookedly. "That makes *you* my friend, mate. I'm not sure you're ready for that."

"I am. After all, it's my job." *And my only chance to save the work-release program. To save myself.*

"Then who have you got?"

Zeke scrolled to the appropriate page in the client database. "The person I have in mind is a näkki."

"A what now?"

"A näkki. A Finnish shapeshifter. They're nonbinary—all näkki are since their shifting doesn't restrict them to a particular gender. Or physical form, for that matter. They're water-based —"

"Hold on. The shapeshifting, nonbinary thing is cool, but I'm a kangaroo. Plains, woods, sure, but water?" Hamish rubbed his palms on his pants. "Even Oregon is too soggy for me. I expect to find moss growing between my toes."

"Do you think that's a deal breaker? These days, näkki don't necessarily *reside* in streams and lakes as they did in the old days, although they're always more comfortable near bodies of water."

"I suppose it'll be all right, as long as they don't expect me to dive down to their home under the sea."

Zeke lifted an eyebrow. "They're not selkies, for Lucifer's sake. Plus, they're known for their musicianship. Violins, mostly, and vocals."

Hamish perked up. "Yeah? That's a plus." He drummed a little riff on his thigh and punctuated it with a slap on the desk. "Pair us up."

Zeke had to control his first reaction—to reach across the desk and grab Hamish's hand to still it. Or perhaps to slap him upside the head. Hadn't he paid attention to anything Zeke had said? With the AI just itching to zap him again, though, he took a moment to fold his hands in his lap. "It's not that simple. I'll need to contact Olli to see if they're amenable to a date outside the ordinary Supernatural Selection service. They may not be."

Although of all the clients, whose reactions had ranged from irritation to outrage when Zeke had called to inform them of the delay, Olli was the only one who'd seemed truly forlorn.

Zeke felt a twinge of unease as he studied the big, bluff, hyperenergetic Hamish in his cargo shorts (in Portland in February?). Olli wasn't the most forceful of personalities, but they had their standards where fashion was concerned.

On the other hand, they'd endured significant bias over the course of their life because of human misappropriation of näkki culture: after centuries of being cast as a bogey to frighten children into obedience, Olli had some severe self-esteem issues. And näkki had been targets of supe hunts too. Blustering ruffians eager to prove their courage had terrorized any näkki unfortunate enough to draw their attention, justifying their thuggery as "protecting the children."

Ridiculous, really. The supposed threat was an entirely human invention—and how much prowess did it take to subdue a violinist anyway?

Would Olli see Hamish as someone like those bullies? Or would they see Hamish as a protector? Although Olli had never said so, Zeke suspected that they were searching for a champion as much as a lover or life partner.

Zeke tried to ignore the increasing glare on his monitor as the AI flared brighter behind his shoulder, but he couldn't see the screen anymore. Unfortunately, he couldn't tell it to shut up in front of a client. He stood up. "Will you excuse me for a minute, please?"

Hamish leaned back in his chair. "Take your time, mate. I'm in no hurry."

Zeke strode down the hall and into his tiny, cluttered office, the AI on his heels. He shut the door, but kept his voice low anyway. "What are you trying to do?"

For an instant, the AI flared bright purple, then faded to an apologetic lavender, which didn't fool Zeke for one instant.

"You are *not* only thinking of the client. Hamish and Olli are a *possible* match based on a few superficial, similar preferences, but personality-wise—"

A magenta flash.

"Oh shut up. You're my monitor. You're supposed to be protecting the Upper World—"

Blue flashes.

"Fine. To you, it's the Lower World. To me, it's the Upper World. So what? To the fae, it's the Outer World. It doesn't matter what we call it. What matters is that you're trying to interfere."

The AI grew until it brushed the ceiling, gold erasing the other colors.

"Don't be so self-righteous. You're supposed to be an observer, not a participant. And trying to force me to match Hamish with someone unsuitable is definitely participating."

It shrunk, the gold shading to silver.

Zeke rolled his eyes, barely stopping himself from a disgusted groan. "Don't pretend to be hurt. I'm not falling for that again." A glimmer of pink grew in its center. "I mean it. How am I supposed to prove the viability of the work-release program if it's not *my* work?"

A blurp of yellow made Zeke's eyes water.

"Exactly my point. Now if you don't mind, I'd like to call Olli and ask them if they're amenable to a date with Hamish. I don't suppose you'd agree to step out while I'm on the phone? You cause a lot of interference on the line."

Red snaked up from the floor.

"Yeah, I didn't think so. Just keep the comments to yourself, okay? All this chatter is very distracting."

Zeke settled himself behind his cluttered desk and punched the landline's hands-free dialing button. "Hecate, call Olli."

"Calling ... Olli." The automated assistant's voice was far more pleasant than the AI's incessant harping.

"Hello?" The timber of Olli's voice changed depending on their aspect. Today it was a clear tenor, as breathless and melodic as ever.

"Good evening, Olli. This is Zeke Oz from Supernatural Selection. Have I caught you at a bad time?"

"Zeke! Oh no. This is fine. I was just watching *Project Runway* reruns. Has the spell come back online already?"

Zeke shifted uneasily in his chair. Olli sounded so hopeful. *Well, maybe this would work.* "No. But I have another option for you, if you're interested."

"Another option?" Doubt crept into their tone. "Something different than what you've shown me before?"

Zeke's palms started to sweat. "Yes. This isn't a new service, per se. More a . . . a retro service."

"Retro?"

The AI quivered with pulsing green, like electric lime gelatin.

Zeke mouthed, *Shut up.* "Yes. While we're waiting for the spell to be brought back online, how would you feel about going on an old-school date?"

"I've never . . . That is, I was hoping you would take care of . . . A date, you say?"

"Yes. You needn't make any kind of commitment, of course. And if you're not comfortable with the notion, that's perfectly all right."

"Well . . ." Olli's sigh was audible, even over the crackly connection. "Could you tell me something about my, um, prospective date?"

"His name is Hamish Mulherne. He—"

"Wait. Hamish Mulherne? The drummer for Hunter's Moon?"

"Yes, that's him."

"Ooohhh."

"Is that a good *oh* or a bad *oh*?"

Olli chuckled. "Good. Definitely good. I'm a big Hunter's Moon fan."

Uh-oh. Did that mean that Olli was technically a groupie? Hamish's deal breaker? "You are?"

"Yes. Their fusion of traditional Celtic and rock is quite compelling."

Is it? I wouldn't know. "Well, Hamish is a newly registered Supernatural Selection client."

"Really? I would have thought he'd have no trouble finding partners on his own. The band certainly has enough rabid followers." Olli's tone was decidedly tart, which comforted Zeke somewhat. *They're not a pushover, despite being a bit timid.*

"Hamish isn't interested in a relationship with a groupie."

"Ah. And is he? Interested in a relationship, that is?"

Zeke glanced at the AI, whose muddy red could only be described as *avid.* "He is. But he understands"—*at least he'd better*—"that without the spell, we can't guarantee a perfect match. Would you be interested in perhaps meeting him for dinner? To see how you get along?"

"Yes." Olli's voice was shy and tinged with hope. "I'd like that very much."

Zeke heaved a relieved sigh. "Excellent. I'll set it up and get back to you. I won't disclose your contact information to him— that will be up to the two of you once you meet. But, Olli— please understand that you are under *no obligation* to Hamish. Even the evening of the dinner, if you decide you don't want to go through with it, or if you want to leave in the middle because you feel uncomfortable, you can—"

"Zeke. It's okay. I'm not exactly an assertive person, but I can take care of myself. So please set up the dinner. And thank you for thinking of me."

"You're welcome. I'll be in touch." After Olli disconnected, Zeke collapsed back in his chair. "That went better than I'd hoped."

Although with the way the AI was pulsing, smug and pink again, Zeke wondered if he'd missed something.

No matter. He had a date to arrange. Which would be much easier to focus on if Hamish would only stop drumming on every available surface—from what Zeke could hear, he'd graduated to something large, hollow, and metal. *Probably my trash can.*

He sighed and pulled up the OpenTable app. Where to send a näkki and a kangaroo?

Surf and turf it is.

Chapter Five

Hamish laid his knife and fork back on the table, smiling an apology at the couple at the next table. "Sorry. Guess not everyone wants metal percussion accompaniment to their dinner."

He rubbed his hands along his pants—dress pants, for crying out loud. Zeke had given him stern instructions about the proper attire for this date. Seemed Olli was a clothes-horse of sorts. It was apparently a näkki thing, and February in Portland —in a moderately fancy waterfront restaurant—wasn't the best time or place to wear cargo shorts and a tank.

He'd had to ask Josh to go shopping with him. The afternoon they'd spent at Nordstrom still gave Hamish the shakes.

The server, a cheerful woman with curly hair pulled back in a ponytail, cruised over to the table. "Everything still good? Would you like a drink while you wait for your other party?"

Great. Now he looked like a loser who was getting stood up. "Nah. I'm early. I'm sure they'll be here soon."

Her brows drew together in as close to a frown as was acceptable for customer service. "'They'? Are you expecting more than one person? This is a two-top and I'm not sure we can—"

"No worries. It's just the one."

She blinked, eyes widening for an instant. "Oh. Got it." She flashed a smile, one that seemed more genuine than her customer-service one. "Is tonight a special occasion?"

Hamish rubbed his hands along his pants again, wishing like hell for his drumsticks. "First date." *Why does it feel like I'm cheating? Tiff never wanted me. We were never together.* He forced a grin. "First impressions and all that."

She topped off his water. "Well, I wouldn't worry too much about that." She leaned down to whisper conspiratorially. "You'll wow them."

"Thanks." *I think.*

She bustled away, leaving Hamish to stare morosely at the massive aquarium that separated the restaurant proper from the entryway. The fish inside were bright and tropical, nothing like the halibut, salmon, and swordfish on the menu. But Hamish couldn't help thinking that their unblinking stares were a tad reproachful.

Then a tall, slender person appeared next to the tank. Their high-collared, knee-length black coat was buttoned across one shoulder and their pants matched the blue of one of the neighboring tropical fish.

Zeke hadn't given him a picture of Olli before setting up the date. *"There'd be no point,"* he'd said, *"their appearance is fluid depending on how they feel like presenting themselves on the day."*

But this person—with their fine bone structure, white-blond hair with a fringe of brilliant blue and green falling over their high forehead, and a look of anxious inquiry on their face—had to be Olli.

Hamish half stood, and relief washed over Olli's face. Right. Zeke had no doubt given them Hamish's photo. *The only time I ever change is when I shift.* And Hamish doubted this restaurant served kangaroos.

Olli glided between the tables toward Hamish, with a grace that rivaled a swan shifter. They held out a hand. "Hamish, right?" Their voice was light and musical. Tenor? Contralto? *Huh. Never thought about how gender-restrictive vocal ranges were before.*

"That's me." Hamish struggled the rest of the way to his feet as Olli unbuttoned their coat, studying Hamish with a faint smile on their face, head tilted to the side. "Oh. Right." He edged around the table. "May I, um, take your coat?" *Strewth, I'm bad at this.*

Olli chuckled, letting their coat slide down their arms to reveal a jacket of the same tropical blue as their pants and a shirt dotted with tiny flowers that matched their hair. "I can manage that." They folded the coat and handed it to the hostess who'd followed them to the table.

Hamish pulled out Olli's chair. *See? I'm not a total bogan.* "Have a seat?"

"Thank you." Olli settled in the chair and glanced around, gaze snagging on the aquarium. "This place is . . . er . . ." They met Hamish's eyes, their own a trifle too wide. "They don't serve us out of that tank, do they?"

"I think that's just for show. Although it's a bit morbid, now that you mention it. I mean, if we're lounging about here, gorging on seafood, what are those blokes going to think? 'Oi, mate. Those tossers are eating Nemo.'"

Olli shuddered. "Don't."

"Sorry." Hamish took a gulp of his water. "Have a little filter problem sometimes. My gir— That is, *friends* have hinted I might be a tad insensitive sometimes. So apologizing in advance, eh?" He downed half the glass. "But contrary to what she—what *they* say, I *can* be taught, so call me on it, like you just did, and I'll try to do better."

The server bustled over just then, saving Hamish from doing something else idiotic, although he couldn't depend on her to save him for the rest of the date. *A date. What the hell was I thinking? I'm not ready for this.* But then he remembered the heated looks Tiff had exchanged with Luci—and Vitor—after the last concert, and decided to grow a pair.

The server smiled down at them as she topped off their water glasses. "Hi, I'm Leslie, and I'll be taking care of you tonight. Can I get you two something to drink?"

Olli glanced at Hamish from under their lashes—they had really pretty eyes. Kind of like opals or something. Hamish swallowed, his throat burning as he remembered Tiff's coffee-dark eyes. Then he realized Leslie and Olli were both watching him expectantly. *Shite, am I supposed to order for us both? How can I do that? I don't know anything about them yet.*

He cleared his throat and gestured for Olli to go ahead. They flushed, and for an instant, the shadow of scales appeared on their throat.

Olli fumbled with the wine list. *I should have handed that to him. I am a total bogan.* "Can you recommend an Australian wine, Hamish? I'd like to try something from your country."

"Couldn't say, mate. Haven't lived there for—" Hamish clamped his lips shut before he revealed just how long he'd been away from Queensland. Probably way before the server's grandparents had been born, but that wasn't something to flaunt in front of humans "—years. Anyroad, more of a beer man myself." He winced, wishing he had a drumstick so he could jab it into his eye.

Olli's tentative smile trembled, then disappeared. "Oh. Well." They looked up at Leslie. "What do you recommend?"

She pointed to a spot on the list. "If you want to try an Australian selection, I'd recommend this one if you're ordering fish. If you're going for beef—"

"No. Fish, definitely."

"Then the Semillon for sure."

Olli nodded. "Then I'll take a glass, please."

"Excellent." She turned to Hamish. "And you, sir?"

"Pint of Guinness, I guess." He'd been drinking with Niall so much lately that he'd developed a taste for it.

"I'll bring those right out."

She whisked away, leaving an awkward silence in her wake. Hamish and Olli stared at each other for at least two eight-counts before Olli broke, unfolding their linen napkin and apparently trying to smooth every wrinkle out. Hamish gulped another half glass of ice water, which succeeded in nearly freezing his vocal chords.

"So," he croaked. "You play the fiddle, then?"

Olli hands stilled, and they glanced up. "The violin. Yes. But not so much anymore."

"Why not?"

Their lips lifted in a crooked smile. "It takes the joy out of it when the neighbors accuse you of trying to kidnap their children every time you practice."

"They what now?"

The wrinkles in Olli's brow were almost hidden by their colorful bangs. "You *do* know I'm a näkki, don't you? Zeke told you." Their eyes widened, alarm chasing across their delicate features. "Oh Ahto, he didn't, did he? You don't know—"

"Hey hey hey." Hamish reached across the table, palm open in invitation. Olli didn't take the offered touch, but Hamish wasn't offended. *They might be like Josh, then.* Or it might just be too soon. "He told me. But I don't know much about what a näkki is or does. It doesn't really matter to me, right?"

"It doesn't? Why not?"

"Why should it? *What* you are isn't as important as *who* you are. At least that's how I see it."

"I . . . suppose."

"I mean, yeah, I'm a—" he glanced around to make sure nobody was close enough to hear "—kangaroo, but that's just an accident of genetics, right? I'm more about the choices I make, the things I like to do"—*the people I unfortunately love*—"than what I look like when I shift."

"Oh. Yes. I guess that makes sense. I, um, don't always look like this."

"So? You change who you are inside?"

Olli chuckled. "Of course not."

"Then we've got no problem."

Leslie returned and set their drinks down. "Can I start you out with an appetizer? We've got a lovely octopus carpaccio tonight."

Olli turned faintly green and swallowed convulsively. "No. Thank you, but no." They dipped their chin for an instant, then looked up at Leslie. "Just some bread, perhaps?"

"Of course." She zipped away.

Hamish peered after her, giving Olli a chance to regain their composure. When he glanced across the table, Olli was staring at the aquarium again. "You okay?"

"Yes. I'm fine, it's just—" They raised their wineglass in shaking fingers. "Octopi are so— Well, a lot of my friends are octopi. Just the idea . . ." They shuddered. "I get out so infrequently, but I should have realized that a seafood restaurant might—"

"No. I get it." *Geez, who picked this place?* "Would you rather bail on this place and go to a hot dog cart or something?"

They shook back their hair, an earring sparkling in the light. "Of course not. I'll be fine as long as we don't— We don't—"

"Eat your friends."

"Yes." They took a large swig of wine. "If you don't live in Australia anymore, where do you live? Here in Portland?"

"Nah. We're just here as part of the latest tour. I've got a place in Indio."

"Southeast Asia?"

"No, Indio. Southern California. It's near Palm Springs."

Olli blinked. "In the desert?"

"Yeah." Hamish grinned. "It's one of the only places that's hot and dry enough for me."

"Oh," Olli said faintly.

"Where do you live?"

"In a spruce mire."

Hamish picked up his Guinness. *Leslie better keep these coming, because this is going to be a really long night.*

Zeke paced his office, gnawing on his thumbnail, certain that his life in the Upper World was about to implode. Why had he ever imagined he could facilitate a match without the spells? He was a *demon*. The very definition of his race was "disaster waiting to happen."

I'm sure I thought of everything. Didn't I?

He'd chosen the spot for Hamish's date with Olli because the collective had a translocation outlet in the restaurant, in a dimensional pocket right behind the host's station. Olli was very shy and nervous in unfamiliar surroundings. Zeke had wanted to make the transportation as low-stress for them as possible, so he'd arranged for Faerie's new supe transit service, the Fae Transportation Association, to escort Olli directly there.

Had that been a mistake? The FTA didn't have much of a track record—it had only been introduced recently as part of the King's initiatives to give the fae a purpose in their newly unified realm. Supernatural Selection had been an early adopter, but sometimes the escorts could be a bit alarming: you never knew whether you'd get a giant, glowering trow or a tiny, big-eyed bwci.

Not that trows could help glowering. That was just the way their faces were made.

But Olli might not know that. *I should have requested a dryad. Or maybe a sylph.*

The urge to run up the stairs and slip through the translocation door was enough to make him wish that demons had souls. Because if he'd had one, he'd be tempted to sell it for a peek inside the restaurant.

He patrolled around the office again. At least the AI had finally gotten tired of dogging his steps and had retreated to the corner in a glimmer of sulky gray. *Small blessings.*

Zeke checked his watch. Only forty-five seconds since the last time he'd checked. Lucifer's balls, you'd think he was in a time loop, because the last hour had felt like days.

Screw this. He strode out of his office and took the stairs two at a time, using a little of his demon anti-grav to smooth and speed his ascent.

The AI, of course, followed him in a veritable strobe of orange-red.

"Yes, I'm going to check on them. What about it?" Suddenly, the AI was in front of him, blocking the top of the stairs, pulsing the most self-righteous gold in the history of the multiverse. "I'm not 'rampaging.'" The AI's brightness increased by a factor of three. "Nor am I soul-cruising. I'm simply stepping through the translocation door into a bespelled dimensional pocket which, technically, is part of Supernatural Selection, since I can get there without going outside. Plus, it's totally job related. So."

Zeke bit his lip, ignoring the AI's nagging magenta flashes. He probably should try to be inconspicuous, though, right? Supes were fond of this restaurant, and Zeke knew a number of them because they'd passed through Supernatural Selection. It wouldn't be great for his probation if it got back to the magistra that he was . . . bending the rules.

He glanced irritably at the AI. *The stupid thing will probably snitch on me, like it always does.*

But the magistra had told him to make Hamish happy, no matter what. It might violate the letter of his visa, but in spirit? The primary clause of the work-release contract was to fulfill the expectations of his employer. Zeke could totally support the trip. *My boss told me to do it. Sort of.*

With a grin, he turned and float-galloped down the stairs again to snatch his hoodie off the hook in his office.

He zoomed back up the stairs, all the way to the fourth floor, the AI yammering indigo sparks at his heels the whole way. He stopped in front of the translocation door to catch his breath and flip his hood over his head, pulling it down to shadow his face.

He took a deep breath, excitement warring with trepidation. This was his first time venturing somewhere in the Upper World other than Supernatural Selection. Was everyone right about demons? Would he suddenly feel the urge to rampage? To try to talk some human out of his soul?

Won't happen. I'm not rated for soul collection. But he'd definitely keep a lid on his desire evaluation, just in case.

He punched the restaurant's code into the keypad next to the door and slipped through—although not quickly enough to keep the AI from following.

His senses were immediately bombarded—the low murmur of the patrons from the dining room beyond an enormous aquarium, coupled with the clash of dishes, and the calls of the staff from the kitchen to his left. And the smells. Lucifer's balls, the *smells*. The aromas of roasting meats, baking breads, caramelizing onions . . . Vanilla. Burnt sugar. Cinnamon.

He inhaled deeply. *The falafel restaurant has nothing on this.* He'd have happily stood there for hours, letting it all wash over him.

But then the AI's sullen green glow reminded him why he was here.

"Stop whining. You didn't have to come." Gold pulsed at Zeke's chest level. "And that martyr act isn't fooling anyone."

Zeke shuffled to the edge of the dimensional pocket, which presented as a dark-paneled alcove with a poster advertising the Waterfront Blues Festival. But the doorway was narrow, so he couldn't see anything except a small stretch of hallway and the giant aquarium with lights that rivaled the AI in color and intensity.

If I want to see what's happening, I have to go out there. Tingles chased up his spine, lifting the hair at his nape. He could get sanctioned for this. Repatriated into Sheol faster than he could say Beelzebub.

Hamish was a Supernatural Selection client, which meant he was entitled to a perfect match. And with no spells between them, it felt *personal*. Yes, if everything went up in flames—literal or virtual—Zeke would have no one to blame but himself. But if it worked? If he could make Hamish happy? Now *that* would be something to be proud of.

Besides, I'm merely following my employer's instructions.

That was his story, and he was sticking to it.

Zeke waited until the hallway was clear and then sidled out of the alcove. The AI, of course, stuck to him like a neon limpet.

"Could you turn the wattage down a little," he whispered. "It's hard to be inconspicuous when you're practically shining a searchlight on me." It flared even brighter. "I don't *care* if you're not ashamed. This is not about you."

The AI pulsed again, in passive-aggressive turquoise, but at least it toned itself down so it could be mistaken for the glow cast by the aquarium.

Better take advantage of that.

He darted across the hall to stand behind the aquarium, peering through the water with its lacy, fernlike plants and the bright, flashing bodies of its fish.

The fish seemed to regard the diners on the other side of the glass forlornly. Zeke commiserated. There was a place in Sheol like this—where prisoners awaited their own judgment as they watched all those in front of them meet their doom.

Kind of insensitive, isn't it? On the other hand, maybe the aquarium fish were more like the AI—gloating that they were safe and protected while others of their kind were not.

But just then, he caught sight of Hamish and Olli at a table by the window. Olli's back was to him, so Zeke couldn't tell if they looked happy or at least interested. Were their shoulders a little tense? It was hard to tell. Hamish *seemed* to be focused on Olli's face, but his expression was unreadable.

"Can I help you?"

Zeke started at the voice at his elbow. He tore his gaze off his probably mismatched clients to face the hostess. Her eyes were narrowed as if against a bright light. *Uh-oh.* He'd been so intent on, well, *spying* on Hamish and Olli, that he'd forgotten that standing with his nose almost pressed against the aquarium wasn't exactly *stealthy*. And his own personal floodlight didn't help.

"No, thanks. I'm, er, just waiting for a friend."

"Do you want to put your name on the list for a table?"

"I'm not sure when he'll be here. I'll let you know, though. Is that okay?"

She nodded and retreated to her podium, with one last dubious glance at Zeke in his downscale gray hoodie.

"Nice going," he muttered. "Maybe next time you can bring the full angelic chorus." He frowned at the AI. "And *don't* you dare say a word. Not. One. Word. The glare is bad enough as it is."

He turned his attention back to the table, but an iridescent blue fish blocked his view. In fact, *all* the fish in the aquarium were grouped together directly in front of him, staring at him like rubberneckers at a crash scene.

Great. Apparently demon stealth doesn't work on fish either.

He flapped his hands at them, but they didn't move. He edged sideways, but they followed him. "Shoo," he murmured, then rolled his eyes at himself. Did fish even have ears?

"Zeke? What are you doing here?"

Zeke whirled, clutching the front of his hoodie. "Olli. Oh. Hi. I was just, um, coming along to see how your date was going."

Olli glanced over his shoulder, toward the window table where Hamish was still sitting, glaring their way with a scowl on his face. "It was going fine. I think. But I have to go."

"Go?" Zeke shoved his fists into his hoodie's pockets so he wouldn't reach for Olli, to pat their shoulders or take their hands. Not many people—not *any* people, if it came to that—wanted a demon's touch. But Olli's expression was devastated. "Did Hamish say something? Do something? If he—"

"No, no." Olli ran a shaking hand through their hair. "I just got a message from my neighbor. Someone set my house on fire."

"What?" Zeke's outraged squawk caused the hostess to turn and stare at him. *So much for being inconspicuous. And this time I can't blame the AI.* "That's— That's—"

"Business as usual." Olli sighed. "Trust me, it's not the first time it's happened." They brandished their phone. "Hence the emergency protocols. I need to get back to my place."

"Yes. Of course. I'll take you back through the translocation door immediately."

"That won't be necessary." They nodded toward the restaurant door. "My ride's already here."

A scowling man strode through the front door, zeroing in on Olli at once. The hostess blinked at him, but didn't approach— not that Zeke could blame her. The fellow was nearly as broad as the hallway, and he made Hamish look short.

"Olli." The giant fellow draped an arm across Olli's shoulders.

"Hello, Aarni. Thank you for coming for me."

Aarni said something in another language—probably Finnish, and since Zeke wasn't one of the demons with Tongues in his skill repertoire, he had no idea what was said. But the tender expression on Aarni's face as he gazed down at Olli told Zeke that maybe Olli didn't need Supernatural Selection's services after all. Although Olli appeared to be oblivious, they did lean against Aarni's side.

Olli turned to Zeke. "Thank you for thinking of me, Zeke. I liked Hamish. Maybe we can set up another date—"

"Date?" Aarni's tone was laced with menace. "No." More rapid Finnish, which caused Olli to blush.

"Aarni, don't be silly. I'm in no danger." They pointed at Hamish. "He's the drummer for Hunter's Moon."

But despite Olli's protests, Aarni bundled Olli out of the restaurant, with one fulminating glare at Hamish.

"Hoo boy," Zeke muttered. He glanced at the table. Hamish was still glowering, but his attention wasn't focused on Olli and his mega-escort. No. He was aiming a death glare at Zeke. *Uh-oh.*

Pink blinked in the AI's middle. "Stop that. It's not funny. I need to go talk to him. And you—" He jabbed a finger at the aquarium. "Wait here. This isn't a revival meeting, and the other patrons didn't come here to be blinded by the light."

Chapter Six

Figured that the first date Hamish had had since he fell for Tiff in 1969 would get derailed by a house fire, of all things. But catching sight of Zeke peering at him through the aquarium fronds was the kicker that sent Hamish's mood into the crapper.

What, didn't the nosy demon think Hamish could be charming enough to entertain a date through a single dinner? Zeke was the one who'd set this up anyway. If he didn't trust Hamish, at least he should trust himself.

Zeke edged out from behind the fish tank and slunk toward Hamish's table just as Leslie arrived with his and Olli's entrees.

She set Hamish's ribeye in front of him, and Olli's plate at their empty spot, then signaled for another server to approach with a small steaming silver pitcher. "Will your companion be back shortly?" She took the little pot from her assistant. "I'd hate for them to miss the sizzle effect."

"Go ahead and sizzle." Hamish picked up his fork. "They've had an emergency and won't be back."

She blinked. "Oh. Should I take this back?"

"Nah." He waved his fork at Zeke, now lurking tableside. "I've got a backup plan."

Leslie smiled brightly. "In that case . . ." She tipped the pitcher, drizzling browned butter over Olli's abandoned fish. She was right. The sizzle effect was nice, as was the aroma of hazelnut butter. "Enjoy!"

She bustled away, followed by her minion.

Hamish picked up his knife and sawed a hunk off his steak. "So. Didn't trust me not to bollix up the date?"

"No. I mean, I wasn't sure— I just wanted to see if—"

"Since you're here, you might as well eat Olli's dinner."

Zeke eyed the fish. "I really don't think—"

"You want that fish to have died in vain?" He leaned forward. "Those blokes in the aquarium are already gawking at you like you're a serial killer." He popped the steak into his mouth. *Gawds.* Whatever else he could say about this disaster of a night, at least the food was good.

"I wouldn't want—" Zeke cast a guilty look over his shoulder, although his expression morphed into an annoyed scowl. Probably because that bloody AI was playing buggers with the restaurant's lighting. The hostess kept fiddling with a light switch, trying to balance things out. "That is, it wouldn't be right. I should—"

"*Can* you eat?"

"Yes, of course. But—"

"Then sit down and do it. You promised me dinner, and I'm not leaving until I've had it."

"I actually didn't promise anything of the sort. I only—"

"Sit. You're attracting attention."

Zeke glanced around, eyes wild behind his glasses and the glimmer of his vision spell. Truthfully, nobody had looked twice at them, but Zeke plopped down in Olli's abandoned chair, tugging his hoodie forward.

Hamish took a satisfying swig of his beer. "Can't you get rid of your sidecar?"

"Sidecar?"

"That bloody AI."

"Well, no. Not technically. It's required to monitor me continually and since I'm not really supposed to be here anyway . . ." He shrugged. "Trust me. I tried. But it seems to think making any concessions—either for secrecy's sake or anyone else's convenience—are beneath it. It is an angel, after all."

"And that makes it better than us?"

"It's an *angel*. Of course it's better." Zeke slumped in his chair. "At least in its own opinion," he muttered, with more than a touch of snideness.

Hamish grinned. "Glad to see you're not buying into that myth."

"It doesn't matter whether I buy into it or not. I have to deal with it."

"Then you might as well get a good dinner out of it, right? Go ahead."

Zeke peered around, but nobody was looking their way. He picked up his fork as if it might leap out of his hand and stab him in the chest. "I've never . . ."

"Never what? Hijacked somebody else's dinner?"

Zeke straightened in his chair, outrage flickering across his face. "I didn't. If Olli's house hadn't been set on fire—"

"Chill out, demon dude. I'm just messing with you. You've never what?"

"I've never eaten in anybody else's presence before. Let alone in public."

"What, they send you into a closet for meals down in whatchamadooger?"

"Sheol. And no. It's not necessary. Demons of my order don't eat."

Hamish dropped his fork onto his plate with a clatter. "You what now?"

"We don't eat. We don't need to in order to survive." He picked up his knife. "That's one of the nice things about the work-release program. Yes, the AI is annoying, especially since I have to share living quarters with it, but at least I'm not hungry all the time."

"You're joking. They *starve* you to death?"

Zeke smiled crookedly. "Not to death, obviously. It's supposed to keep us from getting complacent. If a demon is satisfied with their lot, they won't be motivated to serve the upper echelon."

"Then that tears it." Hamish pointed at the plate. "Eat. Because as far as I'm concerned, controlling somebody by withholding food is cruel and unusual punishment."

"All right." Zeke teased a morsel of fish onto his fork and lifted it to his mouth. As soon as his lips closed around it, his eyes widened. He chewed carefully and swallowed, then exhaled on a low *ooohhh*. "What *is* this?"

The look of bliss on Zeke's face was enough to make Hamish's dick perk up and take notice. And *that* was certainly a first in very long time. "Trout. Something or other French. *Grenobloise*, that's it."

"This must be what food at the angelic buffet is like." He took another bite, this one including a tiny lemon cube. "That's— Lucifer's balls, this is *amazing*."

Hamish chuckled. "Eat up, mate. After all, Supernatural Selection is picking up the bill."

Despite how delicious his steak was, Hamish got more enjoyment out of watching Zeke's face as he ate. His initial skepticism over an asparagus stalk versus his moan when he tasted it was better than porn.

Not that Hamish would know about that. Much.

After Zeke had chased the last grain of rice and popped it into his mouth, he settled back in his chair, looking relaxed for the first time since Hamish had met him. Content. Happy, even. And without the tension in his shoulders and the stress creases around his mouth and eyes, he was about as cute a guy as Hamish had ever seen—and he'd seen the entire raft of fae royalty, for cripes' sake.

"I don't suppose *you're* in that famous Supernatural Selection database?"

"Me?" Zeke's eyes widened, and he shot a look over his shoulder at where the AI was still terrorizing the aquarium fish. "No. Demons aren't allowed to date."

"You're not? So, hookups are the only way you have sex?"

Zeke's fair skin turned blotchy with red. "We don't have sex. Unless having sex is the point."

"But sex *is* the point of a hookup."

"Not the point of the hookup. The point of the *demon*. Like incubi or succubi. Even the dynastic 'cubi, the ones who managed to escape Sheol"—and was that a note of wistfulness in Zeke's tone?—"still arrange their lives around their, er, nutritional requirements."

"'Nutritional requirements,' eh?" Smirking, Hamish beat a soft tattoo on the edge of the table. "I take it they're not vegan."

As he'd hoped, Zeke's blushes spread. "No! They've got, um, you know . . ." He glanced around, then shrunk into his hoodie like a retreating turtle. "Certain nonfood *appetites*. Related to their demon nature."

"Speaking of appetites . . ." Hamish leaned back in his chair, his smirk widening into a grin. "How does *your* demon nature feel about dessert?"

"Dessert?" Zeke's eyes grew as round as Hamish's cymbals. "I've never had dessert."

"You're telling me that in the whole time you've been up here, you've never once scarfed down a bag of Oreos or a pint of Ben and Jerry's while you watch the nightly demon news, or whatever?"

"I don't have the money."

Hamish lost all desire to smile. "Wait a mo. Doesn't bloody Supernatural Selection pay you? You're not their indentured servant, are you?"

"Oh, they pay me. Salaries are mandated by the work-release program, but they didn't specify a minimum wage."

"So ask for a raise, if it doesn't give you enough to afford a treat now and then."

"That's not—" Zeke snuck a glance at the AI again. "I have to turn over most of my paycheck to my supervisor."

"One of the witches is shaking you down? What the hell, mate?"

"Not my Supernatural Selection supervisor. My *other* supervisor. The demon I serve when I'm in Sheol."

Hamish gripped the edge of the table so he wouldn't slam his fist into the window. "So you have to *pay* for the privilege of not starving in a lightless cave with no music?"

"When you put it like that, it sounds like a fair trade, doesn't it?"

"No, it bloody well doesn't. It's like they're trying to create Sheol here on earth—at least where you're concerned. What do you do in your free time?"

"Considering I don't have any money and I'm not allowed outside, not much. Although it's a lot easier to read in a place that's not dark 24/7."

"I imagine." Hamish kept his tone dry, even though he wanted to let his rage bleed out. He wasn't angry at Zeke, after all. But it was so bloody unfair.

"There's cable TV, too. Although the AI doesn't let me watch anything that it thinks is inappropriate."

"So reruns of *Dr. Quinn, Medicine Woman* and *Little House on the Prairie*, eh?"

Zeke's red blotches staged a return. "No. Or not only that." His expression turned wistful. "Although I'd like to watch *Star Trek*. Or maybe *Dr. Who*."

"Bloody hell," Hamish muttered. "They let you out of one prison and stuck you in another."

Zeke leaned forward. "I'm not complaining. Please don't think that. This is *so* much better. And as long as I make you happy, I won't have to—" His eyes widened and he clapped both hands over his mouth.

"Hold on. What do you mean, make me happy?"

Zeke shook his head without moving his hands. He made some kind of *meep* sound, like that skinny orange Muppet with the stand-up hair—the lab assistant one.

"Give over, Zeke. You might as well tell me the whole story. Seems like we're in this together, right?"

He lowered his hands with a sigh. "The thing is, Supernatural Selection guarantees a perfect match, or at least one that meets the client's requirements. But without the spells . . ." He smiled crookedly. "When Magistra Lenore gave me the ultimatum about taking you on as a client, though, she didn't say I had to find you a perfect match, or a match of any kind or length. She just said I had to make you happy. That's the only requirement. As long as I meet it . . ." He shrugged.

"And that's your out? As long as you make me happy, you can stay out of Sheol?" Although as far as Hamish was concerned, Zeke's current life wasn't much better.

"Yes. And since words make a huge difference when they're spoken in that building, and by a witch of Magistra Lenore's stature, I'm pretty sure I can take them to the bank."

"In that case"—Hamish's grinned threatened to split his face —"what would make me happy . . ."

Zeke leaned forward. "Yes?"

"Is for you to have dessert."

Dessert. Lucifer's balls, Zeke had thought the trout was divine, but this? He was convinced he'd been elevated to the Sheol C-suite or perhaps to the angelic host because clearly this . . . this . . . *salted caramel chocolate tart* was fit for the most exalted ranks.

Hamish had insisted that Zeke have two of them, and now he was settled back in his chair, observing Zeke with an indulgent smile. "So. You're a demon. What do demons *do*, anyway?"

Zeke chased the last bite of tart crust across the plate with his fork. "Depends on the demon."

"You mean—what did you call the place? She-something-or-other?"

"Sheol."

"Yeah, that. Does it have an HR department? You go in and apply for a job, pass the interview, and boom? Or is it more like an audition?"

Zeke sighed and left the last delectable bite where it lay. *I really must get better at using Upper World cutlery.* "No. It really depends on the demon. We're . . . I guess you'd say we're purpose-built."

Hamish's eyebrows rose. "'Built'? What, like infernal elves assemble you in some underworld workshop?"

"I suppose 'spawned' would be a better description. Or conjured. Or manifested."

"So when a mommy demon and a daddy demon love each other very much—"

"Shut up. We're not *born*. We're materialized because there's a need for whatever service we're intended for."

Hamish leaned back in his chair, his fingers beating a soft but distracting rhythm against the edge of the table. It was muffled by the tablecloth, but Zeke still felt it vibrate his bones. "So you're like those industrial robots? You can do one thing well, but nothing else?"

"No. We can learn. We're not *stupid*. But there's not exactly room for advancement in a place where everyone is bred for their position." He pleated the edge of the tablecloth in his fingers. "And these days, when there's not as much attrition from enforced summoning, there's no need for—"

"Hold on a minute. 'Enforced summoning'? What the hell is that about?"

Zeke blinked. Hamish sounded almost angry. *Not exactly making him happy, am I?* "In the days when alchemy was popular, magicians and wizards used to summon demons into a restraining circle and compel them to do their will. It was a thing."

"A bloody revolting thing," Hamish muttered. "Can't you refuse to go?"

"No. If someone knows the appropriate ritual and has a demon's true name, we've got to obey. Luckily, it's out of fashion these days."

"Out of fashion? Why?"

"There are easier ways to get what demons used to provide them. Plus Sheol is much more vigilant about security and identity theft, so it's harder for unscrupulous magic users to discover our true names."

"Harder? Not impossible?"

Zeke shrugged. "There are hackers everywhere. In fact, they sort of originated in Sheol, same as the internet and cell phone technology."

Hamish grinned, and for some reason, that sent a shiver up Zeke's spine. "Demons invented modern communication tech? That explains so much."

Zeke glanced at the AI. Could it hear the conversation from where it still lurked behind the aquarium? It hadn't occurred to him to test the AI's range, since it was never more than a room away, and usually stuck right at his shoulder. This kind of subversive conversation was exactly the sort of thing the Sheol C-suite had been worried about when the supe council had proposed the work-release program. Plus, he never should have let on that his success with Hamish's match controlled his fate— or what the definition of *success* actually was.

Hamish followed the direction of Zeke's gaze. "Oi. Not exactly subtle, is it? Was that thing purpose-built to be a pain in the arse?"

"I don't *think* so. I mean angels and demons are part of the same host administratively—"

"You mean there's bureaucracy in heaven and hell?"

Zeke frowned. "Sheol and Elysium, please, and you have no idea. We share payroll, HR—"

"So there *is* a human resources department."

"Technically, it's Host Relations, but it amounts to the same thing. Elysium's management structure, particularly regarding the lower echelons, isn't quite as, er, proprietary as Sheol's."

"Maybe you should put in for a transfer. Because I've got to tell you, your current gig's got some problems."

If only I could. "It's not quite that simple. When we're spawned, we fall along a sliding scale." He held up his hands, flat, parallel to the table. "On the one hand is concern for others." He wiggled the fingers of his right hand. "On the other is concern for self. The higher the one—" he raised his left hand "—the lower the other—" he lowered the left an equal amount "—with the most empathetic and helpful being the top level in the angelic host, the least helpful the C-suite demons. Low-level minions like me are just under the midpoint. We can't be so selfish that we won't follow our masters' orders—they don't want to spawn their own rivals—but we need to be a bit self-serving so we'll be inclined to avoid punishment."

"Wait, so angels and demons are the same under the skin?"

Zeke nodded, then realized he was keeping time to Hamish's continued drumming. "Essentially yes, regardless of what the skin looks like."

"Hmmm. Your skin seems all right." Hamish's gaze raked Zeke from the top of his head to where his body disappeared behind the table.

For some reason, that look made Zeke fumble for his water. He misjudged the distance when he set the glass on the table, hitting the edge of the dessert plate with a *clink*. "S-skin is irrelevant in terms of placement in the host ranks, as is the number and configuration of heads and limbs, and whether wings are involved. Paimon, my supervisor's supervisor, for instance, manages both angelic and demonic hosts."

"Is that odd? Dealing with demons and angels at once?"

"If you're of sufficiently high rank—and he's a king—your authority spans the whole pantheon regardless of where you fall on the selfishness scale. I think he prefers the infernal host though. Their rules aren't as rigid, and he's a little, um, eccentric."

"And if you asked me, nobody with absolute power over others can be completely unselfish, whether they claim to be angelic or not."

"Yes. Well. Um . . . Maybe we should discuss your date. How did you and Olli get along? Do you think you could be happy with them?"

Hamish's brows drew together and his fingers tapped harder and faster, earning annoyed glances from several nearby diners —although one or two others were surreptitiously aiming their cell phones his way. "Eh, they'll do, I reckon."

"'They'll *do*'?" *Yikes, that was too loud.* He leaned forward and made an effort not to access a little demon anti-grav and levitate Hamish's fork into his eye. "What's that supposed to mean?"

"It means they'll do. They seem nice. I told you, I'm not picky. Although next time, I'd like to get through the date without them ditching me." He lifted an eyebrow. "And without our counselor spying on us from behind the guppies."

"Those aren't guppies. They're— You know what? Never mind. But tell me this. Are you serious about finding a life partner? A perfect mate?"

"I told you. I'm not—"

"Yes. Not picky. I've gotten the memo. But if you're not emotionally available, then what's the point? I mean, *you* may not be picky, but your partner might expect something more from you than *You'll do. Let's get married.*"

"Whoa there." Hamish held up his hands, which *thankfully* stopped the cadence resonating in Zeke's chest. "I'm not a total bogan. We'll get to know each other first before I pop the question." He grinned again, the jerk. "I reckon that'll take at least a week. We can announce the engagement at the wedding."

Zeke leaned back and crossed his arms. "No."

"What do you mean, no?" He waggled a finger. "If that's what'll make me happy, isn't it your job to make it happen?"

"Not if it means making Olli *un*happy. They're romantic, whether you are or not. I refuse to shackle them to somebody who can't care for them, even if it means I go back to Sheol on the next infernal elevator."

Hamish blinked. "You get to Sheol via elevator?"

"That's not the point. The point is I can't be a party to mating someone as vulnerable as Olli to somebody who won't care for them, both emotionally and physically."

Hamish's scowl deepened. "You think I'm incapable of caring?"

"You haven't shown much inclination so far. Or at least not an inclination of caring about anybody but the one person who's out of your reach."

Hamish's eyes narrowed. "Who told you about that?"

"You did, if you recall." *Although I peeked at a little more than you volunteered.* "Why should I believe you'll change for Olli's sake?"

Hamish pushed himself away from the table. "I'm not having this conversation here. Supernatural Selection is handling the bill, right?"

"Yes. It's prepaid. But—"

"Then let's go. We both need to cool down, and a walk in the balmy February breeze is exactly the way to do it."

"A walk?" Zeke gulped. "You mean outside?"

"I'm bloody well not talking about a jaunt around the dining room."

"But I can't. I'm not allowed to go outside." Zeke tugged his hood forward as Hamish pulled his wallet out of his pocket and tossed several bills on the table. "I told you. It's taken care of."

"This is a tip. Leslie shouldn't have had to deal with our drama. Now come on." He stood up and shrugged into his coat. "It will make me *happy* to walk back to Supernatural Selection with you." He bared his teeth. "You wouldn't want me to be *unhappy*, would you?"

"But—but the AI—"

"The AI can stuff it." Hamish turned and stalked away, leaving Zeke goggling after him. At the hostess stand, he turned and jerked his head toward the door.

Zeke scrambled to his feet, dropping his napkin on the floor, then banging his head on the edge of the table when he bent to pick it up. By the time he'd stumbled across the room, Hamish's scowl had turned to a smirk.

"Smooth, mate. Let's go." He took Zeke's elbow and led him toward the door, only to be stopped by the AI, its glaring gold only partially camouflaged by its position under a lighting fixture. "Back off, Super Trooper," he murmured. "Do you *want* to violate the secrecy pact?"

Zeke frowned at the AI's pulse of red. Luckily, the hostess was away from her podium seating other guests, and the vestibule was empty. "You are *not* being unobtrusive. And you're messing with the restaurant's ambience. That doesn't seem very angelic to me."

"What he said. Now. I'm taking Zeke back to the office. Meet us there, because you'll attract more attention on the street than two perfectly normal-looking guys taking a stroll along the sidewalk."

Hamish towed Zeke out the door and into the brisk breeze blowing off the river. Zeke sucked in a breath, his steps slowing until Hamish stopped.

"Something wrong, mate?"

"No. It's just . . . This is my first time outdoors in the Upper World." He lifted his face to the sky with its scatter of stars. "It's *glorious*."

"Glorious, is it? Feels bloody cold to me. In Australia, this is the middle of summer." He shoved his hands into his pockets. "I haven't lived there for years, but it still seems odd to me that February is cold."

"But the air . . ." Zeke closed his eyes and breathed in through his nose. "Not even a whiff of brimstone or sulfur, and the humidity isn't ninety-eight percent with matching temperature." He shivered, then opened his eyes when Hamish grasped his elbow. "What?"

"Ninety-eight? All the time? Seriously?"

"At least where the lower ranks dwell. I've never been to the C-suite. I hear it's different."

"Overlords enjoying their perks? Trust me, I've seen that scenario before." Hamish led Zeke away from the restaurant, although a glow seemed to follow them down the sidewalk.

Zeke glanced back. Yup. The glow was from the AI, pulsing angry red in the vestibule. But full of delicious food for perhaps the first time in his life, and drunk on the crisp, clear air, a little rebellion stirred in Zeke's chest.

He stuck out his tongue at the AI, then turned and marched down the sidewalk.

"Oi, mate." Hamish loped up alongside him. "You're going the wrong way."

Yes, I probably am. No doubt there'd be repercussions from his little show of defiance, but right now, he didn't care. "Lead the way, then."

Hamish nodded at the corner diagonally across from them. "Thataway." He took off on his long legs, and Zeke lengthened his own stride to keep up. "That hoodie of yours doesn't look very warm. Aren't you uncomfortable?"

Zeke grinned up at him. "Except for the last few months, I've lived in Sheol since I was spawned. Discomfort is pretty much a way of life there."

"Doesn't mean you shouldn't expect something better. Here." Hamish shrugged out of his coat and draped it across Zeke's shoulders.

"Oh." Zeke fingered the soft wool, tempted to rub his cheek against it. It smelled of citrus and what he'd learned was new-mown grass—a scent he'd forever associate with Hamish. "But you just said you were cold. I can't." He started to shrug the coat off his shoulders, but Hamish gripped his wrist.

"I'm a shifter. We run hot." He moved behind Zeke and held up the coat so Zeke could slip his arms in. The sleeves fell below the tips of his fingers. "Doesn't mean I don't like to complain, but I'm feeling no pain. 'Bout time somebody considered your comfort for a change."

Zeke swallowed around a lump in his throat. "Thank you."

"It's nothing. Come on. Since you've never been outside, what do you say we take the scenic route back to your place?" He glanced down. "Where is your place, by the way?"

"I live above Supernatural Selection."

"Of course you do," Hamish muttered. "Bloody council could have made this less like being transported for life."

"I don't mind. Other than not being able to go outside, it's loads better than my cave in Sheol." Feeling greatly daring, he nudged Hamish with his elbow. "Plus I can get groceries delivered when I scrape together enough after my supervisor's tribute."

Hamish muttered something else that Zeke didn't quite catch, but he didn't ask for a repeat because there was a *river*. Right *there*. "Ooohhh." The lights of the city reflected in the water and a boat, big and white and full of laughing people, glided by. Zeke rushed to the railing and leaned over, watching as the boat sailed under a bridge. Or rather, *one* of the bridges. "There are so many bridges!"

"Yeah. That happens when you build your city on two sides of a river. I take it rivers are in short supply in Sheol."

"If you don't count the lava. Oh, it's beautiful."

"Yeah. I reckon it is." Hamish sounded odd, and when Zeke looked up at him, he wasn't looking at the river.

He was looking at Zeke.

"Um . . . I should probably get back. The AI has probably reported me by now, and who knows what that'll mean."

"All right. This way."

Hamish led Zeke along the waterfront, not hurrying, and not complaining whenever Zeke just *had* to stop and stare at something else: the sweeping arch of a bridge, a flock of geese marching across the grass, streetlamps casting shadows through the bare trees. When they finally cut away from the river, Hamish kept looking behind them.

Zeke chuckled. "Don't deny it. You like the river too."

"I'm not denying it. It's nice, but I've seen it before, so I can take or leave it."

"Then why do you keep looking at it? I mean I know why *I* do, but you've checked it out at least half a dozen times."

Hamish gazed down at Zeke, lifting an eyebrow. "I'm not looking at the river, mate. I think somebody's following us."

Hamish's words chilled Zeke more thoroughly than the wind. "F-f-following?" Could it be Melchom? No, he wasn't allowed out in the Upper World either. The AI? But when Zeke peered over his shoulder, he didn't detect any out-of-place lighting effects. "Who? Why?" *You know why. Because demons aren't allowed to* fraternize.

"Not sure. Sometimes Hunter's Moon fans like to get up close and personal. Snap a photo or two. That kind of thing. But I haven't caught anyone out. It's just a feeling—" he rubbed the back of his neck "—right here. Supes have learned to watch their backs, you know what I'm saying?"

Zeke nodded. He knew all too well. And when it came to demons, it wasn't only humans they had to guard against. Other supes—magicians, wizards, even witches, although they preferred to partner with familiars rather than bind demons in service—were the greater threat. Other demons were the greatest threat of all.

Suddenly, Zeke's earlier devil-may-care insubordination seemed extremely foolhardy.

"I'd better get back quickly. I'm already risking censure by being alone with you outside the office setting."

"You can't take a walk with a friend?"

"Demons don't have friends."

Hamish shook his head. "Seriously, mate. You lot need a better A&R man."

"A what?"

"Never mind. But maybe upgrade your expectations a bit, yeah? Because the way you're treated is total bollocks."

Zeke hunched his shoulders under the weight of Hamish's coat, trying not to flinch every time Hamish looked over his shoulder. When they turned the last corner, though, he had to stop and stare.

"What's wrong?"

"It looks so different from this perspective. I only ever see it from above." He could see his own window from here, and the red glow behind the blinds in the living room that told him the AI was home and not happy. *I'll deal with that when I'm inside again.*

He hurried across the street, Hamish's wordless shout of warning barely registering when a car swished by behind him, because right there was the falafel shop, the one with heavenly aromas that tormented him every day. The windows were dark, but he pressed his nose against the cold glass anyway. "It's closed. I wish . . ." He shouldn't be greedy though. He'd already had more than he could ever hope for tonight.

Hamish chuckled from behind Zeke, standing so close Zeke felt the vibration; even Hamish's laughter held a rhythm that called to him. *Stop it.* "You hungry again already?"

"No. Of course not. But I smell this place every day, and I've always wanted to try the falafel. Or the . . . the shawarma."

"Then why don't you?"

"It's a human establishment. Even if they had an entrance inside the building—which they don't—I couldn't go inside."

"So have it delivered."

"They don't deliver. I checked once when I'd saved enough from my paycheck." Hamish muttered something else unintelligible, but Zeke ignored it. He turned around. "Thank you for indulging me tonight—with dinner and the dessert and the walk. You didn't have to. I didn't do a very good job."

"Oi. Your job is to make me happy, right? I was perfectly happy, despite my date ditching me after the appetizer."

Zeke's eyes widened. "They have *appetizers*?"

Hamish laughed, his gray eyes crinkling at the edges. "You have *got* to get out more, mate."

Zeke glanced at the door to the lobby. "Actually, I'm pretty sure I'll be getting out less. But thank you." He attempted to look fierce and intimidating, something most demons were very good at but which Zeke had never quite mastered. "I'm not setting you up on another date with Olli. I'll check the files and come up with another option for you."

Hamish's smile faded. "Are you sure— Ah, never mind. What time do you want me back?"

"Tomorrow morning?"

Hamish studied Zeke for a moment, his head tilted to one side, until Zeke started to squirm. "Make it noon, if that works for you."

"Of course. Oh." He shrugged Hamish's coat off and held it out. "Thank you for the loan."

"You're welcome." He took a half step forward, but Zeke backed away, one hand groping for the door handle.

"See you tomorrow." Zeke darted inside, lifting a hand in farewell once the door was safely between them.

Hamish's mouth quirked, but he returned the salute, then pulled on his coat and sauntered off down the street.

Zeke trudged up the stairs to his apartment. Sure enough, the AI was doing an excellent impression of a red strobe. "Yes. I know I was in violation of the contract. But technically I was fulfilling my directive from Magistra Lenore. And if you don't mind—" he squared his shoulders "—I have something else to do toward that end. I'll see you tomorrow."

Zeke marched into his tiny bedroom and closed the door, ignoring the increasingly intense red light that seeped underneath it.

He punched the hands-free button on the Supernatural Selection phone next to his bed.

He took a deep breath, clenching his fists so that his hands wouldn't shake. "Hecate, call Olli."

"Calling . . . Olli."

The phone rang four times. Five. Six, cranking Zeke's anxiety higher with each metallic buzz.

"Hello?" Olli sounded breathless. Oh no. Had Zeke taken them away from the fire or its aftermath?

"Olli, this is Zeke from Supernatural Selection. Is everything okay? I don't mean to intrude, but—"

"Oh, Zeke. I'm so glad you called. I wanted to thank you. If you hadn't arranged the date with Hamish . . . Well, my life would be very different right now."

Uh-oh. Had Olli fallen for Hamish already? This was going to be harder than Zeke had originally thought. When he could cite the spells as the reason to block a particular pairing, that was one thing. But when it was all on him? He uncurled his fingers and clutched his knees, his palms damp against his pants. "I— That is, I hope the fire damage wasn't too great."

"No. No, in fact—"

"The thing is, I don't think a second date would be—"

"There was no fire at all!"

Zeke stared at the phone, but its bland black keypad gave nothing away. "No fire? But—"

"Aarni sent that text because he was jealous. Can you believe it? I never thought I had a chance with him. I'd never even *thought* about flirting. If it weren't for you setting me up with Hamish, he might never have made a move."

"I take it he, uh, moved?"

"Like you wouldn't believe." Olli laughed, a throaty chuckle. "So thank you. Supernatural Selection got me my perfect match, just like it promised. You're the best. But I've got to go. Aarni is waiting in the sauna."

"O-okay. Congratulations. I'm really glad there wasn't a fire and—"

The line went dead.

Chapter Seven

After Hamish left Zeke at Supernatural Selection, he couldn't face going back to his hotel, so he took an Uber to the rehearsal studio and spent a solid two hours beating the hell out of his skins. He wasn't entirely sure if it was frustration over the date, shame over Zeke's accusation that Hamish wasn't "emotionally available"—whatever that meant—or anger about the way Zeke was treated by pretty much everybody in his life. Demons. Witches. Angels. And Hamish himself, for that matter.

He hadn't been exactly cooperative in his first meeting with Zeke, or given him much to work with. And why? It wasn't Zeke's fault that Tiff didn't love him. It wasn't Zeke's fault that Hamish's heart was currently closed for business.

Hunh. Maybe that's what emotionally unavailable *means.*

Right, then. Zeke had a point. Maybe Hamish should consider Zeke's other suggestion—just opting for the wedding date instead of looking for a partner who was nothing more than a placeholder for the person he could never have.

Yeah, Hamish could see how that would be unfair to the other person. *But as long as I'm straight with them from the start, maybe I'll find somebody who wants the same thing.* A way to get on with life. Make a rich, rewarding, successful relationship, probably with a good amount of affection, even if love was off the table. Why not? He was willing to work at it. Obviously he wouldn't go for somebody who hated music, or hated *him*, or hated that the relationship would never be the fairy-tale, happily-ever-after bull-crap.

He'd come clean about his feelings for Tiff, and as long as his new mate was good with that, Hamish didn't see any reason they couldn't be happy ever after without the fairy tale. A working relationship based on mutual respect and liking. What was wrong with that?

He was wrung out by the time he got back to his hotel. He took a quick shower and flopped down on the bed. *What's wrong with that is you'll still be pining.* Would he ever stop waiting for Tiff to turn around and *see* him? But that would mean . . . what? That she'd divorce Luci and cut off her relationship with Vitor? That she'd add Hamish to the poly relationship? Vitor had said he'd be up for it, even if Luci was only interested in Tiff.

But when Hamish tried to fit his mind around the logistics of all those intersecting *feelings*, he thought his head would explode.

There was a thing . . . What was it again? Vitor had told him about it once when he'd asked Hamish out on a date . . . The feeling that a person in a poly relationship experienced when their partner was happy with someone else . . .

Oh. *Compersion.* Hamish wasn't sure he could manage that. *For Tiff, would I be willing to try?*

But then, if he couldn't hack it, he'd destroy the friendship they *did* have, not to mention jeopardizing band politics—and they'd had *more* than enough personal angst when Gareth had still been pining for Niall.

No. Moving on was the best choice, for Tiff's sake as well as his own. He'd make his new parameters clear to Zeke tomorrow: mutual respect, liking, honesty. Commitment, even if love wasn't an option. *With the right person, I could do it, no problem.*

He rested his hands on his belly. *Zeke.* It's too bad demons weren't allowed to date, because Hamish could totally see the two of them building the kind of relationship he was looking for. The way Zeke greeted each new experience with such joy—it was totally charming. And arousing, considering how Hamish's dick perked up at the memory.

But Zeke didn't know music, so that would be a problem. *But only because they don't have it in Sheol. How would he react when he was exposed to Upper World music? How would he react to* my music?

The thought had Hamish grabbing himself when his dick threatened to get a little *too* perky, because *damn.* That would be *everything.*

"Bugger," he muttered, and launched himself off the bed and into the shower again—cold this time. *Not gonna beat off to a guy who's never had sex and whose whole life is one giant lockup.* Besides, Zeke had essentially been ordered to make Hamish happy or else. Starring Zeke in even a private happy ending seemed like just another way for him to be betrayed, and Hamish refused to do it.

Although his dreams apparently didn't get that memo, because he awoke the next morning tangled in his sheets, his bare chest damp with sweat, and his dick as hard as his sticks. He told himself that his state didn't have anything to do with Zeke.

I lie like a frigging rug.

He needed another good long practice to work off some energy, but rehearsal wasn't until late this afternoon. So he got dressed and left the hotel, walking the streets until he realized he was retracing the route he and Zeke had taken the previous night. He sat on a bench, scowling at the river, until it was time to head to Supernatural Selection for his appointment.

He paused with his hand on the door handle, caught by a clatter and a burst of laughter from inside the falafel restaurant. *What the hell. It's noon, right? Lunchtime.*

So he stepped inside the place. Zeke was right—it smelled great. Hamish ordered two falafel sandwiches to go and took them upstairs to the Supernatural Selection lobby.

It was empty except for the AI looming behind the desk like a pillar of radioactive salt.

"Hey. I'm here to see Zeke. Want to let him know?"

From the vomit-green tinge around the edges, Hamish figured the answer was *Hell no*, or whatever expletives were allowed angels, but at least it left. If it were something other than over-the-top lighting effects, Hamish would have said it'd "slunk."

Speed obviously wasn't its goal because it was ten minutes before Zeke rushed in, his dark curls rumpled and his tie askew, his arms full of manila folders. "Hamish. I'm so sorry. I was going through the files and I lost track of time."

"No worries, mate. I'm early." He held up the bag from downstairs. "And I brought lunch."

"You . . ." Zeke's eyes widened, looking suspiciously shiny. "Is that . . . falafel?" His voice sank to a reverent whisper.

"Absolutely. Got a place where we can eat?"

"I— If we— Yes, of course." His smile dawned like the sun over the ocean. "We can use the conference room on the third floor. Please come this way." The AI surged toward them, and Zeke cast it a glance that Hamish couldn't interpret. "It's *his* request. Refusing would be rude and counter to our customer-service standards." He returned his attention to Hamish. "Just ignore it."

"No problem there. Can you hear what it says?"

"Not *hear*, precisely, but unfortunately I can understand it." The AI flared pink, and he glanced at it irritably. "I said 'unfortunately' and I meant 'unfortunately.' If you want gratitude, you need to *earn* it."

Zeke ushered Hamish up the stairs, the AI dogging their heels. He stopped at an open door. "Will this be all right?"

"Works for me." Hamish turned to the AI. "I didn't bring enough for you though, mate, so since it'd be rude to eat in front of you, suppose you stay out here in the hallway, eh?"

From the burst of angry red, the AI was not a fan of the idea, but Hamish didn't give a crap. Taking Zeke, his mouth agape, by the elbow, Hamish strolled into the room and shut the door in what he assumed was the AI's face.

"You— Lucifer's balls, I can't believe you did that."

"What, stand up to Satan's flashlight? No skin off my pouch. I don't have to answer to him."

Zeke's lips quirked in a crooked smile. "You don't. But I do."

Hamish set the bags onto the table and took Zeke by the shoulders. "Tell me straight. Will that cause trouble for you? Because I admit I did it mostly because the damn thing chaps my hide."

"I can spin it with 'the client's wishes are paramount,' so don't worry. But what I meant was that I can't believe you brought me falafel."

Hamish shrugged. "You said you wanted to try it. I haven't eaten. Figured we'd kill two ostriches with one pita. Or whatever." He let go of Zeke and unpacked the bags. "Falafel. A couple of sparkling waters. We can nosh while we talk about what happens next."

Zeke tore his gaze from the still-warm sandwich. "Next? Oh. Yes. I've got several ideas—"

"Hold up. Let's eat first, before these get cold."

With the speed Zeke sat, folding his hands on the table and looking at Hamish expectantly, he was obviously down with that plan.

"Go ahead. Take one."

"'Take'? But—" Zeke's shoulders rose with his deep breath, and he reached out slowly to snag one sandwich and inch it toward himself.

Hamish eyed him, grabbing his own lunch without ceremony. "You know, I can *see* you, mate. You're not going to convince me the sandwich is staging its annual across-the-table migration, no matter how slow you go."

Red blotches painted Zeke's neck and face. "Sorry. Habit. In Sheol, we either have to move *very* quickly or at an absolutely glacial pace." He dragged the sandwich across the shiny table, caging it between his hands as if it might escape.

Or as if somebody might steal it from him. *Bugger.*

"Well, dig in at your own pace. We're not in Sheol, and there's nobody here but you and me." Which Hamish was pretty sure was true. He supposed the witches could have installed surveillance spells in the room, but he didn't have that spine-creeping feeling of being watched anymore, and the AI was trapped on the other side of the door. He counted it as a win.

Zeke nibbled at the edge of his falafel, and that same expression of bliss washed across his face—until he saw Hamish observing him. Then he quickly set the sandwich down and folded his hands in his lap.

Hamish sighed. "Don't like to be watched while you eat? You didn't seem to mind at the restaurant last night." Of course, that could have been dessert euphoria.

"I was, um, a little overwhelmed then. In Sheol, we're not allowed to eat at all without our supervisor's permission . . ." He shrugged.

"How often do those arseholes *give* permission?"

Zeke screwed up his face, peering up at the ceiling. "Never."

"Figures."

"Well, never when there's also food available. My supervisor has given me permission twice, but the only things in my cave at the time were rocks." He wrinkled his nose. "Not very tasty."

"I should bloody well think not. Look." Hamish leaned forward, extending his hand across the table. Zeke stared at it but didn't take it, so Hamish withdrew it. "As long as we're working together, anytime you feel a bit peckish? Say so and we'll grab lunch or dinner or a goddamn frigging granola bar. Because if you ask me, mate? Sheol is the last place *anybody* should have to live. And I'm from a place with spiders the size of dinner plates, hot-and-cold-running crocodiles, and semiaquatic mammals with duckbills, beaver tails, and poisonous fangs." He tore a bite out of his sandwich and chewed ferociously. "Now eat up. We've got things to discuss. And afterwards? We're getting ice cream."

He brought me falafel.
Zeke's mouth watered from the delicious aroma and the one tiny bite he'd managed so far, but he couldn't make himself eat —not yet. His throat was too tight.

He took an experimental sip from the can of sparkling water and choked because swallowing anything was apparently beyond his current skill set.

"You okay, mate?" Hamish rose halfway out of his chair, but Zeke waved him back.

"I'm all right," he wheezed.

"If you say so." Hamish took an enormous bite of his sandwich. *He* apparently didn't have *issues* about food. No, his issues were all about love and relationships.

Zeke managed to swallow a mouthful of water without another coughing attack. "What was it you wanted to talk about?"

Hamish eyed him, his gaze dipping to Zeke's untouched lunch and back to his face. He cocked an eyebrow.

Right. We're eating first. Not that eating was a hardship for its own sake, because the falafel—Lucifer's balls, it tasted as good as it smelled, and Zeke's eyes drifted closed with his first real bite. He kept them closed, the better to isolate the flavors, humming low in his throat as he ate. After the last bite, he licked his fingers and sighed, letting his eyes flutter open—and uttered an embarrassing *meep.*

Hamish was staring at him, his unfinished sandwich poised halfway to his mouth.

Zeke shrunk down in his chair, noticing the stack of napkins on the table. *Manners. I shouldn't have licked my fingers. It's not polite.* "I'm sorry."

"For what?" Hamish's voice was rough, as if *he'd* been eating rocks.

"I should have used the napkin to wipe my fingers. But it was so good—"

"Bugger the napkins." He shifted in his chair, his tongue flicking out to swipe his bottom lip. "But if your demon overlords ever want to lure someone into throwing caution to the wind, I can tell them how to do it."

Zeke gazed mournfully at the empty sandwich wrapper. "Yes. I think you're right. That falafel would definitely tempt a saint."

"I wasn't talking about the falafel," Hamish murmured. But then he finished off his own lunch in a few large bites, looking almost angry, so Zeke figured he must find it almost unbearably delicious too.

Zeke got up, cleared away the trash, then sat back down opposite Hamish, folding his hands on the table. "You said you wanted to discuss something?"

"Yeah." Hamish's fingers started to tap against his chair's arms. "You were right."

Zeke tried to focus on Hamish's words and not the way the rhythm seemed to drive his own heartbeat. "I was? About what?"

"That I wasn't being fair to my potential partner. That I didn't really know what I wanted. That I wasn't being truthful—with you or with myself."

Zeke blinked. "That's . . . that's a lot of self-realization in less than twenty-four hours."

Hamish chuckled. "What can I say? Blame it on the transformative effects of salted caramel chocolate tart."

"It was pretty transformative."

"You have no idea," Hamish muttered. "But here's the thing. I still don't believe I'll fall in love again, but you know what? That's okay. I figured out what I want. Something based on mutual respect and liking. Common interests. Eventual affection. Do you think you can find me somebody like that? Somebody who'll be up for dating me at least through the wedding and then we'll see where we go from there?"

Zeke couldn't stop his grin. Because this was *exactly* what he needed: a blueprint of what would make Hamish happy. And if he felt a slight twinge of disappointment—once Hamish was happy, he wouldn't be around to share falafel or dessert or distracting rhythms—he ignored it. Because his job was about the client's satisfaction, not his own.

"You know, I think I might have just the persons."

Hamish's brows drew together. "'Persons'? I'm not sure I'm up for a menage. Or even a poly relationship." He stopped drumming to run his hands through his hair. "Those don't really appeal to me. Too many balls to keep in the air. So to speak."

"That's for you to decide, of course. But three of the muses are registered with us—Euterpe, Erato, and Melpomene. Are you familiar with them?"

Hamish nodded. "I've met some of the muses. Not all of them. Kind of intense, you know what I'm saying? Focused."

"Yes, well, they do each have their specialties."

"Is that what you call 'em? I'd call 'em obsessions."

Zeke raised his eyebrows. "I thought you were embarking on a new journey here. Perhaps you should reserve judgment?"

This time, Hamish rubbed his hands over his face—and then started beating another pattern on his thighs. "You're right. Go on."

Zeke opened one of the folders he'd abandoned in the throes of his foodgasm. "According to their profiles, they prefer dating as a group, but would be willing to try one-on-one for the right partner. Now Melpomene, as the muse of tragedy—"

"Nah. Met her once at a Grateful Dead concert in San Francisco."

"The Grateful Dead?"

Hamish grinned. "I know. A little on the nose, right? But she was disappointed because the Dead's music wasn't nearly dark enough for her. She's a big fan of all those doomed teenager songs from the sixties. Also Jim Morrison, but I think that was the hair."

"Not Melpomene, then." Zeke flipped to the next page. "Erato, muse of love poetry, might be—"

"Too much work. All those double entendres get wearing after a while. What about the last one? Euterpe. I've never met her, but she's the muse of music, right? So we ought to have *that* in common anyway."

"Yes. Music, song, and lyric poetry." Zeke skimmed the rest of her profile. "And she's aromantic, which means she won't expect you to play the doting boyfriend. Asexual too, but you said consummation was optional. She might be the perfect match after all."

He took an unsteady breath, an odd, unfamiliar feeling twisting in his belly like writhing salamanders. He should be relieved that Hamish had decided to cooperate, that they'd located someone who—on paper anyway—fit the new parameters he'd outlined. So why did his fingers twitch with the impulse to toss all the profiles in the trash?

Hamish tilted his head, his intense gray gaze making Zeke squirm in his chair. "I'm willing to give it a go if she is."

"Would you like me to arrange another dinner? She lives on Olympus, but according to her profile, she's willing to come down from the heights for the right person."

Hamish's grin was a little crooked. "You going to convince her that I'm the right bloke?"

"It is my job, you know." *I need to remember that myself.* "The restaurant the other night was . . ." He swallowed convulsively, remembering exactly what the restaurant was. "Lovely.

According to this . . ." He peered down at the paper in front of him, trying to make sense of the words dancing in front of his eyes while Hamish's beat resonated in his blood. "She loves Greek food, but it has to be *superlative* Greek food, so a steak and seafood place might be a better bet. You wouldn't want to start your relationship with disappointment."

"I've got a better notion, since I'm obviously not my best in a restaurant . . ." Hamish winked and propped his ankle on his opposite knee. "Tomorrow night, Hunter's Moon is playing this new venue over by the Rose Quarter. A music muse ought to go for a concert, right? All those Olympians dearly love a party, so I'll get her a VIP pass. She can come to the meet and greet before the concert, sit front row center for the show, and come backstage for our postperformance reception afterwards. If I'm not her cuppa, no harm. She'll at least have other musicians to talk to. But if things go well, she and I can move on from there, and you don't have to be triangulated anymore."

"Oh." The salamanders reared up and hissed at that idea. "That could work. I'm not sure—"

"Don't worry." Hamish grinned. "I'll keep you posted on my happiness quotient. Maybe check in on the regular until after the wedding anyway."

Zeke felt the blood drain from his face. "W-w-wedding? But you said—"

Hamish barked out a laugh. "Crikey, mate, your *face*. Not *our* wedding. Mal and Bryce's wedding. You know, the whole reason I'm here?"

"Oh. Right." The blood rushed upward again, no doubt painting Zeke's face in those unattractive red blotches. "I knew that."

"But here's the thing." Hamish leaned forward, drumming an abbreviated cadence on the table with his palms. "It doesn't seem right to make her sit *alone* for the whole show. She needs a companion. A backup escort."

Zeke frowned down at the discarded profiles. "One of her sisters? That might lead them to think a group relationship was on the table."

"Hell no." He pointed a long finger at Zeke's chest. "I'm talking about you, mate."

"Me? But I can't—"

"Don't give me the 'I can't go outside' line." He grinned, and this time it had a decided evil glint. "We've already established the way to get around it, right? It'll make me happy to have you escort my date to the concert. Boom. Mission accomplished."

"But—"

The door burst open and the AI surged inside, all indigo indignation and flashes of self-righteous gold.

"Oi!" Hamish glared at it irritably. "Were you listening at the bloody keyhole? Not very angelic, that. Besides, I told you to wait outside."

The AI ignored Hamish and advanced on Zeke, seeming to grow in height, foot for foot, as it advanced across the room.

"Shut up." Zeke slouched in his chair, arms crossed. "I *know* it's illegal. But it's the only way to make the client happy." Yellow pulsed in the AI's middle. "Well, you'd know all about self-justification, wouldn't you?" Pink fountained from its . . . feet? "Nope. Don't even try to play innocent. I know perfectly well you hold back some of my wages when you exchange US dollars for demon gold. You're *supposed* to be above greed and avarice." Magenta swirled like a cyclone. "It is *not* for my own good. If you—"

"As fascinating as it is to see you argue with a light show, let's stow it, shall we?" Hamish leaned back, tilting his chair on its gimbals. "I want Zeke to be there. According to what the magistra told him, it's within the rules. In fact, it's *required*, because I would be so distracted by thoughts of my poor abandoned date that I might screw up a set. And bollixing a performance doesn't just make *me* unhappy. It makes my whole *band* unhappy." He propped his feet on the table, lacing his fingers across his belly. "And when my band leader is unhappy —did I mention he's the last true bard of Faerie?—royalty gets involved. Believe me when I tell you that you do *not* want to piss off the Faerie Queen."

Zeke stared at Hamish with wide eyes. Lucifer's balls, he'd actually threatened the AI with fae retribution, and *nobody* messed with the angelic host except *their* supervisors or the Host Relations department—and HR was only called in in cases of the most egregious infractions. Even Lucifer, when he'd complained about his demotion to the infernal ranks, hadn't rated HR intervention.

The AI subsided to a sullen ochre, and Zeke had to hide his satisfied grin behind his hand.

"Oh, and another thing." Hamish laced his hands behind his head, his grin morphing from mischievous to downright evil. "You, you bloody overgrown Maglite, aren't invited."

Zeke sat bolt upright, goggling at Hamish, as the AI burst into a veritable fireworks display of rage. He caught Hamish's gaze. "In case you didn't get the picture, it's not happy about that. It says it'll report me to the work-release oversight committee."

"Why? It's not your idea. Besides, take a look at that." He pointed to the AI, who was still sparking and shimmying like a downed power line. "Even when it's not throwing a bloody hissy fit, it'll fuck up the lighting effects for the show. And between you and me, mate?" Hamish dropped his feet off the table, leaning forward to whisper conspiratorially. "I think it's a little unbalanced."

Well, *that* caused a definite increase in the fireworks. In fact, the AI moved toward Hamish. If it touched Hamish, it would—

"Stop!" Zeke leaped to his feet. "If you hurt a client—an Upper World citizen—you'll be downgraded, maybe right out of the angelic host." The AI froze, then inched toward Zeke with a menacing pulse of orange. "It is *not* justified. He's a *client*. And as you've reminded me approximately sixty times a day since I arrived, the client's wishes always win." Pink trickled down, merging with the orange. "I won't make him take it back, because look at you. You're proving his point for him. He can't trust you not to ruin his show."

Hamish stood slowly, circling the table until he was standing distractingly close to Zeke. "Like I said. Mission accomplished. I'll messenger the tickets to you this afternoon." He clapped Zeke on the shoulder. "Now who wants ice cream?"

Chapter Eight

Two hours before the concert, Hamish stared at his reflection in the dressing room mirror, tugging irritably at the collar of his dress shirt. By this time preshow, he'd normally already be in a tank and shorts, ready to perform. Comfortable, in other words. He yanked at his collar again, causing the top button of the shirt to pop off and ping against the wall.

"Bugger."

"Hamish?" Josh laid his violin in its case and edged over to stand next to him. "What's wrong?"

"*I'm* wrong. Look at me." Hamish jabbed a finger at the mirror. "I'm tarted up like a stockbroker or a bloody evangelical preacher."

Josh chuckled. "I don't think that's entirely the case. Why are you so nervous?"

"Nervous? I'm not nervous."

"You've been beating a steady cadence on every available surface in the dressing room since you arrived. You managed to drive Spence out of the room, and you know he *never* gets more than three feet away from me prior to showtime."

Hamish dropped his hands to his sides, resisting the urge to tap his fingers against his thighs. "I envy that, you know? That you've got someone who wants to make sure you're okay. To let you know he's got your back."

"Actually, I think it's Spence who needs the reassurance."

Hamish glanced down at him, eyebrows lifting in surprise. "*Spence* gets nervous before a show?"

Josh nudged him with an elbow. "Stage fright like you wouldn't believe. But don't let on that I told you."

"Your secret is safe with me." Hamish glared at his reflection again. "I look a right Charley."

"You look fine. Not exactly like yourself, but fine."

"That's it, you know? That's the problem." He gestured to himself. "I'm in a bloody disguise. If I'm trying to meet a person and see if we hit it off, shouldn't I show her the real me? Not somebody else's idea of what I ought to be?"

Josh's white-blond eyebrows drew together. "Whose idea was this outfit?"

"Well. Yours."

"Mine?" His eyebrows shot up until they were hidden behind his bangs. "I wouldn't— Oh. These are the clothes we bought at Nordstrom the other day." He laughed and patted Hamish on the shoulder. "Those were for a date at a fairly upscale restaurant, not a Hunter's Moon concert. You're right, Hamish. You should change into your usual clothes and show your date who you are. Because pretending to be somebody else? That never works in the long run."

Both of them glanced at the door, where Gareth had just entered, and Josh's words hit home. Gareth and Niall's relationship had begun when Niall was hiding his true nature, and it had nearly destroyed them both. Sure, they were solid now, but it had taken a couple of centuries of unmitigated suffering on both their parts.

No way was Hamish signing on for that kind of grief.

"Thanks, mate."

"No problem." Josh gifted Hamish with one of his sweet smiles. "We can all get up in our heads sometimes. Makes it hard to spot the obvious."

Too right.

A little of Hamish's anxiety unwound once he was in his familiar concert clothes, although he had to catch himself from pounding on the dressing table or the sofa back or the bloody frigging walls. He checked the clock. Zeke should be arriving with Euterpe for the meet and greet at any moment. He smoothed the front of his tank top. Should he have chosen a different color? What was Zeke's favorite color? He—

Wait a minute. Why am I worrying about Zeke's favorite color? Shouldn't I be focused on Euterpe? Not that he knew anything about her. *I wonder if she likes falafel?*

Del poked their head in the door. "Hamish. Your guests are here."

Hamish frowned at them. Del was stoic at the best of times, at least on the job—he'd seen them crack a smile maybe twice. But their bland expression and inflectionless voice was a comment all on its own. "Is there a problem?"

"Not yet." They stalked out of the room.

Gareth leaned over to peer down the hall after them. "What's up with Del? I've never seen them so pissed."

Hamish blinked. "That's Del being pissed?"

"Sure. Didn't you know?"

"Nah." People had called him clueless, oblivious, *emotionally unavailable.* Maybe they all had a point. "They've never exactly chirped merry. I figured this was just another nuance."

Gareth chuckled as he cracked open a bottle of water from the mini-fridge. "They must never have been pissed at you. You're lucky." He downed half the water. "It's not very comfortable being on the receiving end of Del's ire."

"I take it you've been there?"

"More times than I can count. Before Niall came back"— Gareth's face took on the special glow he always got whenever Niall was around, or even mentioned—"Del was on my case pretty much constantly about my behavior with all of you. Trust me, I've got more reasons to be grateful for Niall's return than just having him in my life again." He grinned. "Rehearsals and business meetings are much less stressful too."

"Is Niall already at the meet and greet?"

Gareth's grin faded. "No. He's going to be late. Something about the case he's working on now. He promised to be here for the show, though."

Niall never missed any of the band's performances, and hadn't since he'd gotten released from his underworld captivity back in the fall. He always staked out a spot in the wings of whatever venue they were in where Gareth could see him from onstage. Lately either Luci or Vitor joined him, so Tiff was always sending heated looks offstage too.

Hamish rubbed his suddenly tight chest. Would he ever have somebody who'd never miss his shows? Who'd wait in the wings so Hamish would know they were there, even if he couldn't see them every minute?

Maybe Euterpe would be up for that, being the muse of music and all. But as Hamish left Gareth to his preconcert vocal warm-ups, it was Zeke's dark eyes and the glint of his glasses that Hamish imagined standing behind the curtains.

He snorted and strode down the hall. *Never gonna happen.* And probably just as well. Any more band spouses backstage and there wouldn't be room for the roadies.

A low murmur floated out the open door of the lounge where the meet and greet was already in full swing. These days, Hunter's Moon had one before every show, which made Del happy (Hamish assumed) and made their publicist happier still. When Gareth had still been in semimourning for Niall, he'd only agreed to mingle with the VIPs every half-dozen gigs. In a way, that had made the notion of "VIP" more special. On the other hand, now they were able to meet a lot more fans face-to-face, which was always a kick for Hamish.

He wasn't the only extrovert in the band—Spence was technically an extrovert too, but he was too grumpy and focused on Josh to be much good at glad-handing with the guests. They all depended on Hamish to be the happy face of the band, and he was glad to oblige.

Tonight, though, it was different. He wiped his damp palms on his shorts. Shite, he was actually *nervous*. Weird. He was never nervous before these things. Chatting up fans, charming the press, arranging selfies with the band for contest winners—Hamish could ordinarily do that in his sleep. But now . . .

Shouldn't surprise me. I could be meeting my future mate. It was natural to be nervous, right? Natural to want to make a good impression. He glanced down at his brown tank. *I should have worn the blue one.*

Too late now. He took a breath, donned his best company grin, and walked into the room. The place was full of chattering people, but despite the crowd and the noise, the first person Hamish saw was Zeke.

He was standing against the wall on the far side of the room, nearly hidden behind one of Hunter's Moon's hulking security staff. His eyes were enormous behind those cute Harry Potter glasses, and his lips were slightly parted. While everyone else in the room seemed to be holding a glass of champagne or sparkling water or some damn thing, Zeke's hands were empty and his arms were hugging his torso, like he was trying to keep himself from flying apart.

Hamish recognized that look. He'd seen it on fans who'd waited months for a chance to meet the band. On kids waiting in line for Santa. On the crowd before a championship footie game. He snagged a couple of brimming champagne flutes from the tiny bar and headed across the room.

Dimly, he registered that people were speaking to him, looking at him, somebody even put a hand on his elbow, but he cast them an apologetic smile and kept moving forward. When he was about halfway across the room, Zeke spotted him, and the smile that bloomed on his narrow face . . . *Strewth.* Hamish practically leaped the rest of the way.

For a moment, he could do nothing but gaze down at Zeke and grin. Then he finally found his missing voice. "Hey. You made it."

Zeke nodded, and the security guard saluted and stepped aside, revealing a tall woman in high heels, narrow black trousers, and a shimmery white blouse that called togas to mind. Her dark hair was twisted in a sleek updo and winking with diamond pins, and her full lips were pursed like she'd been sucking lemons for the last hour.

Zeke's shoulders rose and fell, and his Adam's apple bobbed as if he'd had trouble swallowing. "Hamish, this is Euterpe, muse of music, daughter of Zeus and Mnemosyne. Euterpe, Hamish Mulherne."

Shite. I should have worn the stupid dress clothes after all. Because Euterpe was dressed like someone who was about to traipse into an opera, not someone about to watch a rock concert. Hamish glanced at Zeke. Hadn't Zeke warned her what this crowd would be like?

Be fair. He's never been *in this kind of crowd before.*

That's when it hit him: Zeke really *hadn't* been in this kind of crowd before. Euterpe had been swanning around the world for millennia, so she'd have a ton of experience in social situations of all kinds. Rock music wasn't exactly new or secret. She had to have known what it would be like. Hell, she'd agreed to the date, so Zeke had probably prepped her with info about Hamish and the band. Any inappropriate clothing choices were all on her—not that she looked like she was uncomfortable. More like she was disappointed that the current crowd wasn't up to her standard.

Not exactly a bonza beginning.

Zeke was wearing a version of the same outfit he'd worn at all their other meetings: white button-down, dress slacks, subdued tie, along with that same gray sweatshirt, its hood mashing his curls. Didn't he own any casual clothes?

Wonder what they're wearing in Sheol this season? Assuming they wore clothes. Hamish's mouth went dry at the thought, so before he could down both glasses of champagne—and he never drank before a show—he presented them to Zeke and what's-her-name.

"Nice to meet you. Can I offer you both some of our exclusive second-rate champagne?"

Zeke chuckled. Euterpe did not. "No, thank you. I only drink spring water."

Good to know. "We've got some of that. The band lives on the stuff before and during our shows."

The security guard said, "I'll handle it, Mr. Mulherne." He shouldered his way through the crowd. Hamish stared after him, not really wanting to turn back to his prospective mate.

Prospective mate. Right. He suppressed a shudder. Still, he needed to make an effort. Maybe she didn't like crowds.

The glasses were taken gently from his hands, causing him to finally turn back. Zeke smiled at him crookedly. "Thank you. I've never had champagne before." He set one glass on a nearby table and took a sip of the other. His eyes widened. "It's . . . it's like drinking stars."

Hamish chuckled. "You know, that's what the guy who invented champagne said the first time he tried it."

Zeke's blush-blotches made an appearance. "I'm sorry. But it's like magic."

No, mate. The magic is all you.

Champagne. Lucifer's balls, how had he never had this before? Well, he knew how. Even if it existed in Sheol, no demon of his rank would ever get near it. But this wasn't about *him.* He gulped the rest of it down, ignoring the temptation to savor it, because clearly he was screwing up the meeting between Euterpe and Hamish.

Of course, the instant he'd met her at the translocation door, where she'd been escorted by Pan and Mercury, for Lucifer's sake, he'd known the evening was going to be . . . challenging.

The first thing out of her mouth had been a complaint about the weather—and they were inside a building. By the time they'd taken the limo Hamish had provided—the AI glowing a judgmental green at the door—her disapproval had turned into downright disgust.

If Zeke had heard one more comment about how preferable the perfect Olympian weather was compared to Portland, he'd have almost welcomed his cave in Sheol, just to escape from her incessant grumbling.

But again, he had to remind himself that this wasn't about *him*. He needed to make Hamish happy, and if it made him happy to be in a non-romantic relationship with a woman who leaked disapproval from every perfect pore, well, that was his business.

Zeke grabbed the champagne he'd set aside earlier and downed that too, choking a bit as Hamish made awkward small talk with Euterpe. Or rather didn't make small talk. Euterpe was observing the crowd with half-lidded eyes, accepting water—in a crystal glass instead of plastic—from the security guard without bothering to thank him, or even acknowledge him for that matter. She simply held out her hand as if she expected it to be filled.

Maybe that was the way things worked in Olympus. Zeke wouldn't know.

Hamish cast Zeke a rather desperate glance. *Right. Do my job. Facilitate this meeting.* Although in the normal course of events, he shouldn't be here at all—as the AI had reminded him approximately six hundred seventy-three times since lunch— which was another falafel sandwich delivered to the Supernatural Selection office, courtesy of Hamish.

"Would you two like to have a little more privacy to chat?" Zeke had checked in with Del, the band's rainbow-haired manager, when he'd arrived, and Del had assured him there'd be a quiet place if needed.

"No." Euterpe sipped her water, leaving a crescent of red lipstick on the rim of the glass. She finally lifted her gaze to Hamish. "I understand your band leader is Faerie's last true bard. You may introduce me."

"Ah . . ." Hamish rubbed the back of his neck. "He's not here at the mo. Doing his warm-ups."

Her eyes narrowed. "If you introduce me, the warm-ups won't be necessary. You *are* aware of who I am, are you not?"

"Yeah." Hamish met her narrow-eyed gaze with one of his own. "Got that memo."

"Well?" She lifted an eyebrow.

Lucifer's balls. This is a disaster.

Zeke grabbed another glass of champagne from a passing server and took a huge gulp. "Perhaps you could tell Hamish . . ." Tell him what? She'd done nothing so far but complain about the weather. *Well, better than nothing.* "About your impressions of Portland so far. He's from Australia, you know."

"Australia." Her tone dripped with scorn. "The penal colony. What did you do to deserve transportation?"

Hamish crossed his arms, glaring down at her. "In case news hasn't filtered up to your ivory Olympian tower, that story's been over forever."

She flicked her fingers dismissively. "I rarely attend to anything as irrelevant as politics. My sisters and I have a higher calling."

Is it a higher calling to be rude to somebody you've just met—and with whom you're supposed to be developing a relationship?

Zeke downed the rest of his champagne and stared at the empty glass mournfully until it was refilled by that same helpful waiter. He smiled at the man, the room suddenly seeming much brighter and full of cheerful chatter.

He blinked at Hamish and Euterpe. Maybe this was a standard way for people to engage with one another when they were first trying to determine compatibility. After all, if they got their *worst* behavior out of the way first, then things were bound to get better afterward, right?

He cupped his hands around his glass and raised it to his lips, two-handed, but before he could take a sip, it was lifted out of his grasp and deposited on a passing waiter's tray.

"Hold on there, mate." Hamish's voice was soft and amused, and Zeke wanted to wrap it around himself. "I think you should slow down a bit, this being your first time and all."

Zeke gazed up into Hamish's kind, gray eyes. "Oh. Yes. You're probably right. Have I introduced you to Euterpe?"

"Yeah, mate. You took care of that." Hamish glanced over his shoulder.

Zeke squinted in the same direction. "Wait. Is that her?" A woman who looked like what Euterpe probably looked like from the back was slinking her way through the crowd, aimed at a curly-haired man who'd just walked in the door. "Why isn't she talking to you? Why aren't you talking to her? Is this the way you handle sexual foreplay in the Upper World?" He blinked. "No wait. It wouldn't be sexual foreplay. She's *a*sexual." He blinked again. "Although that doesn't mean she doesn't want sex, you know. I looked it up." He leaned toward Hamish, and kept leaning until he was propped comfortably against Hamish's shoulder. "There's a whole *range* of asexual behavior. Did you know?"

Hamish smiled down at him. "Yeah, mate. I do. Couple of my bandmates are ace too."

"They are?" Zeke glanced around. "Which ones? Oh. Wait. Is that rude to ask?"

"Well, it's not really something that's anybody's business, yeah? Not unless they're clients of Supernatural Selection."

Zeke's belly plummeted as if it were on the elevator to Sheol. "Clients. Yes. I'm here on a job. I should make sure that you and

Euterpe have a chance to bond." He looked up at Hamish. "I want you to be happy."

"And I appreciate that."

Hamish's voice held something—like a buried laugh. Did that mean he was happy? Zeke had so little experience with that particular emotion, although he was starting to build up his recognition of happiness tells since he'd been working for Supernatural Selection.

Everybody was different, he'd learned that much. Maybe it made Hamish happy to stand around in this little room while people snapped selfies and drank stars from tall narrow glasses. Maybe it made Euterpe happy to be rude to everyone and imagine that her Olympic heritage made her superior.

He frowned, trying to make those two things mesh. "Something doesn't make sense."

"Considering you've drunk about half a bottle of cheap champagne in about ten minutes, I'm not surprised. But you know what? I need to go rescue Gareth from the Olympic Inquisition. Think you'll be okay here on your own for a bit?"

Zeke nodded, easing himself away from Hamish and immediately missing his solid warmth. "Of course. I shouldn't be here at all, you know."

"You most certainly should. If I have to put up with her, then I should at least be rewarded occasionally with your smile."

He walked away, leaving Zeke gaping in his wake. *He likes my smile?* Was that a good thing? *Hamish's* smile—with that dimple peeking out of his scruff—was *lethal*. Zeke didn't know how Euterpe could resist it.

He tried to think back to his first meetings with Hamish, which was difficult because, for some reason, everything was a little hazy now. He seemed to recall being irritated with Hamish at first, when he hadn't wanted to *engage* in the process of finding his perfect mate.

His mate doesn't have to be perfect. They only need to make him happy.

Maybe Euterpe just needed more time to warm up to Hamish, the same way Zeke had. He sighed and sagged against the wall, watching as Hamish laughed with a little cluster of young women who were all waving their cell phones. He paused and let them all take selfies with him before he moved on to stand with Euterpe and the curly-haired fae whom Zeke recognized from the band photos in Hamish's profile as Gareth Kendrick.

Zeke peered at the young women. They all seemed quite taken with Hamish, and rather more cheerful than Euterpe. Would one of them do as a mate?

He shook his head. No. They were obviously human, which made them far too fragile and short-lived for interaction with the supe communities, even if the Secrecy Pact allowed such a thing.

Other than at the restaurant the other night, when he'd been distracted by the food—*and Hamish*—he'd never been near humans before. So he wouldn't be tempted to watch Hamish obsessively now, he peered at the crowd.

As he squinted through inexplicably bleary eyes at a huge man in a T-shirt with *Security* emblazoned across the chest, something shifted in his perception.

Gambling.

Zeke blinked. *His weakness. I've evaluated him. How? Why?* He tried to shut down his demon sensitivity, but he couldn't turn it off.

He glanced at Hamish, whose hand was hovering over Euterpe's back. He tore his gaze away, because better to scan a few random humans he'd never see again than violate Hamish's privacy. *Again.*

A waiter paused in front of Zeke. "Champagne, sir?"

"Yes." Zeke almost snatched the cup from the tray. Taking a gulp, he checked out the laughing man in the leather jacket who was standing next to the security guard.

Alcohol. Hmmm. Maybe Zeke should give the waiter a hint not to serve that guy any more champagne. He shifted his focus to the women who'd stopped Hamish: *Food. Money. Fame.*

Zeke straightened up. Hey, this was easy—and kind of fun. If he wanted, he could offer each one of those people the exact bargain that would make them offer their souls willingly in return. The images were right there in the forefront of their minds, like teasers for the television shows that Zeke was never allowed to watch. *Breaking the bank at the Bellagio. Drinking all night with no aftereffects or guilt. Eating anything without gaining weight. Unlimited funds for clothes and parties. Living like a Kardashian—*whoever they were.

Of course, Zeke had no ability to procure those things. Only the upper echelon demons had those resources. But if he had similar access? He could totally rock the demon stereotype.

He frowned, his belly squirming uneasily, and shoved his hands in his pockets. *I don't want to tempt anybody. I don't want to make them give up their souls. I don't want to condemn anyone to eternity in torment.*

He much preferred his job at Supernatural Selection, helping people find their true partners.

Making people happy.

Unbidden, his gaze locked on Hamish again. He was laughing. *That's good, right?* Euterpe was not, but Gareth was smiling fondly at Hamish. It warmed Zeke's chest. *Laughter. Smiles. Love. Much better to promote those than screams of torment and anguish.*

Oh look. Euterpe was smiling. *See? It just took a little time.* Although her smile was directed at another man who'd joined the group—a slight man with white-blond hair, wide brown eyes, and something about him that whispered *werewolf* to Zeke's senses. *Joshua Wills, Hunter's Moon's violinist, guitarist, and co-songwriter.*

While Zeke had been woolgathering—or rather fault-gathering—the other members of the band had obviously joined the group.

Hamish's laughter faltered as his gaze followed a woman with dark hair shaved close on one side and falling to her chin in a straight, dark slash on the other. Zeke's stomach roiled, because he recognized her from more than a band photo. He'd seen her when he'd peeked at Hamish's desires.

She's the one. Hamish's weakness. Tiff.

Zeke was tempted to drink two more glasses of champagne in quick succession to blot out that thought, but he settled for one—only enough to bring the sparkle back to the room.

Just then, Hamish brought two fingers to his mouth and uttered a long, piercing whistle. Everybody laughed and turned toward the group at the door. Gareth raised his hands.

"Thank you for coming, everybody. But the show will be starting soon and the band has some preparation to do so we can give you our best." The crowd erupted into a ragged cheer. "So if you would please follow our manager"—he gestured to Del, standing next to the door—"they'll make sure you get to your seats. Enjoy the show!"

The band all disappeared down the hall, with Hamish throwing Zeke one final grin. Although Zeke raised his hand in response, Hamish was already gone. Zeke made his way to where Euterpe was standing in a little island of empty space as everyone else crowded out the door.

"May I escort you to your seat?"

She handed him her lipstick-stained glass. "I'd prefer to watch from backstage."

Del shook their head. "Not an option. Insurance."

Euterpe sighed heavily. "Very well." She sailed into the hallway, Del observing stoically from the doorway.

"Actually," they said to Zeke, "backstage is reserved for family. She'll never be that."

Zeke blinked. "But—"

"Come on. I don't want her at-large anywhere near the band. They need their prep time."

Zeke trotted to keep up as Del powered down the hall in pursuit of Euterpe. They ushered her and Zeke through a nearly hidden door and handed them over to another huge man in a Security T-shirt. He showed them to their seats in the middle of the first row.

Euterpe immediately sat, arranging the folds of her blouse to her satisfaction, then pulled out her cell phone. But Zeke stayed on his feet, agog at the mood of the audience. He'd been in crowds this large in Sheol, of course—the punishment pits were sized for mass torment—but never in one so . . . so *festive*. Everybody was smiling or laughing. Waving at friends. Snapping selfies.

But when the lights dimmed, a roar went up from them that rivaled Beelzebub's fury, and everyone—except Euterpe—surged to their feet.

No wonder Hamish banned the AI—it would have spoiled the effect entirely.

Over the PA, a booming voice announced, "And now, everyone, *Hunter's Moon!*"

The lights went out as another roar shook the walls, and with his Sheol-evolved dark-vision, Zeke saw the band take their places onstage: Gareth, guitar around his neck, at the center microphone; Tiff to his left with her bass, winking at somebody offstage right; Josh with his violin; Spence behind the keyboard, although he didn't move until Josh was in place.

Hamish. *Oh, Hamish.* Enthroned behind his drum kit, bouncing on his stool and grinning, grinning, grinning until Zeke's answering grin threatened to split his face. Then Hamish counted off a beat against the rim of one of his drums, and the stage lights burst on like a supernova.

And Hunter's Moon's magic rolled off the stage.

This. This was music. How had he lived without it? The tinny imitations on client's cell phones, the piped-in travesty that accompanied some of the mating ceremonies—it had never even registered with Zeke as anything more than organized noise.

But *this*. Zeke couldn't have moved if he'd had a soul and it depended on it. Any residual awareness he had for Euterpe disappeared under the spell of Gareth's voice, of Spence's fingers dancing over the keys, of the rolling growl of Tiff's bass, the crystal brilliance of Josh's violin.

But the drums. But *Hamish*.

The random rhythms Hamish had beaten on every available surface had set up a compelling resonance in Zeke's chest, but that was *nothing* compared to this.

To the way his entire being—blood, heart, mind—answered the manic thunder of Hamish in performance.

He bore the band along, the wind in their sails, the waves under their hull. Yes, Gareth's voice was electric velvet. Yes, Josh's violin could make the angels weep. But *Hamish*.

How can anyone see him like this and not fall in love with him?

As Hamish tossed back his hair, sweat glistening on his face, Zeke forced himself to look away lest he fall under the spell. He glanced down at Euterpe and was shocked at the expression on her face—*avarice* was the only way to describe it.

So she feels it too.

But then he followed the direction of her gaze. She wasn't looking at Hamish.

She was looking at Josh.

Chapter Nine

The show tonight was one of the best—at least from Hamish's point of view—that the band had played since their first days together. They weren't even thrown off when Gareth switched out a song in the second half of the show for one of the old woe-is-me-love-lost numbers that they hadn't played since Niall came back.

Hamish hadn't missed the glances Gareth cast at Niall's usual place backstage between songs. It was the first concert Niall had missed since his return, so maybe Gareth was feeling a little . . . what? Hurt? Anxious? Let down?

Hamish could finally understand the feeling, because tonight, for the first time, *he* had somebody there just for him, and that had infused the experience with so much *more*. Even though he couldn't see beyond the stage lights, he knew they were there. Euterpe. Zeke. And the idea that he was playing for *them*? Well, it was different, that's all.

He could understand Gareth's little burst of melancholy, because he wasn't sure he could handle not having that personal audience again. Would future shows seem flat if they weren't there?

Hamish gave himself a mental facepalm. *They* wouldn't be there. Zeke was just his Supernatural Selection counselor, and once he'd made Hamish *happy*, he'd chalk up another successful match for the company. Hamish hoped it would be enough to keep the poor little bloke out of Sheol.

A world without light, food, or music. Hamish couldn't even imagine.

He bounded offstage after their third encore, sweat dripping in his eyes, but Rowdy, the roadie who usually handed him a towel, wasn't there. Oh well. He didn't want to face Zeke and the music muse in all his postconcert funk. He had time—they wouldn't be able to get through the crowd for a few minutes, so he zoomed down the hall, through the dressing room, and hopped in the shower.

When he stepped out of the bathroom in a billow of steam, toweling his hair dry and with nothing but another of the skimpy venue towels around his waist, he squawked and nearly retreated.

The band was all there.

That wouldn't be such a bad thing—they had little modesty between them after decades of touring together—but Zeke and Euterpe were there too. He hadn't planned on exposing quite so much of himself until they were better acquainted. Luckily, Euterpe wasn't looking his way, and Zeke was frowning at her as she spoke earnestly to Josh.

For an instant, Hamish was tempted to draw Zeke's attention. He lifted a hand, but before he could wave, he caught Tiff's smirk and pretended he'd just been adjusting the towel.

Hamish glanced at Spence, who normally gave him the most shite, to see if he'd caught Hamish's blunder, but he wasn't paying attention. He was scowling at Euterpe. Gareth didn't notice Hamish either: he was slumped in a chair in the corner, staring at the water bottle in his hands. *Niall must still be MIA.*

Hamish grabbed his duffel and retreated to the bathroom to change. When he emerged, Gareth was wrapped in Niall's embrace, and Tiff had Luci tucked under her arm on the couch, but nobody else had moved.

Correction: Zeke wasn't frowning at Euterpe anymore, even though she'd slid closer to Josh. He was studying his feet, but then he raised his chin and met Hamish's gaze and *holy shite.*

Hamish's breath stopped somewhere south of his throat. Because the look on Zeke's face . . .

Heart eyes.

Nobody had *ever* looked at Hamish that way, although he was familiar with the expression, having seen it tossed between Gareth and Niall, or Spence and Josh, or Tiff and Luci-slash-Vitor more times than he cared to count.

He took a step forward, but then Spence caught his elbow and towed him back into the bathroom, slamming the door behind them.

"What's the deal with your date, kangaroo? Why's she hitting on Josh?"

Hamish was still reeling from the wallop of Zeke's gaze. "What?"

"That Greek chick. She's got Josh all but backed into a corner, cooing at him about his talent and why should he want to waste himself in a rock band playing derivative Celtic fusion when he could be a soloist with this or that symphony, *all* of whom would jump at the chance to feature one of her protégés." Spence threw a punch at the wall, but Hamish caught his wrist before it connected.

"Steady there, wolfman. Hard to play the keys with broken fingers."

Spence shook him off. "Would you rather I hit you? Because it's on my list of possibilities."

Hamish held out his arms. "If it'll make you feel better. You know I can take it and at least you'll be able to play tomorrow."

"Forget it." Spence propped his shoulder against the wall and shoved his hands into his jeans pockets. "It's not the same if you ask for it."

"Look." He took Spence by the shoulders. "You know damn well Josh is devoted to you *and* to the band. Has he ever said he wanted to play with a bloody symphony?"

Spence shrugged off Hamish's hold. "No."

"Then what's the problem?"

"The problem is it's postshow." Spence gazed at the door as if he could bore through it with some previously undiscovered werewolf laser vision. "You know what Josh is like after a performance. You know what he needs."

"Yeah. Sort of. Not that I want the details, mind." Hamish sighed. Josh was always jittery after a performance until Spence had taken him someplace private for at least half an hour to smooth him out. Hamish had never asked what exactly went on behind those closed doors—it wasn't his business and he had no desire to pry. But on the occasions when it hadn't been possible, Josh had been kind of a wreck for days. "Sorry I wasn't on hand when Zeke and Euterpe showed up."

"Zeke I've got no problem with. He kind of reminds me of Josh, actually—he obviously needs some kind of relief valve."

Hamish blinked. "Relief valve?"

"Yeah. He's wound tighter than a pig shifter's tail." Spence cracked a smile for the first time. "I think he really liked the show."

"It's his first one. They don't have music in Sheol."

Spence's eyebrows shot up. "No music? Shit, man. I'd opt for a silver bullet over that."

"It's what he's used to. He never complained about it."

"I think he might now. We've got ourselves a fan." Spence's scowl returned. "But the other one. She treats all of us except Josh—even Gareth, for crap's sake—like something she scraped off the bottom of her stiletto. What gives her the right to act so fucking superior?"

"Well, she is a demigod," Hamish said dryly.

"So? The King of Faerie came to our last barbecue and *he* didn't . . . Ah, shit." Spence scrubbed his hands through his hair. "Is she really your date?"

"She's supposed to be." Hamish joined Spence in frowning at the door. "But now you mention it, she doesn't seem to like me much above average. Rather less, actually."

"Do you? Like her above average?"

Hamish reviewed Euterpe's dismissive attitude. "Now that you mention it . . . No. I don't."

She certainly didn't make him happy. In fact, she hadn't made the least effort to even be pleasant to him. So why had she agreed to the date in the first place? It wasn't like she didn't know who he was and what he did.

Unless it was the only way she could get to the rest of the band. To Josh. Maybe the muse of music was in a slump and was looking for a new project.

Not on my time, sister.

Still, he owed it to Zeke to at least make the effort. Then they could chalk her up as a no-go and move on to somebody else.

It's a damn shame Zeke *isn't in the dating pool, because I would so* —

Nope. He couldn't think that way. Zeke had made his stand clear. He had rules he had to follow, and even though Hamish wasn't a fan of rules, he also wasn't a fan of somebody else getting punished for his own misbehavior.

Hamish clapped Spence on the shoulder. "No worries, mate. I'll take care of her. You spirit Josh away for whatever it is you two get up to after our shows." He held up his hands in mock surrender. "Just don't give me any details."

Spence barked a laugh. "In your dreams, kangaroo."

Hamish opened the door and headed straight across the room to where Euterpe had indeed backed Josh into a corner, practically breathing into his ear while Zeke wrung his hands. Zeke glanced up. For an instant, the heart eyes returned, but then he shut them down.

"I'm sorry, Hamish," Zeke murmured. "Every time I try to get her attention, she tells me to shush, and she's a *client*."

"No worries, mate. She's my date, right? Guess we both better remember that." He edged past Zeke, whose breath hitched in a way that made Hamish's southern regions stage a brief rebellion. *Back off, southern regions.* He wasn't interested in having that kind of relationship with Euterpe, not anymore.

With Zeke though . . . Gah! Not an option.

He didn't feel like touching Euterpe, so he nudged Josh with his hip. "Great show, mate." He gazed down at Euterpe as he insinuated himself between her and Josh. "Did you enjoy it?"

She glanced up at him, a single furrow between her classic eyebrows. "It was very . . . illuminating."

"That so?" *If the AI were here, it would have been illuminated a bit more.* "Oh look, Josh. Spence needs you. Off you go." He gave Josh a little push, directly into Spence's waiting arms, then turned back to Euterpe. "You were saying?"

Whoa. Spence's earlier laser-eyeball thing had nothing on Euterpe. Good thing muses didn't have that kind of power, or Spence would have been filleted and fried.

Zeke appeared at her elbow, a tentative smile on his face. "I thought the show was brilliant."

She didn't bother to glance at him. "You would."

Hamish bristled on Zeke's behalf. "What's that supposed to mean?"

"He's a demon." She flicked her fingers. "You can't expect him to understand the nuances of melody and pitch and time signature. He can't possibly appreciate the subtleties of Joshua's performance."

"I'm pretty sure that Josh wasn't the only one on the stage." Hamish glared down at her. "What did you think of Gareth's vocals? Last true bard of Faerie and all that."

"He was pleasant enough, but you have to admit that the melodic lines of your music were rather . . . simplistic without the embellishment of Joshua's violin."

"Simplistic, eh? If you—"

"Hamish." Zeke's tone held an edge of desperation. "I'm sure Euterpe doesn't mean any disrespect. After all"—the smile he directed at her was a tad manic—"you're the muse of *all* music, correct?"

She aimed her hooded gaze at him. "All *good* music." She turned to Hamish. "Where's the ladies' room?"

"Down the hall on the right."

She turned and left the room. *Thank all the gods.*

Zeke gazed after her. "What a *horrible* woman." He frowned, his eyebrows disappearing behind his glasses. "She could never make you happy."

"I'm pretty sure she could never make *anyone* happy. She was about to give poor Josh heart failure."

Zeke peered up at Hamish. "I'm so sorry about that. She started *devouring* him with her eyes during the concert, and then she practically burned a path backstage afterward. I'm not entirely sure she didn't toss several security guards over her shoulder on the way."

Hamish chuckled. "Nice one."

"I'm not joking. Ask them if you don't believe me." He scrubbed his hands through his curls. "And then, once we got here, I couldn't get her to leave him alone. I'm really sorry."

"You don't need to apologize to me, mate. Now Spence— that's another story."

"I don't mean about the way she monopolized Josh— although I am sorry about that. I mean I'm sorry I ever thought she'd be a possible match for you." His shoulders slumped. "I'm obviously a *terrible* matchmaker."

Hamish rested his hand on Zeke's shoulder. *It feels good there. Can I leave it there forever?* "Don't beat yourself up. No harm done, and we can give it another try tomorrow."

He nodded. "Thank you." He peered up at Hamish, leaning slightly into him, causing a bit of a stir in Hamish's southern regions again.

Then . . . return of the heart eyes, and Hamish couldn't suppress the, er, southern uprising.

"The concert was— Well, I've never experienced anything like it. It was wonderful," Zeke whispered. "Really. Wonderful."

Maybe it's you that's wonderful.

And maybe Hamish was totally fucked.

Lucifer's balls, could I be any less articulate? Wonderful? *Seriously?*

The word was so inadequate for the experience, for the way the concert had turned Zeke's world on its head. If the AI hadn't been banned from attending, Zeke would have suspected it of spotlighting Hamish in brilliant silver until Zeke could barely see anything else.

But since the AI was back at Supernatural Selection, he couldn't blame it for the way Hamish was suddenly *illuminated* —to use Euterpe's word—in Zeke's sight.

Euterpe wasn't nearly good enough for him. Zeke wasn't sure anyone was.

"You okay, mate?"

Hamish's concerned voice jolted Zeke out of his reverie. He restrained himself from blurting *You glow like the sun.* Barely. "Yes. Yes, I'm fine."

"Then come here. I want you to officially meet the rest of the band." He hooked his hand around Zeke's elbow, his touch electric through hoodie and shirt. *What would it feel like against my skin?*

He pushed the thought away as Hamish led him toward Gareth, who was wrapped in another vaguely familiar dark-haired fae's arms, murmuring in his ear.

Zeke tried to hold back. "Hamish, I don't think we should disturb—"

"Nah. They're always like that. If they wanted privacy, they'd duck into another room." He towed Zeke the last few feet. "Gareth, Niall, this is Zeke. He's my . . . friend."

Niall held out his hand. "I thought I recognized you. I saw you at Supernatural Selection the other day. Angel, right?"

Zeke cast an alarmed glance over his shoulder, but luckily no disapproving pillar of light was lurking in the corner. "No. Hamish didn't want it to come along tonight."

"Not an angel? But . . ." Niall's eyes grew unfocused for an instant. "Never mind."

"Don't mind him. He hears voices." Gareth smiled, disengaged himself from Niall, and shook Zeke's hand. "Nice to meet you. You're the demon on work-release, right? My brother mentioned you." Gareth chuckled. "You don't know how long Alun's been trying to get demons mainstreamed into supe society. When you finally volunteered, I thought he'd weep with joy."

"Oh." Zeke was glad of Hamish's hand in the small of his back, anchoring him, because the idea that someone was *glad* he was here was enough to send his head reeling as if he'd downed a hogshead of champagne. "Thank you?"

Niall smiled at them all and then turned to kiss Gareth on the temple. "I've got to run, sweetheart. I'm sorry the case kept me so late, but I promise I didn't miss the show. I watched it from the back of the house. You were transcendent, as usual."

To Zeke's intense interest, Gareth blushed. "I wasn't. I was in a snit because I thought you'd forgotten."

Hamish chuckled, elbowing Niall in the ribs. "Hope you caught that downer song in the second act. That was one of our *old* staples, when Gareth was determined to depress all our fans into therapy or Xanax."

"Shut up." Gareth scowled at Hamish, but leaned into Niall's side when the taller fae draped an arm across his shoulders. "You'll note that the fans seemed to like the throwback."

"Maybe." Hamish lifted the back of his wrist to his forehead. "Although I may go into a decline."

Niall laughed. "You'll recover presently. Now let me say goodbye to my boyfriend properly." He nodded at Zeke. "Pleased to meet you, Zeke. Demon, eh? Funny, I could swear . . . Oh well. Hope you enjoyed the show." He led Gareth away.

Zeke gazed after them. "Why do you suppose he mistook me for the AI?"

"He didn't say that. But Niall's got his secrets. Especially now that he's a private investigator."

"An investigator?" A chill slithered down Zeke's spine. Had Niall been speaking with the magistra because he was investigating *Zeke*? He remembered Hamish's conviction that they'd been followed from the restaurant the night of the dinner with Olli.

Lucifer's balls, if Niall reports that *to the magistra . . .* Or to the council. Or, infernal imps forbid, to *Melchom*. He shivered. He didn't want to think what the consequences would be. Plus Niall had seen him here tonight, and he'd admitted that he'd ditched his AI observer. *I'm doomed.*

"Something wrong, mate?" The concern in Hamish's eyes matched the tone of his voice. "You've gone a bit pale. Well, pal*er*."

Zeke took a shaky breath. He couldn't burden Hamish with his worries because that wouldn't make him happy, now, would it? And making Hamish happy was the only thing that might possibly save him from an express elevator to Sheol. "Must be the aftereffects of that champagne." *Not answering is* not *the same as lying.*

Hamish studied him, head tilted to the side and eyes narrowed as if he could detect the lie like an oracular raven. "If you say so." He smoothed his hair back. "Now come and meet Tiff."

Tiff. This was the woman who'd turned Hamish against love. Zeke was predisposed to be annoyed with her, but as they approached where she was cuddling with a man and a woman —both shifters; big cats if Zeke was a judge—his irritation faded. Clearly *she* was a big proponent of true love.

Just not with Hamish.

And Zeke could hardly blame her for that, even though he couldn't understand it. Hamish was a lovable guy—not to mention crazy talented, handsome, and *built*. But people loved who they loved.

"Tiff, Luci, Vitor—this is Zeke." Hamish grinned down at him. "He thought tonight's show was wonderful. Really."

Zeke felt the blotches bloom on his face. "Do you have to mock me?"

Hamish immediately looked contrite. "I wasn't. I thought it was sweet. And way better than Euterpe's review."

Tiff lifted one pierced eyebrow. "Euterpe? That Greek harpy with a permanent stick up her ass about rock music?"

"That's the one. She said we're simplistic. Except for Josh. She thinks he should be playing with a symphony somewhere."

Tiff snorted. "Like he'd ever leave Spence. Or us."

Vitor, a darkly handsome man with a brilliant smile, shook his head. "That's not it. I have heard of this one. She likes to be the *inspiration*. Perhaps she zeroed in on our Josh because he's the only one in the band who's not supremely confident in their music. He is brilliant, but insecure."

Tiff shook her head. "I think you're confusing insecurity with being a peacemaker. Josh doesn't like to rock the boat."

"That is certainly not one of Euterpe's failings," Vitor said.

"Speaking of Euterpe . . ." Hamish peered around the room. "Did she fall in the toilet?"

Just then, Spence strode back in the room, his face like a thundercloud. "Has anybody seen Josh?"

"Oh no." Zeke clutched Hamish's arm. "She's after him again." Zeke let go of Hamish and rushed out of the room, Hamish and Spence at his heels. He paused in the hallway. Where would she have gone?

The hallway was empty, but the stage door was propped open, and somehow Zeke *knew*. He sped toward the stage door, dread engaging his anti-grav so only one foot touched the floor every other step. He burst onto the stage, where, sure enough, Euterpe had Josh backed up against a stack of amps. From the way his gaze skittered away from her face, he wasn't buying what she was selling, but that didn't mean she had the right to hector him.

"Hey!" Spence's shout echoed in the empty venue. "Get away from him!"

Euterpe startled, stumbling back a few steps and turning to glare at Spence. "He's wasted with you. I could make him world famous." She advanced on him, and Spence matched her until they were nose to nose in the middle of the stage.

Zeke stared at them in horror as they started sniping at each other in low, angry voices, but when he glanced at Hamish, he was grinning. He winked at Zeke and turned his attention back to the face-off.

I should do something. Intercede. But when demons negotiated, it usually resulted in more conflict, not less. He'd heard some of the upper-echelon demons comparing stories, trying to one-up each other, something Zeke had never understood.

Nevertheless, he was about to at least try to defuse the situation when he caught a movement out of the corner of his eye. He snapped his head around. Josh was still cowering against a stack of huge amps, but that wasn't what had drawn his attention. The top amp was trembling, wobbling, teetering . . . and started to topple.

He shouted wordlessly, raising his hands to lasso the amp with anti-grav, straining to hold it, and panting as his muscles cramped.

Then Hamish leaped across the stage, caught Josh around the middle, and hauled him out of the way. None too soon, because Zeke's anti-grav failed and the amp crashed to the stage an instant later.

"Josh! Oh my god, Josh!" Spence rushed across the stage and grabbed Josh out of Hamish's arms, crushing him to his chest and burying his nose in Josh's hair. "I'm sorry," he murmured. "So sorry. I should have been taking care of you, not—"

"Shhh." Josh ran visibly shaking hands down Spence's spine, as if he were smoothing down Spence's hackles. "It's not your fault."

Spence shook his head, then turned to fix Zeke with an intense gaze. "Thank you. If you hadn't been here . . ." He swallowed, closing his eyes and pressing his lips together. When he opened them again, he turned to Hamish. "And you. You were faster than me."

"If Zeke hadn't raised the alarm first— Shite." Hamish scrubbed hands through his hair. "Doesn't bear thinking of."

Hamish gripped Spence's shoulder, so Zeke crept backward to grant the three of them a little privacy. When he turned around, though, he discovered that the entire band, along with their significant others, the manager, the stage crew, and all the security guards were clustered at the edge of the stage.

Time to do my job.

He straightened the knot in his tie and stalked toward Euterpe, who was staring at the smashed amp, one hand clutching her pearls. "I think it would be best if I escorted you home now, don't you? It's clear this match will never be perfect."

Chapter Ten

Hamish reached Zeke's side in time to hear him offer to escort Euterpe home. While he agreed that this match was made in hell, he ought to be the one to endure her toxic presence. She was supposed to be his date, after all, and he didn't want Zeke to be subjected to her anti-demon bias any longer than necessary.

Besides, judging by how the band was advancing on Zeke, he was about to get some richly deserved hero worship, something Hamish doubted had ever come his way before.

"Nah, mate. That's my fate, er, privilege." He held out his elbow. "Euterpe?"

She glanced down her nose at it, then over to where Spence was still holding Josh in a clench like he was a bloody life preserver. "I want to—"

"That's *never* happening, so let's move on, right?"

She sniffed and turned on her heel, not taking his arm and not acknowledging Zeke, although she did incline her head at Niall. *Bloody snooty demigoddess.* Trust her to acknowledge royalty—Niall was technically a fae prince—and ignore Faerie's last true bard because he was a commoner like the rest of the band.

He followed her into the hallway, where she powered right past the security guards who should have kept her off the blooming stage in the first place.

For that matter, where were the roadies? How could they have stacked that amp so precariously? He slowed for a moment. *Could* the amp be stacked precariously? There were safeties. Tie-downs. Anchors, or some bloody thing.

He caught sight of Del at the end of the hall and loped toward them, overtaking Euterpe. Who cared if it was rude? As far as he was concerned, she'd lost the right to any consideration.

"Del, what the hell is up with those amps? Weren't the roadies—"

"Later." Their lips were pressed together and steam was almost visibly shooting out of their ears. "I'll arrange for your . . . guest to be escorted home. You have that interview."

"Interview?" Hamish frowned in confusion. "After a concert? We never—" Del glared at him with a don't-be-dense glint in their eye. "Ooohhh. The *interview*. Right." He turned to Euterpe, who was apparently pretending neither one of them existed. "It's been grand, but don't wait for my call."

Her nostrils flared as she drew herself up. "You—"

"This way." Del nodded toward the door, signaling for two of the largest security guards to flank Euterpe. "We're closing up for the night."

Hamish didn't bother to watch Euterpe's judgmental ass march down the hall and out the door. *Life's too short, even for someone as long-lived as a shifter.*

He sprinted back to the stage, only to find it empty except for a couple of roadies clearing away the remains of the amp and the maintenance crews cleaning up the auditorium.

"Shite," he muttered, and legged it to the green room. *Success!* Or at least he thought so at first. Yes, Zeke was there, but he was surrounded by the band and their partners. Spence was shaking Zeke's hand, although his other arm was still holding Josh glommed to his side. Josh, for his part, simply smiled, with his head on Spence's shoulder.

Tiff was speaking to Zeke earnestly, and Vitor was pressing a glass of champagne into his free hand.

Uh-oh.

"A toast," Vitor called as Luci passed out champagne to everyone, including Hamish. "To Zeke. Thank you, *mi amigo,* for saving our brother Josh."

"To Zeke!"

Everyone raised their glass except Zeke, whose skin had gone blotchy again, and whose gaze darted from side to side as if he were a rabbit cornered by a whole den of foxes.

Hamish set down his cup—he preferred water after a performance anyway—ready to leap to Zeke's rescue, but unless he wanted to fling his bandmates out of the way, he didn't see how to do it.

"Poor bugger." Niall appeared at Hamish's side. "I'm guessing he's not used to being killed with gratitude or dog-piled by fans the way you lot are."

"I'm not sure he's ever been thanked by anybody." Hamish racked his brain, trying to remember if he'd ever expressed appreciation for Zeke's efforts on his behalf. Heat rushed up his neck when he couldn't remember a single instance.

That's going to change. Tonight.

Niall sipped his champagne. "We had an interesting—though brief—chat before everyone suddenly wanted a piece of him. He and I have something in common, something that the rest of you have never faced."

"You mean because you've both lived in the underworld?"

"'Lived' is an interesting description, and although the heat in Govannon's forge may be similar to Sheol, I doubt it could be compared in any other way other than lack of sunlight. No, I mean that both of us know what it's like to have our lives completely at the mercy of somebody else." He tossed his empty cup into the recycling bin. "As an Australian, that might resonate with you from a historical perspective, but unless you're older than I think, you've never personally experienced it."

Niall wandered over to Gareth's side, leaving Hamish gaping in his wake.

Completely at the mercy of someone else.

It had amused Hamish to take the piss out of the AI, because the way it tried to control Zeke was rubbish. But the AI wasn't the only one with chains on Zeke's life.

Forget the witches, or the demons, or the supe council—I'm just as guilty. He'd considered Zeke's mandate to make Hamish happy —or else—as more of a joke, something to be exploited to skirt around the rules. *Although the rule-bending was primarily for my benefit.*

And although he'd been outraged over the idea that Zeke would be punished for Hamish's own failure to *engage*, he hadn't really considered how much that *or else* might constrain Zeke's relationship with him.

Does he want *to find me a mate?* Would he want to make Hamish happy if he weren't under duress? Had anyone ever bothered to ask for his consent?

I wonder what would make Zeke *happy?*

Hamish studied Zeke, boxed in by his bandmates and friends, his eyes showing white around their nearly-black irises. *Being the focus of attention isn't so jolly, eh, mate?*

Zeke spent most of his time being unobtrusive, attempting to *avoid* undue notice. In fact, he was trying it now, tugging his hoodie forward until it nearly met the top of his glasses.

Well if nobody else was going to consider Zeke's feelings, it was up to Hamish. And nobody had ever accused Hamish of being subtle.

"Stand aside. Kangaroo coming through."

His bandmates groaned, but they cleared a path so he could reach Zeke's side.

"Hey," he said softly. "You did a good thing."

Zeke edged toward him, as if Hamish were his shelter. "I only did what anyone would do."

"But *some* anyones"—Hamish gave Spence a mock glare—"were too busy playing *quién es más macho* with a demigoddess to do anything at all."

Vitor snorted, but instead of snarking back, Spence ducked his head. Holy shite—the werewolf looked almost *sheepish*. "You don't have to remind me. I know I fucked up."

Zeke took a half step toward Spence. "No. You mustn't blame yourself. It was my fault. I should have kept a closer eye on her." He twisted the hem of his hoodie in his hands. "I should have taken her away as soon as I saw how she treated all of you. I'll report to my supervisors and ask to be taken off Hamish's case, since it's obvious I'm not making him happy. In fact, I'm making him—and everybody else—miserable."

Hamish's belly plummeted, and he clenched his fists to keep from clenching *Zeke*. "Now wait a minute—"

"It *wasn't* your fault." Still tucked against Spence's side, Josh's tone was almost fierce, his gaze fixed on Zeke. "The fault was with whoever didn't secure the amp stack properly. It could have fallen at any time—during the concert even."

"We're looking into that," Del said from the doorway. They must have offloaded Euterpe, thank the gods. "The roadie we hired to fill-in for Rowdy is conspicuously absent, and the regular guys swear they saw him lurking over there after the concert."

"Regardless, I'm just glad that you were here when it counted. I didn't . . ." Josh gazed at Zeke with a simple admiration that would have sent Spence into a jealous funk if he hadn't been looking at Zeke exactly the same way. "I didn't realize demons could do things like that."

Zeke pulled away from Josh, cowering against Hamish's chest. It was only natural to put an arm around him, right? "How—how do you know I'm a . . . you-know-what?"

Josh blinked in confusion. "Euterpe said something about it. I'm sorry. Is it a secret?"

"We're . . . we're not supposed to be at large in the Upper World, especially not without an AI monitor. But Hamish insisted, and the client is always right."

Spence growled low in his throat. "That's bullshit. What do they think you're going to do? Take over the world?"

Zeke shrugged, his shoulders brushing Hamish's chest, and suddenly Hamish was no longer interested in finding any other date. "Yes," he said simply.

Niall rubbed the side of his nose. "Tell me, Zeke. Do you *want* to take over the world?"

"No! I've got more than enough to do keeping the Supernatural Selection office running. Although . . ." He sighed. "I haven't been doing such a good job with that lately."

"What do you mean?" Hamish tightened his arm around Zeke's shoulder. "It seems like nobody else over there does anything at all, and the AI is nothing more than a second-rate light show."

Zeke turned in the circle of Hamish's arm, his face a study in misery. "I've screwed up two high-profile matches in the last month, and I'm certainly not doing such a good job with you."

"What are you talking about? You—" Hamish glanced up and noticed the far-too interested expressions on the faces that surrounded them. "Sorry, mates, but could you give us some space here?"

Tiff linked her arm with Luci, Vitor at her back, matching smirks on all their faces. "Sure, buddy. We'll see you at the show tomorrow. And don't think you're getting out of the paintball war, even if you don't have a date."

Everybody filed out, most aiming another "Thank you" at Zeke, who bobbed his head in acknowledgment and seemed to shrink further inside that bloody hoodie.

When the door closed behind Del, Zeke exhaled heavily and turned to Hamish. "Paintball war?"

"Yeah. The day before the wedding, Mal and Bryce are hosting a paintball tournament for their bachelor party. Don't ask me why. But every time they talk about it, they spend the next ten minutes making heart eyes at each other, so I'd wager it has some sentimental significance."

"I expect you're right. I've seen that with the couples I've helped at Supernatural Selection." He sighed. "I'll miss that. The way they all looked at their partners during the mating ceremony. I always loved seeing how happy they were together."

"I'm sure you'll see it again."

Zeke shook his head. "No. Once I get back to the office, I'll resign. After tonight . . ." He pressed his lips together, closing his eyes. "I may not want to take over the world, but it's obvious I'm still a danger."

"Bullshite." The word came out with more force than Hamish intended, and Zeke's eyes flew open. Hamish hated—absolutely *hated*—the alarm on Zeke's face. "Sorry." He grasped Zeke's shoulders. "You're not a danger. You're a hero. Any one of us here tonight will testify to that."

"Yes, but don't you see? I stepped outside my purview. Even the magistra might question whether my actions were directly related to making you happy. And if"—he swallowed convulsively—"Melchom should find out, I could be dragged back to Sheol for Upper World interference and conduct unbecoming a demon."

"Interference?" Hamish frowned. "What kind of interference?"

"If I were a proper demon," he said, his gaze riveted on his feet, "I would have let the amp fall." He lifted his chin, and his eyes were shiny with unshed tears. "The misery quotient from Josh's death—"

"Don't. I don't even want to think about that."

"I have to. To make you understand who I am. What I am. All of you—the band, your lovers, especially Spence—would have been so devastated that it might have been enough to elevate me above minion rank, once a spot in the upper echelon opened up. And if *I* get promoted, it means my supervisor moves up too. If Melchom finds out I robbed him of that chance . . ." Zeke shuddered. "*I* don't want to think about *that*."

"Then he won't find out. I'll tell the others that we have to keep it all on the down-low. They know how to keep their mouths shut. They're supes. Discretion is our life."

"Really?" The hope that dawned on Zeke's face was a beautiful thing. "You'd do that for me?"

"Absolutely."

"That's . . ." His face fell. "There's just one problem. Euterpe." Hamish swore under his breath. "Euterpe."

"I don't think she was very happy with how the evening turned out."

Hamish screwed up his face, thinking, then snapped his fingers. "Del. They can handle anything, and they were *not* impressed with the meddling muse. Don't worry about her any more. I've got a much more pressing problem."

"Y-you do?"

"Mm-hmm. Tell me . . ." Hamish gazed down into Zeke's night-dark eyes. "What did you think of the show?"

"The . . . the . . ." With Hamish gazing at him so intently, as if Zeke's opinion actually mattered, he could barely form words, let alone sentences.

"The show. The concert. Hunter's Moon. You know." Hamish grinned crookedly, tapping a little rhythm against Zeke's collar bone with his thumbs. "Music."

"Oh." That little cadence brought the feelings surging back, drowning Zeke's worries about Euterpe and Melchom and possible exposure. "I can't even— Hamish, it was so wonderful. Magical. *Alive*. And your drums were its heart." Zeke pressed his hand against his chest. "It was as if you were driving my blood through my veins. It was— Mmmfph."

Zeke couldn't speak for another reason now—because Hamish's lips were on his—heat and pressure and *want*, and Zeke *wanted* right back. *Is this how 'cubi feel? That their soul is being fed by a touch so simple and yet so profound?*

But then Hamish broke free, stumbling away until he fetched up against the wall. "I'm sorry. Gods above and below, Zeke, I'm sorry."

Zeke touched his lips, still warm from the ghost of Hamish's kiss. "I— It's— Um . . . sorry for what?"

"I kissed you."

"Yes. I noticed."

"Without asking for permission."

"Permission? From whom? Does the shifter council have to grant permission before you kiss somebody? Or is it because I'm a demon?" He choked on something that might have been a laugh if he weren't so devastated. "Of course it's because I'm a demon. They wouldn't want you consorting with—"

"Fuck the council. I didn't ask for permission *from you*."

"Is that a thing?"

"Are you kidding me?" Hamish's face clouded, but Zeke didn't think he was mad at *him*. "Hell yes, it's a thing. Consent —consent is *everything*."

"Oh." Zeke couldn't drag his gaze away from Hamish's mouth. "Would you . . . If I asked . . . Would you do it again?"

Hamish's lips curved up. *What would it feel like to be kissed by a smile?* "I might. If you're sure."

Zeke nodded. "I'm sure."

"Then brace yourself, mate, because I'm coming in."

Zeke clenched his eyes shut, bracing himself as ordered, but Hamish's fingers drifted over his cheek. "I didn't mean that literally, you know.

Zeke cracked an eye open. "You didn't? Then what should I do? I've never kissed before. I mean other than just now." He'd never even considered it, actually. It didn't seem like something he'd ever want to do. But now, he fairly vibrated with the need to feel Hamish's lips on his. "Are there rules?"

Hamish's smile turned wry and impossibly tender. "I forgot. You're a virgin."

"In just about everything. Is that bad?"

"Not at all. Just means I need to be a little more mindful than I'm used to."

"I'm sorry."

"Don't be. It's not a bad thing. In fact, it's probably good. My bandmates are always telling me I have a tendency to rush the groove. So first things first. I never asked. I assumed. You identify as male?"

"Er . . . yes." Zeke was sure his blush-blotches must cover his entire body by now. "From the time I was spawned. Although I've heard that some demons have changed gender and identity at the order of their masters."

Hamish's face grew stormy. "Without your consent? That's total shite. It's *your* life."

Zeke shrugged. "According to them, our lives belong to them, since we wouldn't *be* alive without them."

"Yeah, I've heard that argument before from homophobic and transphobic Neanderthals. Doesn't make it true."

"Try telling that to the Sheol C-suite and see how far you get."

"I'd like to get as far away from them as possible, thanks." Hamish glanced down at his feet, his chest expanding with a deep breath, then squared his shoulders as if he were bracing for a blow. He raised his chin to meet Zeke's eyes. "Are you gay?"

"I— Maybe? I don't know. Would that be okay?"

"Why not? I've told you before, I'm—"

"Not picky," they said in unison.

"But—" Hamish held up a finger. "Labels are just a convenient way to compartmentalize things, and sometimes they get in the way because, well, assumptions. All that matters is what you want. What you like."

"I liked kissing you."

Hamish grinned. "Good. Because I liked kissing you too, and I'd like to do it some more." He tugged on one of Zeke's curls. "You asked about rules. The only rules—for kissing or for anything else—are the ones we set together. And even those can be changed if we decide it's what we both want."

"Okay." Zeke took his courage in both trembling hands. "Then what I want is to kiss you some more. If that's what you want. And if you can teach me how it works so I don't do something stupid or awkward or that you don't like."

"No worries, mate. We can take it slow. My first rule—" he reached out and took Zeke's hand "—is that you can touch me. Anywhere."

Zeke's breath sped up. "Anywhere?" His voice squeaked and heat bloomed on his skin. He almost didn't care because there were some places on Hamish's body that he'd *love* to explore.

"Anywhere. I don't have many no-fly zones, but if something feels uncomfortable, I'll say so—and you don't have to be upset or embarrassed by it because we're *both* learning here. After all . . ." He grinned, tracing a path of fire along Zeke's cheek and down his throat. "You're my first demon."

"Then you can touch me too. *Please* touch me."

"All right. Though I'll warn you . . ." Hamish's voice turned low and smoky. "I don't always touch with just my hands."

Hamish leaned forward, his face getting closer, closer, closer, until his breath ghosted against Zeke's jaw, and Zeke was positive he was about to get his second kiss. *Yes. Oh yes please.*

But then Hamish changed direction, and Zeke felt a warm, *wet* touch on his throat. *Lucifer's balls, is that his tongue? Do people do that?* The idea of using his tongue on Hamish, maybe on the skin between those clever fingers, sent a wave of heat to Zeke's groin and *something's happening down there.*

"Mmm." Hamish hummed against Zeke's neck. "I've always had a weakness for a good Adam's apple."

"We . . . we don't call it that."

"What *do* you call it?"

Hamish's lips moving against his skin had short-circuited Zeke's brain. "Er . . . Satan's apple. After all, according to popular myth, he had it first."

Hamish chuckled, and the vibration resonated in Zeke's bones until he nearly melted onto the floor. "I like it. And it definitely explains the temptation."

To keep himself upright as Hamish delved into places Zeke had never even considered to be sensitive—*Behind my ear? Really?*—Zeke clutched Hamish's shoulders. But then, the heat of Hamish's skin on either side of the narrow straps of his tank top called to Zeke, demanding that he release his death grip and explore with his fingertips instead.

Hamish's skin was so smooth on the ball of his shoulder, but as Zeke followed the edge of the shirt, he encountered crisp, curly hair on Hamish's chest, the texture so fascinating that he nearly forgot to move on until a groan from Hamish startled him.

"You're killing me here, mate."

"Sorry!" Zeke immediately jerked back, but Hamish chuckled, pulling him forward again.

"I didn't mean that literally. I just meant that what you're doing feels really good." Hamish pressed a kiss to Zeke's temple. *Oh. Kisses work everywhere.* "Feel free to keep going."

Zeke nodded, relishing the way Hamish's lips slid over his skin at the movement. He continued his exploration, up the column of Hamish's throat to his jaw. Intrigued by Hamish's springy scruff, Zeke carded his other hand through Hamish's hair. *Soft. Like silk.* "You have so many different kinds of hair."

"I've got some in other places too."

Zeke's mouth went dry. "Other places?"

"Yup. But I can't show you here. Anyway, we have to clear out so they can close up the venue. Would you . . ." Though an instant before, Hamish had been his usual brash, confident self, in control and sending Zeke to unimagined places, he suddenly seemed almost shy. "Would you come back to my hotel with me? We don't have to do anything you don't want, but at least we'll have privacy."

"And you'll show me your other hair?"

Hamish grinned, and the edge of wickedness that was so much a part of him returned. "Absolutely. It comes with a few accessories that you might be interested in too."

Did he mean . . . Ooohhh. "Yes, please."

"I was hoping you'd say that. Let's go."

Hamish took Zeke's hand. When they got to the door, Del met them, holding a large black duffel.

"I think you'll need this. They're about to lock up." Their gaze flicked to Hamish's and Zeke's joined hands, and Zeke tried to tug free, but Hamish just squeezed more firmly. "I'll see you tomorrow."

"Thanks, mate. Oh. By the way. Could you make sure Euterpe keeps mum about what happened tonight?"

Del smirked. "Don't worry about it. She's so mortified that she failed to 'inspire' Josh that she's trying to pretend she was never even here."

"Excellent. You're the best, Del."

"I know. Now get out of here."

Hamish let go of Zeke to take the duffel and sling it over his shoulder. He grinned down at Zeke and jerked his head toward the distant door. "Coming?"

He loped down the hall on his long, *powerful* legs. Zeke was so caught up in watching the play of muscles in Hamish's calves that he nearly tripped over his own feet.

Walk now. Ogle later. He trotted to catch up. "Where are you staying? Is it far from here?"

"Nah. Just across the way. We can walk. In fact, a little time in the cooler air might be a good thing."

"Oh? Are you still overheated from your performance?"

Hamish stopped, causing Zeke to overshoot until Hamish reeled him back in against his chest. "No, mate. I'm overheated from you." He threaded his fingers through Zeke's hair, causing Zeke's nerves to ping like during one of the AI's hissy fits, and when their lips met again . . .

Ooohhh. Zeke sighed into the kiss, and Hamish's tongue flickered against his. *Tongues can do that too? I have so much to learn.* The anticipation of being taught by Hamish nearly set his skin on fire.

Hamish broke the kiss. "Let's get to my room before I disgrace myself."

"Yes. Can we run, please?"

Hamish threw back his head and laughed. "Absolutely."

As they burst out of the door and raced across the paved courtyard in front of the theater, Zeke had just enough functioning brain cells to come to a very important conclusion.

He's happy. I'm making him happy.

The warmth coursing through Zeke had nothing to do with job satisfaction, meeting a client's expectations, or preserving his position in the Upper World.

Even the frigid wind was inconsequential, because for the first time in his life? Zeke was happy too.

Chapter Eleven

Hamish's heart was pounding harder than one of his manic drum solos, as he and Zeke ran across the courtyard, hand in hand. How long had it been since he'd held hands with anyone in public? He couldn't remember. Before he'd met Tiff for sure—which meant pre-Woodstock. He hadn't wanted to hold anybody's hand but hers since then, and she'd never shared any touch with him except their preshow fist bumps or an occasional punch in the arm when he annoyed her badly enough.

He grinned down at Zeke, who'd pulled his hoodie so far forward he looked like one of those alien blokes in Star Wars—Hamish couldn't remember what they were called, but their hoods were so deep that all you could see was the flashes of their eyes.

His eyes. Hamish seriously loved Zeke's eyes, so different from his own insipid gray. Dark and deep—although the occasional flashes of red or gold were a bonus. Should Hamish have been alarmed by the occasional flashes of red when Zeke got pissed off?

Nah. He'd never hurt me. He'd never hurt anybody. Whoever thought demons were too great a risk to allow near humans had never met Zeke Oz.

Hamish swung their hands, Zeke's palm warm enough to counteract the chilly wind, laughter burgeoning in his chest. But then Zeke pulled his hand away.

"I can't." Zeke tugged his hood practically down to his nose —seriously, how could he even see anything but his feet?

Laughter dying, Hamish shoved his hands in his pockets. "It's okay, mate. Like I said, you can change your mind anytime. Want me to walk you back to your place?"

Zeke stumbled to a halt and peered up at Hamish, his eyes flashing gold behind his glasses. *Jawas. That's what those aliens were called.* "Do *you* want to change your mind?"

"Nah. Course not. But you said you can't, so—"

"No, no! I meant I can't hold your hand in public." He glanced around. The courtyard wasn't especially busy—it was nearly midnight after all—but it wasn't empty either. Music fans were notorious night owls. "I told you that demons don't have . . . you know."

Hamish smiled down into Zeke's earnest face. "Sex, you mean?"

"Relationships. *Connections.* The only reason any demon would initiate one is to get something from the human in return. Usually their soul, since for some ridiculous reason, demons like to collect them." He rolled his eyes. "It's like the Sheol version of Pokémon Go, only they invented it at the dawn of time."

"Demons are a weird bunch, no mistake." Hamish stepped closer, the heat of Zeke's body like a campfire on a cold beach. "But you're making me happy, so it's all good."

Zeke fidgeted with his hood drawstring. "But if anyone sees me touching you in a way that is inappropriate for my job—"

"Ah. Right. You need to stay on the down-low. So no PDA."

"PDA?"

"Public displays of affection. No worries, mate." Hamish nodded in the direction of the hotel. "I'll keep my hands to myself until we get to my room. But then?"

"Th-then?"

"Private displays of affection. How's that?"

"That sounds . . . perfect."

"Then let's go."

They crossed the street, Zeke glancing furtively behind himself every hundred paces or so. Zeke's nervousness bled over to Hamish, because *he* started doing it. But nobody seemed to be lurking unduly, so he shook it off until they *finally* reached the funky little hotel Hamish preferred over the higher-end places downtown.

Hamish lifted a hand to the night desk clerk and led Zeke to the old-fashioned cage elevator. "I'm on the third floor. Elevator or stairs?"

"Which is faster?"

"Are you kidding? I'm a kangaroo. Stairs."

Zeke flashed a grin. "And I'm a demon. Want to race?"

"You're on."

Hamish held the stairwell door for Zeke, but by the time it shut behind them, Zeke was already two flights up, laughing down at Hamish from over the railing. Hamish caught up with him on the third-floor landing, but only because Zeke was leaning against the door, waiting for him.

"So demons have superspeed?"

"Not all. But low-level minions like me have to be fast. We serve a lot of masters and they don't like to wait."

Hamish's stomach knotted as he pushed Zeke's hood off his curls. "I don't like to think about that."

"About waiting?" Zeke's tone was teasing, almost lighthearted, something Hamish hadn't heard from him before.

"Well, that too. But about these 'masters' of yours. You shouldn't have to serve anyone. You should be able to do what you want."

Zeke tilted his head and placed one of those fever-warm hands against Hamish's cheek. "Doing what we want is what got demons relegated to Sheol in the first place. Nobody can do entirely what they want with no thought about the consequences."

Hamish closed his eyes and leaned into the touch. "I could name you a dozen people who do that every day. And some of 'em are in charge of entire countries."

"Then they've probably sold their souls to a demon."

Hamish snorted a laugh. "That explains so much. But I don't want to think about those arseholes right now. Not with my room less than two bounds down the hallway." He captured Zeke's hand, pressing it against his cheek for one last instant before he laced their fingers together. "Holding hands all right where nobody's watching?"

Zeke nodded. "More than all right."

"Then I'm going for it." He dropped a kiss on the back of Zeke's hand and was rewarded with a hitch in Zeke's breath. "Come on."

He led Zeke out of the stairwell and down the hall to his corner room. Once inside, he threw the dead bolt as Zeke crept across the floor toward the window seat.

"This is . . . charming."

"Yeah." Hamish joined him by the window. "It's a historic building. One of the local colleges owns it and uses it to train their hospitality students. But you know what?" Hamish lowered the crimson shades, closing the two of them inside. "I don't want to talk about it now."

"You know what?" Zeke unzipped his hoodie and tossed it on the window seat. "Neither do I."

Hamish sent his own coat after it. "I was hoping you'd say that." He took both of Zeke's hands. "But we should talk about what you want. You've never done this before. I don't want to hurt you or . . ." He swallowed against a lump in his throat. He was about to debauch a virgin demon, for cripes' sake.

A smile touched Zeke's mouth, amusement lighting his eyes —literally. "You're thinking about corrupting a demon, aren't you?"

"Well. Yeah."

"Don't. I'm here because I want to be. Since it is my . . . my first time, I might not want to do *all* the things." He bit his lip. "I don't even know what *all* the things *are*. But I want to do them with you. I've . . . I've never wanted that before, so even if we don't do anything but stand here holding hands, I've already won." His gaze flew to Hamish's. "That is, if *you* don't mind."

Hamish drew their joined hands up between their chests. "You know something? Nobody—and I mean literally nobody —has ever looked at me the way you did after the show tonight."

Zeke blinked. "Really? I can't believe that. You were so . . . so *vibrant.*"

"I'm in a band where the front man is the last true bard in Faerie. You think anybody ever even notices that the band *has* a drummer?"

Zeke shook his head, and this time, he kissed the back of Hamish's hands. Both of them. "You sell yourself too short. Everyone knows the band has a drummer. Your bandmates certainly do. You carry them on your back, or rather you let them sail on the swell of your drumbeats, keep them from devolving into chaos. The audience knows too. They can't help it. You're the beating heart of the band."

Hamish's throat was so tight he could barely swallow, let alone speak. But he managed to croak, "See? I've already won too. But I would really, really like to kiss you now."

Rather than answering, Zeke rose up on his toes and pressed his lips against Hamish's. *So sweet. Not practiced. A little awkward. Yet so bloody hot.* Because it was completely, utterly, absolutely sincere.

Not to mention one of the bravest things Hamish had ever witnessed.

Zeke was defying his frigging masters, the judgmental AI, the supe council, the witches—pretty much everybody who held power over him—to be with Hamish now.

Fuck me dead. He won't regret it. Not if I can help it.

He let Zeke guide the kiss, responding to a change of angle here, an increase of pressure there, and *fuck*, the guy was a fast learner. When his tongue flicked along Hamish's lower lip, Hamish jerked.

Zeke pulled back, eyes wide. "Did I do something wrong? I thought that it was all right to use tongues that way."

Hamish laughed shakily. "Trust me, it's very okay to use tongues that way, and you didn't do anything wrong. You're just really turning me on. And I'm afraid of going too fast."

Zeke's smile was blinding. "Really? I turn you on? That's never happened before. I mean, my clients tell me what turns them on all the time"—he wrinkled his nose—"even when it's not necessary, given that the spells do all the work. But none of it ever applied to me."

Hamish rested his hands on Zeke's narrow hips. "Can I ask you something?"

"Of course."

"Do I turn *you* on?"

Zeke glanced down at his groin, framed by Hamish's hands on his hips. "I know I don't have much experience, but I'm pretty sure that the erection is a prime indicator."

"So that's a yes? Because male bodies are notorious for having minds of their own."

"That's a yes." He cupped Hamish's face with his hands. "That's *definitely* a yes."

Hamish rested his forehead against Zeke's. "Thank the gods for that."

"So, um, is now when we're supposed to take our clothes off?"

"I—" Hamish had a hard time controlling his laughter, but he didn't want Zeke to feel like he was laughing *at* him. But it was just so . . . refreshingly direct. How often had Hamish ever been with someone who wasn't trying to hide something—usually their own insecurities—with bravado or aggression or sickeningly sweet coyness?

When Zeke asked a question, it was because he really wanted to know the answer, and Hamish could totally get down with that.

"We can take our clothes off if you want to. I'd love to see you, touch your skin. But if you're not comfortable with being naked in front of someone else—"

"I'm always naked in Sheol. All low-level demons are. But—" he glanced up shyly "—it feels different with you. I'm afraid you won't like what you see."

"Remember what I said? Not picky. But I'm pretty sure I couldn't be disappointed anyway, because it's you. I want to feel *you*. I want to make *you*—" Hamish sucked in a breath and backed off. "Wait a minute. Are you here— Is this all because you're supposed to make me happy?"

"What?" Zeke's eyes widened, but didn't change color. "No! I mean, yes, I want to make you happy because that's the reason to do this, isn't it? To make us both feel good?"

"Yeah, but it's your *job* to make me happy. If I'm doing this against your will—"

"Stop." Zeke advanced on him like a prowling panther. "I'm off the clock. Okay?"

"Okay. But here's the deal. For tonight, I want you to forget about making me happy."

"But—but—"

"No buts. Tonight isn't about me. It's about you. Tonight, it's my job—no, not my job. My *privilege* to make you happy." He twined his fingers with Zeke's. "So tell me, Zeke. Would taking off our clothes make *you* happy?"

For a moment, Zeke couldn't find his voice. Hamish wanted to make Zeke happy *on purpose*? Zeke had been thrilled enough that he'd experienced joy simply by being in Hamish's presence, but if Hamish was *explicitly* focused on Zeke's pleasure . . .

Lucifer's balls. If Hamish went at it with the same ferocious attack with which he played the drums, Zeke might not survive.

On the other hand, wouldn't it be worth it?

"Yes. It would make me very happy if we took off our clothes."

He started to unbutton his shirt, but Hamish gently grasped his wrists. "Let me."

So Zeke let his hands fall to his sides while Hamish unbuttoned Zeke's shirt as carefully as if he knew it was one of only three that Zeke owned. As he slid it down Zeke's arms, he pressed a kiss to Zeke's shoulder.

"You're so smooth. Like milk."

"P-p-pale, you mean. Like a corpse."

Hamish laughed, his lips vibrating against Zeke's skin. "No. No corpse has these gorgeous flowers blooming on them." He nuzzled Zeke's neck, where, judging from the heat coursing throughout his body, his stupid blotches were staging a riot.

"A parboiled corpse, then."

Hamish drew back and folded Zeke's shirt over his arm. "Hey. Don't dis the way you blush." He laid the shirt over a chair back. "I happen to think it's cute as hell." He winked. "If you'll pardon the expression."

Cute. Zeke turned the word over in his mind. He'd never heard a demon called *cute* before. In fact, most demons would be highly insulted—they strove for terrifying, threatening, awe-inspiring. Never *cute.*

Zeke decided he liked it.

And when Hamish kissed each and every blotch on his chest, throat, and face? Zeke decided he *loved* it.

He grabbed Hamish's ears and pulled him into a kiss—and suddenly, Zeke knew *how* to kiss. Their mouths fit together and then *tongues.* Yes! Tongues could totally do this—stroke and curl and dance around each other as if they could mate all on their own.

If Zeke had thought salted caramel chocolate tart was delicious, it had nothing on the taste of *Hamish*. Not sweet like wine, but with definite intoxicating overtones. If champagne was like drinking stars, kissing Hamish was like dining on fireworks.

Zeke's hands scrabbled against Hamish's shirt until he rucked it up and his hands touched *skin*.

Hamish's chest vibrated. Oh! He was laughing into Zeke's *mouth*, and Zeke wanted to devour every chuckle. But Hamish broke the kiss.

"You want me to take my shirt off?"

"Yes please. I mean no. *I* want to do it."

Hamish held out his arms. "Be my guest."

Zeke gathered the bottom of the soft tank in his hands, then lifted up, getting stuck around Hamish's armpits. "If you don't raise your arms all the way, this is never going to work."

Hamish chuckled again, and Zeke realized his nose was inches away from Hamish's chest and all that fascinating hair and— "You have an earring in your nipple!"

"Pretty sure it's not called an earring unless it's in your ear."

"Doesn't it hurt?"

"Nah."

Zeke touched the little silver bar with a tentative finger, then gave it a gentle tug. When Hamish hissed a breath between his teeth, though, he let go. "I'm sorry. But you said it didn't hurt."

"It doesn't. That wasn't a pain response."

"No?"

"No."

"So if I do this . . ." Zeke leaned forward and flicked the bar— and Hamish's nipple—with his tongue, and this time Hamish moaned. *Tongues are so powerful! Who knew?*

"If you don't get my shirt the rest of the way off so I can lower my arms and touch you . . ."

"Oh. Sorry!" Probably more experienced, less awkward people could take their lover's shirt off without catching it on their nose and one ear. Though Zeke clearly wasn't one of those people, he eventually got Hamish's shirt over his head.

"That's better." Hamish wrapped his arms around Zeke's back and pulled him close until they were chest to bare chest.

If Zeke had thought Hamish's chest hair had felt wonderful to his fingers, it was nothing to the way it felt against his skin. He wanted to climb all the way inside Hamish, just so Hamish would know how wonderful he was making Zeke feel.

Instead, he tucked his head under Hamish's chin—he was just the right height for it.

"Mmm." Hamish's low hum vibrated along Zeke's skin. "You're just the right height for me."

Zeke snuggled closer and, feeling greatly daring, plucked at Hamish nipple bar.

"If you keep doing that, mate—"

So Zeke did it again, and then Hamish's mouth was on his— hot and intense and demanding. Zeke met the kiss with heat of his own, certain his blotches were now a solid carpet of red across his skin.

If I had this to feast on, I'd never have to eat again.

But Hamish pulled away, leaving Zeke dizzy with some nameless *want* that was trying to roost somewhere between his heart and his groin. He whimpered in protest, but Hamish stroked his hair until the whimper turned into a purr.

"How would you feel about losing the rest of the clothes?"

"I would feel really good about that. Great. Spectacular, in fact."

"Then let's do it."

Before the last word left Hamish's mouth, Zeke had removed his own pants. "Would you like me to help you with yours?"

Hamish was staring at him, wide-eyed. "Demon superspeed comes in handy, I reckon." He licked his lips. "Damn, Zeke. You are *fine*."

Zeke glanced down at his body. It wasn't too different from any other demon of his rank. Thin, of course—that happened when you never ate—but stringy with muscle too, since a weak minion was no use to the overlords. He blinked at his penis. It was so *big*. And when he poked at it, it bounced back against his belly.

"I— It's never done *that* before!"

He'd seen erections on other demons, of course—incubi were notoriously well-endowed. He'd just never imagined he could match them. He peered up at Hamish anxiously. "Is this okay?"

"Trust me. It's very okay." He shucked his own pants, and Zeke forgot how to breathe.

Because Hamish hadn't been lying about having hair somewhere else. A line of golden brown arrowed down his belly to point right at his—

"Are you sure you're not an incubus?" Zeke croaked.

"Nah. Just a kangaroo." He held out a hand. "Come here?"

"Can I— Can I touch you?"

Hamish grinned. "I wouldn't object. But let me show you a way we can touch each other at the same time."

Zeke nodded, and embarrassingly enough, his penis leaked a little. He stared down at the smear on his belly, mortified. "I'm sorry. I don't know—"

"Hey. It's okay." Hamish stepped closer, close enough to take both of Zeke's hands in his. "If you note, mine's doing the same thing."

"It is?" Zeke checked, and Hamish was right. A pearl of moisture gathered at the end of Hamish's— "What should I call it? I mean, I've heard some of the . . . the nicknames, but they all seem so rude." Nothing that fit the beautiful curve of Hamish's . . . Or the color. Or the skin that stretched so tight and smooth over the head.

"Since you're looking down there, I assume you're talking about my cock—"

"'Cock.' Is that the right word?"

"Cock. Dick. Prick."

"But 'dick' and 'prick' are terms used for people who aren't very nice." Zeke couldn't take his eyes off Hamish's . . . "And that is *very* nice."

Hamish chuckled. "You could call it a johnson, then, if that makes you feel better."

"Johnson?" That was almost . . . friendly. Not alarming at all. In fact, one of his last clients had been named Johnson, and even though he'd punched the wall when Zeke had given him the bad news about his messed-up match and unavailable spouse, he was really very nice. *Johnson, then.*

Then Zeke forgot about nomenclature, because Hamish stepped closer, right *there*, right *here*, their johnsons snug against each other's, pressed between their bodies, with skin touching *all* the way down. His knees buckled.

"Hey." Hamish caught him with arms wrapped around Zeke's waist. "What do you say we make use of this very comfortable bed? Then we don't have to worry about how well our legs work, because I've got to tell you—kangaroos may have powerful legs, but you're making me weak at the knees too."

Zeke nodded, the sensory overload of Hamish's body—the heat of his skin, the texture of the hair that furred his chest and groin and legs, the hard length of his johnson—rendered him incapable of speech.

Hamish led him to the bed, laid him down tenderly, and then joined him there. With his head propped on his hand, Hamish toyed with one of Zeke's curls.

"You really are beautiful, you know. Are all demons this beautiful?"

Zeke tried to ignore the way his johnson bounced at Hamish's praise. "You said 'cute' before."

"I said your blushes were cute. But that was before I saw you naked. 'Cute' doesn't cut it anymore."

It was a good thing Hamish liked Zeke's blushes, because they were back with a vengeance. "Is there something I should be doing?"

Hamish nuzzled Zeke's hair. "What do you want to do?"

"I don't *know!*" he wailed. "I want *something*, but I can't describe it."

"Let's try this," Hamish murmured against Zeke's temple. "If you don't like it, if you want me to stop at *any time*, you just say so."

"O-okay." Zeke raised a trembling hand to Hamish's face. "Can I kiss you first?"

"Absolutely."

So Zeke laced his fingers behind Hamish's neck and drew him down—slowly, because he didn't want this to end too soon, and he had a feeling that *something* was about to happen, a line he was about to cross that could never be uncrossed.

Hamish didn't rush him. He let Zeke set the pace. But when their lips were a breath apart, Zeke couldn't stand it anymore. He lifted his head and met Hamish's mouth with his own—open, so that *tongues* could get involved because *Lucifer's balls*, tongues were the *best*.

Then Hamish jerked back. "Hold on. I should have asked. How old are you?"

Zeke blinked, still dizzy from the kiss. "Old?"

"Yeah. Your age. You look so young. Last thing I want to do is —"

"One thousand three hundred forty-seven."

Hamish blinked. "Seriously?"

"Give or take a few years. I wasn't counting at first."

Hamish grinned. "Well, then. I don't feel at all guilty about doing this."

He kissed Zeke's jaw. His Satan's apple. His collar bone. His . . . *nipple!* Zeke levitated six inches off the bed, but Hamish stroked his hip until he settled back onto the mattress.

"Shhh." He kissed Zeke's jaw. "I won't do that if you don't like it."

"N-n-no. It's okay. I liked it." Zeke swallowed, gasping when Hamish followed his Satan's apple with his mouth. "I *really* liked it."

"Then let's see how you like this." Hamish climbed over Zeke until he was propped above him on his elbows. "You're smaller than me, so maybe—"

Zeke wrapped his arms around Hamish's back and *pulled* with his demon strength.

"*Ooof.*" Hamish's eyes twinkled—yes, they actually twinkled, and Zeke hadn't known that anyone outside the angelic host could manage that. Not that he'd ever seen one face-to-face— the AI didn't count, since it was encased in its light column— but he'd heard stories. Sometimes the twinkles could turn a man into a pillar of salt. But Zeke figured that was just hype.

"Demon minions are sturdier than we look." They had to be, considering the punishment the C-suite could dole out. "And I —" Hamish flexed his hips and *oh!* His johnson stroked Zeke's with velvet fire, and this time Zeke levitated an entire foot, taking Hamish with him.

"Fuck me dead. Midair sex. How did I never—" Hamish hooked his arms under Zeke's shoulders and did that hip thing again and then . . . and then . . . and then . . .

Fire gathered in Zeke's groin, burned in his blood, sizzled in his bones, until he couldn't contain it anymore, and it burst free. *Oh.* Zeke's back arched as heat erupted from his . . . his . . . *Oh! It can do* that *too?* Something wet and musky and *wonderful* shot onto Zeke's belly, hotter than his skin, silkier than water. *It feels almost as good out as in.* He sucked in air as Hamish's grip tightened, and then it was coming *again,* and that was even better than before.

"Oh," he breathed. "More stars."

"Gods above and below," Hamish growled. "You are so fucking . . . *Gah!*"

Hamish buried his face in Zeke's neck, his body stiffening in Zeke's arms while his hips jerked in sharp little pulses and there was more warmth flooding between them.

Slowly, but still far quicker than Zeke wanted, the euphoria faded, and he drifted back onto the mattress.

Zeke stroked Hamish's hair—*soft and silky*—while his beard—*rough and springy*—tickled Zeke's shoulder. "So this is what sex is like?"

Hamish chuckled, raising his head to smile down at him. "This was just the starter, mate."

Zeke blinked. "You mean there's *more*?"

"Yeah. I take it sex education wasn't big in Sheol."

"No."

"Porn?"

Zeke scoffed. "Not for the minions. We just have to clean up after."

"Speaking of cleanup . . ." Hamish rolled off and padded to the bathroom.

Zeke ran a tentative finger through the mess on his belly. *This came from me. And from him. We're joined together in . . . in messiness.* He lifted a finger to his mouth and tasted it. *Together we taste like a Beltane bonfire on the beach.*

It was a flavor Zeke could get addicted to—even more than salted caramel chocolate tart.

"Hey, Zeke. I was thinking," Hamish called from the bathroom, "I'm gonna need a date for the bachelor party as well as the wedding."

The last remnants of euphoria faded. *Remember who you are. Remember who he is. Remember your job.* "All right. I can look up some more options when I get back to the office."

"That's not going to fly."

"It's not?"

"Nah." Hamish poked his head out of the bathroom. "I want *you* to be my date."

Zeke's heart tried to escape from his rib cage. "I—I can't."

"Why not?"

"Because . . . because . . ." *Because I'm not good enough for you either.*

Hamish grinned and leaned against the doorjamb, and all rational thought fled from Zeke's brain. "Still waiting."

"What would your friends think if you brought a demon to the party, let alone the wedding?"

"They'd think I was a lucky sod. After what you did last night, they all worship you anyway. They probably like you better than me."

"Don't say 'worship.'" Zeke shuddered. "So many demons got into trouble by thinking they deserved worship."

"All right." He ducked back into the bathroom, calling over the sound of running water. "No worshipping. But don't blame me if they mob you like a bunch of crazed fans."

"Seriously, Hamish. I can't go. Demons aren't supposed to fraternize with humans—"

"Newsflash: I'm not human."

"We're *really* not allowed to fraternize with supes. The C-suite has never gotten over the whole 'cubi dynasty thing. They'd consider it a threat to their power."

Hamish snorted "They should be grateful. Consider it continuing education for your job with Supernatural Selection. I mean how can you make a decent match for somebody else when you don't know what a decent match feels like?"

From what Melchom had said, the overlords would probably prefer indecent matches. *More misery to mine.*

Hamish, still naked, returned with a washcloth in his hands, his johnson soft between his legs. Zeke glanced down at his own.

"I guess these things need to recharge?"

Hamish crawled onto the bed and sat cross-legged at Zeke's side. "Yup." He ran the washcloth over Zeke's chest, pausing for a moment to stare at Zeke's groin. "Or maybe not."

Zeke's blotches started to bloom again, and he put his hands over his misbehaving johnson. Maybe if he poked it with one of his claws, it would deflate? He extended one, but Hamish grasped his wrist.

"Hey. This isn't a bad thing. In fact, if you want, I can show you something else on the sex roster."

Zeke pointed at Hamish's johnson, which, now that he was paying attention, had started to perk up. "Should I wait for yours to inflate?"

Hamish laughed. "Nah. I'll catch up. Just remember—" he gazed somberly into Zeke's eyes "—if you don't like it, say so, and I'll stop."

Zeke nodded. "I promise."

"Okay, then." Hamish lay down again, but weirdly with his feet toward the head of the bead and his head—

"Lucifer's *balls!*"

Hamish's mouth around Zeke's johnson was hot and wet and his *tongue* . . . Then Hamish did something else, something with his lips and suction and Zeke's back bowed, stars going supernova under his skin, and that . . . that *thing* happened again. *Who needs anti-grav? With him, I can fly.*

But when he realized Hamish had *actually swallowed*, that what had come from Zeke was now *inside* Hamish, a part of him, at least for a little while? He flailed as if he were falling from the ceiling, from the roof, from the sky, scrabbling madly for something to hold on to. And Hamish's arm was there, catching him, grounding him, cradling him, because of course it was. "That—that— What *was* that?"

"That, my lovely little demon, was a blowjob."

"Really?" Zeke hauled himself up using Hamish's arm as leverage. "Can I do that too?"

Chapter Twelve

I may never sleep again. Zeke's nerves buzzed with the memory of Hamish's touch, the taste of Hamish's spend still on his tongue, Hamish's breath tickling the curls over his ear. But with the steady beat of Hamish's heart under Zeke's palm, he closed his eyes, the better to let his own heart synchronize.

I'll close them for a minute, just a minute.

But when he opened his eyes, sunlight was spilling in from under the blinds.

Shit. I am so demoted.

He wriggled out from under Hamish's heavy arm and gazed down at him. His hair—Zeke's fingers twitched with the urge to touch it—was rumpled and captivating, and a tiny smile curved his lips.

I made him happy last night. I know I did.

His heart spiraled down to his toes when he remembered Hamish's request. Zeke couldn't be his date, not for the bachelor party and not for the wedding. Zeke would be lucky if he wasn't hauling fuel for the Sheol boilers by noon.

Which could be any minute. *No. The light is wrong. It's early. Not far after dawn.* Maybe he could make it back to the apartment before anyone found out.

He winced. The AI would know. And how likely was it that it could keep its mouth shut?

Zeke used demon speed to scramble into his clothes, distracted by the scent of Hamish still clinging to his body. He should take a shower, but he didn't have time and he didn't want to wake Hamish. At the door, he indulged himself with another look at Hamish, long and golden, the sheet only covering one leg.

"Thank you," Zeke murmured. "I'm glad my first and only time was with you."

He hustled down the stairs and into the wan morning light, clouds the color of ash drifting across the sky. The streets weren't busy, but they weren't empty either, so he had to restrict his speed to that of a hurrying human. Consequently, it took him longer than he'd hoped to get back to the Supernatural Selection building.

The falafel restaurant was still closed, as was the metaphysical bookstore run by the witches' collective. The building looked deserted, but that didn't always mean anything.

Zeke scheduled the bookings for all the Supernatural Selection altar rooms himself—they weren't only used for mating ceremonies—and he knew the witches preferred time slots were in the midnight to 3 a.m. range. He couldn't remember anyone ever booking a dawn ritual—that was more of a druid thing. He might at least be able to avoid Magistra Lenore.

He crept up the stairs, checking the lobby for activity, but everything was quiet, so he took the chance and sped up the remaining flights to his apartment.

He breathed a sigh of relief and allowed a bit of his euphoria to return. A smile tugged at his lips as he eased the door open and slipped inside.

Only to be faced with the AI, in blaring green and gold, and Melchom, wearing a three-piece white suit with wide lapels and bell-bottom trousers.

"Uh-oh," he whispered.

"Indeed." Melchom strode forward and slapped Zeke across the face. "You were abroad." Another slap. "You evaded your monitor. You—" Melchom's nostrils flared, and he seized Zeke's jaw in one hand, his claws digging into Zeke's skin when he squeezed. *Hard.* "You've dallied with a *human*. Don't bother to deny it. I can *smell* him on you."

Zeke couldn't shake his head, not in Melchom's merciless hold. The pain caused his eyes to tear up, but he held back a sob, even though he knew that was what Melchom wanted—and giving Melchom what he wanted sometimes cooled his temper.

But this time, Zeke wasn't willing to give in, because that would somehow betray Hamish. "I didn't." His words were garbled because of Melchom's iron grip on his jaw. "He's a supe."

"So." Melchom flung Zeke against the wall. "You admit it." He glanced over his shoulder at the AI. "I didn't believe your claim, but for once, your spite and the truth aligned."

Zeke rolled to his knees, keeping his head bowed. "I'm sorry, Supervisor. But I was following the magistra's orders."

"*Her* orders? What about your nature? What about *my* convenience? I've endured the infernal *din* of that wretched disco for *hours*, and just as I was about to close the deal on a hedge fund manager's soul, I got pulled out." He closed his eyes and rubbed his temples. "Beelzebub's balls, how can humans tolerate it? My head is *pounding*."

"Would you, er, like some aspirin, Supervisor?"

Melchom's eyes snapped open. "Silence! And *then*, when I returned to the blessed peace of Sheol, the screams of the tormented had barely begun to soothe me before I was treated to a tongue-lashing from that weasel, Adramelech, about not being able to control my minions." He brushed the sleeve of his white jacket. "Ridiculous. He's nothing but a *launderer*, regardless that the wardrobe he maintains is Satan's, and I'm in charge of *all* civil service. Do you *know* how annoying that is?"

"No, Supervisor."

Melchom glared down at Zeke, his eyes blazing red. "That wasn't a question."

"Of course not, Supervisor. But by the articles of the work-release, I must answer to her while I'm in the Upper World."

Blue swirled in the AI's pillar, and Zeke risked a glare of his own. *I do not answer to you, you . . . you . . .* What had Hamish called it? *You jumped-up follow spot.*

"Congratulations, Ozul-y-Kalon." Zeke blanched at Melchom's use of his true name in front of the AI. "You may have just obliterated the entire work-release fiasco. And despite how happy that will make the C-suite overlords, there's still the little matter of the soul you cost me." Melchom grinned, showing *all* his pointed teeth. "So you'll collect one in its place."

"But . . . but, Supervisor. I'm not rated for soul collection."

Melchom flicked a finger at Zeke, and Zeke nearly doubled over with the pain in his head. "You are now. One soul. By Monday." He strolled forward until his white patent-leather boots jabbed into Zeke's kneecaps. "In fact, I'll make it easy on you. I wouldn't want to strain your abilities by making you search. You already have a connection to this *supe* of yours. His soul will do nicely."

Zeke stared up at Melchom—and got another clout for daring to meet his supervisor's eyes without permission. But that was nothing to the horror curdling his blood. With his ears ringing, his head still pounding, he tried to find a way out.

"Supervisor, he's a client. I can't—"

"Silence!" Melchom kicked Zeke in the ribs. "His soul. By Monday. No excuses."

And he disappeared in a burst of disco music and brimstone-laced smoke.

The sun on his face woke Hamish from the best sleep he'd had in forever. Eyes still closed, he grinned sleepily, reaching for

Zeke. But when his hand patted nothing but empty sheets, he opened his eyes and could tell in an instant that he was alone.

For one thing, Zeke's clothes were gone. For another thing, the little frisson that played along his skin whenever Zeke was within ten feet of him was missing.

Maybe that was what had been nagging him whenever they'd been out in public: they weren't being watched; Zeke was just setting off his *holy-fuck-hotness* proximity alarm.

He blinked at the digital clock radio on the bedside table. What the fuck? He was never awake by eight, or rather, if he *was* awake by eight he was usually cursing a blue streak because the band had to be on the road to their next gig and Del was a sadistic piece of work.

Nah. Del was freaking royalty, the way they'd gotten rid of Euterpe last night with that straight-faced lie about an interview.

"An interview! Shite!" Hamish untangled his foot from the sheets and scrambled out of bed. Sure, he hadn't had an interview last night, but Del hadn't been completely untruthful. The whole band was supposed to appear on a local TV show this morning. Hamish was surprised Del wasn't already pounding on his door.

He raced to the bathroom and took the quickest shower in his life—although he was slightly distracted by finding a stray flake of Zeke's jizz on his thigh. He grinned as he soaped up and rinsed off. *His demon.* Yeah, there'd probably be all kinds of council negotiation crap—not to mention crap with his own band leader. There usually was for cross-species matings. But Gareth had loosened up considerably after Niall had come back, and after both his brothers had found their happy ever after with non-fae partners.

And as for the council—hadn't it been their idea to mainstream demons into the Upper World? Hamish would totally help them out with that—full immigration was the only way to really be fair, right?

Because now that he'd met Zeke, gotten to know Zeke, *tasted* Zeke . . . well, no one else would do.

He dried off and scrambled into clean pants and a long-sleeved shirt—might as well give winter at least a passing nod—grabbed his jacket, and flung open his hotel door in time to face Niall's raised fist.

"Whoa, there, mate. I'm not late enough to warrant a haymaker, am I?"

Niall chuckled and lowered his hand. "No. But I've been sent to retrieve you. You're dead late and . . ." Niall's eyes widened. "You got laid. By an angel?"

"What? Not bloody likely. I wouldn't have an angel any more than one'd have me." He shrugged into his coat.

"But the *ethera*—"

"*Ethera*? Those the voices you hear?"

"Yes. They like to keep me up-to-date with the news. And *they* say you got busy with an angel last night."

"They're barmy, your voices."

"The *ethera* are never wrong. Annoying sometimes. But never wrong." He stood aside and gestured for Hamish to exit the room.

"They're wrong this time." He smirked as passed Niall in the doorway. "Or maybe something got lost in translation."

"That's . . . a point, I suppose. They say they can see the tracks of grace on your heart, but they occasionally have a little trouble with interpretation." He kept pace with Hamish as they hurried down the stairs. "They might mean love."

"Love?" Hamish scoffed. "I don't do love, remember? However—" he shoved his hands into his coat pockets as he followed Niall onto the street "—I had a *very* good night."

"Glad to hear it. Did Supernatural Selection come through for you, then?"

Hamish winked. "In a manner of speaking."

Niall grabbed his elbow. "Tell me it wasn't that horrible, highly *un*inspiring muse from last night."

"No worries there." Hamish shuddered. "I wouldn't have her as a present."

"Then . . ." Niall's hand tightened. "*Zeke*? Goddess, are you mad?"

"I've been told. But not this time." He shook Niall's hand off. "Where's the car?"

Niall pointed to the sleek black Town Car idling at the corner, then powered after him as Hamish strode down the sidewalk. "Hamish, demons are tagged with more restrictions and warnings and bloody *rules* than anybody outside of necromancers." He frowned as he opened the car door. "In fact, back in the day when summoning was still popular, demons were *frequently* outside necromancers. And sometimes inside, if the necromancer was rubbish enough not to set the wards right and let himself be possessed. Or eaten." He smirked as Hamish folded himself into the car. "Although I suppose then they were technically outside the bloke again."

Hamish stared out the window as Niall joined him in the back seat and the car pulled into traffic. "He's not like that."

"That's what they all say."

"Let's leave it, shall we? What have I already missed?"

"Well, the rest of the band is probably halfway through the interview by now, so you'll be heading straight into the performance."

"What's the song?"

"'Lover's Reel.'" Then he grinned, the smug bastard. He was allowed, Hamish supposed. After all, Gareth had written the song for Niall back when they'd first met.

Hamish could play "Lover's Reel" in his sleep, so he wasn't worried about that. "Niall? Do you really think there'll be a problem with me and Zeke? I mean, you've met him. He's not *evil*. He saved Josh's life, for cripes' sake."

A hint of worry flickered across Niall's face, but then he pasted on a reassuring smile. "The *ethera* are ready to vouch for him—not that anybody can hear them except me. But the testimony of the King of Faerie's brother has got to be worth something, right?"

"As long as nobody remembers you're Unseelie and lied to the love of your life for a couple of centuries," Hamish muttered.

"Hey! Seelie and Unseelie are all one big fae family now, and I wasn't exactly underfoot and in constant contact for most of that time."

"Just saying."

"Look, Hamish. I know you. The band knows you. Your fans know you—"

"Nah. The fans *think* they know me, but they only know the public me. Zeke, though . . . Zeke knows the private me. As much as you or the band." As much as anybody except maybe Tiff. "This isn't just a one-nighter for me, Niall. He's the one. I feel it." He thumped his chest with his fist. "Right here."

"All right, then." Niall squeezed Hamish's shoulder. "You can count on me to back you up. You can count on Gareth too, and if Gareth adds his voice to your case . . . well, nobody in any realm can say no to Faerie's last true bard."

"Not even a bunch of arseholes who rule a realm with no music?"

Niall blinked. "No music? Seriously?"

"That's what Zeke says."

"Must be different than Govannon's corner of the underworld, then, or even beyond the Styx. Orpheus conned Hades into releasing Eurydice with music. And Govannon pulled himself out of his own fire for the sake of a song." A sly, wicked smile grew on Niall's face. "If these blokes have never heard music before, then they've got a troll's chance at midday of resisting Gareth."

That thought carried Hamish through the rest of the drive to the television studio, through the performance—which he very well might have done in his sleep, or at least in a Zekedaydream-induced trance—and all the way to the rehearsal studio for the run-through for tonight's show.

Hamish caught Josh's elbow at the door. "I'll be right in. I've got to make a call first, okay?"

Josh smiled, although his customary sweetness had a definite side of smirk. "Sure, Hamish." He headed into their usual practice room but paused at the threshold. "Tell him hello for me."

Hamish barked a laugh. *Cheeky little bugger.* But he supposed Josh might be almost as fond of Zeke as Hamish—although not in the same way. Josh's liking was based on gratitude. Hamish's on flat-out lust. He rubbed his chest. *And maybe more than lust.*

As he pulled out his mobile and wandered down the hall into another empty studio for privacy, he wondered if Niall's *ethera were* always right.

Was he in love?

He'd been sure he'd been in love with Tiff for decades, but that had always been laced with hurt and anger and hopelessness. He'd always dreaded seeing Tiff again as much as he'd been desperate to do so, because he'd always known she'd shut him down again.

With Zeke, it was completely different. As he punched in the Supernatural Selection number—did Zeke have a personal mobile phone?—he whistled a random tune, then chuckled when he realized it was "Lover's Reel." *Maybe the* ethera *are onto something after all.*

"Supernatural Selection. This is Zeke. How may I help you?"

"I can think of a lot of ways we could help each other. Most of them require a bed and no clothing."

"M-M-Mr. Mulherne. Good morning."

Mr. Mulherne? Seriously? They'd axed that shite forever ago. All right, maybe it was only a few days, but it *felt* like forever. *Oh.* "AI hovering at your shoulder, is it?"

"I should let you know, Mr. Mulherne, that you're now—" there was a pause, and then the quality of the call changed "—on speaker."

Fuck. "Got it."

"After last night's . . . events . . . I don't think it would be appropriate for you to continue as a Supernatural Selection cli— *Augh!*"

Bloody AI probably zapped him again. Hamish ground his molars together. If he had his way, that thing wouldn't come within a dozen miles of Zeke. *Wait. What?* "Not appropriate? But I need—" *You. I need you.* "A match. You promised."

"Yes, but— *Augh!*"

Damn it. Hamish wasn't going to let the AI electrocute Zeke. But clearly, arguing about this wasn't going to work.

He took a deep breath. "So what do you suggest I do . . . to be *happy.*"

Even over the echoing phone line that made it sound like Zeke was at the bottom of a barrel, Hamish could hear his quick intake of breath. *Yeah, babe. I went there.*

"There aren't any other supe-only agencies, but there are several who have a mixed clientele. I could give you their— *Augh!*"

That does it. "Fine. I'll figure it out for myself."

He punched disconnect before Zeke had a chance to respond, then shoved his phone into his pocket. He flung open the door and stalked down the hall to where Hunter's Moon was already tuning up.

Fucking AI. It was probably taking it out on Zeke that Hamish had banned him from the concert last night.

He slowed his headlong rush. But *Zeke* seemed like he had been trying to cut Hamish loose, and got zapped by the AI with every attempt. Why? Did he regret last night?

Hamish's throat closed, mouth going dry. Had he done something that Zeke wasn't comfortable with, hadn't really wanted? Zeke had *said* it was all okay, but he was used to submitting to everybody—the witches, other higher ranked demons, the bloody AI. Would he be able to distinguish Hamish from all those other arseholes?

Hamish wanted to think so, but . . .

He stalked into their practice room and took his place behind the drum kit without a word, even though everyone—including Tiff—greeted him as usual.

Gareth cast him a quizzical glance. "Are you okay, Hamish?"

"Yeah. Let's just get on with it." Josh wordlessly handed Hamish the set list. "Lover's Reel" was the opening number. *Bloody marvelous.*

Somehow he made it through the rehearsal—although his bandmates apparently had a different opinion.

"What the fuck is wrong with you, Hamish?" Spence slammed a dissonant chord on his keyboard. "We've got a rock concert tonight, not a funeral and not a charge into the Valley of Death—and you can't even decide which of *those* you're playing for."

"Just having an off morning."

"An off morning? You fucked up the lead-in to 'Orfeo' *six times.*"

Hamish didn't launch a stick at Spence, but it was a near thing. "Didn't think you could count that high."

"You need to get laid."

"Stuff it, Spence. I mean it." Pretty fricking pathetic that he'd spent years *not* getting laid, and the one time he did, his drumming suddenly tanked. His respect for Gareth rose about a million percent. *He managed to keep it together for two hundred years, and I can't even manage one day.*

"Hate to break it to you, but it's afternoon." Spence joined Josh by the door. "We're grabbing lunch and then taking a nap. Try to get your head on straight by tonight."

Spence left *or else* hanging almost visibly in the air. Hamish scooted his stool back so he could lean against the wall, eyeing his duffel. He needed to change his shirt, but he'd stowed his mobile in the duffel, and if he had it in his hand, he'd break down and call Zeke again. He didn't need that kind of drama if he intended to *get his head on straight*, per instructions.

Gareth came over to him while Tiff was arranging some kind of meal deal with Luci and Vitor. "Hey." He kept his voice low, leaning against the wall next to Hamish. "Niall told me you'd found somebody."

Hamish grunted and shot Niall a glare. Niall shrugged sheepishly. *I should have known he wouldn't keep anything from Gareth.* At least not anything of this magnitude. *"Hamish got laid! Alert the media!"* Maybe it was already on the band's Twitter feed.

"I take it by your attitude that something went wrong."

"You think?"

"I think this is the same song, different verse." Gareth glanced sidelong at Tiff. "You were pining after Tiff for all these years because it was safe. It meant you didn't have to actually engage."

"Engage?" That's what *Zeke* had said—that Hamish couldn't engage emotionally. Well, he'd engaged all right. "If the other person doesn't engage back, then you're screwed."

"For years, you gave me grief for . . . let's see, what did you call it? Oh yeah. My 'love-lost-woe-is-me lyrics.' Turns out you were mired in the same shit."

"Stuff it."

"'Woe is me, I'll never have the one I want.' But really, it was 'Hot damn. I don't have any baggage.'"

"You've got no room to talk. You pined for two frigging centuries!"

"Actually, I'm the only one who does have room, for exactly that reason." Gareth picked up his guitar. "So I'm the only one who can tell you—figure it out. Whatever it takes, my friend. Figure it out."

"That's bloody helpful," Hamish muttered as Gareth strolled out of the room with his arm through Niall's, leaving him alone in the room.

Except for Tiff.

She faced him over her open case. "Heart troubles?"

He huffed a laugh. "That obvious?" She shrugged one shoulder. "Apparently you're not the only one who has no trouble resisting me."

"I'm guessing this is about Zeke?" When Hamish nodded, she chuckled. "Yeah, he seemed pretty into you at the concert." *And I was pretty into him after the concert.* "And please *don't* give me the obvious response because what you get up to in bed is way TMI."

"Based on our recent conversation, he doesn't seem into me anymore."

"You sure?"

Hamish rubbed his chest, trying to ease the ache. "Pretty sure."

"Hunh." She tugged on her earring. "Maybe . . . instead of smashing your drum kit to bits, you should ask him the big question."

"The big question?"

"Yeah. The one you never got around to asking me." She snapped the latches on her bass case. "Why?"

"'Why?' That's it?"

"Why doesn't he want to be with you, and be ready to take no for an answer. He doesn't have to tell you. Nobody's owed another person's time or affection—or even an explanation. But if he's willing, it'll at least give you an idea of what to work on the next time you're attracted to somebody." She studied him, her head tilted to one side. "You never pushed me. But you never asked me why either."

He attempted a grin, but only made it halfway. "Maybe I was afraid you'd tell me. And then I'd have no hope." He started to flip the drumstick, but set it on the snare instead. "So I'll ask now. Why, Tiff? And you don't have to tell me if you don't want."

She picked up her case. "I love you like a brother, Hamish, but you're a one-person guy." She paused in the doorway and gave him a smile that held both amusement and apology. "And I am *so* not a one-person girl."

Chapter
Thirteen

"You did *what*?" Zeke goggled at the AI, whose smarmy gold was laced with smug turquoise. But the truth of what it had done was staring at Zeke from his monitor—a 1:30 p.m. appointment with Hamish Mulherne. "You of all people . . . things . . . *whatever* should want him to stay far away from me. You *heard* what Melchom said. I thought you lot *objected* to having people's souls stolen."

Silver, which Zeke didn't buy for a minute, bloomed inside the AI's column.

"Supes are too people. Are you saying the angelic host only cares about humans? Kind of racist of you, isn't it?"

Zeke shoved his chair back and stormed out of his office. An indigo glare sent his shadow leaping out in front of him, but he ignored it. It simply proved his point: bigots were always the first to claim they weren't prejudiced.

The AI could just stuff it.

It followed him, of course, so he ducked into the restroom and locked the door. He lowered the toilet lid and sat down, his head in his hands. He had no idea how soul collection worked. Was it a compulsion? Would he suddenly leap on Hamish when he walked in the door and try to suck his soul out through his mouth?

Calm down, idiot. That only happens in fantasy books. You know better.

The soul extraction could only happen after the bargain had been struck, when the Sheol C-suite could claim that the victim had consented fully to the process. *A process that would render them nothing more than fuel in the Sheol boilers.* Eventually.

Of course, they'd get what they desired first. For a while. But Zeke had been assigned to boiler duty more than once, and he knew that nobody who was down there, awaiting their next cycle in the enormous furnace that powered Sheol's technology, thought the deal was worth the cost.

Somehow, he had to keep Hamish from the same fate. *I could just refuse.* But if he did, would Melchom take Hamish anyway? *Maybe I could substitute somebody else.*

But his belly cramped at the thought. He couldn't sacrifice another innocent person. Nobody deserved that. And Hamish was walking into this blind, thinking Zeke didn't care for him. He'd be vulnerable. He'd want *something*, even if it was only revenge for Zeke's behavior. And that *want*, that *desire*, would render him vulnerable to a soul swap bargain.

Zeke raised his head slowly. *But if he knows about the danger, maybe he can avoid it.* Hamish had friends—powerful friends. They could help protect him too. Zeke could then refuse Melchom's order, and if it meant a return to Sheol and a few decades of torment, so what? That would always have been on the plate anyway, given how angry the C-suite had been when they'd been ordered to comply with the mainstreaming solution.

At least this way, Hamish would be safe.

How to warn him though? Zeke couldn't very well pull him into the restroom for a private chat, not with the AI sticking to him like a neon burr. That would be bound to raise an alarm.

But if I arrange another date for him, one that requires my presence but that the AI can't attend . . .

He burst out of the restroom, dodging around the AI, who was lurking in a green funk outside the door, and raced back to his office. He pulled up the Hunter's Moon official website, and sure enough—they had another concert tonight. Zeke just had to find the perfect date for—

A grin that probably rivaled Melchom's spread across his face. The AI loomed over him in a toxic cloud of magenta.

"I'm doing my job, of course. That's what you're here to verify, isn't it?" Pink tinged the magenta. *What a drama queen.*

"Then you shouldn't have set up that appointment. I have to find Hamish another date, so if you could go sulk in the corner? The glare interferes with the monitor."

The AI retreated, inching across the floor so slowly a snail could lap it. *Yes, yes. You're annoyed. I get it.*

But Zeke was past caring what the AI wanted. It had set him on this path by informing on him anyway. Now his only mission, his only goal, his only *desire*, was to save Hamish.

Good thing demons don't have souls of their own. Zeke would be a prime candidate for collection if that were the case. If he had one, he'd gladly trade it to save Hamish. But since that wasn't an option, he had to get creative.

By the time Hamish slouched through Supernatural Selection's door at precisely one thirty, hands in the pockets of his coat and his hair mussed by the wind, Zeke hoped he'd done enough.

"Good afternoon, Mr. Mulherne."

Hamish glanced at Zeke from under the fall of his shaggy—*so soft*—hair. "Really? We're back to that? And setting the appointment by text? Least you could have done is call me. I almost decided to blow it off."

Zeke swallowed, then attempted a customer-service smile although the hurt in Hamish's tone nearly gutted him as viciously as any demon scimitar. But the AI was quivering at Zeke's shoulder like a parti-colored greyhound, so Zeke couldn't explain.

He could only move forward with his plan.

"It was the most efficient method of communication"—*not by me*—"since I was aware"—*I wasn't*—"that you were occupied this morning. But I have good news!"

"Yeah? What is it?" He flopped into the chair across from Zeke. "That a comet is on a collision course with earth and I won't have to deal with this shite anymore?"

Zeke laughed nervously. *This isn't going well. If only he'd drum on something.* But Hamish stayed uncharacteristically still. "Of course not. But I've arranged another date for you. Someone who's thrilled with the thought of attending the Hunter's Moon concert this evening."

Hamish sneered. "Because *that* worked out so well last time."

Although his smile threatened to slip off and scurry across the floor to hide from Hamish's fully understandable anger, Zeke clutched the edge of the reception desk, his claws extending to bite into the wood, and kept pushing onward.

"I assure you that *this* person has no interest *whatsoever* in any of your other bandmates"—*or in anything other than himself, for that matter*—"so the little contretemps with Euterpe won't be repeated. *Everything else*"—Zeke tried to load his voice with meaning—"will happen exactly as *you* could wish."

Hamish's gaze sharpened. "As *I* could wish, eh? You sure you know what that is?"

Thank Lucifer. He's getting it. The AI pulsed brown with suspicion though, so Zeke dialed it back a notch.

"Yes, I believe I do. Do you think you could arrange tickets? I realize it's too late for the same amazing seats as last night—"

"Nah. I can manage something decent. Or Del will. They can do anything."

"Excellent. You needn't send the car. Your date will arrive on his own. Do you—" Zeke aimed for a completely neutral tone, but he wasn't sure he managed, since Hamish raised an eyebrow and the AI twitched like it was the one who'd been goosed for a change. "—wish for me to accompany him, as I did with Euterpe?"

Hamish's gaze flicked to the AI, now a blazing ball of red-orange rage. *Maybe it'll go supernova and give us all a break.* "Yeah. I do. It sucks for someone to sit through a show by himself." He leaned back in the chair, and his fingers beat out a sprightly rhythm on its arms. *Finally.* "Course your electric sidecar can't come along."

"Yes. We understand." Zeke looked at the AI. "Don't we?"

Pink stained the wall behind it, with a little green burst at waist level.

Hamish laughed. "I'm guessing that's the AI version of blowing a raspberry."

Or turning its back while flipping us off. "Something like that."

"Okay. Who's my date tonight? Somebody I know?"

Here's where it gets tricky. "You might have heard of him. Paris."

"Paris." Hamish blinked and his fingers stilled. "*The* Paris? The one who ran off with Helen of Troy?"

"Yes, but *that* relationship is *so* thirty-three centuries ago."

"Wasn't *he* over thirty-three centuries ago? You setting me up with a ghost?"

"No, no. Paris is naturally still paying for his transgressions, but Aphrodite intercedes on his behalf every time Hera and Athena want to load him onto Charon's boat with a one-way ticket." Zeke cleared his throat and pretended to read from his monitor. "He loves long walks on the beach, watching *America's Next Top Model*, and is an avid video game enthusiast. *Grand Theft Auto* is a favorite."

"Bloody marvelous. This is the best you can do?"

"Believe me, Mr. Mul— Hamish. I'm trying my best to make you happy."

"Yeah? Well, that remains to be seen, doesn't it?" He stood up. "I'll ask Del to leave the tickets at the box office for you. I suppose he'll expect the VIP treatment?"

"Well, he *is* used to hobnobbing with goddesses—although not always with the best results."

"Grand." He strode toward the door, but stopped at the threshold. "Just warning you—this is the last time I'm going through this."

"I—I understand. I really believe tonight will be a turning point for you. If not, I'll let Magistra Lenore know that I've failed and you've decided to terminate your agreement with Supernatural Selection."

Hamish held Zeke's gaze for a moment, then nodded sharply and walked out.

Zeke slumped in his chair, blowing out a breath. Of course the AI had to express its suspicion and disapproval in a strobe of yellow and blue, with a little green thrown in for good measure. Zeke closed his eyes against the glare.

"I don't know what you're talking about. Another concert date makes the most sense—it presents Hamish at his best and provides his partner with perks that few others ever see—Augh!" Zeke shot upright, rubbing his arm where the AI had zapped him. "Stop that! I *know* because I saw it in action last night. My mandate may be to make Hamish happy, but his match needs to be happy too."

Letting Hamish go certainly won't make me *happy. But if it saves him from soul collection, it'll be worth it.* At least Zeke would be able to see Hamish play one more time.

And *that* would definitely make him happy. Right before it ripped out his supposedly nonexistent heart.

After leaving Supernatural Selection, Hamish made his way to the Bullpen, the shifter bar in Portland's Old Town. Or rather, he made his way *downstairs* at the Bullpen, where shifters could work off a little steam by punching the shite out of each other in the fight arena.

The last time Hamish had been down here was right after Gareth had found out Niall had been lying to him from the beginning. Gareth, as a fae, had no business challenging a bear shifter to a fight—and ended up with the black eye and broken hand to prove it—but he'd had to work off his anger somehow.

Hamish steered away from a couple of surly bears and a panther—no way was he ever fighting a big cat—but the hyenas in the corner? He grinned and beckoned to both of them. Because he could take one with no problem—and where was the challenge in that? Two, though. Two would let him work off his frustration, hurt, and yeah, anger.

Because what was Zeke playing at? All those hints had to mean something. But what?

When Hamish shifted, his height didn't change—still six three—so he had *that* advantage over the hyenas. But he had another advantage—the hyenas' main weapon was their bite: their teeth and jaws were made for ripping apart animal carcasses. They barked that crazy hyena laugh at him, expecting him to use his arms, which—although his claws were wicked—didn't have the reach of his human arms.

But Hamish fought with his feet.

Balancing with his tail, he took out both hyenas with less than half a dozen well-placed kicks. When they tapped out, he shifted back.

"Not much of a challenge after all." Maybe next time he *would* go for the bear.

He walked back to his hotel and showered. Wiping the steam off the mirror afterward, he noticed that his hair needed a trim, the way it always did after a shift. Hamish threw the towel at the mirror, not even bothering to comb his hair. The fans wouldn't care—and by the end of the concert, he'd look like he'd run a marathon anyway.

Would Paris—self-proclaimed judge of beauty, and self-absorbed, narcissistic bastard—expect anyone who scored a date with him to match his expectations for looks, grooming, and wardrobe? *Too bad. He'd take his bloody chances.*

In front of the hotel, he waved away the car Del had sent and walked to the venue to bleed off his nuclear fidgets.

Consequently, he was about fifteen minutes late. The VIP reception was already in full swing, the chatter drifting down the hall as Hamish approached.

He ducked into the dressing room to stow his duffel. The walk in the wind hadn't done his hair any favors—he looked like he'd been dragged behind a horse for a mile or two. He sighed. What were the odds he could just hide out here until showtime?

Slim to never, mate, so stop being a bleeding princess and go face your "date."

And the demon you love.

He squared his shoulders and marched down the hall and into the reception room.

And fuck his luck, the first person he saw was Zeke. Hamish turned away before Zeke could meet his eyes and pretended to be listening to what Gareth was saying to a reporter.

He didn't have to hear Tiff's voice to know what she'd say: *Real mature, Mulherne.* But sod it, his hands were shaking. If he was in this bad a state now, this morning's rehearsal would be Grammy-worthy compared to what he'd be like onstage tonight.

Ordinarily he never drank anything but water before a performance—none of them did. But tonight, he needed something to smooth out his nerves and let him meet Paris with the pretense of pleasure. Or at least not active animosity.

And maybe to keep him from dragging Zeke into the nearest convenient broom closet.

So he grabbed some champagne and took a gulp. Before he could down the rest, though, Del grabbed his wrist and pried the glass out of his hand.

"No," they said, and handed the glass to one of the waiters.

"But—" Hamish followed the retreating glass with his gaze.

"No." They turned away, but Hamish knew better than to do an end-run around them to snag another drink. They'd know. They always knew. *Fucking oracles.*

Ah well. Might as well get this over with. He sneaked a glance in Zeke's direction—although not directly at him, because what if he was looking back?—in an attempt to locate Paris. It shouldn't be hard. The arsehole had never tried to be inconspicuous.

But the room only contained his bandmates and their significant others, the usual fans, and the caterers—although there did seem to be more security goons tonight than yesterday.

Finally, Hamish sighed and looked straight at Zeke—and apparently he needn't have worried about meeting Zeke's gaze, because Zeke was huddled against the wall, staring at his shoes, while Josh spoke to him earnestly. *Of course, Josh speaks to everyone earnestly, so that doesn't mean much. Does it?*

Time to face the music. Hamish made his way through the crowd, stopping to smile or take selfies with fans along the way, until he reached Zeke and Josh.

"Remember what I said, okay?" Josh's gaze flicked to Hamish, then he reached out and squeezed Zeke's shoulder. *What the—* Josh never touched anybody. Not even Spence on some days.

Zeke nodded, but didn't lift his chin. Josh shot Hamish what could only be described as a death glare—another thing Josh never did—so *something* was going down.

Too bad neither one of them was telepathic, because Hamish had no clue what the message was.

He shoved his hands into his pockets to hide their trembling. "Hey."

Zeke looked up—and *strewth*, the desolation in his eyes. *Talk about despair.* "Is there somewhere we can speak privately?"

"Uh . . . sure. We can use the dressing room. Everybody else is in here . . ." Hamish scanned the room again. "Except apparently my date. Paris isn't out hitting on one of the roadies, is he? That gorgeous but apparently inept one from yesterday?"

Zeke's lips twitched. "You noticed him?"

"Hard to miss. He acted like he was always in his own personal spotlight, too busy striking poses to do his job, which was almost a disaster." He edged closer. "But it wasn't, thanks to you." But when Hamish lifted his hand toward Zeke's face, Zeke flinched away.

"Please, Hamish? A few minutes in private?"

Hamish pocketed his hand again. "Sure, mate. This way."

Zeke kept his head down on the way across the room, but it seemed to Hamish as if every one of his bandmates tried to give him some kind of mental message—from Josh's second glare, to Spence's grin and thumbs-up, to Gareth's head tilt and lifted eyebrow. Tiff at least didn't depend on nonexistent mind-reading. She mouthed, *Why*.

Yeah, *that* message Hamish got, although he didn't need her reminder: it was an answer he really wanted.

He led Zeke down the hall and into the empty dressing room, closing the door behind them. He leaned against it, crossing his arms. "Okay. We're private. You want to tell me where my alleged date is?"

Zeke fiddled with his hoodie drawstring, the way he always did when he was nervous. "He didn't show. I knew he wouldn't. He *always* stands up his dates."

Hamish scowled. "Then what the fuck, dude? Did you *want* to humiliate me in front of my bandmates?"

Zeke spread his hands in apparent surrender. "It was the only way I could think of to speak to you alone. Without the AI listening in"—he gestured spasmodically to the room—"since it's not allowed at your concerts."

"Wait . . . It's *spying* on you?"

Zeke gave him a get-real look. "It's *always* spying on me. That's what it's *for*."

The knot in Hamish's belly started to unravel, a grin stretching his cheeks. "Why not just tell it to sod off? You're never exactly polite to it."

"Because of what I'm supposed to do." Zeke paced across the room, wringing his hands. "Because of what I *can't* do."

"Babe, stop wearing out your shoes." Hamish stepped into Zeke's path and took him by the shoulders. This time he didn't flinch away, thank the fates. "What is this awful thing you're supposed to do?"

Zeke clenched his eyes shut. "My supervisor—"

"Magistra what's-her-name? The witch?"

He shook his head. "No. The other one. My Sheol—"

"Don't say 'master' or I may have to punch the wall."

Zeke clapped his hands over Hamish's. "Don't do that! Your hands! You couldn't play, and then—"

"Easy, mate." Hamish kissed Zeke's forehead. "Just a figure of speech. Go on. Some arsehole from Sheol wants you to do a job for them, I take it."

Zeke nodded miserably. "Melchom, my—my supervisor, found out about last night."

Hamish's fingers went cold, despite the warmth of Zeke's hands covering them. "That you slipped the AI's leash, you mean? That was my idea, and I'm the client, so I must be right. Right?" Hamish grinned, trying to get an answering smile from Zeke.

Instead, Zeke's mouth trembled. "Not only that. He knows I was with you. That we . . . you know."

"Ah shite." Hamish drew Zeke, unresisting, into his arms. "He played the *demons don't date* and *only sex demons have sex* cards on you, didn't he? Can't you lay that one on me too?"

Zeke leaned back enough to gaze into Hamish's face, but didn't try to escape his embrace. "I couldn't. Because I wanted it too. I wanted it more than anything."

"So? Just lie to him."

"I *can't*," Zeke wailed. "Demons don't lie. It's a . . . a thing, because it's too great a liability in contract negotiations. We *can't* lie to our betters."

"Nobody is better than you," Hamish growled. "I don't care what the high and mighty arseholes tell themselves."

Zeke dashed a tear away, but judging from his fierce expression, it was a tear of rage. "The point is that we can't lie. We can only misdirect. There's no way I could misdirect about my feelings for you."

"Misdirect. That's what the Paris date was—misdirection."

"Yes. Because I had to tell you. I had to let you know." Zeke's breath caught. "If anything were to happen to you . . ."

"It's not easy to take down a kangaroo shifter. We're tough. We have to be."

"Not tough enough," he muttered.

"So tell me. Why, Zeke? Why did you try to *misdirect* me away?"

"Because . . ." He took a deep breath. "Melchom ordered me to collect your soul."

Hamish blinked. "He what now?"

"Collect your soul. It's one of the primary mediums of exchange in Sheol—souls and gold."

"Why the fuck would they want souls? What do they even do with them?"

"They use them to power the realm."

"Like batteries?"

He shook his head. "More like firewood. Souls are resilient. So they can recover to be burned again and again."

Ice crept up Hamish's spine. "Half a mo. They *recycle* souls? Like plastic or old newspapers or beer bottles?" Zeke nodded miserably. "So why do they need more? Are the overlords just a bunch of greedy sods?"

"Well . . . yes. But since the industrial revolution, and even more since the internet came along, Sheol's energy requirements have grown. Before that, heating the place to acceptable levels was the only concern, but now there's *technology* to maintain. A power grid. *Infrastructure.* Besides, it isn't only their usefulness that demons crave. They . . . they thrive on chaos, on the misery of others. If you take someone's soul, you've—" he make a jerking motion with his fist "—amputated their empathy. So not only will Sheol eventually get the use of their soul after the term of their bargain runs out, but the soul-impaired create *more* misery in the Upper World during their lifetime because they care only for themselves."

"So when we talk about soulless arseholes—"

"They might actually *be* soulless."

Hamish tapped his thumbs gently against Zeke's collarbone. "Why does this Melchom of yours want me?"

"Apparently when the AI summoned him after I didn't come home last night, he failed to close negotiations on a valuable soul, one that would have increased his status. Given him bragging rights with the other mast—supervisors for bagging such a prize. So I don't think he's interested in you per se—" Zeke's eyes widened. "Um, no offense."

Hamish grinned down at him. "None taken."

"He's trying to punish me. And he could tell that would be the worst possible punishment." His gaze dropped to Hamish's collarbone. "He even promoted me so I could do the collection. I've only been able to evaluate before."

"Evaluate?" Hamish was trying to pay attention, but holding Zeke in his arms was distracting him in the best possible way.

"I can look at someone and know their deepest desire—what they'd be willing to trade their soul away for."

"Could you tell that with me?"

Zeke looked away. "I won't. Not again."

"You mean you did already?" When Zeke nodded, Hamish kissed the top of his head. "It's okay. When?"

"At your first appointment. I could see what you felt about Tiff. But even then, you wouldn't have been willing to *make* her love you at the expense of her own happiness or the happiness of her partners."

Hamish huffed a laugh. "Yeah, well, that desire might have changed lately."

Zeke looked up, his eyes wild. "Don't tell me! I don't want to know. What if this new power means I'll *want* to collect your soul?"

Fuck my soul. You've already collected my heart.

Hamish cupped Zeke's face—and look at that: his hands weren't shaking anymore. "So demons don't lie. Tell me, would you date me? Do you want to be with me?" Hamish waggled a finger. "No misdirection now."

Zeke caught the finger in his fist. "I wouldn't do that. Not here. Not now."

"No. Only set me up on a date with the most notorious self-promoting sociopath in history."

"That was different! There was a reason for that."

"Is Paris even registered with Supernatural Selection?"

"Actually, yes. He is. Aphrodite insisted, since the whole thing with Helen didn't work out. She's convinced he only needs the right partner to change his ways."

"You think that'll happen?"

Zeke scoffed. "Are you kidding? Only if somebody works a duplication spell on him so he can date himself. He gives Narcissus a run for his money."

A knock sounded on the door. "Five minutes, Hamish," Del called.

"Be there in half a mo."

Zeke tried to pull away. "I should go."

"What? No way. I need you to be out there, in the audience."

"But—"

"Please." Hamish kissed Zeke's lips, and was rewarded with a tiny moan. "I played like shite at rehearsal today because I was twisted up about you. But if I know you're there, if I can play for you? I know I'll be brilliant."

"Well . . ." Zeke bit his lip. "Technically, nobody else knows that Paris was a no-show, so I suppose I could stay. For the sake of the band, of course. And the fans. We wouldn't want them to be disappointed."

"Right. The fans. The band." He traced the crest of Zeke's cheekbone. "And afterward, we can discuss our next date."

Zeke's eyes widened. "But I *told* you. The AI. Melchom. Your soul. I—I can't."

"You just leave all that to me. I've got an idea." He kissed Zeke again, and this time he didn't hold anything back—and to his satisfaction, neither did Zeke. "For now? Enjoy the show." He grinned. "I know I will."

Chapter Fourteen

Best. Show. Of his fucking *life*.

And Hamish wasn't the only one who thought so—even Spence commented on it, and he never said anything to Hamish postshow unless it was a complaint. For the first time, Hamish had fans screaming for *him* after "Lover's Reel"—but none of that mattered as much as the look in Zeke's eyes when the security guard escorted him backstage.

For a moment, Zeke simply gazed at Hamish. *Heart eyes. I can seriously get used to this.*

But when Zeke didn't say anything and didn't say anything and *still* didn't say anything, Hamish shifted nervously from foot to foot. "So. Did you like the show?"

Then Zeke *launched* himself past the rest of the band—from halfway across the room, so Hamish *knew* levitation had something to do with that incredible trajectory—right into Hamish's arms. *Where he fucking belongs.*

"You were incredible. The band was incredible. The music—"

"Was incredible?"

Zeke grinned. "Have I mentioned that you were incredible?"

"Little bit." Hamish kissed him. "But it always bears repeating."

"Well, you were." Zeke kissed *him* this time, and strewth but his little demon was a fast learner, because Hamish's knees threatened to buckle. *That's all right. My cock can probably catch me before I hit the floor.*

"Come back to the hotel with me." Hamish pressed an open-mouthed kiss on Zeke's Adam's—no, *Satan's* apple, which always made him moan and go boneless.

But Zeke surprised him this time. "I can't." He slid down Hamish's body, although there was a bit of a snag when their cocks—*heh, johnsons*—interfered with a smooth ride. "I need to pretend this was the arranged Paris date, or you could be in even more danger."

"Don't worry about me. I can take care of myself."

Zeke rested his hands on Hamish's chest. "I can't risk it. I can't risk *you*. That's why I—" He swallowed, not meeting Hamish's eyes. "Why *we* can't see each other anymore."

"Hey now." Hamish placed a finger under Zeke's chin and lifted until they could see each other's eyes. "We talked about this. I've got an idea."

"It won't matter. When I tell Melchom I'm refusing to comply with his orders, I'll be sent back to Sheol immediately."

Alarm pinged Hamish's nerves like an out-of-tune guitar. "What? No."

"I'm disobeying a direct order from my supervisor." He shrugged. "There's really nothing else I can expect."

"Bollocks to that. Hold off on the confession, all right? Wait until you hear from me again."

"I don't know if I can. Melchom could be there when I get back. It depends on whether he went back to the disco."

"Figures a demon lord would dig disco," Hamish muttered. "There's no other explanation for the whole fucking genre."

"Oh, he's not there by choice. He hates it. It gives him a headache." Zeke smiled sadly. "He much prefers Sheol's chaos and soothing screams of torment."

Hamish shuddered. "Then let's hope he's gone back to enjoy them. Otherwise, stall, okay? I'll get word to you as soon as I can."

"All right. But remember, the AI will be watching—and eavesdropping."

Hamish allowed himself a grin. Zeke blinked at him. Was the grin evil? It certainly felt like it—and that felt *awesome.* "Don't worry about that either. I've got a plan."

"A plan? What kind of—"

Hamish cut Zeke off with a kiss. *No point getting his hopes up until the plan is more than a gleam in my eye.* The distraction worked, although Hamish wasn't sure who was more distracted, because one kiss turned into three. Or maybe twenty-seven. But eventually he sent Zeke off, dazed and smiling, with one of the band's drivers.

Then he went to find Niall—which wasn't hard: where Gareth was, Niall was too. Although it took a bit of effort to catch his attention, since he was busy playing with Gareth's curls, which had finally grown back after last autumn's unfortunate haircut.

"Niall? A word?"

"Sure, boyo." Niall gave Gareth a quick kiss—which earned Hamish a dirty look from Faerie's last true frigging bard, but who cared? This was *important.* Gareth could pash Niall later all he wanted.

Hamish led Niall into the corridor. "Listen, mate. I need a favor."

"I'd say 'anything,' but with you, that's a dangerous commitment to make."

"I hope this won't be a stretch for you. You on good terms with your brother these days?"

"Eamon? Sure."

Hamish rubbed his hands together. *It pays to have a mate whose brother is the King of bleeding Faerie.* And coupled with Gareth's bard status, Hamish had an in with the Queen too. "You think His Majesty would be willing to strong-arm a witch for me?"

Niall's wicked grin probably matched Hamish's—that was why they got on so well. "I'm sure I could persuade him. What do you have in mind?"

"Oh . . ." Hamish rocked from his heels to his toes. "Nothing much. Just starting a revolution in an underworld or two. You in?"

Niall barked a laugh. "You've come to the right bloke. Tell me what you want me to do."

As Zeke had told Hamish, he was half-afraid Melchom would be waiting for him in his apartment when he got home. Luckily, only the AI was there, sulking in a muddy violet by the window. *Who'd have ever thought I'd be grateful that the AI was here?*

It didn't move from its spot overlooking the street, but green snaked through the violet.

Zeke just walked toward his bedroom. "I don't have to answer to you. Stay out here and sulk if you want. I'm going to bed."

Judging by the rainbow strobe effects that bled under his door for the next hour, the AI had decided to throw a temper tantrum to rival an entire crèche full of infernal imps. Zeke finally rolled over and closed his eyes. He couldn't sleep—not with the worry still eating at him from Melchom's ultimatum, combined with Hamish's dear—but no doubt futile—vow to "handle it."

Handle what? It wasn't as though anyone had ever been able to change Melchom's mind. He'd decided on Hamish's soul, and he'd accept no other. But Zeke had done a little research into Sheol's by-laws regarding soul collection—clauses he'd never had access to before Melchom upgraded him—and he'd discovered that delegation, as Melchom had done when he'd assigned Hamish to Zeke, was irrevocable.

So the only thing I need to do is make certain I'm not in a position to succeed.

Unfortunately, the only way he could see to make that happen was to voluntarily return to Sheol. He could renege on his work-release articles. All that would take was venturing out on the street with no work-related mandate to do so.

Maybe tomorrow I'll go down to the falafel restaurant myself. That would do it. He'd even turn himself in, to speed things along. Removing himself from the Upper World, from Hamish's orbit, was the only way to be sure.

He must have dozed off, at least for a while, because when he opened his eyes, dawn was peeking through his curtains. As he rolled out of bed, rubbing his eyes, he saw the message light blinking on the bedside phone. He picked up the handset, fingers shaking. *Who would have left me a message at this hour?*

When he punched the voice mail code, Magistra Lenore's voice rolled out, obviously displeased. "Zeke. My office. Six thirty. Don't be late."

Then a second message: "That's 6:30 *a.m.*"

Zeke glanced at the clock: 6:15. *Lucifer's balls!* He leaped out of bed and raced in and out of the shower so fast he actually dodged the water and failed to get wet, so he had to go back in and force himself to stand still, vibrating in place with the urge to hurry.

After he raced downstairs at full demon superspeed, he paused for a moment outside the magistra's door to run shaking fingers through his hair. *Fat lot of good that will do.* He probably looked like he'd been caught in a supernatural cyclone.

I wish I could be dropped in the middle of Kansas right now.

He took a deep breath and knocked, fist trembling. *Is this the last time I'll do this?*

"Enter."

Zeke opened the door and slipped inside. "You wanted to see me, Magistra?"

In full Mother mode, she was seated in the carved oak chair behind her desk, her fingers steepled. "I had an unexpected visitor last night."

Icicles speared Zeke's belly. *Melchom.* Or worse—Paimon, *Melchom's* supervisor. "Y-y-you did? I hope you weren't unduly disturbed."

"I was extremely disturbed." She frowned at him over her steepled fingers, Crone mode flickering over her face. "The weeks since we accepted you as a work-release placement have been the most . . . disruptive weeks in Supernatural Selection's entire history."

He hung his head. "I'm sorry, Magistra," he whispered. "I never intended to be a bother. I've loved working here."

"You speak in the past tense, Mr. Oz. We are not there quite yet."

Zeke peeked up from under his curls. "You're not firing me?" He winced. *Firing,* when it came to returning to Sheol, had a rather more literal meaning.

"No. While your time with us has been disruptive, disruption is not by itself disadvantageous. Uncomfortable, perhaps, to discover that our magic has, shall we say, *vulnerabilities* that we didn't anticipate. But illuminating nevertheless."

"Has something else happened?"

"I believe I mentioned a visitor?"

"Yes. Of course. Sorry, Magistra."

She waved a scarlet-lacquered nail. "Stop apologizing, Mr. Oz. There's no need to be so abject. Believe it or not, I am not your enemy. Other than the latest . . . quirks in your clients' matches, and despite any comments I might have made under stress, your work here has been exemplary. Your organizational skills and attention to detail are remarkable."

"I'm a low-level demon, Magistra. A minion. We're spawned to handle unpleasant details for our masters."

Her lips pursed in a moue of distaste. "I dislike the notion of ownership that the word 'master' implies. But that's beside the point. Last night, as I was about to attend a pre-equinox planning meeting, I was visited by the King of Faerie."

Zeke's eyes popped so wide he was surprised they didn't spring out on stalks. "The King? But I've been told he *never* leaves Faerie."

"Apparently," she said, her tone dry, "he made an exception. For you."

"M-m-me?" Zeke croaked. "But I don't know him."

"Perhaps not. But he seems to know you, or at least *of* you. It seems that his brother's . . . brother-in-law? The relationships were a bit murky. Anyway, a close connection of his is getting married, and he wishes you to attend not only the ceremonies and receptions, but the prewedding festivities as well."

"Ceremonies?"

"Really, Mr. Oz. Need you repeat everything I say? Perhaps I spoke too soon about your attention to detail."

"Sorry, Magistra."

"There will be two ceremonies and two receptions. Apparently the King's brother's . . . whatever, who is a high lord of the Sidhe, is marrying a druid, so they will wed in this realm as well as in Faerie. You will attend all events. Escorting your present client, Mr. Mulherne."

Waves of alternating heat and cold swept through Zeke's chest. *Hamish.* He'd told Zeke he'd take care of everything. Is *this* what he meant? That he'd pull rank and do an end-run around Zeke's wishes for them to stay away from one another?

"With all due respect, Magistra, there are extenuating circumstances"—*like the loss of Hamish's soul*—"that would make it most imprudent for me to—"

"Enough. Mr. Mulherne is our only active client. You've already filed every scrap of paper within an inch of its life, and you have no other duties. What possible reason have you to refuse?"

"The danger—"

"Nonsense. You will attend, representing Supernatural Selection in a professional and responsible manner. I would hate —" she fixed him with a baleful stare "—for our brand to suffer another blow because you are unable to meet this simple request. A car will arrive for you this evening at six. Don't be late." She waved him away. "That's all."

He turned, fumbling with the door handle.

"Oh, and Mr. Oz?"

"Yes, Magistra?"

"The AI is not invited. Please inform it to remain in its quarters. We have rituals booked in the altar rooms this evening that require darkness, and I can't have it wandering the halls, *disrupting* things. Really, from the perspective of annoyance and inconvenience, *that* has been more of a problem than hosting a demon."

Zeke stumbled up the stairs. *How am I going to get through this? What if Melchom shows up today?* He stopped outside his apartment door. *What if Melchom shows up tonight?*

But surely he wouldn't. Not in the middle of a party full of fae and druids and who knows who else. Zeke swallowed, although his Satan's apple seemed lodged firmly at the base of his neck.

Who will be there? Surely the King of Faerie wouldn't attend. It'd been intimidating enough being around the Queen during the hearing about Ted Farnsworth's Secrecy Pact violations. And Elder Bowen, the druid? *Brrr.* How could Zeke, Sheol minion and *disruptive* influence, mingle with dignitaries like that?

Stop it. You know you're just avoiding the elephant shifter in the room.

Hamish.

Zeke was going to be forced into close proximity with Hamish for hours on more than one occasion. And while that in itself wasn't a hardship—his mouth dried at the memory of Hamish's touch, Hamish's kiss, Hamish's *tongue*—it could only increase the danger for both of them: For Hamish, the danger of losing his soul. For Zeke? *The danger of losing my heart.*

Although really, that boat had crossed the Styx long ago.

He sighed and entered the apartment, only to nearly bolt outside again from the AI's eye-watering glare of alternating red and green. *It looks like a psychedelic Christmas tree.* If it weren't for Zeke's bespelled glasses, he'd probably have been blinded by the light.

"Stop shouting." He shielded his eyes with one hand as he closed the door. "I can't help it if she wanted to speak to me privately." He turned his back and walked into the kitchen to put the kettle on. He really needed some tea.

Unfortunately, the kitchen was so small that when the AI followed him in—still at full throttle—it was like being trapped inside an incandescent bulb.

"If it bothers you so much, complain to *her*, not me. It's not like I can do anything about it."

The AI blared orange and retreated, probably aiming for the front door. Zeke grinned as he pulled his favorite Voodoo Doughnuts mug out of the cabinet. "Oh, by the way—you're on house arrest. The witches are doing a bunch of pre-equinox preparation rituals tonight, and you muck up the required darkness."

That did it. The AI was back in the kitchen, and this time the kaleidoscopic light show rivaled the effects at Hunter's Moon's concerts.

"If it bothers you so much, learn to tone it down. I mean, you don't *have* to glow all the time, do you?"

The AI faded to a sullen silver glimmer. Zeke froze with the tea strainer in his hand.

"You're kidding?" He'd never considered that the AI had its own restrictions. "You *can't* turn it off? At all?" He plunked the strainer in his mug and poured boiling water—that he'd urged to heat faster—over it. "Wait. Do you mean you're actually unable to do it, or that you're not allowed to, like I'm not allowed outside?" The glimmer pulsed in the equivalent of a shrug. "So much for entertaining angels unawares, I guess."

The AI emitted a brief tell-me-about-it flash of orange.

If it weren't so annoying—and so prone to zapping him when he didn't do what it wanted—he'd almost sympathize with it. But it *was* annoying, not to mention too quick with its Taser effects, so he felt barely a twinge of regret when he added, "By the way, I'm going out tonight. And you're explicitly not invited."

The strobe effect was back, brighter than ever, but Zeke didn't respond or apologize. He took his tea and his book and retreated to his room so he could freak out in peace. During daylight hours, it was easier to ignore the light leaking in from under the door as the AI continued to rage.

By the time Zeke crept out of his bedroom late that afternoon, though, the AI wasn't in the living room or kitchen, and its door was closed. He was able to zip into the bathroom and clean up for his date without interference.

My date. And this time, it really was his—not one that he'd hijacked under false pretenses or inherited by default. This time, Hamish wanted to date *him*—wanted it badly enough to have brought in one of the biggest of big guns. *Wow. I rated intercession by the King of Faerie.* And anyone who rated *that* had to be worthwhile, right?

His throat vibrated oddly as he hurried downstairs at 5:58. He stopped inside the glass doors, although the car was already idling at the curb. *Humming. I was humming.* It was one of Hunter's Moon's songs, the one that got Hamish a standing ovation last night. Zeke didn't know what it was called, but that hardly mattered.

Even if he was pulled back to Sheol this instant, Hamish had given him something he'd never forget.

He's given me music.

Hamish was pacing in front of Mal and Bryce's house when the car pulled up with Zeke peering out of the back window, mouth agape as he viewed the street with wide eyes. Hamish looked around—the neighborhood didn't seem that awe-inspiring to him. Yeah, it was one of those planned "green" communities, and Gareth had told him Bryce had been instrumental in its design. *Trust a druid to keep the earth happy.*

Hamish tried to look at it from Zeke's perspective as he sprinted to the driveway to open the car door. *I suppose if you're used to darkness and hellfire and hot and cold running torment, this place would look pretty bloody good.*

Then Zeke stepped out of the car, his smile brighter than the moon, and Hamish forgot everything except the need to have him in his arms. And since Hamish was never one for delayed gratification, he swept Zeke up in a tight embrace, twirling him around in a circle, and surprising a startled "*Meep!*" out of him that was so fucking cute Hamish just had to kiss him immediately.

Which Zeke—judging by the way he moaned into Hamish's mouth, meeting every stroke of his tongue with one of his own—didn't object to at all.

A discreet throat-clearing from somewhere behind them eventually prompted Hamish to set Zeke on his feet. He grinned down at him. "In case I didn't make it clear, I'm really glad you're here."

Zeke glanced over Hamish's shoulder, and those adorable blotches bloomed on his face and neck. "I'm glad, too, but I have *words* for you about your methods, especially the secrecy. You could have *told* me. I mean, seriously, Hamish? The Faerie King? And you totally ignored my warnings. But"—he lowered his voice, jerking his head in the direction of his glance—"someone's watching us."

"Doesn't matter to me. I'm used to performing in front of a crowd."

Zeke frowned at him. "Well, I'm not, remember?"

"Ah right. You're on the down-low." Hamish grinned again. "Maybe you should have thought of that before pashing me in the driveway."

Zeke's hands flailed helplessly until Hamish caught them and kissed each palm. "I couldn't help it. I mean, *there you were.*"

"Yeah? Irresistible, am I?"

More blotches. "Never mind that. Don't you think it would be polite to acknowledge him, whoever he is?"

"Fine." Hamish turned, but it wasn't one of his bandmates who was waiting to take the piss out of him. It was Gareth's brother-in-law, David, whose husband, Alun, was the Queen's Champion.

As Hamish understood, David was an *achubydd,* a magical healer—the only one alive, as far as anyone knew. Despite being married to a fae with one of the biggest ethical sticks up his arse *ever,* David still looked more like a cheerful club boy than a fellow with enough power of his own to almost raise the dead. He wasn't wearing one of his signature bow ties today—he was dressed in jeans, trainers, and a purple University of Portland sweatshirt.

David hurried over, a bundle of some kind in his arms. "Hello! You must be Zeke. I'm David Evans-Kendrick, Mal and Gareth's brother-in-law." He gestured to the neighboring house with one elbow. "My husband, Alun, and I live next door." He smiled apologetically, tossing his bangs out of his eyes. "I hope you don't mind, but I found out that your wardrobe is limited to business not-so-casual, and since I'm sure nobody"—he glared at Hamish—"bothered to tell you *what* this evening's festivities entailed, I thought you might like to borrow some clothes so yours don't get spoiled." He studied Zeke, his head to one side like an inquisitive magpie. "Gareth was right. I think we're about the same size. Come on. You can change inside."

"Hey!" Hamish captured Zeke's hand as he started to follow David obediently. "Don't steal my date."

David stuck his nose in the air. "He'll be much more comfortable in these than in what he's wearing. I mean, who plays paintball in a shirt and tie, let alone wool slacks?"

Zeke turned a round-eyed gaze on Hamish. "Paintball. Oh. I forgot."

"You could have *reminded* him." David clucked his tongue. "Honestly, Hamish, you supes are *so* bad at communicating."

"Watch it, mate. You're a supe too."

"Yes, but I thought I was human for so long that I learned not to *assume* like you all do. Now go get Zeke a beer while I take him to get changed."

Hamish knew better than to think he could withstand Hurricane David, so he gave in with as much grace as he could muster—that is to say, not much—and went in search of beer.

He found Gareth in the kitchen, staring morosely at his feet. Since Niall wasn't attached at his hip, Hamish guessed at the reason. "Niall running late again?"

Gareth startled as if he hadn't noticed Hamish's arrival, then shrugged. "He's still working that same case." He sighed. "I'll be glad when one of two things happen." He held up a finger. "One, he wraps up this case, or—" he held up a second finger "—two, Mal gets back from his honeymoon so Niall isn't the only one on deck." He frowned down at his beer. "I suppose there could be a three—they hire more help. Mal and Niall both complain that they spend way more time filling out forms and reports and inter-realm permits than they do actually investigating their cases."

"Cheer up, mate. Won't be long now." He nodded toward the archway into the living room, where Mal and Bryce were mooning at each other as if nobody else were in the room. "From the looks of it, they may launch the honeymoon tonight. Then we'd have no need of a bachelor paintball party, right?"

Gareth chuckled. "Oh I'm sure there'll be premarital sex tonight. Maybe during the game, if we're not careful. But Mal is determined to do this right. He wants Bryce to be officially his—and vice versa—no matter what realm they're in."

Hamish gazed at the kitchen doorway. *Still empty, sod it.* "Yeah. I get it."

"Goddess," Gareth murmured. "I think you finally do."

Chapter Fifteen

"Thank you for the clothing loan." Zeke peered at his reflection in the full-length mirror on the wall of David's guest bedroom, twisting to check out his rear view. He'd never seen himself head to toe before—there weren't any mirrors in Sheol, and his apartment above Supernatural Selection only had one not-very-generous mirror over the bathroom sink. "Are you sure I look all right? These pants seem a little tight."

David chuckled. "Oh, sweetie. Trust me. You look fine, and Hamish is going to *love* those pants."

The little flame that had kindled under Zeke's heart when he'd seen Hamish waiting for him burned brighter. "Really?"

"Absolutely." He grinned. "My husband certainly loves them on me. Have you met Alun yet?"

"Um, not here. But he, um, kind of showed up at Supernatural Selection to arrest Ted last fall."

David wrinkled his nose. "Oh. Right. I remember that night. He was in full-on Queen's Champion mode, which is just the *grimmest*. I was there too, but I didn't get a chance to really meet you then. Don't worry though. He's not nearly as scary when he's at a party." He tapped his lower lip with one finger. "Well, I suppose it depends on the party. But he's perfectly cheerful tonight, although he can get quite competitive during paintball, especially with his brothers. Now, if—"

A knock sounded on the door. "David?"

David scrunched up his face. "Excuse me. That's Mal." He scurried over to the door and cracked it open. While he spoke to Mal, Zeke stared at his reflection again, smoothing the front of the borrowed sweatshirt. It was a little brightly colored for his liking, but it had a hood. He pulled it up and forward so it shaded his face. Barely. *This doesn't conceal* anything. *Has my camouflage* always *been this thin?*

"Zeke?" David called from the door. "I have to deal with a quiche emergency. Will you be okay?"

"Yes. Of course."

"Just come out whenever you're ready." He jerked a thumb over his shoulder. "Bathroom's across the hall if you need it."

"Thank y—" But David was already gone. With one last glance in the mirror, Zeke made his way out of the bedroom and down the hall to the living room. It was deserted, the windows darkened with nightfall, although a fire burned in the fireplace. Unlike the flames of Sheol, however, this one seemed cheerful and welcoming rather than savage and menacing. Voices murmured from the dining room and kitchen, and outside, several people shouted with laughter.

Other than his Supernatural Selection apartment, Zeke had never been in an Upper World household. The hotel—heat swept down his body, and if he weren't so *nervous*, his johnson might have misbehaved—the hotel didn't count because it didn't belong to the people who stayed there.

This house, though . . . this house was lived in. *Loved* in. Zeke blinked as misty images of two large men, both dark-haired, flicked in and out of sight. Laughing, kissing, sometimes doing nothing but sitting on the comfortable-looking sofa. But always, always aware of each other.

Melchom must have given me more in that upgrade than I thought. Demons with the right abilities could read the shadows of the past and use the knowledge to their advantage in crafting a soul-collection contract.

For Zeke, the glimpses of companionship, of happiness and contentment, filled him with hopeless yearning. *I can never have this.*

He edged closer to the fire, the only familiar thing in this new world. He started to wipe his hands on his borrowed jeans, but thought better of it, clenching his fists instead.

"Zeke! Hey! Hi!"

Zeke whirled at the sound of that familiar voice and found himself face to chest with . . . with . . .

"Oh. Hello, Mr. Farnsworth," he said faintly.

"We're all guests here." The big bear shifter brandished the bowl of chili in his left hand. "You can call me Ted."

That hand dwarfed the bowl, and Zeke's gaze caught on the gold wedding band—and on the missing joint of Ted's little finger.

Zeke's blood rushed from his head, and he wobbled. "I'm so sorry about your . . . your body-part sacrifice. If I'd been better at my job—"

"Hey." Ted set the bowl down on the mantelpiece. "If it wasn't for you, Quentin and I would have never met. Or if we did, it would have been as somebody else's husband." He laughed, a deep, rolling sound. "Imagine how awkward *that* would have been." He waggled his finger. "I don't even miss this. In fact, I kinda like the reminder. I never want to forget how far Q-Bert and I were willing to go so we could be together."

Would someone go that far for me? In a way, Ted's missing finger joint filled Zeke with a wistful longing. In another way, guilt threatened to consume him from his toes to his borrowed hoodie.

"If you say so. Does—does Mr. Bertrand-Harrington feel the same?"

"Sure! It was his idea to invite you to our wedding. I'm sorry you couldn't make it." He grinned. "I guess Boston's kinda far away and you were probably busy."

No, I just wasn't officially allowed in the Upper World until today. And the Bertrand-Harrington ancestral home was definitely in the Upper World. In the deep recesses of Sheol, stories of the 'cubi dynasties who had successfully migrated were legends, only whispered about when the supervisors couldn't hear.

"I wish I could have been there too. You look very happy."

Ted slapped Zeke's shoulder, knocking him off-balance. "You bet." A grin split his beard. "Speak of the devil. Here's Q-Bert now."

Zeke's stomach tumbled when Quentin Bertrand-Harrington hurried across the room to Ted's side. *I wonder if anyone would notice if I crawled into the fireplace?*

But Quentin simply gave Zeke a harried smile before grasping Ted's arm. "You'll never guess who just arrived. Casimir Moreau and Rusty Johnson."

Ted blinked. "Wait. You mean *your* Casimir?"

Quentin laid one hand on Ted's chest and the other against his cheek. "He was never *my* Casimir, you infuriating bear." Quentin's tone was infused with an affection that belied his words. "But—"

"So . . ." Casimir appeared in the doorway, the light gleaming on his caramel-colored hair—and his fangs.

Maybe behind *the fireplace. Or somewhere in the next county. Demon superspeed. I could do it.* Except Casimir was a vampire, and they were nearly as fast. So Zeke started to edge toward the safety of the hallway, a centimeter at a time.

Casimir flung the end of a silk scarf over his shoulder and glided up to Ted. "This is your famous bear shifter, Elmer darling?"

Quentin growled low in his throat. "He's not—"

"Stop stirring the pot, Cas." Rusty Johnson strolled into the room to drape an arm across Casimir's shoulders.

Eep! All of them in the same room! Even if Rusty and Ted hadn't been so massive—with Quentin not far behind—the room would have felt too small for Zeke. As it was, he gasped for air like a startled pixie.

"Wow. So you're Rusty." Ted held out his hand. "Nice to meet you. Although I've got to say, I'm glad it didn't happen until now."

Rusty chuckled as the two enormous men shook hands. "Likewise."

Casimir leaned into Rusty, but turned his laser-eyed gaze on Zeke. "I understand Rusty's oh-so-stodgy clan is making trouble for you because of our little matchmaking do-si-do."

"Um . . ." Zeke tugged on the neck of the hoodie. "You mustn't think I begrudge their complaints. The shifters and vampires were understandably concerned over your match."

"Wait. The vampires?" Casimir exchanged a glance with Rusty. "We didn't lodge a complaint."

"But—" Zeke glanced from Casimir to the other men who were part of his most infamous foul-up. "Magistra Lenore said —"

"Oh, some members of the council wanted to, but I convinced our chief to delay while I proved to them Rusty and I were meant for each other." He glanced at Rusty from under his lashes. "Leaving out a few pertinent details that are none of their business, of course."

Rusty's cheeks reddened above his beard. "Cas. Not here."

"In fact—" he turned his fanged grin on Quentin and Ted "— I'm delighted to meet the two of you, because I'm determined to hold *our* wedding as the inaugural event at your new resort. I understand you haven't booked anything officially yet."

With the four men absorbed in their conversation, Zeke began his sideways migration again. *Slowly. Don't draw their attention.*

"No," Quentin said. "We wanted to get the construction finished first. We've been having some issues with one of our contractors."

"Really?" Rusty pulled a business card out of his shirt pocket and handed it to Quentin. "I might be able to help with that. Give me a call on Monday and we can set something up."

"There, you see? Problem solved. Now." Cas tucked his arm in Quentin's. "Let's discuss the *fabulous* wedding that will launch—what's your resort called again?

"The Weasel Pit." Ted grinned and winked at Quentin.

"The name isn't finalized yet." Quentin was obviously smothering a laugh. "But it is most definitely *not* the Weasel Pit."

Casimir shared a wicked glance with Rusty. "I would dearly love to be able to announce to my council chief that I'm getting married at someplace called the Weasel Pit, but I can understand that might be a long-term marketing disadvantage for you. Now, shall we?"

Quentin shot a bemused glance over his shoulder, but allowed Casimir to lead him away.

Almost there. Another foot, then maybe I can hide in the bedroom all night.

But as Zeke was about to take the last step into sheltering darkness, Ted's massive arm dropped across his shoulders. "Think about it, Rusty. If it weren't for Zeke here—" Ted buffeted Zeke's shoulder, then let go to retrieve his chili bowl "—you and I would be hitched and those two would be married to each other by now."

The two big men looked at one another, then at their retreating partners, their expressions darkening. "Over my dead body," they both growled.

Their faces cleared and they both laughed. Rusty slapped Ted's shoulder. "Glad we're on the same page. Want a beer?"

"Yeah. And some more chili. Come on. I'll show you where everything is."

"I know. I've been here before."

Ted's eyebrows rose. "You have? When?"

"A few times," Rusty muttered, his blush returning. "But never mind. Beer?"

They headed into the kitchen, Zeke stumbling along in their wake.

But if the vampire chief didn't demand the investigation, who did?

When two guys, obviously shifters and the only ones at the party bigger than Hamish, cleared the kitchen door, Hamish's heart tried to beat out of his chest. Because there was Zeke, in borrowed trainers, UP sweatshirt, and—*fates preserve me*—a pair of skinny jeans. He smiled shyly as he tugged his hood over his curls, and at that moment, Hamish knew.

I'm in love. And I never want him to have to hide again.

He forced himself to breathe, then took Zeke's hand. "Ready to meet everyone?"

Zeke glanced at the two big shifters as one of them handed the other a beer out of the fridge. "I've already, um, met a few people."

David slid a tray of miniature quiches, redolent of bacon and cheese, out of the oven and set them on the stove top. He nodded to the French doors in the dining room. "The rest of the gang is out on the patio, pretending it's not freaking cold. We were just waiting for you to get here."

Zeke's gaze darted between Hamish and David. "Me? Why?"

"Well, not only you." David grinned slyly. "But we couldn't start without Hamish, and he was too busy wearing a path in Bryce's native fescue lawn to pay attention to anything else. Even my outstanding chili."

"Shut it, David." But Hamish couldn't work up a convincing grumble. He was too busy trying to keep his heart from floating out of his chest. On the other hand, David had a point about the food. He draped his arm across Zeke's shoulder. "You hungry?"

Zeke glanced furtively at David and at the other people milling about outside. "Um . . ."

David was immediately contrite. "I was only teasing Hamish. The game isn't starting until everyone finishes eating." He gestured to the table and breakfast bar. Hamish hadn't noticed before—David was right about his level of distraction—but there was enough food laid out to feed a horde of hungry trolls.

"Come on. Let's eat so we can get the party started." Hamish snagged a couple of beers from the fridge and held one out to Zeke.

He took it, turning the bottle in his hand. "What's India red ale?"

"Beer."

"Oh. I've never had that. How does it work?"

Hamish chuckled. "Remember the champagne?" Zeke nodded, eyes widening. "It has bubbles too, but the effect might be a bit different. Would you rather not try it?"

"No! I mean yes, I want to try it. I want to try *everything*."

So they did, Zeke getting rather giggly halfway through his beer.

Then he nibbled the edge of one of David's tiny quiches and his eyelids fluttered closed, near-ecstasy flooding his face. He snarfed the rest down in a single bite, and between one blink and the next, he was cradling three more in a napkin.

Hamish laughed softly. "I guess this is the flip side of the falafel cross-table creep, eh? Demon dinner party speed?"

"I'm sorry. Was that rude? I keep forgetting." Zeke gazed at his contraband mournfully. "Should I put them back?"

"Nah. There's plenty more. David never stints on the food." He grinned. "I could watch you eat them all night long."

Well, maybe not all night.

"Oi! Hamish!" Mal called from the door. "It's time to get this party started."

"Keep your pants on, Kendrick." Hamish made a show of savoring the last bite of his chili. "Your paintballs aren't going to catch fire because you waited for us to finish dinner."

Spence stalked over to set his bowl next to the sink. "Maybe not," he muttered. "But his other balls might. He's been all but humping Bryce's leg all night."

Zeke crumpled his napkin, face blotches blooming. "Sorry. I didn't mean to be so slow. I can—"

Hamish stopped his apologies with a kiss. "Don't mind Spence. Mal *always* acts like that around Bryce. Finish your dinner." He handed Zeke another quiche, with a bonus glare at Spence. "That's part of the party too."

"Yeah, yeah." Spence smirked at them. "Like you two aren't eye-fucking over the guacamole."

Zeke uttered that adorable little *"Meep!"* But he polished off the quiche in two bites. Hamish intended to make it his life's work to ensure Zeke would never be hungry again.

Besides, half the other guests were still eating or indulging in another beer. Zeke's reaction to beer had been worth the price of admission.

After Zeke finished, Hamish grabbed a couple of more beers for them and followed Spence onto the patio, where the rest of the band greeted Zeke enthusiastically—much to Zeke's embarrassment. Hamish took his hand, but Zeke tried to pull away, tugging his hood practically down to his nose.

"Zeke. Seriously? This is a private party. Everyone here knows us. You don't have to be afraid of anybody judging you."

"That's what you think," Zeke muttered. But he sighed and let Hamish take his hand again. Hamish counted it a win when Zeke leaned against his shoulder too.

Bryce strode to the edge of the patio and turned to face the group. "Good evening, everyone. Thanks for coming to our bachelor party. I hope everyone has had a chance to fill up on dinner, because you'll be working it off over the next ninety minutes."

"I can't believe you're gonna let us have a paintball war in your precious wetlands, Bryce," Gareth said with a grin.

"Are you kidding?" Bryce glared at them all in warning. "The wetlands are a fragile ecosystem. I'd never let you jokers crash around in there. Especially Hamish."

"Hey!" Hamish pretended outrage. "I'm not nearly as destructive as Mal."

Mal buffeted Hamish's shoulder as he swaggered by to stand next to Bryce. "I'm not the one who pounds the daylights out of inoffensive drums for a living. These days, I can float through the wetlands leaving no more damage than a butterfly."

Hamish snorted. "Right. I mistook you for a swallowtail just now."

Mal simply grinned and hooked a paintball tagger to his belt.

"Mal's claims notwithstanding," Bryce continued with a mock-glare at his fiancé, "I'm not willing to risk the wetlands. The paintball game will take place in Faerie."

Zeke tugged on Hamish's arm. "Faerie? Hamish, I can't go *there*."

"Why not?"

"I won't be allowed in." He gave Hamish a seriously-dude look. "I'm a *demon*."

"So?"

"So the Faerie threshold won't let me pass. It's supposed to keep out evil."

Mal scoffed. "Trust me, boyo. That's a load of codswallop. I can tell you stories—"

"Not now, Mal." Bryce smiled kindly at Zeke. "You don't need to worry." He held up a tiny object between his thumb and forefinger. It glinted in the light spilling out from the dining room. "I'll give each of you a talisman like this. They're official invitations by the Faerie monarchs to use the forest around the Keep for the paintball game—not to mention to retire to the Keep afterward for dessert."

"Dessert?" Zeke's tone was laced with longing. "Really?"

"Undoubtedly. The Keep's staff likes to show off a little when they have Outworlder guests." Bryce passed everyone a little gold disk. "Stow those in a pocket, and you'll be able to pass the threshold at will until dawn."

As everyone complied, Mal strolled over to a table laden with paintball taggers. "Before we head across the threshold, come over and choose your weapons." He gestured to another table with face guards and padded jackets. "Protective gear's over there." He picked up a tagger and tucked it under his arm. "We were going to have to juggle the teams a bit since Niall's been delayed." He shot an apologetic glance at Gareth. "But with Zeke joining us, we're even again."

Mal stepped back from the table, the tagger still in his hands. Tiff pointed to the one attached to his belt.

"Why do you get two weapons and we only get one?"

Mal grinned at Bryce and patted the tagger at his hip. "This one has sentimental value."

Bryce cocked an eyebrow at him. "You really think you'll need to combat evil at our bachelor party?"

Mal's grin widened. "You never know. Maybe you'll need to use it on me. I'm having some definitely evil thoughts where you're concerned."

Bryce just laughed and set off across the lawn, but Zeke shivered under Hamish's arm.

"I need to keep out of the way. Do you suppose I could sit out the game?"

Hamish squeezed Zeke's shoulder. "You don't need to worry about Mal's evil intentions." He pulled Zeke out of the nimbus of light and kissed him, long, hard, and hot. "Mine, on the other hand . . ."

Zeke chuckled, tucking his head under Hamish's chin. "I'm not worried about *you*. Or Mal. But see those guys over there?"

Hamish glanced in the direction of Zeke's gaze, where two enormous guys who had to be shifters were chatting with another guy nearly as big, and a pale, elegant man about a foot shorter. "What about them?"

"They're former clients. The one with the red beard, Rusty Johnson, was supposed to—"

"Johnson?" Hamish pulled Zeke's hood away from his face. "Really?"

Sure enough, blotches crept up Zeke's neck. "Hamish." His voice held an edge of anguish. "*Please.*"

Hamish kissed his forehead. "Don't worry, babe. I won't torment you. But why are you worried?"

"I *screwed up*. They weren't supposed to end up with . . . with who they ended up with. If it hadn't been for me—"

"Are they all happy?"

"Yeeesss. They sort of said so earlier." He screwed his face up. "At least I think they did."

Hamish glanced over his shoulder, where Rusty had tucked the pale man against his side. "Don't sound so uncertain. That looks like a definite yes to me. I'd say you did them a favor. So what do you say," Hamish murmured into Zeke's ear, "we . . . play some paintball?"

Chapter Sixteen

Paintball was *awesome!*

Zeke peeked out from behind a gigantic tree and caught Hamish's signal to move out, and Gareth's acknowledging nod.

Because Tiff, Luci, and Vitor had wanted to be on the same team, Gareth had joined Hamish and Zeke, and the three of them were *killing* it. So to speak.

Part of that was due to Zeke's demon speed. At first, he'd been afraid that would be cheating, but Hamish had reassured him.

"All's fair in paintball war, mate."

So the three of them had staged a series of lightning raids on all the other teams, even Zeke's former clients. He'd tried to avoid them at first, but when he'd bailed on a clear shot at Ted, Hamish had pulled Zeke behind a boulder while Gareth kept lookout, and taken him to task.

"What's up? If that Quentin bloke wasn't such a terrible shot, he'd have nailed Gareth right in the chest."

Zeke hunched over his tagger. "Surely I've done enough to them. I don't need to splatter paint all over them too."

Hamish gripped Zeke's shoulder. "All's fair, remember? So come on. I want to see you hit that big Johnson dude square in the back."

"I—I couldn't!" Zeke peered around the rock, and spotted Rusty and Casimir creeping along a stream bank. "Could I?"

"Absolutely."

So he'd done it. Multiple times, in fact, and it was *glorious*.

For his part, Hamish had targeted Spence the most—although never Josh—so Spence's vest was almost completely covered with their team's garish neon-green paint.

And when Spence tried hiding in a thick copse of trees? Gareth had sung a quiet song and the trees had *moved out of the way*, giving all three of them a clear shot.

"Hey!" Spence shouted. "I protest! No fair pulling out the bardic tricks!"

Hamish had cackled with glee. "You know what they say—"

"All's fair in paintball war!" the three of them had chorused, and zipped off to find another target.

As Gareth skulked through the underbrush ahead of them, Hamish caught Zeke's hand. "Come with me."

Zeke glanced from Hamish's grin, to Faerie's incredible violet sky, to Gareth's retreating back. "But the game—"

"It's almost over. Besides, we've massacred the other teams, thanks to you and Gareth."

"And you. When you hopped over that boulder and tagged Mal?" Zeke shivered at the memory. He'd never seen Hamish shift before—and since he'd had to doff his clothes beforehand, it had been doubly thrilling.

Zeke *might* have spent a bit too long helping Hamish get dressed again. *There are times when superspeed has its drawbacks.*

So with that memory replaying in his head, Zeke let Hamish lead him in the opposite direction, away from Gareth and the occasional shouts when one of the other teams scored a hit.

They passed a rock that looked vaguely like Beelzebub picking his nose—something Zeke had seen far too often for his own peace of mind. "Wait. I recognize that. Aren't we close to the threshold?"

"Yep. It's right over there."

"But—"

Hamish lifted his own face guard, then reached out and lifted Zeke's. Zeke didn't resist—or not much anyway—when

Hamish pulled him in for a kiss. "As much as I like kicking ass in any kind of competition, I'd rather have some time alone with you before we have to join everyone at the Keep. Chances are the royalty might make an appearance, and then we'd have to be all proper and shite." He stepped away, but took Zeke's hand. "If we sneak back to the Outer World, we'll have Mal and Bryce's lawn—and for that matter, their living room—to ourselves."

"O-o-okay. But can we get back again?"

"Yep. I know the spot, and remember Bryce said the talisman isn't a one-and-done thing. It'll let us pass again, and we'll get to the Keep in time to share some salted caramel chocolate tart."

Zeke grinned at him. "What makes you think I'm going to share?"

Hamish's wicked smile turned tender. "Because you're the most generous person I know. Of course you'll share."

Zeke swallowed against a lump in his throat. *With you. I'll always share with you.* And since their time was limited—Zeke had no confidence that the King's request would keep him out of Sheol after the wedding festivities—he let Hamish draw him down a little slope and across a tinkling brook.

Zeke felt the change in the air immediately. Faerie had been, if not balmy, at least comfortable. The Outer World was teetering on the far edge of winter.

"Now . . ." Hamish pulled off his face guard and moved to toss it on the ground, but Zeke stayed his hand.

"Not here. We need to get out of the wetlands and up the slope."

"See? The world's most responsible demon."

"Not quite."

Zeke froze at the sound of that voice, so out of place here among the murmur of water and the rustle of tiny life in the bushes. *Melchom.* He turned slowly, keeping his body between Hamish and danger.

Melchom was leaning on the trunk of an evergreen, in a three-piece black suit and bowler hat, and carrying an umbrella with a wicked point.

He pushed himself off and sauntered toward them. "If Ozul-y-Kalon were *that* responsible, he wouldn't be flouting the rules of his work-release," he said, studying his fingernails. "If Ozul-y-Kalon were that responsible, he wouldn't be consorting with his employer's client. If Ozul-y-Kalon were *that* responsible"— Melchom fixed Zeke with blazing eyes—"he would have followed *orders*."

"Supervisor, please—"

"*Silence.* You *do not* have leave to address me."

"Here now." Hamish's tone held more anger than Zeke had ever heard from him before. "You've got no right to talk to him that way."

"I have every right. He is my minion. He belongs to me, no matter what the ridiculous work-release program might claim."

Hamish stepped out from behind Zeke and strode toward Melchom, with Zeke trying ineffectually to drag him back by holding on to his arm. "And no matter what *you* might claim, he has rights. He doesn't belong to anyone except himself."

Melchom's shark-toothed grin made Zeke shake in his borrowed shoes. *Please, Hamish. Don't provoke him.* "That's where you're wrong. When the C-suite overlords signed the treaty for the work-release, they never agreed to actually *releasing* any demon from Sheol citizenship. Ozul-y-Kalon is still a citizen of Sheol, subject to our laws, and therefore he owes his allegiance to *me*. Not to the Upper World. Not to Supernatural Selection. And certainly not to *you*. Unless . . ." His grin widened as he turned it on Zeke. "Is this part of your plan to complete your assignment? Lull him into complaisance until he'll give up his soul willingly in exchange for unlimited access to any of your orifices he chooses to fill?"

"No! It's not like that." Zeke turned to Hamish. "You know it's not like that." Hamish's mouth tightened. *Surely he doesn't believe that's why—*

"Tell me something, arsehole." Hamish's tone was harsh, and Zeke flinched. But when he looked up, Hamish was glaring at Melchom, not staring accusingly at Zeke. "Zeke told me a demon's true name is a weakness. That some bastard of a wizard could conjure him up and enslave him if they found it out."

Melchom flicked a finger at Hamish, as if shooing away a gnat. "What of it?"

"You've just trumpeted his name at least four times by my count, so I've got to ask . . ." Hamish stepped forward, fists clenched at his sides. "What the actual *fuck*?"

Melchom chuckled. "Perhaps I'm hoping some unscrupulous wizard *will* hear. We're on the very threshold of Faerie, not to mention a druid's doorstep. If some ambitious magician were to take advantage of the knowledge and enslave Ozul-y-Kalon . . ." He shrugged. "It would be no more than he deserved."

"You bastard. You—"

"No. Hamish, please. He's *trying* to provoke you."

Hamish glared at Melchom. "It's working."

"But if you're not thinking clearly, it gives him an advantage, don't you see? I told you about this last night."

"You *told* him?" Melchom's roar shook the bare branches of the trees around them. "You're stupider and more incompetent than I ever imagined—and only a stupid and incompetent demon would *volunteer* for that benighted work-release charade."

"Charade?" Zeke hated how small his voice sounded. "But the treaty . . . the application process. The—the interview. Surely that was—"

"For show." Melchom bared his teeth, no longer even pretending to smile. "With the combined supe community putting pressure on us for *rights violations*, of all things, we had to prove how utterly preposterous the idea of mainstreaming demons in the Upper World would be. We had you in mind from the beginning. The mortification of the flesh and ritual cleansing torture?" His eyes sparked. "We just did that for fun."

"You—" Hamish lunged forward, but Melchom wasn't there, using his demon speed to appear on the other side of the clearing.

"Really. Haven't you learned anything about demons by now, even after fucking one?" Melchom brushed nonexistent lint off his sleeve. "Even after he *told* you your fate. You might be a match for him after all. You seem equally stupid and inept."

Hamish barked a laugh. "Insult me all you want, arsehole. I've heard it all before, and worse—probably more than once. But you're wrong about Zeke."

"I'm never wrong. Not about him." Melchom stared at Hamish, his expression turning avaricious. "And not about you. I can see your desire as plain as the oversized nose on your face."

"No," Zeke protested weakly. He didn't want Melchom to humiliate Hamish by parading his devotion to Tiff, even if there was nobody here but the three of them. *Is it Hamish's feelings you're worried about, or your own?* "Please don't."

Melchom rubbed his hands together. "Excellent. Nothing adds more spice to negotiations than when two parties are desperate for different outcomes. As I was saying, your desire is clear." He jerked his chin at Zeke. "When I spoke of you having access to all his orifices, did you think I chose those words at random? Tormenting Ozul-y-Kalon was simply a bonus."

"Shut it," Hamish growled. "You don't know shite."

Melchom raised one eyebrow. "Don't I?"

Hamish turned and took Zeke by the shoulders. "You know that's not true, right? I mean, sure I want you. But not like that. I want you because I—"

Zeke put his fingers over Hamish's lips. "Don't say it." He desperately wanted to hear those words, the ones he suspected, the ones he hoped for. But a declaration of love in front of Melchom was a recipe for even greater torment. "I don't care what he says. I know you." He smiled crookedly. "Although I have to admit, I'd have picked a much more appropriate time for you to finally *engage*." *Like any time before I'm banished to Sheol forever.*

"Come, come, Ozul-y-Kalon. You have your orders. Fulfill them. I have other things to do tonight."

"Can I brain this arsehole with a rock?" Hamish mumbled behind Zeke's fingers. "Because that makes seven."

Seven? Oh, seven times Melchom had revealed his name. It hardly mattered. After leaving Hamish behind, Zeke couldn't imagine any other punishment would compare. And really— could an unscrupulous wizard be any worse than Melchom, or the demon C-suite who'd decided that Zeke would be the best way to court failure for their own benefit?

Zeke smiled at Hamish for the last time and turned to Melchom. "No."

"No, I can't brain him with a rock? How about one of Mal's anti-evil paintballs? I'm sure he'd be on deck for that."

Zeke blinked back his tears before Melchom could see them. "I doubt we could get him here in time. But I wasn't talking to you." He jerked his chin at Melchom. "I was talking to him."

"You dare to tell *me* no?" This time, Melchom's roar could have been heard in Sheol. "You have no choice. I am your *master*. Obey me!"

Zeke shook his head. "No."

Melchom's eyes narrowed. "You know what that means."

"Yes." Zeke forced the word out of a mouth gone dry, not from what awaited him in Sheol—eons of backbreaking labor interspersed with excruciating torture—but from the *true* torment: never again to see Hamish's face, taste his mouth, hear his music. But it was worth it to spare Hamish's soul.

"Very well." Melchom raised his hand.

"Hold on there." Hamish gripped Zeke's shoulders. "What's going on?"

"Stupid," Melchom muttered. "Just as I thought." He pointed at Zeke. "*He* refused to collect the soul to which he was assigned —yours, to be precise. For gross disobedience to his rightful master, he must return to his previous duties for all eternity."

Zeke had expected no less. "I understand, Supervisor. I'm sorr—"

"And *in addition*," Melchom said, raising his voice to a near bellow, "he is sentenced to two thousand seventy-five years, give or take a century, of—" he waggled his hand "—whatever we want to do to him." He bared his teeth in what passed for a gleeful grin. "This is going to be such *fun*. It's been *centuries* since we've had an insubordinate minion to torment."

"No! What if I let him colle—"

"Stop!" Zeke broke out of Hamish's grasp. "I won't. So don't even *think* of that as a possibility. Please, Hamish." Zeke took one big hand in both of his. "Stay here. Make—" He swallowed. "Make music. I can handle anything if I know you'll be up here, happy and safe."

"But how can I be either?" Hamish's voice broke on the last word. "How can I be happy without you?" He uttered a broken laugh. "I'll be begging Gareth to add the woe-is-me songs back to our set list, because I can't imagine ever wanting to play anything upbeat again. Not when I know you'll be"—he gestured to the ground—"suffering."

"It'll be okay." Zeke's lips trembled, but he forced a smile. "I'm a demon, remember? We're tougher than we look."

"Zeke . . ."

But using his demon speed, Zeke darted to Melchom's side. "I'm ready to submit to your judgment, master."

"While it's been amusing to witness this touching display of mutual distress—" Melchom twirled his umbrella like a Regency dandy on the strut "—may I say that it's about. Fucking. Time." He drove the ferrule into the grass.

And the ground opened up at their feet.

Chapter
Seventeen

Hamish teetered on the edge of the stinking pit that had suddenly appeared in Bryce's pristine wetlands.

"No!" Zeke shouted. "Hamish, stay back."

"Like bloody hell I will."

"By all means, ignore his warning." Melchom prodded Zeke in the back with his umbrella, driving him toward the pit. "Then I'd have you both—although your body might not stand up to the rigors of a Sheol residency. A pity, but—" he flashed those revolting sharklike teeth, and Hamish wanted nothing more than to knock them down his throat "—those are the fucking breaks."

Then he pushed Zeke over the edge, where he plummeted like a stone.

"No no no!" Hamish fell to his knees at the edge of the pit, peering down into the murk despite the noxious stench that rose from it. "Zeke!"

"Ta. It's been grand." With a jaunty tip of his bowler, Melchom stepped out onto nothing and glided downward as if he were on the world's swankiest lift.

"You bring him back, you sodding wanker," Hamish growled, snatching up a rock as big as his fist and hurling at the smug arsehole's head. A direct hit—but it bounced off as if he were made of rubber.

Melchom brayed with laughter.

Hamish lay down on the ground, his head and shoulders over the pit. "Zeke? Answer me!" But the only thing Hamish could hear was a faint discordant chorus of shrieks and wails. Then even that began to fade. "Zeke, gods damn it!" He scrabbled for another stone and flung it into the darkness.

He didn't hear it land. Gods, how far had Zeke fallen? Would he be hurt? Broken? Hamish clutched the edge of the hole, grass crumpling in his fist. *I've got to get him out of there, away from those motherfucking—*

"Oi, Hamish." Hamish flinched at Mal's cheerful voice. "No sneaking off in the middle of the game for a little— What the bleeding *fuck*?" Mal strode over from the Faerie threshold, three-quarters of the way around the pit. "Bryce is going to shit a whole pallet of bricks."

"About what?" Bryce shimmered into being at the Faerie threshold, several yards behind Mal.

Mal tried to block his path. "Nothing."

"Nice try." He stepped past Mal, his eyes widening. "Hamish, get the fuck away from that."

Hamish glared at them across the abyss. "Fuck that. Zeke's down there. I've got to—"

"I said get *away*." Bryce's voice cracked like thunder, and suddenly two sets of very large hands grabbed Hamish as Ted Farnsworth and Rusty Johnson pulled him to his feet and towed him backward, away from the pit. *Away from Zeke.*

Hamish dug his heels into the soft earth, but resisting two bigger guys was futile. "Let go, damn it!"

Ted complied immediately, but Rusty glanced at Bryce for permission first. At Bryce's nod, he released Hamish's arm—but caught him again when Hamish lunged for the edge of the pit, a tortured sob catching in his chest.

"Hamish." Bryce was digging something out of a vest pocket. "Listen to me. This is a transdimensional wormhole."

Hamish wanted to kick with a kangaroo's full strength, but it wasn't Rusty he wanted to injure. *Let me at that Melchom arsehole.*

One round in the fighting pits and he'd be done. "I don't care if it's a bleeding TARDIS. Zeke's in there."

"Technically, he's not *in* there." Bryce tossed something into the pit that vaporized in a puff of red smoke. "He's already passed through it to another location."

"So the fuck what? I need to get him back." Hamish struggled against Rusty's iron grip, the urge to kick nearly irresistible. "Let go. I'm going after him."

"How?" Bryce tossed something else into the pit and, to Hamish's horror, the hole started to shrink. "Do you know where he went?"

"His bloody supervisor showed up dressed like Mr. fucking Steed from *The Avengers* and hauled him off to Sheol."

"Yes, but where in Sheol?"

"Who cares? I'll go down there and look until I find him."

"It may not be that easy. I'm Quentin Bertrand-Harr—"

"I know who you are," Hamish snarled, "and I don't care. I just need to get Zeke back!"

Quentin nodded curtly as Ted moved to his side. While Ted's paintball vest was splattered with every color in the game, including Hamish's team's, Quentin didn't have a drop on him, as if Ted had been throwing himself in front of his husband to keep him from being tagged. "Sheol isn't one place. Or rather, it occupies a single *geographical* space, but it contains hundreds— or perhaps thousands, by this time—of alternate dimensional pockets. Think of it like different frequencies. Each node occupies the same space but resonates with a different frequency. Those unique resonances keep the dimensional pockets distinct, keep them from collapsing in on themselves, or from merging with one another. Unless you know the correct frequency for the pocket where Zeke is, you won't be able to locate him, even if you search every corner of the Sheol where you land." He grimaced. "And it's not small, even without the multidimensional thing thrown in."

Hamish sagged in Rusty's grip, whimpering as the pit closed completely, the only sign it had ever been there a circle of brown grass in the lush wetlands. "I have to get him back." His voice was as ragged as a ten-pack-a-day smoker's. He jerked his arm out of Rusty's hold. "I *will* get him back. There must be a way."

Quentin edged toward Hamish, carefully avoiding the brown grass. "Why was he taken? As I understand it, he was the sole constituent of the work-release program. The supe council will expect an explanation of why he was recalled without at least notifying them."

"Yeah." Gareth dodged Bryce, who was sprinkling some kind of liquid over the dead grass. "Especially since the King of Faerie arranged for him to be here tonight. Even the Sheol overlords tread carefully where fae royalty are concerned, especially now that they've consolidated the Seelie and Unseelie power bases."

Hamish's legs, so tense and ready to lash out before, gave way, and he arse-planted on the ground. "That Melchom arsehole wanted Zeke to collect my soul, whatever that means. Zeke refused."

Quentin's eyes grew round. "He *refused*?"

Hamish scrubbed his hands through his hair. "Is that a big deal? I mean, yeah, it must have been since Melchom used it as an excuse to haul Zeke into the earthly bowels, but—"

"Zeke is a low-level minion," Quentin croaked.

"Yeah. He's told me that." *More than once. I never asked him what it meant though.*

"They *can't* refuse orders from a superior, particularly one in their direct chain of command."

"Oh."

"And further, a demon's nature is acquisitive. For 'cubi— sorry, incubi and succubi—that translates into seeking the life energies of their—" he glanced sidelong at Ted, who grinned "—partners. But for most demons, it's the quest for riches of another kind."

"Souls," Hamish muttered.

"Well, yes. Most of the time. But you said Zeke refused yours?"

"Yeah. At the concert last night, he warned me Melchom wanted him to do the deed. That's why he was trying to avoid me before."

This time, Quentin goggled like a bubble-eyed goldfish. "He *told* you? About a supervisor's orders? And tried to *evade* them, even if it meant increasing his collection?"

"He doesn't have a collection. He says he wasn't rated for it, but Melchom gave him an instant upgrade or something."

Quentin dropped to the grass just like Hamish had, and Ted crouched next to him.

"Q-Bert? You okay?"

"Yes. Yes, of course." He patted Ted's paint-splattered shoulder, then ran the same hand through his dark hair, apparently not caring that he'd just given himself hot-pink highlights. "But it's unheard of. I'd met Zeke myself, yet I had no idea he was so . . . so . . ."

"Weird?" Ted asked helpfully. "Wacky? Freakish?"

"Special." Hamish pushed himself off the ground. "He's special. And I'm getting him back, no matter what."

"That may not be easy," Quentin warned.

"I don't care. He's worth it. And I—" Hamish swallowed hard, his gaze locked on his clenched fists. "I love him."

"Ah," Quentin murmured.

Wait a minute. Hamish jerked his chin up and pointed at Quentin. "You're an incubus. How the bloody hell did *you* escape from Sheol?"

"I didn't personally. I was born in the Upper World. My many times great-grandmother emigrated when she mated with a dragon shifter."

A tiny spark of hope flared in Hamish's chest. "So there *is* a way? A— an immigration policy? Supe INS or what-the-fuck-ever?"

"Not really. It was sort of a one-time deal."

"I don't care. If it happened once, we can make it happen again. If we can find him, bring him back, I'll pull in every fucking connection I've got—"

"You can count on me to help," Gareth said. "And Niall. All of us."

"Right then. Let's pull him out." Hamish turned to Bryce, who was tucking a glass vial into a vest pocket. "I know what his name is. His true name. You're a druid, Bryce. Can't you conjure him?"

"That wouldn't help," Bryce said gently. "He'd then be enslaved to me."

"So release him!"

"If I did, he'd simply revert back to his position in Sheol. Besides, the preparation necessary for the ritual takes several weeks, so it's not an immediate solution, even if the druid council would countenance it. Which they won't. I'm sorry."

Hamish paced across the glade, only belatedly noting that the grass over the former pit was now as green as the rest of the place. "Then we have to do something else." He whirled and jabbed a finger at Bryce. "The witches. That magistra. She practically ordered him to come to the party after Niall's brother paid her a visit. She's got the magic mojo to wrangle something and she *owes* him. He's her employee, even if she treats him like a bloody serf."

Bryce shook his head. "Zeke chose to go with Melchom of his own free will."

"It was not *free will!*" Hamish roared. "That arsehole tried to force him to take my soul."

"But he chose not to do it. From the witches' perspective, Zeke's reaping the natural consequences of his choice, and they never budge when it comes to letting those play out."

Hamish growled low in his throat and resumed pacing. Something tickled the back of his mind, but he couldn't think, couldn't grasp it. His brain jangled with dissonance, worse than an out-of-tune orchestra playing six different pieces. "Fuck, there has to be *some* way to break him out of that place."

"Well . . ."

Hamish's head snapped up at Quentin's cautious word. "Do you know something? What? How?"

"There *is* certain legal precedent," Quentin said. "Not with Sheol per se, but with underworlds in general."

"What kind of precedent?"

"Orpheus. Inanna. Hermod." He shrugged apologetically. "Not that any of those ended particularly well."

Hamish pounded his thigh. "Yes! *That's* what I was trying to remember. Niall made a joke. Something about Orpheus. What the fuck did he do?"

"You know what he did," Gareth said. "We play 'Orfeo' in nearly every concert. We played it just last night."

Hamish blinked at him. "Fuck me dead. That's the same bloke?"

"More or less. The Greek Orpheus traveled to the underworld and bargained with Hades to rescue his wife, Eurydice, who'd died from a snakebite. The Orfeo in our song rescues his lady from the acquisitive Faerie King. But the principles are the same. Both men won their mate's release through music."

"That's what Niall meant. He said nobody would be able to resist the last true bard of Faerie. If—if the band could play for the demons with the real power, maybe we could bargain to get Zeke back."

"There's a slight problem with that," Bryce said. "While I could arrange a transport spell to translocate one person to Sheol, I couldn't do it for the whole band."

Gareth stepped forward. "I'll go." He smiled at Hamish. "After all, as you've pointed out, I've been to hell before."

"No." Hamish grabbed Gareth's shoulder. "I know you've got the whole bard-power thing going, but this is *my* battle. You've already gone through hell—literally—for your own lover—"

"Actually," Mal said, "his lover got out of hell himself. Gareth just passed through after the fact."

Hamish ground his teeth together. "Not the time, mate."

"Hamish is right," Quentin said. "The only possible way this can work is if the person making the request has skin in the game. My own ancestor, a dragon shifter, petitioned the lords of Sheol so that his succubus lover could emigrate to the Upper World."

"How did he work that?"

Quentin shrugged. "Sadly, the details are rather sketchy, but it may have involved a large portion of his hoard, since demons would have scoffed at the threat of burning the place down with dragon flame."

There's got to be a way. Hamish paced the clearing, punching a fist into the opposite hand. The dissonance in his brain was finally sorting itself into something resembling harmony, and he could finally *think* again.

Wait. He stopped dead. *Dissonance? Resonance?* He slowly turned to face Quentin, hope blooming under his heart. "You said the frequencies of those blasted pockets keep Sheol from collapsing on itself, right?"

"That's right."

"What if we interfere with those frequencies? Inject a resonance they're not expecting, that they're not prepared for?" *Stupid bloody realm with no music. What were they thinking?* "You think that might get someone's attention?"

Quentin's eyes lit up. "*Yes.* It would. The balance is quite delicate, really, considering the weight of the infrastructure it has to support. That's why the overlords need so many minions —they're constantly shoring up the place and adjusting the distribution of soul-powered energy."

Zeke's voice whispered in Hamish's brain. "*They thrive on chaos,*" and "*your drums drive the music, keep it from devolving into chaos.*"

"I've got an idea."

"If you don't stop pacing, you'll piss Bryce right off by wearing a groove in those recycled concrete pavers of his."

Hamish spun at the sound of Mal's voice, scrubbing his hands through his hair. He peered through the French doors into the dining room, which was empty except for David and Ted, who were clearing away food and empty bottles. "Shite, mate. Sorry. Guess there's nothing like having one of your guests kidnapped by hell-spawn to break up a party."

After a rather intense and distinctly *un*festive debriefing, almost everyone had gone, either home to rest or off on missions of their own. Quentin had remained to bring Bryce and Hamish further up to speed on Sheol, but when Quentin urged Ted to go home, Ted said, *"If you stay, I stay."* David, of course, being David, had stuck around to help. Besides, he lived next door.

Mal sauntered closer, offering Hamish a tight smile. Although the rest of the paintball gear had already been packed away, Mal still had his "sentimental" tagger attached to his belt. "Not a lot of merriment to be had with one of the grooms holed up in his druid lab, cooking up your anti-Sheol potions, and the other on call with the supe council—"

"You're on call? Why?"

"You might not have noticed, but Alun about burst a vein when Quentin filled us in on some of Sheol's, shall we say, less than enlightened policies? He dragged Gareth off with him to invoke a special session, with yours truly on deck for additional testimony if required. Although"—his smile turned a bit more genuine—"as I understand it, you've already got my business partner stirring things up on behalf of our favorite demon."

Hamish choked on a laugh. His and Niall's plans to shake up the Sheol hierarchy hadn't moved nearly fast enough. Yeah, their first shot had been to spring Zeke for the wedding. But they should have aimed higher faster. Granted, the King of

Faerie was right up there, but the Queen was the senior ruler, and this called for more firepower. All of it. The full council. He'd correct that today. Now. This instant or sooner. "Anything you need from me, I'm there. Or will be, once I get Zeke back." He peered at the sky, the stars dimmed by the moonlight. *Zeke can't see the stars. Or the moon.* His belly cramped, fingers curling into fists, and he wanted to throw back his head and howl like a werewolf. He forced himself to unclench his hands. After all, he wasn't the only one whose world had been upended. "I'm guessing this isn't how you want to start your wedding day."

"The wedding's postponed."

Hamish's jaw sagged. "What? But—but you've been practically glowing with anticipation ever since you proposed."

Mal grinned full-on this time. "My brothers have been less than complimentary about my behavior, but"—his expression turned serious—"do you honestly think we'd go through with it when our friends are hurting this way? What kind of celebration would that be? Nah, I'm not ready to start my mated life with that kind of bad karma."

"But—"

Mal gripped Hamish's shoulder. "It's done, mate. David handled canceling all the arrangements and notifying the guests with his usual efficiency—although most of the guests were at the paintball party anyway, so it wasn't exactly a surprise."

Hamish couldn't help the guilt that threaded through his worry and panic. "If you're sure . . ."

"Absolutely. We're thinking the vernal equinox. It'll give everyone time to recover after we bust Sheol wide open." He chuckled. "Bryce is happier about that date anyway. Now that they've promoted him to elder, he's totally invested in the whole druid natural-balance thing."

Tiff trotted around the corner of the house. "We've got your drum kit. Shake your lazy ass and help us unload it. Bryce needs to give it the druid once-over after we set it up in the wetlands."

Hamish joined her. "Is he protecting the kit or the wetlands?"
She grinned crookedly. "Both, probably."

With help from her, Mal, and Vitor, Hamish set up his kit on
the exact spot where Melchom had opened the pit. They left
Bryce muttering druid mumbo-jumbo and hiked back up the
hill, hitting the patio just as Quentin emerged from the house.

He handed Hamish a pair of glasses with thick black frames.
"Here."

"Thanks, but I can see fine, mate."

"In the Upper World, yes. But Sheol is a dark realm. These
contain the inverse of the spell on the lenses Zeke and I use to
adjust dark-adapted vision to daylight. You'll need them."

"All right, then." Hamish slipped them on. "Do I look all
'sexy geek' like Bryce now?"

Tiff snorted. "You look like Chris Hemsworth as the dim
receptionist in *Ghostbusters*."

"Well, that can't be bad. Although I've always fancied myself
more like his brother, Liam."

Her expression turned somber, and she moved forward to
grasp his shoulder. "Be careful, asshole."

He forced a grin. "Yeah. The band wouldn't be the same
without me."

Her grip tightened. "The *world* wouldn't be the same without
you."

Hamish jerked a nod, a lump forming in his throat. As little
as a week ago, he'd have been thrilled with this kind of
admission from Tiff. Today, he appreciated it because it meant
he was important to her, but he wasn't disappointed that it
didn't mean anything more. He didn't *want* it to mean anything
more.

He gripped her hand. "Thanks, mate."

She squeezed his fingers. "We'll see you when you get back."
Then she and Vitor disappeared back around the corner of the
house.

Bryce appeared at the edge of the patio, patting a couple of his vest pockets. "It's time."

Quentin kept pace with Hamish as he practically raced down the hill, Bryce following more slowly. Although Hamish was grateful to Quentin for all the Sheol intel—list after list of things to do and things *not* to do—by now, Hamish had heard it so many times he was only half listening.

"Just remember, when you start the negotiations, *do not* say you'd give anything to get Zeke back. That will give them the opportunity to demand your soul in exchange."

"Seems like a bargain if it means getting him back."

Quentin glared at him. "Then you'd defeat the entire purpose of this exercise. Zeke surrendered expressly to keep from being forced to collect your soul. And while I understand some of your bandmates consider you mildly annoying at times, without your soul, they'd find you insufferable."

"Right. Don't offer up my soul." But Hamish had no intention of letting Zeke suffer, and if the price was giving up something he wasn't sure was doing him any good, he'd pay it.

Bryce handed him a vial filled with a murky yellow liquid. "Drink this."

Hamish took it gingerly. "What is it?"

"It's a flame-retardant potion. You'll still feel the heat, but you won't burst into flame. Don't get overconfident though. It won't protect you if you try to actually walk through fire."

"Good to know." He downed the stuff, and it wasn't nearly as nasty as rumors about druid potions had led him to believe. "That's not bad. Tastes better than some of those bloody energy drinks."

Hamish settled himself on his stool behind his drum kit, running his fingers over his snare skin. It didn't feel any different after Bryce had cast his druid anti-Sheol spell, but what did he know?

"Are they going to be able to hear me? The spell doesn't muffle the sound, does it?"

"Shouldn't do." Bryce sketched a sphere in the air with his hands. "It's like a protective bubble, preventing any damage from Sheol's environment or demon offensive magic. As long as you're seated, it'll cover you too." He glanced at the loose snare at Hamish's feet, its strap coiled on its skin. "But the spell's range is based on the mass of the full set, so if you go mobile, while the drum will be all right, I can't guarantee the same for you."

"That's just insurance. Backup. It won't have the carrying power of the full kit, but . . ." Hamish shrugged.

"Don't worry," Quentin said. "The acoustics in Sheol are legendary for their excellence. Otherwise the screams wouldn't echo satisfactorily. Now." His eyes turned serious behind his glasses. "It's unlikely to an astronomical degree that Zeke will be anywhere near where Bryce's spells land you, so when you strike your bargain, insist that they bring him to you." Quentin moved out of the way as Bryce finished sprinkling some kind of powder in a circle around Hamish. "Just remember—"

"No offering my soul. Yeah, mate. I got that memo."

"And make sure safe passage back to the Upper World is included in the deal."

Hamish stopped fidgeting with his snare stand. "Will they try to fiddle with that?"

Quentin smiled, and while before he'd looked like any buff, geeky guy, Hamish could suddenly see the demon in him. "They'll be pissed as all get out. They *hate* giving anything away —they're worse than dragons, really. So if they can trick you by giving you Zeke, but not giving you a way out? You bet your ass they'll try it."

"Good to know." Hamish picked up his sticks and saluted his friends. "Wish me luck."

Mal raised a hand. "You'll bring him back. I've got faith."

"Thanks, mate."

Bryce muttered some kind of Gaelic incantation, and greenish fire flared up, blunting Hamish's hearing and clouding his view of the clearing just as Alun, Niall, and an unfamiliar man with a camera looped around his neck burst out of the house and pelted down the hill. Niall was shouting something that made everyone else turn—and then *all* of them started shouting at Hamish.

"What? Sorry, mates. Can't hear you."

Fat lot of good that'll do. They probably can't hear me either.

Then Bryce started gesturing frantically, but when the ground seemed to drop out from under Hamish's feet, he was too busy trying to hold on to his drums—not to mention the contents of his stomach—to worry about it.

He'd get the story later, when he got back. *With Zeke.*

Failure was not a bloody option.

He managed not to upchuck—barely—as sweat beaded on his forehead. Sheol wasn't just hot—it was *hot.* He shuddered to think what it would have been like without Bryce's fire-retardant potion—he might have spontaneously combusted.

He dared a lightning-fast touch on the snare's rim, and while it was hot, it didn't burn. *Small favors, I reckon.* He hoped the spell covered the havoc this kind of heat could wreak on the skins. He'd just have to trust that Bryce was as good as rumor said he was.

Hamish gazed around him. He was in a cavern of blackened stone, its ceiling so high as to be out of sight, only the teeth of a few stalactites hinting that it was there at all.

He tilted his chin down and peered over the rims of his glasses. *Black. Total, unrelieved black.* Thank the fates for Quentin Bertrand-Harrington and his geeky bespelled glasses. *Not to mention his inside knowledge of Sheol.*

Of course, Quentin hadn't ever been here—none of his family had been for generations. But his intel was better than anything else they had, so Hamish would go for it.

He glanced around the cavern again. While the space near him was empty, shadows moved and flickered at the edges, behind rocks and in and out of the dozen or so openings that gaped in its walls.

The only sounds were that same discordant chorus he'd gotten a taste of before: shrieks, wails, the occasional crack of something that sounded suspiciously like a whip. A muted crackle—flames, perhaps? A sub-aural hum that he felt in his bones rather than heard. *Is that the frequency of this pocket?*

Guess it's time to announce myself.

Hamish tapped out a four-count on the snare's rim and launched into the drum solo from "Wipe Out"—because that thing set *his* teeth on edge, so it was bound to get the attention of a bunch of arseholes who didn't know the meaning of rhythm or back beat or syncopation.

Quentin was right about the acoustics. The cavern amplified his sounds like a high-end amp. But even over the echoes, he could tell that the cries of agony and despair had changed. They were coming from a different direction, for one thing—for another, they were liberally mixed with rage.

Hamish grinned and started his first encore. That was the thing about "Wipe Out"—he could play the damn thing in his sleep. By the time he'd swung into the third iteration, three blokes had come rolling out of the biggest cave mouth. One of them had green scales, bat wings the width of a Cessna, and a grimace that put the Notre Dame gargoyles to shame. The second looked like some kind of bird, maybe a stork—if you didn't count the fact it was wearing gray flannel trousers on its troll-sized legs. The third was an okay-looking bugger, assuming you were into guys with three heads.

"Cease that this instant!" one of the heads roared.

"Don't think I will." For a change, Hamish switched to Ringo's solo from "The End," just because it had a few rests that would lull the demons into thinking he might be tiring. *Not likely, arseholes. I can do this forever.* Especially if it helped Zeke.

"You will cease or we will incinerate you where you stand." Apparently that one head was the spokesdemon.

"Don't know if you've noticed"—Hamish segued into Gene Krupa's percussion arrangement for "Sing, Sing, Sing"—"but I'm not standing. Sitting here, in a very nice druid spell circle." He grinned. "Pisser, ain't it?"

The three demons gnashed their teeth—or in one case, beak. Hamish nearly laughed because he never thought he'd see somebody actually *do* that. What was next? Rending of garments?

Since these guys were wearing suits that could pass with no trouble at Paris Fashion Week despite their anatomical challenges, Hamish would bet *that* would get their knickers in a right twist. But he didn't feel like screwing around.

"You lot have someone I want."

"If you're referring to the soul of a loved one, *all* the souls here are legally contracted," Spokesdemon barked. "You have no right—"

"Keep your souls, though I have no idea why you'd want them. I'm after a demon."

The gargoyle bloke's scales changed from green to red. "No human can tell us what to do!"

"I'm not human," Hamish said, increasing the tempo. "Shifter."

Gargoyle spread his wings, like *that* would intimidate Hamish. "No *anybody* has the right to punish a demon but someone in its direct reporting line."

"I don't want to punish one. I want to break him out of this literal hell hole and take him home. With me."

All three of them reared back at that, and a boulder detached from the wall, seemingly on a collision course with Hamish's drums. Hamish braced himself, setting his jaw and trusting Bryce's preparation, not letting his beats falter. At the last moment, the enormous rock veered to the side, toward the trio, and they had to scramble out of the way.

Hamish grinned. *Hot damn, that druid magic is some good shite.* "Nice try, mates. But your tricks aren't going to work."

"Fine, fine. Stop that infernal racket and we'll talk."

"Ah, ah, ah. Think I'm an idiot?" Hamish added an extra paradiddle and punctuated it with a clash of the high hat. "This keeps up until you agree to free Zeke Oz from this joint for good."

They glanced at each other—Spokesdemon glancing between each of his heads as well—with the same bewildered expression, adjusted for stork beaks and gargoyle grimaces. "Zeke Oz?"

Bollocks. Of course, after that Melchom wanker had bleated it all over the wetlands, Hamish could hardly forget it. "Ozul-y-Kalon."

"He's nothing more than a low-level minion," Stork-head squawked over the sound of the drums. "And an unsatisfactory one at that. He *volunteered* to work among humans with no possible ROI."

"Then you won't miss him."

"But what could you possibly want with him?" Spokesdemon narrowed all six eyes in suspicion. "If you think to avenge yourself on his managers, you—"

"Nah. I don't give a rat's ass about anyone else." Hamish added an extra flourish on the snare, offset with the bass, and a stalactite detached from the distant ceiling and smashed to bits on the cavern floor. All five heads exchanged nervous glances, and winced simultaneously when Hamish hit the bass again. "I'd hurry if I were you. I'm powered by druid juice, so your house'll crash around your ears before I run out of steam. I want Zeke, and I want him now."

"So." Spokesdemon's shifty eyes telegraphed his intentions as loudly as if he'd shouted them from all three mouths. *These blokes should never play poker.* "We show you Ozul-y-Kalon and you'll stop?"

"No chance. I don't let up until you give me Zeke and we shake Sheol's bloody brimstone dust off our feet. Permanent residency for him in the Upper World. No more kowtowing to your bleeding management structure or being ordered to collect random souls."

Stork-head's beak gaped. "But—but that's what demons *do*. It's what we're *for*."

"Not Zeke. He's more than that. Now bring him here. Then we'll leave." Hamish added a little Keith Moon intensity to his latest improvisation. "Do you want to make a bargain, or do I bring this place down?"

"Yes, yes, *yes!*" Spokesdemon didn't have enough hands to block all of his available ears. "We agree to a negotiation. But for Beelzebub's sake, *stop it!*"

Elation flooded Hamish's chest. *We did it! This is going to work!* "Not yet." He punctuated his words with the crash cymbal. "You know my terms." *Clang.* "Zeke's freedom in exchange for me not destroying the place." *Clang.* Gods, he wanted to laugh at the sour expressions on their faces. "Although if you ask me, a little destruction couldn't hurt." *Clang.* Three more stalactites crashed to the floor, and Hamish could detect a dissonant vibration building beneath his feet like an impending earthquake. "There, see? The place looks better already. So tell me. Have we got a deal or what?"

"Here are *our* terms," Gargoyle bellowed over the driving beat of the bass. "You must promise never to return."

"Deal! I won't darken your door again." Hamish grinned and doubled down on the tempo. *Clang. Crash. Boom.* "Not unless you ask *really* nicely."

Chapter Eighteen

Zeke trudged along the narrow tunnel that led from the boilers to the soul repository, the heavy chain that shackled his ankles clanking with every step. The cuffs around his wrists were red hot—not that it mattered much to him. But it was a measure of how angry Melchom—and presumably the other C-suite demons—were with him that they'd expended their own energy on a useless symbolic gesture.

"Here. If you were human, you'd be in agony right now. Remember that."

It was stupid, really. The real agony was being separated from Hamish. It was as if Melchom had borrowed Cerberus from Hades to gnaw out Zeke's entrails—only to have them restored and go through it again.

Now I know how Prometheus felt.

But on every tortuous trip since Melchom had thrown him down here—he'd lost count by now—he staged his own tiny rebellion: he hummed under his breath.

On the way from the repository to the boilers, his back laden with shrieking, struggling souls, he crooned the song from last night's concert. Then on the return journey, this time weighed down with the moaning remains of nearly incinerated souls off to recover before the next cycle, he tried to time his steps to one of the rhythms Hamish was always playing on any available piece of furniture—and in their absence, on himself. *And once— that one glorious night—on me.*

But the chains made his footsteps too clumsy to maintain the beat. It didn't stop Zeke from trying, of course—because what else did he have to do? In fact, this time, he could swear he'd almost gotten it right, his bare feet slapping in time with the pulse of that remembered rhythm.

He almost smiled—but then he realized that the pulse wasn't only in his mind. He stood still, head cocked. "Shhh!" he hissed to the souls on his back. "I need you to be quiet for just a minute, please."

The soles of his feet vibrated with the kind of organized sounds—*music*—that had never occurred in Sheol before.

But how? Why? And more importantly, *Who?*

I'll never know. Not stuck down here for the next couple of millennia. He shook his head and started toward the repository again.

But before he'd gone two steps, Melchom appeared in front of him in a red brocade dressing gown, a heavy woolen scarf wrapped around his ears.

Zeke backed away from the fury on Melchom's face. "Supervisor? What—"

"Shut up and come with me."

"But—" Zeke gestured to the load on his back. "I have to return them to—"

"Leave them. For Beelzebub's sake, stop stalling!"

That was hardly fair, since Melchom had only appeared seconds ago. *But when has Melchom ever been fair?* He lowered his burden to the rocky tunnel floor.

"I don't understand, Supervisor. Have I done something wrong?"

"Shut up." Melchom grabbed Zeke's arm and yanked, his claws digging into Zeke's biceps, and then they were rising up, up, up, through the rocky tunnel ceiling. Then they zipped sideways, scenes of other souls in torment flashing past them like the fast-forward feature on the DVR in Zeke's Supernatural Selection apartment.

He tamped down the surge of pain at the memory. Not about the DVR—he'd never had much chance to watch it since the glare from the AI made the screen impossible to see—but about the Upper World. Falafel. Salted caramel chocolate tart. Music. *Hamish.*

He concentrated on the pain from Melchom's increasingly tight grip instead. The added discomfort was almost a welcome respite from the tedium of his life in Sheol.

But as they moved through dimension after dimension, Zeke realized that the vibrations he'd detected down in the lowest tunnels hadn't vanished. In fact, they were louder, clearer, cleaner—and with every beat, Melchom whimpered and his grip tightened on Zeke's arm until tendon and muscle were crushed against bone.

They slowed to a halt in a tunnel leading to one of the nexus caverns where many paths converged, one Zeke was familiar with because it was directly under Portland. Melchom finally released him, and Zeke rubbed his aching biceps.

"In there." Melchom pointed one shaking claw at the entrance to the cavern. "Go in there."

"Are you coming with—"

"Go! Now! Beelzebub's bloody horns, how can anyone stand this?" Melchom sank quickly through the tunnel floor and out of sight.

Oookay. Zeke crept down the tunnel, but then he recognized the vibrations for what they were.

Drums. And not just any drums. He'd recognize that passion anywhere. *Hamish.*

Lucifer's balls, what the *fuck* was he doing here? Had Melchom finagled some deal with a C-suite demon to sidestep Hamish's soul-collection assignment to Zeke? He'd never heard of a way to rescind the assignment and allow a second demon to approach the same victim, but then nobody ever told minions anything.

He broke into an awkward run. Although hobbled by his chains, his bare feet still slapped against the stone floor in time with the beat as he hurried though the passage and burst into the cavern.

Hamish.

Zeke's heart stuttered, because there he was—enthroned behind several drums, sticks flying across their heads, grinning maniacally at Ronwe, Shax, and Haborym, three of the most powerful upper echelon demons.

Haborym took his hands off the ears of one of his heads long enough to gesture peremptorily at Zeke.

Zeke didn't have to be asked twice. He sped across the cavern until he reached Hamish's side.

"What are you doing here?"

Hamish tore his gaze from the overlords and his grin softened, but his drumming didn't falter. "Oh hey, mate. Was wondering when you'd get here."

"Hamish, answer me. Did Melchom do it? Did he collect your soul? Did one of them—" Zeke waved a hand at the overlords, whose faces were screwed up as if in agony, even Shax, whose stork head was usually impassive. *A change for them. Usually they're dispensing agony, not enduring it.*

"Nah. I came to get you. Pack your bags." Hamish glanced at Zeke's nakedness. "Although guess you don't have a lot of luggage, eh?" He glared at the overlords. "Oi, you lot! Get rid of these chains!"

Zeke cringed, expecting a burst of retaliatory fire. "Hamish, you can't—" The chains clinked to the ground, leaving Zeke's wrists and ankles free.

"That's more like it." He jerked his chin at Haborym. "These buggers have agreed to let you go as long as I stop drumming." He shook his head sadly. "Everybody's a critic."

Joy bled through Zeke's terror, although it didn't banish it completely. "You . . . you came here? For me?"

"Course I did, mate." Hamish's smile faded, and the look in his eyes behind the unfamiliar glasses melted Zeke's bones. "I love you. Can't let you languish down here. Because I've got to tell you . . ." He leaned toward Zeke and spoke out of the side of his mouth. "This place sucks."

He loves me. A laugh burbled up in Zeke's throat. "Yes," he choked. "It does."

"So what do you say we get out of here?"

"I'd like nothing better."

"Good. 'Cause we're leaving. Now."

Haborym's three mouths stretched in identical sharklike grins. "You can try."

"What the fuck?" Hamish half rose from his stool. "We had a deal."

"We do." Haborym nodded at the remains of Zeke's chains. "His freedom in exchange for you not destroying Sheol and never returning. Those were your exact words. He's technically free, in that he is no longer restrained." He grinned wider. "And of course, you can't return if you never leave. Now keep your side of the bargain and stop that infernal racket."

"Bollocks." Hamish's eyes widened, and one drumstick hit the rim of the snare instead of its head. "I mentioned leaving earlier. I'm sure I did. I think. Your Upper World residency too."

"Ah-ah-ah." Haborym waggled a finger. "That was *before* we agreed to negotiations. Therefore, it's not included in the final contract."

Zeke glanced at the overlords, whose expressions, although still pained, were infused with evil glee. "Timing is just as important as words. Any demands prior to both parties formally entering deliberations are considered coercion and therefore invalid."

"*Shite!* Quentin should have told—" He bashed his cymbals with both sticks. "Fuck. He did, and I rushed the groove again. But so what?" He cast a determined glance at Zeke. "We'll renegotiate. We'll renegotiate for as long as it takes."

"You've already given them your main bargaining chit—your music. You don't have anything to negotiate *with*, except your soul, and *I* won't allow that."

Hamish grimaced, and his rhythm slowed but didn't cease. "I'm so sorry, babe. But I was so desperate to see you, to make sure you were okay, that I screwed up. I did exactly what Quentin told me not to do." He glared at the overlords. "But if they're gonna get pissy about language, then I can too. I only promised not to destroy the place, not to stop drumming, and if it keeps them reaching for the earplugs, I can tone it down but keep going until I drop."

"They'll pounce at the first opportunity." Zeke bit his lip, glancing around the cavern. It was empty except for the overlords, all the other demons driven away by the organized tempos that threatened their comfortable chaos. "I know a way out, and since I'm *technically* free, they *technically* can't stop me from leaving. Technically, they can't stop you either, since you've never been under their jurisdiction. But it's a bit of a hike, and they won't make it easy. Once you stop drumming, they'll pull out all the stops."

Hamish grinned. "No worries there." He nudged a shorter drum at his feet, a black strap draped over its head. "I brought my old marching drum. It might not be enough to bring the place down around our ears, but it should keep these blighters at a distance."

"But your other drums . . ." Zeke bit his lip. "We'll have to leave them behind."

"You think I care about that? I can always get another kit. But you, love?" Hamish's smile was tender. "You're irreplaceable."

"How quickly can you transfer to the marching drum?"

"Less than a minute. The sling's already in place."

"That may be too slow." Zeke winced. "Demon superspeed, remember?"

"Nah. We'll be okay. I know how to keep them distracted." He switched to another song, one that Zeke didn't recognize.

The overlords immediately groaned and dropped to their knees. "They hate this one."

Zeke gazed at some of the most powerful demons in Sheol, writhing on the floor like any tortured soul. "What's it called?"

"'Wipe Out.'"

"I *love* it." Zeke edged closer and kissed Hamish's sweaty temple. "But not as much as I love you."

"Then what do you say we scarper? Because I could really use a beer about now."

Hamish grabbed the drum from the floor and looped the strap over his head. Zeke had underestimated his speed—he was beating out a brisk cadence that had Zeke moving his feet almost before the last echo of "Wipe Out" faded from the cavern. "Can you grab the bass drum, though, just in case?" Hamish nodded at the big drum at the front of the kit, and Zeke snatched it up. It was unwieldy but not heavy, at least not for a demon. "Good man. Now you lead, and I'll follow. Just don't go all superspeed on me and leave me in the dust."

"Never." Zeke nodded to a tunnel widdershins from where they stood. "That way."

Hamish increased the tempo, and it reverberated in Zeke's bones, his mind, his heart—not to mention his feet. It was just so *freeing*. He had no trouble holding his speed down because Hamish's music wouldn't let him do anything other than march to the beat, knees high, feet slapping the floor in time, heart lifting with every downbeat.

Beside him, Hamish chuckled. "I was going to ask if the rhythm bothered you, but I see it doesn't."

"No. It's wonderful."

Hamish glanced behind them as the tunnel mouth faded from view. "The acoustics aren't great in here. Will they be after us?"

"As long as you keep playing, nobody will get close." Zeke raised his voice to be heard over the drums, as Hamish had.

"All the minions will be scurrying around, trying to maintain the domains for their masters—"

"Oi. You know I hate that word."

Zeke shot him a wry smile. "I know. But it's the nature of Sheol. No point in denying it."

"I reckon you're right. Doesn't mean I have to like it."

"This way." Zeke turned into a narrower tunnel, its ceiling low enough that Hamish's hair nearly brushed the rough rocks overhead. Both of them had to tuck their elbows in, and Zeke had to hunch over the bass drum.

Hamish swore under his breath. "You sure you know where we're going, mate? 'Cause this looks an awful lot like a trap."

"It leads to the portal that soul collectors use to get to the Upper World. Two days ago, I wouldn't have been able to use it." He grinned over his shoulder at Hamish. "But I got an upgrade."

Hamish barked out a laugh. "Hoisted with their own what-the-hell-ever, eh? Does it go to wherever you want?"

"No. There has to be a translocation gate on the other side, but luckily I have access to the one at Supernatural Selection." His steps faltered. "At least I think I do. I doubt Melchom bothered to tell Magistra Lenore that he pulled me back to Sheol. She won't look for me until after the wedding festivities. So I guess . . ." He glanced at Hamish, whose face was runneled with sweat. "Keep your fingers crossed?"

"Fingers are a little busy now, but I'm not worried. You know what you're doing—as long as clueless arseholes like yours truly don't try to bollix things up for you."

Zeke whirled to face him. "You're *not* an arse— asshole."

Hamish grinned at him. "I notice you didn't argue with the clueless bit."

Zeke shrugged. "Well . . . demons don't lie. Sorry?"

"Never mind that. Just get us out of here and you can teach me how to overcome all my shortcomings."

Zeke's heart swelled in his chest until he was in danger of levitating. "It's a deal." Ahead of them, a faint shimmer marked the portal. "There it is." He increased his pace, but the faster he hurried, the farther away the portal seemed to get, until it was no bigger than a mouse hole in the distance clouded with increasing smoke.

Behind him, Hamish coughed. "Those blighters are cheating."

"They don't see it as cheating." Zeke peered at the walls, which seemed to be closing in. "They see it as fully exercising the terms of the contract."

"Is there another way out?"

"There's the one Dante used, but he had to go all the way down before he could go back up."

Hamish hacked harder, his cadence faltering. "Bollocks." His voice was raspy. "I'll have to tell Bryce to add smoke inhalation to his anti-Sheol potion."

Zeke clutched the bass drum tighter, his grip snapping the pedal. *He's not suited for Sheol. I can wait this out, but he's not going to make it. Not unless I strike a bargain.* And for once, Zeke had something to bargain with: his freedom. Considering how angry the overlords *still* were about the incubus migration, they'd jump at the deal in a heartbeat.

He turned around, but before he could suggest a retreat, the corridor behind them was engulfed in flames.

Hamish glanced over his shoulder. "Looks like—" he choked, obviously trying to smother his cough "—our options are shrinking."

Zeke wanted to take Hamish in his arms, soothe him, somehow protect him from smoke and fire and the spite of the overlords. But his hands were occupied with the drum and the broken pedal with its round-headed stick.

He stared at the stick, an idea blooming in his brain. *By the terms of Hamish's contract, by the overlords' own admission, I'm free.*

That means I don't have to abide by my former masters' orders.
"Hamish . . ."

"Yeah, love?" he croaked.

"*You* agreed not to destroy Sheol." Zeke brandished the stick.
"But *I* didn't."

Hamish pulled a grin out of the tail end of another coughing
fit. "Too right. Do it."

Zeke listened carefully as Hamish swung into a cadence he
recognized—"Lover's Reel," a song buried so deep in Zeke's
heart that he had no trouble adding a strong bass beat to
punctuate it, support it, *become* it.

As he marched forward, Hamish at his heels, the portal
zoomed toward them, smoke clearing and walls receding, as if
the overlords had realized their mistake. *Too bad. This time I'm
not backing down.*

When they reached the portal, the hallway had widened so
much that they could stand next to one another. Zeke turned
around. The fire still blocked the end of the extremely
foreshortened corridor. *They* want *us to leave now. Too bad.*

"Uh, Zeke?" Hamish wasn't coughing anymore. "Shouldn't
we get the hell out of here?"

"In a minute. Keep playing." Zeke pounded the drum,
adding an extra beat for emphasis.

Hamish grinned. "You're learning, mate. Keep it up."

So they did. Until Zeke too was dripping with sweat from the
exertion. But when the walls started to crumble and stones
dropped from the ceiling, he just beat harder until tremors
underfoot almost knocked him off-balance.

He threw down the drum and grabbed Hamish's wrist.
"Now!"

As the tunnel collapsed behind them, Zeke yanked Hamish
through the portal, and straight into the corridor on the fourth
floor of Supernatural Selection.

And face-to-face with the red and green glare of an extremely
pissed-off AI.

Hamish ignored the pulsing AI and caught Zeke around the waist, letting his sticks clatter to the floor. Hamish had finally stopped coughing, although both of them were still breathing hard, smelling of smoke and brimstone and leftover terror. He buried his face in Zeke's curls because *fucking hell.*

"That was intense," he murmured.

Zeke's shoulders shook, whether with laughter or sobs or simply relief, Hamish couldn't tell. "You think?"

"What I think is that we both need a shower, a drink, some clean clothes." He raised his head. "And to get rid of this fucking AI." He ripped his see-in-the-dark glasses off and shoved them in his pocket to return to Quentin before the veritable strobe of bright, angry red fried his retinas.

Zeke's spine stiffened as the AI sparked like a shorting amp, lifting his head from Hamish's chest to face it head-on, although he squinted against the glare. "For your information," he said, his voice shaking, "I have every right to be here. Hamish bargained for my release."

"That's right. He's not under Sheol's jurisdiction anymore, so you can just sod right off, you electric wanker." He kissed Zeke's temple. "How does your place do for hot water?"

Zeke chuckled weakly, drawing Hamish along with him as he staggered toward the stairs. "Adequate."

"That works for me."

Zeke led Hamish up the stairs and into a tiny apartment, the AI dogging their heels. The place had a narrow galley kitchen, a couple of rooms that might be bedrooms (although they looked more like shoeboxes to Hamish), a living room the size of Hamish's loo, and a loo the size of Hamish's closet. *Bloody hell. Couldn't the witches spring for a decent crib for their staff?*

"I, um, won't be a long." Zeke ducked into the loo and closed the door, leaving Hamish alone with the AI.

"You might as well leave off the light show, mate, because I don't know what you're on about and I wouldn't care if I did." The flash of bright pink as Hamish wandered over to the narrow window was probably the AI's version of profanity. "Yeah, yeah. Big talk."

He gazed down at the street, the aroma of the falafel restaurant detectable through the ill-fitting windows.

Hamish wondered how many hours Zeke had spent here, gazing down at the street and at sidewalks he was forbidden to tread, sniffing food he couldn't afford to eat even if he *could* enter the restaurant, watching people walk by who might have relationship problems, money woes, or job stress, but who were all free in a way that Zeke had never believed he could be.

That's all changed now. It had to be better, right?

He sighed, plucking at the slightly charred hem of his tank top. He ought to contact Bryce. Let him know the potions had worked a treat—except for the smoke inhalation—and that Hamish and Zeke were back and safe. But for one thing: he didn't have his mobile. Bryce had offered to Sheolify it, but Hamish hadn't wanted to take the time.

For another, he wanted a few moments with Zeke without the threat of retribution hanging over them from the Sheol overlords, the witches, the bloody AI, or even the self-righteous supe council, who hadn't been blameless in the way Zeke had been treated. A few moments to adjust to this new truth—that Zeke was free, that he had choices, that they could be together in the open.

But if he has choices, will he still choose me? Hamish thought so. He *hoped* so. But at the very least, he owed Zeke the opportunity to decide based on his new circumstances. The last thing Hamish wanted was for Zeke to feel a different kind of trapped —the insidious trap of gratitude and obligation.

Zeke emerged from the bathroom, clad in a pair of flannel sleep pants, settling a rather battered pair of glasses onto his nose. *Good thing he had spares.* "There's a clean towel in there. You should have plenty of hot water."

Hamish peered into the tiny bathroom. The mirror had zero fog. "You took a cold shower, didn't you?"

Zeke shrugged. "The water temperature doesn't really matter to me." Something must matter though, because tiny tremors were chasing across his skin.

"Oi." Hamish took Zeke's face between his hands, nudging his chin up with his thumbs. "You don't have to do without. That's not what this relationship is about. All right?"

Zeke smiled tremulously, not saying yea or nay—or anything else for that matter—although he didn't protest when Hamish kissed him, and even clung a bit to Hamish's shoulders. "I'll wait for you in the bedroom."

At Zeke's announcement, the AI surged across the room toward him, but Hamish blocked its path. "Be gone. You have no power here." He tossed his best grin over his shoulder at Zeke, hoping for one in return. "I've always wanted to say that."

Zeke *might* have smiled before he slipped into his bedroom, but it was hard to tell. The AI's glare played bugger-all with the room's shadows. He took great pleasure in shutting the bathroom door in its figurative face.

When he got out of the shower, he stared at his Sheol-infused shorts and tank with revulsion. *Nope. Not putting those on again until I have to.*

He left them hanging over the shower curtain for the moment, and wrapped one of Zeke's flimsy towels around his waist. It covered him. Barely. When he stepped out of the bathroom, he expected the AI to get up in his face, but it wasn't in the living room, and the bedroom door opposite Zeke's was closed.

Small favors for which I should be thankful, I guess.

He eased Zeke's door open and slipped inside. Zeke was standing next to a narrow bed, its blankets tucked in with mathematical precision. Still barefoot and shirtless, he was staring at the hoodie hanging limp in his hands.

"Are you okay, love?"

Zeke didn't raise his chin, but Hamish saw his lips press together as if he were trying to hide their trembling.

Crossing the room in two steps, Hamish wrapped him in his arms, knocking the hoodie to the floor. "It's all right. You're safe now. We're both safe."

"I don't even know what day it is." Zeke murmured, his cheek warm against Hamish's chest, his curls tickling Hamish's neck. "Is it stupid that that's what bothers me? That I don't know if I've missed Mal and Bryce's wedding?"

"You haven't."

Zeke drew back. "How do you know? Do you know what time it is?"

"Nah. Don't have my phone." He smoothed Zeke's curls back from his forehead. "But they've postponed the wedding."

Zeke jerked out of Hamish's hold. "They what? Why?"

Hamish reeled him back in where he belonged. "The Kendrick brothers. They're not perfect. Gareth's a moody SOB, Mal's a snarky wanker, and Alun has a stick up his ass the size of the Sydney Tower. But they'll always—always—be there for victims of oppression and injustice. And now, that includes you."

"They postponed the wedding for me?" Guilt flickered across Zeke's face. "But—"

"Not only you. For everyone like you. Demons. Angels too, assuming they're not all arseholes." He kissed Zeke's forehead. "What can I say? It's a crusade I'm behind one hundred and ten percent."

"But the wedding—"

"They've only put it off for a while. Maybe until the equinox." Hamish grinned. "Think that's enough time to mount a revolution?"

"R-revolution?" Zeke's eye widened. "Wow."

"And now that I've seen Sheol firsthand? I'm behind it *two* hundred and ten percent." Hamish shivered and settled Zeke against his chest, because the notion of him being trapped there forever? *No. Just no.* "Have I told you," he murmured, "how fricking *amazing* you were?"

"No." Zeke's lips whispered against Hamish's skin. "That was you. Nobody else has faced down the demon overlords since Quentin's ancestor challenged them for his succubus mate." He eased back until he could meet Hamish's gaze, a smile teasing his lips. "You realize you've now become a legend."

"Legend? Me? Nah. I'm nothing but a kangaroo shifter who was lucky enough to score a gig with Faerie's last true bard. Now *there's* a legend for you."

Zeke's eyes glinted red. "Don't say that. They're *lucky* to have you. There's nobody else like you. You're the bravest, most daring, most—"

The phone on the bedside table shrilled, making Zeke jerk in Hamish's embrace. "Damn. Just when things were getting good." He sat on the bed and pulled Zeke into his lap. "Ignore it."

"I can't. It's my boss."

"How do you know?"

"She's the only one who has the number."

But when Zeke tried to wiggle off Hamish's lap, Hamish tucked him closer. "Stay put. My arm span is good for things other than reaching the crash cymbal." He plucked the receiver off the base and handed it to Zeke.

"Yes, Magistra?" He blinked, his mouth rounding with a barely voiced *Oh.* "How did you get this— Yes, thank you. I'm fine. We're both— Of course. Here he is." He held out the handset. "It's for you. It's Niall."

Hamish raised his eyebrows. "What does he want?"

Zeke's lips quirked up in a ghost of his former smile. "Maybe you should ask him."

"Too right." Hamish held the phone to his ear. "What?"

"You need to get back to Mal and Bryce's place." Niall's voice was clipped, his tone tense. "Now."

"Fuck that. I'm staying with Zeke."

Niall let out an exasperated huff. "He needs to be here too."

"Come on, Niall. The poor guy's been to hell. Literally. You think you could give us a minute? How'd you even know we were back?"

"The *ethera*. They've taken a liking to Zeke, so I asked them to let me know when they could sense him again. Please, Hamish." Niall's voice turned coaxing. "I know Zeke's got to be shaken up—"

"You could say that."

"This is important. Critical. I tried to stop you before you went after Zeke to tell you, but—"

"And leave him there for one more second? Not a chance, mate."

"Well, now that you're back, waiting any longer could endanger him again."

Hamish tightened his hold on Zeke, earning a tiny *meep*. "Endanger how?"

"I don't want to discuss it over the phone. We've already sent a car for you. It should be out front now." He hung up.

Hamish cursed softly and smacked the handset back into its cradle.

Zeke gazed at him somberly. "I guess you have to go."

"Not just me. They want us both."

"Oh." He blinked. "Why?"

"He didn't say. But no matter what Niall says—and the fae, especially royalty, can be right bossy—we don't have to go if you're not ready."

"I don't mind. I'd rather be there than here."

Hamish glanced around, shifting his arse on the rock-hard mattress. "I don't blame you. I've seen empty lockers with more personality, not to mention more space and comfort."

Zeke laced their fingers together. "I *meant* I'd rather be there because that's where *you'll* be."

"Oh." Hamish pressed a kiss to the back of Zeke's hand. "That's all right, then. Besides, anyplace without that blasted AI is a step up." He glanced down at his bare chest and terry loincloth. "Shite. Guess I better put my clothes back on, eh? Although the way they smell . . ." He wrinkled his nose.

"Oh. Just a minute." Zeke rose and took the two steps necessary to reach the dresser. He pulled a plastic-wrapped black T-shirt out of the top drawer and held it out. "This is left over from a promotion the agency did on Samhain. It's never been worn."

Hamish took it and peered at the label. "Double extra-large? I'm not sure if I'm flattered or insulted."

Zeke's blush flowered like a field of poppies. "The only other size I've got is extra-small and I *know* that won't work. I'm sorry."

"Hey." He stood, and *he* didn't have to take a step to reach Zeke and drop a kiss on his forehead. "This is bonzer. Especially if the only other option is skin or smelling like Sheol." He ripped open the package, pulled the shirt over his head, and smoothed it over his chest. The Supernatural Selection logo was blazoned on it in lurid red—and the hem hit the top of his thighs. "Not sure the micro-mini is a good look on me. Might get picked up for indecency just dashing from the door to the car."

"I've got another pair of sleep pants, if you'd like to borrow them. They'll be too short, of course—"

"And probably too small around the middle."

Zeke finally grinned. "They've got a drawstring. They're adjustable."

"Bring 'em on, then."

* * *

When they got to street level, the car was waiting at the curb, just as Niall had promised. Hamish held the door for Zeke to slide in, and once he joined him, he didn't waste any time in taking Zeke in his arms.

As the car started to move, Zeke sighed, snuggling in closer. "I still can't believe you came after me."

"Hey. After all the work you put into finding me the perfect mate, I couldn't very well let a little thing like a hellmouth get in my way."

Zeke drew back, his eyes wide and dark behind his glasses. "P-p-perfect? Mate? Me?"

"What, you don't think so?" Hamish's belly did a slow roll. "Are you saying you don't want—"

"No! I mean yes. I mean—" Zeke huffed an exasperated breath. "I get so confused about how to answer those double negatives. Yes, of course I want you. I thought that was *obvious*. But I don't know how that will fly with Supernatural Selection."

"Hey. Magistra what's-her-name herself okayed you to be my date to the wedding."

"I believe her words were 'escort' you. I'm an employee." His brow wrinkled. "At least I *think* I'm still an employee. But even if that's changed, I don't think she intended her orders to benefit *me*." One shoulder lifted in a shrug. "It's not exactly the Supernatural Selection brand to match their counselors with high-profile clients. That's a *different* business model altogether."

Hamish chuckled. "Maybe. But it doesn't change the fact that you did exactly what Magistra what's-her-name—"

"Lenore."

"Yeah, I know. But she doesn't deserve recognition yet. I'm reserving judgment until I see her do the right thing by you. Like give you a decent place to live. Seriously, what is with that lousy roach motel?"

Zeke drew back and glared at Hamish. "There aren't any roaches," he said indignantly. "Or bedbugs either."

"Yeah? What about room to breathe?" The car pulled in to Mal and Bryce's driveway. "And stowing the bloody AI in a broom cupboard somewhere away from you?"

"The accommodations are way better than the ones in Sheol. Besides, I knew the parameters of the job when I took it, including the AI monitor requirement."

"I don't care." Hamish climbed out of the car and held out his hand for Zeke. "That tosser is borderline abusive. What did it say when we got back from Sheol? More crap about you and me?"

Zeke smiled wryly as he took Hamish's hand and stood. "Some. But more outrage and astonishment that I dared show my face in the Upper World after . . ." Zeke's eyebrows drew together. "Wait a minute. How did the AI know I'd been to Sheol? It wasn't there when Melchom showed up, and Melchom wouldn't have given it the time of day. He hates the thing."

"Then what—"

The door burst open and David rushed out. "Oh thank goodness! You found him!" He flung himself at them, hugging first Hamish and then Zeke. When he let go, he blinked, his gaze flicking to their rather unconventional outfits. But he shook his head and tugged on Hamish's arm. "You both need to come inside. Matt says—"

"Who's Matt?" The name was vaguely familiar, and Hamish dimly recalled some kind of fuss as he was taking the express elevator to Sheol. There'd been an unfamiliar bloke with a camera . . . *Got it.* "He's the photographer who's working with Niall, right?"

"Yes." David herded them toward the house. "Doing surveillance, and he's found out something—"

A familiar pillar of light rose out of the ground between them and the door—blazing gold, then red, then—

"I've never seen it go *black* before," Zeke murmured.

David's mouth sagged open. "What is *that*?"

Hamish groaned. "It's the bloody AI stool pigeon. And it's not supposed to be here since it *wasn't invited*."

"The homeowners' association is going to have a *fit!*" David said. "We're not allowed to have outdoor lighting that bright."

"The supe council is going to have an even bigger fit. Secrecy Pact violation, anyone?" Hamish grabbed Zeke's hand. "Let's at least take this around back before the neighbors all come out to see who's staging illegal fireworks."

Hamish hustled Zeke down the grassy path next to the garage, David trotting to keep up, their shadows stretching out ahead of them like misshapen giants. *Bloody AI.*

When they got to the patio, they found all three of the Kendrick brothers—Mal, Gareth, and Alun—speaking urgently to Niall, Bryce, and the unfamiliar bloke who must be Matt. Quentin Bertrand-Harrington stood with them, a massive binder in his arms, while his husband loomed behind him, slurping from a giant mug, a doughnut in his other hand. Alun and Mal both had enormous swords strapped to their backs, and Mal still had his paintball tagger attached to his belt.

Niall looked up, shading his eyes against the AI's glare, his expression flickering between relief and shock and something that looked an awful lot like righteous indignation. *Where the hell did that come from?* Hamish could have sworn Niall had never had a righteously indignant thought in his life.

Niall broke away from the Kendricks and strode toward Hamish. "Hamish, get Zeke inside. Now."

Zeke clutched Hamish's hand tighter. "Did the overlords follow us? Melchom?"

"No. It's—"

The AI surged forward, caroming into Zeke and sending him flying through the air. Zeke's sharp cry cut off when he landed in a heap halfway across the lawn.

"Zeke!" Hamish lunged after him, only to be blocked by the AI, swirling gold and turquoise. "Get the *fuck* out of my way, you sorry excuse for a tiki torch." Hamish tried to dodge around it, but it matched his movements, and Hamish's pulse beat as savagely as any of his drum solos. *If only it had a neck I could wrap my hands around.*

"Don't worry, Hamish." David scurried across the patio. "I'll take care of him."

The AI lunged toward David, and Alun Kendrick's battle roar split the air, followed by the *zhing* of an unsheathing sword. But as he charged, a paintball flew past him and splatted against the AI's pillar. And another. And more, in rapid fire until Hamish lost count.

The pillar of light fritzed like a shorted-out fluorescent, then blinked off to reveal a tall man with long, golden hair and the profile of a classical Greek statue. He was wearing a toga, to add to the effect, although Hamish had never seen a statue wearing that look of petulant outrage.

"Ow!" He glanced down at himself, his expression morphing to horror. "You—you *materialized* me! How could you? I'll be corrupted!"

"Since those paintballs only affect creatures whose nature or intent is evil," Mal said, holstering his tagger, "I think that ship has already sailed." He glanced at Bryce. "Fighting evil is kind of our brand, eh, love? Guess we can't just turn it off for our bachelor party."

"Should we tell him that toga parties aren't really a thing anymore?" Ted murmured around a bite of doughnut.

Hamish was tempted to test the hands-around-the-bastard's-throat scenario, but when he saw David's worried face as he bent over Zeke, he tabled that thought—for the moment.

He leaped across the patio, only to have the AI block his path. "Stop!"

"Bugger you," Hamish growled, and shoved the blighter on his arse.

"You can't do that!" he wailed from the ground. "I'm an angel!"

"What you are is a bloody pain in my arse. And what *I* am is fed the fuck up with your shite, so stay out of my way."

"I won't! You can't—"

"Allow me," Mal said, and planted his boot in the middle of the AI's chest.

Hamish shot Mal a grateful smile, then hurried to Zeke's side and dropped to his knees. Alun gripped David's shoulder while David pressed both of his hands to Zeke's chest. David's eyes were closed and his face was pale. Alun looked as grim as Hamish had ever seen him—and that was saying something.

"Is he okay?" Hamish murmured.

Bryce knelt next to Hamish. "He will be."

Hamish fisted his hands on his thighs, barely resisting the urge to punch something, kick something. Sadly, even though Mal had pulled the AI to his feet, the arsehole was too far away to pummel. "How do you know? He's so still."

"Because I survived something very similar." He looked up at Alun. "This looks like the same type of magical electrocution that Rodric Luchullain used on me."

Alun nodded curtly, but didn't take his attention—or his hand—off his husband.

"But—"

Zeke took a gasping breath and opened his eyes. David sagged in Alun's grip, but kept his hands pressed to Zeke's chest.

"Zeke?" David's voice was thready, and Alun's expression grew darker, which Hamish would have sworn was impossible. "Pardon me for touching you without permission, but you needed immediate care. May I—"

"Please," Zeke croaked. "But only if it doesn't hurt you."

David gave him a wavery smile. "Not anymore."

Zeke's hand flopped in the grass, so Hamish took it gently and pressed a kiss to its palm. "Don't scare me like that. After I went to all the trouble to pull an Orpheus for you, it would be too cliché for you to pull a Eurydice."

Zeke chuckled weakly. "That would be terrible plotting, wouldn't it?"

"Damn straight."

David sighed and sat back, leaning against Alun's legs. "There. How do you feel?"

"I . . ." Zeke blinked, and Hamish realized his glasses were missing.

"Here." The unfamiliar bloke passed Zeke's folded specs to Hamish. "These flew off when he, um, went airborne."

"Thanks, mate. Matt, isn't it?"

His eyebrows shot up and he blinked rapidly. "That's right. We haven't actually met yet, but there's something you need—"

"Can you give me a mo? We'll talk later, I promise. Soon as he's back on his pins." Hamish turned away and pressed the glasses into Zeke's palm, but when he had trouble aiming them at his face, Hamish guided his hands until the glasses were settled on his nose. "How *do* you feel?"

"I feel . . . pretty great, actually." Zeke pushed himself up on one elbow, so Hamish wrapped an arm across his shoulders and helped him sit. "Not that I don't enjoy cuddling, but I'd like to stand up now, please."

Hamish grinned, relief flooding him at the edge of acerbity in Zeke's voice. He leaped to his feet and extended a hand. "Allow me."

But as soon as Zeke stood, Hamish wrapped him in a tight embrace. "I don't know what I'd do if you—"

"Shhh." Zeke's voice was muffled against Hamish's chest. "I'm fine." He lifted his face, pressing a kiss to Hamish's jaw. "Thanks to you."

"Thanks to David, you mean."

Zeke's blotches appeared. "Of course. I didn't intend to discount David's efforts—"

David laughed. "Don't worry about it. I know what you mean." He glanced up at Alun. "Having a reason to recover always makes healing go faster."

Zeke still looked adorably flustered. "Yes, but I didn't want to appear *ungrateful*." He gazed around at the rest of the group. "To any of you. I know all of you . . ." A wrinkle appeared between his eyebrows. "Hamish," he murmured. "Who's the guy in the mini-toga? I don't remember meeting him before."

"*That*," Hamish growled, "is your AI without his bloody light shield."

Zeke's jaw dropped. "But . . . but . . . how?"

"Seems like the blighter wasn't as benevolent as he wanted us to believe. Mal hit him with his anti-evil tagger and—" Hamish gestured to the AI. "Bob's your uncle. Instant angel."

"I don't have an uncle," Zeke murmured. He shot a glance at Hamish.

"And that's no angel," Gareth said. "That's the incompetent temp roadie from the concert. The one who nearly dropped an amp on Josh's head."

Chapter Nineteen

"My *name* is Athaniel."

"Angel of incompetence," Hamish muttered. Zeke tried to smother his laugh, but from the amused glance Hamish shot him, he hadn't fully succeeded.

"I am *not* incompetent. My job, my *calling*, is to protect the Lower World and its human denizens from the rise of evil and abominations." Athaniel's voice dripped revulsion on the last word, and something broke loose inside Zeke's chest.

"'Abominations'?" Zeke stepped away from Hamish, half-afraid the heat behind his eyes, building in his chest, would boil over and scald everyone nearby. "Like me?"

Athaniel's gaze lingered on Quentin before flicking to Ted, then Hamish, then returning to Zeke. "This plane must be kept pure and safe for humans. Any other . . . incursions are against the true order of things."

Bryce stepped forward to stand next to Zeke. "Bullshit."

Athaniel drew himself up. "I do not bulls— do that. I'm an angel!"

"Bugger," Hamish muttered, dragging a hand through his hair, "I am so tired of that excuse."

Athaniel crossed his arms over his perfect chest and turned away. "I don't wish to speak to you any longer."

Hamish grinned. "I'm good with that. I'd be even better if you'd bugger off."

Athaniel didn't deign to answer. He just stuck his nose in the air, his mouth turned down in a highly unattractive pout.

Okay, now I believe he's the AI. Zeke had been treated to precisely that kind of sulk on a daily basis, although admittedly with more lighting effects.

Niall studied Athaniel speculatively, then shrugged. "Apparently our uninvited guest is refusing to leave."

"Hadn't you heard?" Ted said. "He's an angel."

"So?"

Ted turned wide, innocent eyes on Niall. "Sorry. I thought that excuse covered everything, from poor manners to attempted murder."

"I didn't!" Athaniel cast a contemptuous glare at Zeke. "Demons can't be *murdered.* Only exterminated. And as for the incident at the concert—"

"So you admit it? You attacked Josh deliberately." Gareth's curls fairly writhed around his head. *Scary.* Zeke drew closer to Hamish.

"Of course." Athaniel's noble brow bunched in confusion. "Don't you see? I had to *prove* how disastrous it is to have demons at large in the world. None of you were paying the least attention to the threat."

"Seems like the only threat was from you," Gareth said, his voice vibrating with a power that raised the hair on Zeke's neck.

Wait a minute. Horror knotted Zeke's belly. "You mean you nearly killed Josh just to make a point? Because I was there?"

"Naturally. I'm an angel. It was my *duty.*" Athaniel shrugged. "And no humans were ever in danger. Only a shifter, and a werewolf at that. They hardly matter."

Hamish growled. "Watch yourself, arsehole, or I'll show you how much we *matter* by ripping your fucking throat out."

Athaniel drew himself up, a look of outrage on his perfect features. "You *can't.* I'm an *angel.*"

"You keep saying that like it's an excuse. In case you haven't gotten the memo, labels aren't worth shite. What matters is how you behave. And you?" Hamish flipped him off. "Behave like a motherfucking. Entitled. *Arsehole*."

Athaniel lunged, but Mal's grip on his arm jerked him back, and he flailed for balance. Zeke felt Hamish tensing as if to spring, so he wrapped his arms around Hamish's waist. Part of him was thrilled by Hamish's defense, but another part was terrified for his safety. *If he goes, I go with him.*

"Enough!" Niall planted himself between Hamish and Athaniel. "Both of you need to stand down."

"He started it," Athaniel said, jerking the hem of his toga down. *Thank Lucifer for that. I have no desire to discover what angels wear under their raiment.*

"Nah." Hamish held Zeke tight against his side. "I'm pretty sure you started it. The way you've treated Zeke—"

"I said, *enough*." Niall divided his glare between Hamish and Athaniel, as if daring them to make another move. They didn't, although Hamish muttered something under his breath. "As I was trying to say before we were joined by our visitor from on high—"

"If he's from on high," Ted said in an audible whisper, "why'd he rise up from underground?" When Niall glared at him too, Ted grinned unrepentantly. "I saw him through the kitchen window when I was grabbing a doughnut, and it made me wonder. I mean, if he didn't take a shortcut through Sheol, how'd he get here anyway? The sewers?"

"A point we'll consider later," Niall muttered, but turned back to the group. "Alun, I need you to put on your Queen's Champion hat, because the investigation that's been kicking my arse lately is the Secrecy Pact violation."

Ted straightened. "You mean the one from November? The one that implicated Matt and me?"

Hamish glanced between Ted and Niall. "Did I miss something?"

Quentin tucked his hand in Ted's arm. "Soon after Ted and I met, he was accused of leaking information about the supe community to the press."

"And the press bought it?" Hamish scoffed.

Ted's ruddy cheeks turned even redder above his beard. "I'd sort of done it before."

"You did?"

"I, um, sort of phoned in Sasquatch sighting tips to Matt and lumbered around the woods in partial shift."

David goggled. "That was *you*? No wonder Alun had a fit when I brought those tabloids into the office."

Matt rubbed the back of his head. "That wasn't the only scam I fell for. At least I don't think so. I thought there was something involving vampires at Mount Hood, but I must have dreamed it, since I can't find anything in my files."

Bryce cleared his throat. "Yes, well. Memories can be confusing. However, everything, ah, worked out in the end. It's all good."

Athaniel whirled around. "It is *not* all good! You—"

"Hey!" Hamish said. "I thought you weren't going to speak to us anymore."

"Not everyone." Athaniel gave Hamish the angel version of the stink-eye. "Just you." He nodded at Ted. "And him."

"Lucky me." Ted popped the last bit of doughnut into his mouth.

"And them." Athaniel gestured broadly.

"That seems like everybody," Zeke said. "Maybe you really should leave."

"Silence, demon!" Athaniel roared. "You have no right to speak to me!" He lunged for Zeke, but suddenly Mal was between them—*and wow, he can draw that sword fast.*

"That's enough out of you. This is my house. My yard. And you're not welcome."

Athaniel drew himself up, his face a mask of outrage. "I'm an *ang*—"

"And I'm a fae who doesn't give a rat's arse about rank. So you can take your fat angelic head and—"

"Danu's tits, Mal." Niall gripped Mal's shoulder. "You're supposed to be part of the solution, not the problem. Could you stand down? Please?"

"He started it," Mal muttered, earning him an eye roll from Bryce and a snicker from Ted.

"Let's get through the rest of my announcement without further interruptions, shall we?" Niall released his hold. "You can smite him later."

"Fine. But smiting is definitely on the table if he doesn't take himself off then."

"To be fair," Bryce said, "I'm not sure he can. You hit him with three of those bespelled paintballs. They won't wear off for a while yet, so he can't just leave the way he arrived."

"Then he can take a bloody Uber. I don't want him in our house."

"Mal." Niall's tone held exasperation.

"Fine." Mal stalked over to stand next to Bryce, but he didn't sheath his sword.

"Now, as I was saying . . ." Niall glanced around. *Probably waiting for somebody else to interrupt him.* "This case has been Quest Investigations' top priority. We had not only leaks to the press, but also blackmail attempts. We've been monitoring the man who had been in contact with the blackmailer—"

"Larry," Quentin muttered, his tone laced with fury.

"But there had been no further contact," Niall continued. "Until now."

Mal's chin jerked up. "You got a break in the case? Why didn't you tell me?"

Niall tipped his head in Bryce's direction. "Because I didn't want your fiancé to turn me into a newt for pulling you away from your wedding."

"So what was the break?" Mal asked.

"The blackmailer placed another call to Larry, directing him to a location where the students from the shifter primary school were going to be practicing safe shifting techniques."

"The kids. He did that last autumn too," Ted murmured. "Why does he always target the kids?"

Niall spread his hands out, palms up, as if to say *It's obvious.* "Because he knows that's what will motivate the council to action the quickest."

"Did . . ." Zeke swallowed. "Did Larry take the job?"

"No. We intercepted it, of course. But we traced the call." Niall's gaze caught Zeke's. "It originated from a landline in Portland. From the apartment above Supernatural Selection."

All the blood drained from Zeke's head until he wobbled, sick and dizzy, as everybody turned to look at him. *That's how Niall got the number.* "But I didn't. I swear I—"

"There! You see!" Athaniel threw his arms out in an overly dramatic gesture that would definitely have been a fuchsia starburst if he'd still been encased in his pillar. "Demons can't be trusted. He'll jeopardize all your supe enclaves. He belongs in Sheol!"

"'Your' supe enclaves?" Hamish said. "Last I checked, arsehole, you're a supe too."

"I'm not a supe! I'm an—"

"Yeah, yeah." Hamish leaned down and murmured into Zeke's ear, "Can you believe this bugger? He's worse than Euterpe."

Zeke clutched Hamish's arm. "I didn't make that call, Hamish. I wouldn't. You know I wouldn't."

"Nobody will believe *you*," Athaniel sneered. "You're a demon. Demons claim they don't lie, but everybody knows that's a lot of bullsh— nonsense."

"We don't!" Zeke's gaze darted around the circle of Hamish's friends—who he'd hoped would be his friends too. "We negotiate, and yes, we might try to arrange the terms to our benefit, but who doesn't? And each clause is *always* laid out precisely or the entire contract could be struck down in arbitration."

"You see?" Athaniel crowed. "He admits it! He obviously phoned his contact the instant he returned from that ridiculous concert. Arrest him!"

An angel's word versus a demon's. The conclusion was foregone. Sweat popped out on Zeke's forehead—unheard of for a demon—as he waited for someone to slap the magic-inhibiting cuffs on him.

Nobody moved.

Athaniel stamped his foot. "Are you all deaf as well as stupid? Apprehend this miscreant at once and send him back to the depths of Sheol where he belongs!"

"Tell me, Zeke," Niall drawled. "Where were you at about one, night before last?"

Night before last . . . Zeke glanced at Hamish, heat rising up his throat. *Will Hamish be implicated if I admit the whole story?* "I . . . um . . ." He lifted his chin. "It wasn't Hamish's fault. When I set up the date with Euterpe, I didn't know—"

"Hold on, mate. You don't need to protect *my* reputation." Hamish took his hand and kissed his palm. "And I'm pretty sure everyone here knows what we got up to after the show." He faced Niall, his jaw tight. "He was with me. At my hotel. Why?"

"Because," Niall said with a sly smile, "that's when the call was placed."

Zeke sucked in a breath, clutching Hamish's hand. "If the call came in while I wasn't there, then the only person who could have made it"—he swiveled to face Athaniel—"was you."

Rrriiip. With a crack and a whoosh, a pair of massive black wings divided the group on the patio.

Quentin, his shirt and jacket shredding as his wings mantled, stalked toward Athaniel. "*You.* You're the one who implicated Ted. Who nearly got him tagged. Who nearly got him *killed.*"

Athaniel backed away. "Stay away, incubus. I'm an *angel.*"

"What you are," Quentin growled, "is dead meat."

"Q-Bert." Ted's voice held a note of rebuke. "You promised. No wings in public."

Quentin glanced at Ted, chagrin replacing the fury that twisted his face. "Sorry, darling. Instinct." He furled his wings but didn't retract them completely.

Ted beamed at him. "It's still totally hot though."

Quentin smiled tightly and took Ted's hand before he faced Athaniel again. "Explain yourself. And if you trot out the angel excuse again, I will *not* be responsible for my actions."

Athaniel's gaze bounced wildly around the circle of unsympathetic faces. "It was your own fault, yours and"—he jerked his chin at Ted—"his. I never expected you to *sign* those agreements. They were blood contracts." His mouth pinched in revulsion. "Any sane person would read them before pricking their finger."

"So you were counting on us to raise an uproar and demand Zeke's dismissal."

"That's what any reasonable person would have done. But since you clearly weren't reasonable, I had to take . . . other steps."

"Wait a minute." Zeke let go of Hamish and dodged around Quentin's half-extended wing to stand at his side. "*You* subverted the spell? *You're* the reason the names were switched?"

Athaniel barely glanced at Zeke, focusing instead on Niall. "I had to do *something*," he said, his tone calm and annoyingly matter-of-fact. "A demon was at large in the Lower World. It was a disaster of apocalyptic proportions and everyone was acting as if it was perfectly normal." He made a moue of disgust. "But even *that* didn't work. I had to take . . . other steps."

"Other steps." Heat built behind Zeke's eyes, and he had no doubt they were blazing red by now. "So when I tried to repair the contracts with the blood quill, *you* wiped the corrections?"

"Oh that." He flicked his fingers. "That wasn't me. For some incomprehensible reason, that pestilential matchmaking spell decided the bear shifter and the ... the ..." His chest heaved, and his lips pinched together as if he were trying to keep himself from vomiting. "The *incubus* were a perfect match. But *you* had resorted to blood magic. Blood magic! A demon! And nobody paid the least attention!"

Zeke's breath sawed in and out through his nose until he could calm himself enough to speak again. "Let me guess. *You* lodged the complaint with Supernatural Selection on behalf of the vampire council and the beaver clan, which caused the spells to be taken offline."

Athaniel sniffed. "The vampires, yes. The beavers handled it on their own after I emailed them with the option."

"Did you jigger the website so Hamish could register, even though it was supposed to be shut down?"

"Of course. He's in love with someone unattainable. You were bound to fail, and then we could put this whole debacle behind us." Athaniel's expression—self-righteous innocence overlaid with mild irritation—sent Zeke's anger into the danger zone.

"So you jeopardized the happiness of at least six, no, *seven* people, threatened innocent children, and blackmailed the *supe council* just to sabotage the work-release program? To take me down?"

Athaniel shrugged. "The sacrifice of a few is acceptable collateral damage for restoring the true world order."

"No, it's not," Zeke said hotly. "In fact, that's the kind of thinking I'd expect from a demon."

"Or someone wearing a MAGA hat," David murmured.

"You told Melchom I was at the bachelor party, didn't you? *That's* how you knew I'd been sent back to Sheol. You *set me up!*" Zeke clenched his fists, and he took a step toward Athaniel, whose eyes widened in alarm. "You nearly cost Hamish his soul! For that," he growled, "you're going to pay."

Before Zeke could engage his superspeed and do something stupid—like attack an angel in front of witnesses when Hamish wanted the satisfaction of decking the arsehole first—Hamish leaped in front of him and took him by the shoulders.

"Hold on, mate. You don't want to do that."

"Yes, I do," Zeke said through clenched teeth. "He could have destroyed you, for no reason other than his own selfish desires."

"I am not selfish! I'm an ang—"

"Shut up!" everyone else roared at once.

Zeke gazed up at Hamish. "He can't be allowed to get away with it. He caused so much misery. He's a danger to more people—"

"I never endangered *people*. Only . . . only . . ." Athaniel's voice faded under the chorus of growls that rose from the group.

"I've had enough of this motherfucker," Hamish said, prompting a gasp from Athaniel. "Can't we just do him here? Now? Kill him, beat him senseless, throw him in Bryce's swamp —"

"Wetlands," Bryce muttered.

"—spill hot coffee on his damn toga, for crying out loud. Something!"

"No." Niall stepped forward. "But we can arrest him. He has to appear before the council and answer for his crimes."

"Crimes," Athaniel scoffed. "I can't commit crimes. I'm an *angel*."

"So you've said." Niall's tone was drier than the outback. "However, I have it on better authority"—he tapped his temple —"that you lost the right to use that epithet the first time you tried to sabotage Zeke."

Athaniel sniffed, obviously unimpressed. "You may be a prince of Faerie, but you're hardly an authority on *me*, whatever you think."

"Oh. it's not me. It's the *ethera*. The spirits who bridge the realms. They couldn't give a shit about labels or appearances, but they're infallible when it comes to a person's true essence. And according to them, your essence is blacker than Satan's anus."

Athaniel's jaw dropped. "You *dare* to use such language about *me*? Do you know what I could do to you?"

Mal and Alun flanked Niall, both of them with swords drawn, and Gareth took his place at Niall's side.

"Try anything—" Alun narrowed his eyes as if judging the distance between his blade and Athaniel's neck "—and harsh language will be the least of your worries."

Zeke rubbed his eyes under his glasses, then repositioned them on his nose and peered at Athaniel. "Um, Hamish? Am I seeing things or is that a red glimmer rising around him?"

Sure enough, a faint glow was growing around Athaniel. "Shite. The potion's wearing off. Mal, hit him again!"

"I can't. I'm out of ammo. But we'll take him now. Alun, the cuffs." Mal leaped forward, but when he tried to grab Athaniel, his hand got no nearer than the light pillar, and he let out a harsh grunt. "Gods damn it to all the hells, haven't I had enough hand injuries for a lifetime?"

"If you can't take the shields down again, it's too late," Zeke moaned. "Once they're engaged, nobody can touch him."

Athaniel started to sink through the patio's concrete pavers, the golden light that flared around him not bright enough to obscure the triumphant smile splitting his face.

I'd like to split his face—with my fist. "There's got to be something we can do." Hamish's arm tightened around Zeke. "I'm not letting him hurt Zeke again."

Alun let his sword point drop. "The council's already reviewing Sheol policies in special session, so I'll petition them to add this to the docket. There's no precedent for extradition procedures with the angelic host, but with Niall's evidence and all our testimony, I think we can make a strong case."

"Count on it," Quentin said. "I'll represent the prosecution at the tribunal." His wings rustled on his back until Ted stroked them into stillness. "Trust me. He has no chance."

Zeke stood on his toes to peer around the Kendrick brothers. "Guys? I think he's stuck."

Chapter Twenty

Inside a cylinder of slowly fading silver, Athaniel was struggling unsuccessfully to free himself.

Then, a bloke taller and broader than Ted Farnsworth, and with a wingspan to rival Quentin Bertrand-Harrington's, strolled around the corner of the house. His hair leaped about his head like flames—in fact, as Hamish looked closer, it seemed his hair *was* flames.

But the most notable thing about him, other than those minor details and the fact that his face was more beautiful than Gareth's, was that he was wearing a Hunter's Moon T-shirt with his Nike training pants.

Zeke clutched Hamish's arm. "That's Paimon."

"The bloke you told me about at the restaurant? Your old boss's boss?"

"Yes. My case must have been escalated." Zeke gulped, his Satan's apple sliding under his blotchy skin. "I'm doomed."

"Not if I can help it," Hamish muttered.

"Relax, Zeke," Niall said. "I invited him."

"You invited a C-suite demon to your brother-in-law's *home*?"

"Technically, he's not my brother-in-law yet." Niall glanced around at the solar-powered lights ringing the patio. "And this is technically the yard, not the house.

"Then I hope you all have everything you want," Zeke said, "because any demon who's *that* senior can detect your deepest desires in less time than it takes you to *think* about them."

Niall glanced at Gareth with a wry smile. "If he's trolling for souls here, he'll be out of luck, boyo. Other than a little extra office help, all of us have everything we could ever wish for, and I wouldn't call needing someone to file and answer phones a deep desire, precisely."

Paimon stopped next to Athaniel, who was still shin-deep in Mal and Bryce's patio. "I interrupted my workout for this, so let's make it quick, shall we?" With a flick of his fingers, Athaniel popped out of the ground like a cork, and his light show winked out.

"Ow!"

"Be still. I'll deal with you in a moment."

"You have no jurisdiction over me! I'm an angel!"

Paimon shook his head. "They told me you were an unsatisfactory worker, but they didn't tell me you were criminally stupid. What do you imagine the difference is between the infernal and angelic hosts?"

"It's obvious! We're good and you're evil."

Zeke cleared his throat. "Pardon me, sire, but I understood it was a sliding scale between concern for self and concern for others."

"Indeed." Paimon gave Zeke a look of approval. "I'm pleased that someone pays attention at their Host Relations refreshers. And do you know who I am?"

"Of course, sire," Zeke whispered. "According to the *Ars Goetia* of the Lesser Key of Solomon, you're a king. The past and future is known to you. You can remain underwater indefinitely. Reanimate the dead for a certain time, create visions—"

"Yes, yes. But those are my *powers*. I'm referring to my *responsibilities*."

"You, um, acquire and dismiss minions. You govern two hundred legions, half in the infernal host, and half— Oh!" Zeke blinked rapidly. "Half in the angelic. You mean . . ."

"Yes. This sorry excuse for a minion is in one of my departments. Which, I might add, will be getting a thorough audit in the very near future. And this minion is *definitely* about to be dismissed. With extreme prejudice. Now—"

"Just a minute." Alun sheathed his sword, but his voice held a note of menace. "Do you intend to take him away?"

"Yes. You can't possibly want him here, making more people miserable?"

"Of course not. Release him into my custody. We intend for him to appear before the supe council to answer some very serious charges. They'll want to be assured of his punishment."

Paimon bared his teeth. "I think they'll be satisfied with my solution."

"Nevertheless, I must insist." Alun crossed his arms, doing a spot-on impression of an immovable object.

"Oh, very well. Have your people call my people, and we'll discuss the particulars later. Any other questions?" Paimon's gaze drifted to each of them in turn until he got to Hamish, then he grinned that shark's-tooth smile again. "I commend you on your performance in Sheol. The video has already gone viral. It's playing nonstop on every crystal ball in Elysium."

"Yeah?" Hamish chuckled. "By the way, nice T-shirt."

Paimon glanced down at his chest and smoothed his shirt with one clawed hand. "Yes, isn't it?"

"But I thought demons weren't into music."

"'Demon,'" Paimon said with a huge sigh. "It's such a loaded word and caters to such a rigid mindset." He aimed an eyebrow raise at Athaniel. "I prefer to think of us all as 'the Host.' In any case, it's Sheol itself that can't tolerate music, although I think some of Philip Glass's compositions wouldn't strain its dimensional vibrations much. In any case, I'm a dual citizen of Sheol and Elysium, and"—he grinned in that alarming display of pointed teeth—"I'm a fan. It's delightful to meet some of you in person."

Hamish squinted at him, from his fiery hair to his—shite—cloven hooves. "If you don't mind my saying, you don't look much like an angel."

Paimon snorted, smoke curling out his nostrils. "You've never seen Azrael before his morning coffee." He nudged Athaniel with one hoof. "Don't let this idiot's prejudices influence you. The Host comes in all shapes and sizes. And sometimes—" he studied Zeke, his head tilted to one side "—it's difficult to tell the difference in their relative roles even when you think you know the story."

"Yeah," Hamish murmured, then kissed the top of Zeke's head. "Ain't that the truth."

"So. I believe we're done here." Paimon gripped the back of Athaniel's neck. "Come, Ozul-y-Kalon. It's time to go."

"G-g-go? But . . ." Zeke glanced from Paimon to Hamish. "I thought—"

"Here now." Hamish pulled Zeke behind his back. "He's free. I struck that bargain myself."

"Mr. Mulherne, you may have liberated him from Sheol, but by the definition of the work-release program—which is still fully in force—a member of the Host who's demon-identified cannot reside in the Upper World without employment. Ozul-y —"

"Oi! It's Zeke, you—"

"Hamish," Zeke whispered fiercely, "you don't provoke kings. There are *consequences*."

"There are consequences to them tossing your name about like a hacky sack too."

Paimon sighed. "Very well. *Zeke* is presently unemployed."

Zeke seemed to shrink, his face going pale. "Unemployed?"

"Yes. Apparently your contract with Supernatural Selection has been terminated for policy violations. You've been"— Paimon glanced pointedly at Hamish's arm, currently occupying its rightful place across Zeke's shoulder— "fraternizing with the clients."

"Shite," Hamish muttered, but he kept his arm where it was.

"Someone told Magistra Lenore that Hamish and I were . . . you know?"

"She said it was included in this morning's report from your AI observer."

Hamish gave a disgusted snort. "Figures that arsehole would find another way to bollix things up. Frankly, I'm surprised he sat on that one for so long."

Zeke glanced up at him. "He probably thought siccing Melchom on me was a surer bet."

Paimon's hair flared higher, and from the expression on his face, another black mark had been added to Athaniel's book—and maybe to Melchom's as well. "If you believe there are extenuating circumstances, you're certainly welcome to petition the supe council and the Sheol administration, but that will take time. Until then, Zeke must return to his last place of residence. In other words, Sheol. It's the law."

When Zeke nodded and tried to step toward Paimon, Hamish tightened his hold. "If you think I'm letting him go back to that place, you're barmy. They *tortured* him. They . . ." Hamish's throat thickened with the memory of the chains on Zeke's wrists and ankles, the marks of abuse on his pale skin. "I won't let you take him."

"Indeed?" Paimon's eyes glowed gold. "What are you willing to offer in exchange?"

Zeke turned in Hamish's embrace and clutched his shirt. "Hamish. Don't. Nothing is worth your soul."

Hamish stroked Zeke's curls at the same time that he bared his teeth at Paimon. "I'm not offering *him* a fucking thing. Oi! Niall!"

Niall startled, shifting his glare from Athaniel to Hamish. "What now?"

"You're still whinging about office help. What about it?"

"What about what?" Niall's eyebrows rose until they disappeared behind his wavy bangs. "You mean—"

"I *mean*, Zeke's available. Think he'd be a fit for Quest Investigations?"

Niall barked a laugh. "Are you joking? He can handle *you*, so he's clearly got skills." He smiled at Zeke. "How about it? Do you think you could manage two very disorganized fae who'd both rather be in the field than doing paperwork, and one human with more enthusiasm than sense?"

"Hey!" Matt called. "I've got sense."

"You're working with us, mate." Mal grinned at Matt. "Enough said."

Zeke's gaze darted between Niall and Mal. "You can't— Do you really want me to work for you?"

"Absolutely." Niall left Gareth's side to stand in front of Zeke. "According to Magistra Lenore, you're the most efficient match counselor they've ever had. So much so that the other counselors were all assigned to other magical duties for the collective. In other words, even before the spell was shut down, you were the only one doing any work for Supernatural Selection."

Zeke shrugged. "Demon speed works on filing too." He hung his head. "But pristine filing systems don't offset the fact that I screwed up the contracts for my two highest profile couples."

"Actually," Quentin reminded him, "it was Athaniel who attempted to screw things up. You *fixed* them, sometimes at a not-insignificant personal cost." He curled an arm around Ted's back. "All four of us—Ted, me, Rusty, and Casimir—were certain we knew what we wanted. As it happens, our assumptions were completely wrong. And though you were unfailingly responsive to our demands, no matter how misguided, you nevertheless helped steer us onto the right path, to show us that what we *wanted* wasn't necessarily what we *needed*." He smiled kindly at Zeke. "If anyone ever needed a guardian angel, it was the four of us."

Athaniel sniffed. "As if I would ever—"

"I'm not talking about *you*." Quentin's wings unfurled again, causing Ted to growl. "You made it your business to try to destroy our happiness because you didn't think we *mattered*.

Zeke thinks *everyone* matters. He seems much more like an angel than you do."

"Told you so, Hamish," Niall murmured. "The *ethera* are never wrong."

"The *ethera* you say?" Paimon tapped his lip with one claw. "Interesting. This puts another spin on things. It would seem, Zeke, that by your actions, you've qualified for a transfer to the angelic host, just as this one"—Paimon tossed a dismissive glance at Athaniel—"has proven himself more suited to the infernal ranks."

Zeke goggled at Paimon. "A transfer? I didn't know that was possible."

"Usually it's not, since transfers require a one-for-one replacement. Luckily"—he shook Athaniel, who flopped like a rag doll—"we've got one."

"Um, does that mean I have to hang about inside a pillar of light?"

"Why would you need to do that?"

"That's what *he* always did. He claimed it was so he wouldn't be corrupted by the mortal realm."

Paimon glared at Athaniel. "Really? I'm going to have a serious conversation with whoever conducted your last performance review, because that's . . ." He sighed. "He obviously just didn't want anybody to touch him. Well, that and the light pillar's weaponry component."

"Naturally," Hamish murmured.

"Of course, you'll have to return to Sheol until the paperwork goes through, but then you can relocate to Elysium."

Zeke's belly dropped as if he'd taken the express elevator to Sheol. "Relocate? But . . . you heard them. I've got a job. Can't I stay here?"

Paimon blinked. "You *want* to stay here? As part of the angelic host, you've got other options, you know."

Zeke glanced up into Hamish's dear face, then around at the circle of people who he'd come to know in a very few days—*my friends*—and shook his head. "This is the only option I need."

"If you say so." Judging by Paimon's tone, he wasn't convinced, but Zeke had never felt more sure of anything in his life. "I'll be in touch with the council regarding the charges against this one." Athaniel winced in Paimon's grip, but apparently had surrendered to the inevitable. "Now, if you'll excuse us—"

"Hold on." Bryce strode across the patio to stand in front of Paimon. "I'd appreciate it if you didn't open a pit in the middle of my yard like the last time."

Paimon's eyebrows rose. "Someone opened a pit? Didn't they close it?" Bryce shook his head. "Honestly, the incompetence . . ." He sighed. "Don't worry. We'll take the FTA." He pulled out a cell phone, thumb already flying across the screen as he disappeared around the corner of the house, Athaniel stumbling along by his side.

"FTA?" Matt asked.

"Fae Transportation Association," Niall said. "I'll tell you about it later."

"Grand." Mal clapped his hands, then rubbed his palms together. "Now that's settled, I think we've all earned a beer or seven. Come on inside."

Everyone trooped into the house, but when Zeke would have followed, Hamish held him back. Once the French doors closed behind Bryce, Hamish enveloped Zeke in a hug and just held him.

Zeke was more than happy to be held—and to hold back.

"Fuck me dead," Hamish murmured into Zeke's hair, "I thought they'd *never* leave."

Zeke laughed shakily. "I was afraid they'd leave with one or more of us, so thank goodness for that."

"'Goodness'?" Hamish pulled back to grin down at Zeke. "What kind of a demon are you anyway? Or are you already embracing your job as the newest angel on the block?"

Despite the relief of knowing he was safe from Sheol, and despite Hamish so warm and solid against him, Zeke somehow felt adrift. "I . . . I don't know. I knew my place in Sheol, at least until my unexpected upgrade, and I knew my job at Supernatural Selection. Now I don't have either of those things. I'm not sure who I am."

Hamish stroked Zeke's cheek with the back of his long, clever fingers. "Gotta tell you, mate—that's pretty much how the rest of us feel all the time. We're just doing the best we can and hoping we don't bollix things up too badly."

"Really?"

"Really." He kissed Zeke softly, then rested his cheek on the top of Zeke's head. "So at the risk of serious bollixing . . . I know it's too soon, I know we've only been on a couple of dates and those didn't turn out so well." Hamish's chuckle vibrated in Zeke's bones. "But somebody told me recently that I'm a one-person guy."

Zeke leaned back, desperate to see the expression on Hamish's face. He didn't *sound* like he was joking, but he'd only wanted a wedding date at first. *Has he changed his mind? Does he want what I want?* "You are?"

He nodded, but for some reason wouldn't meet Zeke's eyes. "I'm pretty sure you're my one. I know I'm an annoying sod, and I can't keep still most of the time, and—"

"Hamish." Zeke cupped the side of Hamish's face, his scruff crisp and springy against Zeke's palm. "You went all the way to Sheol to rescue me."

"And I'd do it again, no hesitation." He peered at Zeke from under his brows. "Think of the street cred I'd gain. It's not everybody who picks up his date in hell." He grinned ruefully. "Although I'm just as glad that's off the table. The toll it took on you was totally unacceptable."

Zeke shook his head. "That was nothing. I told you, demons are tougher than we look."

"Ah, but you're not a demon anymore."

There went Zeke's stomach again. "Then what am I?"

"Mine."

Oh. Zeke's heart lifted in his chest—and his feet left the patio, so at least his anti-grav was still a part of him.

And Hamish. He's a part of me too. "I don't know about too soon, but I know I'm not good enough for you."

"Bullshite. You—"

Zeke put his fingers on Hamish's lips, easy to do since he was floating level with his face. "*But* nobody else is either. Certainly not in the Supernatural Selection database, and not in any realm I've visited either. You're the beat of my heart, Hamish, the fire in my blood, and call me an evil, selfish demon—"

"Angel," Hamish said, his smile curving behind Zeke's fingers.

"*Demon.* Because now that I've got you, I'm going to hold on to you forever."

Hamish caught Zeke's wrist and turned his head to place a kiss in its palm. "So what you're saying is that I'm your one?"

Zeke nodded. "The most perfect of perfect matches. And you can trust me on that." He threaded his fingers through Hamish's hair, drawing them together until their lips were a breath apart. "After all, I'm a professional."

Chapter
Twenty-One

Zeke clutched his flagon of mead, trying his best to remain unobtrusive at the edge of the ceilidh glade at the heart of Faerie. It wasn't hard to do—the sheer diversity of the fae who wandered across the mossy clearing or darted between the trees was enough to make a mere demon completely unremarkable.

Except I'm not technically a demon anymore. Thanks to the Realm Accords, I'm simply "of the Host" in terms of rights and privileges. That was hard to believe, still harder to get used to. But thanks to testimony from Hamish, Zeke, and—surprisingly enough—Paimon, the supe council had negotiated massive reforms in both Sheol and Elysium, instituting parity not only between them, but with all the other realms as well.

Zeke hugged himself as he skirted the tree line. It wasn't only treatment of the Host that had changed, but also of the souls confined in both Sheol and Elysium. The Accords stipulated that a review panel would evaluate every contract and adjust for reasonableness and time served. It was scheduled to begin any day, now that the druid conclave had converted the Sheol power grid to geothermal energy. Zeke couldn't quite imagine Sheol without the soul furnaces, but the supe council had the leverage to force the changes.

Leverage Hamish and Zeke had provided.

If I do nothing else with my life, at least I've done that.

Zeke smiled at a big-eyed, green-skinned fae no taller than his chest who was carrying a massive tray of flagons to the tables at one side of the glade. This part of Faerie was so different from the woods where they'd held the paintball war. If it weren't ringed by old—*really* old—growth trees, and if the sky visible through the leaves were star-studded black instead of star-studded violet, it could almost be any high-end wedding venue. *Although I suppose you can't get much higher-end than the company of both fae monarchs.*

The King and Queen were standing on a raised dais at one end of the oval clearing, ready to officiate at Mal and Bryce's long-delayed handfasting ceremony: tall, regal, beautiful as the day—and holding hands like lovestruck teenagers.

A giant hawthorn had spread its branches over the dais and halfway across the glade, white with blossoms, even though it was March and—according to David Evans-Kendrick, Zeke's source of information on All Things Everywhere—hawthorns usually didn't bloom until May.

But after the changes Zeke had undergone personally in the last weeks, a tree blooming out of season was nothing more than *meh, whatever*.

Even before the Accords had passed, his entire *life* had gotten a makeover. New job, new apartment, new clothes. And busy? During the day, he'd taken over setting up Quest Investigations' new Outer World offices in Portland, and none too soon, because their files were a *disaster*! Oddly enough, they'd taken over the offices formerly occupied by Supernatural Selection, since the witches' collective had decided to get out of the matchmaking business.

But he was *not* still living in that apartment, thank goodness. He'd moved into the flat above Alun Kendrick's psychology practice, and he actually took a bus to work! And stopped for coffee and scones. It was gloriously, ridiculously, abnormally *normal*.

The work was satisfying and interesting, his new bosses almost embarrassingly complimentary about his performance, and between that and making his new home a *home*, his days positively *flew* by.

And the nights . . .

Hunter's Moon had been on tour for the last month, so if there was a show, Niall whisked him through Faerie to stand in the wings, where he had a perfect view of Hamish in his element.

That thrill never got old.

Even more thrilling was what they did after the shows. Hamish always came back to Zeke's apartment with him, and Lucifer's balls, the *things* Zeke had learned about tongues and johnsons! He quivered with so much anticipation just thinking about what Hamish had promised for tonight that he had to set down his mead or risk spilling it all over his shirt.

When he straightened up, Casimir Moreau, a flute of sparkling water in his hand, was sauntering Zeke's way. In his exquisitely tailored tux, he was almost more beautiful than the fae. His clean-shaven cheeks were tinged with pink and his gray eyes lit up when he spotted Zeke.

"Good evening, Zeke. How lovely to see you." He gazed around, his smile displaying just a hint of fang. "Isn't this the most delightful gathering? I could almost imagine myself back on the set of some vast DeMille extravaganza." He glanced sidelong Zeke. "Or perhaps in Oz itself."

"Mr. Moreau—"

"Cas, please." He took a delicate sip of his water. "We're old friends, are we not?"

The telltale heat bloomed in Zeke's cheeks. "Yes. Well. Thank you for the wedding invitation."

"I trust you'll be attending? You and your lovely drummer."

"Of course. But the card says it's being held at the Weasel Pit. I thought Ted and Quentin were renaming their resort."

"Oh, they are. But I convinced them to wait until *after* our ceremony. They were happy to agree—well, perhaps Quentin wasn't precisely *happy*, but they were both so grateful for

Rusty's help finishing the construction on time and under budget, they were willing to make the concession." Cas placed a hand over his heart. "And consequently, I was privileged to see my council chief's face when he opened the invitation. It was everything I'd hoped it would be."

Zeke scanned the crowd. "Where *is* Rusty? He didn't get delayed in Sheol, did he?" After the Accords had passed, Paimon had hired Rusty to do a huge renovation to bring Sheol into compliance. He'd already finished half a dozen break rooms, each with the list of supe rights posted prominently between the vending machines and water coolers.

"He's over there." Cas gestured toward one side of the clearing, where Rusty's large figure towered over a group of lesser fae. "He's standing up with Bryce for the ceremony." Cas clucked his tongue. "Poor darling. He's terrified he's going to get the handfasting knots wrong." He cast Zeke a glance from under his lashes. "Despite getting *lots* of practice lately." He tossed off the rest of his water and handed the empty glass to a passing bauchan. "I'd better go soothe his nerves."

He strolled across the center of the glade, exchanging a few words with David. David grinned at whatever Cas said, then trotted over to join Zeke. Since Zeke had moved in above Alun's offices, he and David had become close friends.

"Hey!" David gave Zeke one of his usual enthusiastic hugs, then held him at arm's length to check out Zeke's outfit. "You look fantastic in those clothes. The laced jerkin and linen shirt?" He flashed two thumbs up. "Classic Faerie attire. I approve. Perfect choice for a handfasting."

Zeke raised an eyebrow. "I'd be more flattered if you weren't wearing almost the same thing."

David laughed. "What can I say? I love having a shopping buddy."

Zeke stroked the soft suede of his jerkin, his full shirt sleeves billowing in the playful breeze which, here in Faerie, seemed to come from everywhere and nowhere at once. "Shopping. I still can't get used to the fact that I'll be able to *do* that now."

"It's awesome, right? Nordstrom's having a sale next week. You'd look great in a bow tie, so we've totally got to get one for you."

"Mal and Niall don't require business attire for the office."

"That's because until they hired you, they didn't *have* an office. That's one of the reasons they were so frazzled. You've got your work cut out for you."

"I don't mind. I like to be busy."

"Well, if you have any trouble dealing with them—anything at all—you just call me. I've learned a *ton* about how to handle fae warriors in the last year."

"Here now." Hamish appeared next to Zeke, looping an arm around his waist. "He's not handling anybody but me."

Zeke snuggled closer. "You know I wouldn't. Not like *that*."

"I know." He tilted Zeke's chin up and pressed a soft kiss on his lips.

Zeke shivered at the touch, the public intimacy nothing he'd ever imagined for himself. "I was afraid you wouldn't get here in time."

"What? Gareth miss his brother's wedding? Not a chance. We just got held up at the studio a bit." He grinned. "Tiff had to go all jaguar on the engineer so we could escape."

The rest of Hunter's Moon were setting their instruments behind the dais. Zeke stared—it looked as if Hamish's drums were marching across the moss by themselves until he realized they were being carried by a crew of bauchan. He grinned. *Heh. Fae roadies.*

David smiled at Hamish. "Aren't you playing for the wedding?"

"We'll play for the dancing at the ceilidh afterward, but not for the ceremony itself. Gareth's going to sing." Hamish pointed to the smooth white stones that ringed the clearing, nearly invisible in the thick moss. "Make sure you stay out of the circle unless you want to dance involuntarily."

Zeke blinked up at him. "Involuntary dancing?"

"A bard's voice has that effect on people."

Zeke considered the stones, a bit wistfully. "I don't think I'd mind. I've never danced before."

"Oh, you *have* to dance here!" David bounced on his toes. "Once Hunter's Moon starts playing, everybody does."

Zeke glanced up at Hamish. "But you'll be playing, so I won't have anyone to dance with."

David waved Zeke's protest away as Alun joined his husband. "Oh, that won't matter. You don't need a partner. Most of the fae don't have one anyway."

"But I don't know how to dance."

"No worries." David's smile widened. "I'll teach you!"

"No!" Hamish and Alun bellowed together.

Zeke startled, glancing at David to see if he was hurt by the reaction, but he just looked resigned.

Harp music suddenly filled the air, and the crowd settled down—all except the dryads, who squealed like the younger fans at Hunter's Moon concerts. But they weren't squealing for Gareth—who had started to croon a lovely song in Welsh. They were focused on Bryce, who'd emerged from a flowered avenue on one side of the glade to face Mal, who was standing across from him.

Zeke dared a bewildered glance at David, who whispered out of the side of his mouth. "Bryce is like a rock star to dryads. He's the first druid they ever met."

Alun kissed David quickly. "Time for me to do my duty to my brother." He strode over to Mal as Rusty flanked Bryce. The four of them approached the dais and mounted a lichen-encrusted stair to stand before the Queen.

"Lord Maldwyn. Elder MacLeod," she said, "we greet you with joy. Do you come before us today to declare your commitment, one to the other?"

"We do," Mal and Bryce said together, smiling at one another in a way that made Zeke's heart stumble and his breath catch.

Hamish pulled him closer, and Zeke leaned against him, grateful for the reminder that he, too, had someone who looked at him as if no one else existed.

Mal and Bryce joined hands, Mal's right to Bryce's left, and as Gareth sang, Alun and Rusty twined gold and green cords around their hands in an intricate pattern. Sweat glinted on Rusty's broad forehead, and his jaw was clenched in concentration, but despite his worries, he must have done it right, because he grinned with relief and stepped back with Alun, leaving Mal and Bryce facing each other as the Queen stepped forward.

"Hand to hand," she said. "Heart to heart. Life to life."

"Hand to hand. Heart to heart. Life to life," the men repeated.

"So mote it be." She touched the knots, and the cords glowed brighter than the stars, wind rippling outward and tossing hawthorn blossoms through the air like snow. "In the presence of the One Tree, you are joined in a true mating, together until the last leaf falls."

Everyone cheered as Bryce caught Mal in a deep kiss, their bound hands caught between their chests.

Zeke held out his hand, catching a few white petals in his palm. Hamish chuckled, folding Zeke's fingers in with his own.

"Know what they say about blokes who capture the hawthorn at a fae handfasting?" Hamish's voice was low and intimate, the same tone he used when they were in bed together. It sent delicious tremors down Zeke's spine.

"No. What?"

"They'll be the next ones to tie the knot." He raised Zeke's fist to his mouth and pressed a kiss to his fingers, his eyes glinting with mischief. "What do you think about that?"

"I think," Zeke said, drawing out the words, "that you made that up this instant."

Hamish laughed, head thrown back and the lovely column of his throat on display. *Mmmm.* Zeke kissed that enticing Satan's apple, which made Hamish's laughter falter into a groan.

"You'd be right, love. But that doesn't mean it can't be true. What do you say?"

Zeke glanced around the glade—at Mal and Bryce, still locked in a kiss in front of the Queen. At Casimir, blotting the nervous perspiration off Rusty's forehead with a linen handkerchief as Rusty gazed down at him with a look of complete adoration. At Ted, who appeared to be wearing a leather straightjacket because Quentin's wings were wrapped tight around him, Quentin's tuxedo jacket in tatters on his back.

And for the first time in his very long life, Zeke dared to evaluate his own deepest desire, and—no surprise—found it bound up with the brave, beautiful, talented man standing next to him.

"Zeke?" Worry pleated Hamish's forehead. But Zeke smoothed the wrinkles away, then laid his hand against Hamish's dear, dear face.

"If I wanted to torment you, I'd say, 'You'll do.'"

Hamish grinned down at him. "And *do* you want to torment me?"

"Only a little bit. Because being with you, my kangaroo, my Orpheus, my love? There's nothing I desire more."

Romantic Mythmatched adventures don't end with Supernatural Selection. Next up: frat house werewolves? Join the fun in *Howling on Hold.*

About Howling on Hold

Sometimes it's harder to teach a **young** *dog new tricks.*

That's why werewolves embark on a Howling: a three-year rite of passage in which they're sent to a group residence to wrestle with their wolfy instincts and assimilate into the Wider World. But Tanner Araya's Howling is almost over, and he could be called back to his remote pack at any moment. His twenty-first birthday might be his last chance to act on his strongest instinct and finally kiss Chase Denney.

Chase is RA at the Howling residence affectionately dubbed "the Doghouse," and he takes his job seriously. So seriously that when he realized he was developing feelings for a resident, he forced himself to keep Tanner at a distance. But now that Tanner's twenty-one, he's not Chase's charge any longer. They could be friends or—if Chase is lucky—something more. At least until they both return to their home packs for good, as tradition demands.

It would take a miracle for them to get together—especially when the other Doghouse werewolves insist on "helping."

Warning: Many Frisbees are harmed in this story, forgiveness is not always easier than permission, and the five-second rule does not apply

Zeke's got a new job now, working with Mal, Niall, and Matt. Follow their adventures in the Quest Investigations mysteries, beginning with *Five Dead Herrings*.

ABOUT
FIVE DEAD HERRINGS

Something's definitely fishy about this case...

On my last stakeout for Quest Investigations, I nearly got clotheslined by a grove of angry dryads. I expected my bosses to reprimand me, but instead they handed me my first solo assignment. Me! Matt Steinitz, the only human on the Quest roster!

Okay, so the mission isn't exactly demanding. Obviously, the bosses wanted to give me something they think I can't screw up. I'm determined to show them what I can do, however, so I dive right in with no complaints.

At first glance, it looks as simple as baiting a hook: A selkie's almost-ex-husband is vandalizing his boat with unwanted deliveries of deceased sea life. All I have to do is document the scene, tell the ex to cease and desist, and present the bill for property damages. *Boom.* Mission accomplished, another Quest success, and as a bonus, I get to keep my job.

But then things get...complicated. Suspicious undercurrents muddy up my oh-so-easy case. Nothing is as clear as it should be. And the biggest complication? My inappropriate attraction to the client, who may not be as blameless as he claims.

Turns out those dead herrings aren't the only things that stink about this situation.

Dammit.

Five Dead Herrings is the first in the Quest Investigations M/M paranormal mystery series, a spinoff of E.J. Russell's Mythmatched paranormal rom-com story world. It contains no on-page sex or violence, and although there is a romantic subplot, it is not technically a romance.

a message from
ej

Dear Reader,

Thank you so much for reading about my adorkable Zeke and his high-energy perfect match, Hamish. I'm so happy you've taken this journey with me! I'd be immensely grateful if you'd take a moment to leave a review at the retailer and any other site you use for reviews. Believe me, reviews make an *enormous* difference to the health and well-being of books (and not incidentally, to their associated authors!).

If this is your first taste of my Mythmatched story world, you might want to travel back to the Fae Out of Water trilogy, where it all began. *Cutie and the Beast* is the first in that series, but Hamish and the Hunter's Moon band hit the stage first in book three, *Bad Boy's Bard*, Gareth and Niall's story.

Pop on over to my website, https://ejrussell.com, for all the deets on my books—the rest of my Mythmatched tales, my other paranormal rom-coms and mysteries, my contemporary romances, and my one lone historical. If you're an audio fan, you can find the audio scoop there too. The Supernatural Selection trilogy, for instance, is narrated by the wonderful Greg Boudreaux. (The QR code on the next page will get you there with your smartphone camera or other code reader.)

My newsletter is the place to get the latest dish on new releases, sales, and more. I promise I only send one out when I've got...well...news. You can subscribe here: https://ejrussell.com/newsletter.

All my best,
—E

Also by

ej

Paranormal Romance
Mythmatched Universe
Fae Out of Water Trilogy
Cutie and the Beast
The Druid Next Door
Bad Boy's Bard

Supernatural Selection Trilogy
Single White Incubus
Vampire With Benefits
Demon on the Down-Low

Other Mythmatched Romances
Howling on Hold
Possession in Session
Witch Under Wraps
Cursed is the Worst
The Skinny on Djinni
Assassin by Accident (part of Carnival of Mysteries)

Mythmatched Companion Stories
Rusty's Really Bad Day (free to newsletter subscribers)
Second First Date (free to newsletter subscribers)
First Flight (free to newsletter subscribers)

Quest Investigations Mysteries
Five Dead Herrings
The Hound of the Burgervilles
The Lady Under the Lake

Death on Denial

At Odds with the Gods (A Mythmatched/Purgatory Playhouse crossover)

Art Medium Series
The Artist's Touch
Tested in Fire
Art Medium: The Complete Collection (omnibus edition)

Legend Tripping Series
Stumptown Spirits
Wolf's Clothing

Enchanted Occasions Series
Best Beast
Nudging Fate
Devouring Flame

Royal Powers Series (shared world)
Duking It Out
Duke the Hall
King's Ex

Magic Emporium Series (shared world)
Purgatory Playhouse

Science Fiction
Sun, Moon, and Stars Series
Partnership
Principles

Interdimensional Time Bureau
Monster Till Midnight

Historical Romance
Silent Sin

Contemporary Romance
Camera Shy
Summer Kitchen
The Thomas Flair
Mystic Man
For a Good Time, Call... (A Bluewater Bay novel, with Anne Tenino)

Christmas Kisses (holiday shorts)
The Probability of Mistletoe
An Everyday Hero
A Swants Soiree

Geeklandia Series
The Boyfriend Algorithm (M/F)
Clickbait

Writing as Nelle Heran
(traditional cozy mystery)

Crafty Sleuth Series (with C.K. Eastland)
Die Cut
Mixed Media
Found Objects (*coming soon*)

About the
Author

E.J. Russell (she/her), author of the award-winning Mythmatched paranormal romance series, writes LGBTQ+ romance and mystery in a rainbow of flavors. Count on high snark, low angst, and happy endings.

Reality? Eh, not so much.

She's married to Curmudgeonly Husband, a man who cares even less about sports than she does. Luckily, C.H. also loves to cook, or all three of their children (Lovely Daughter and Darling Sons A and B) would have survived on nothing but Cheerios, beef jerky, and Satsuma mandarins (the extent of E.J.'s culinary skill set).

E.J. also writes traditional cozy mystery as Nelle Heran. She lives in rural Oregon, enjoys visits from her wonderful adult children, and indulges in good books, red wine, and the occasional hyperbole.

News & Social Media:
Website: https://ejrussell.com
Ream: https://reamstories.com/ejr
Newsletter: https://ejrussell.com/newsletter

Acknowledgements

Thank you to the Riptide team who first brought this series to light: Rachel Haimowitz, Carole-ann Galloway, Kelly Miller, Alex Whitehall, Grace Stack, and of course L.C. Chase (who's turned out so many lovely covers for me).

Thanks to my family—Jim, Hana, Nick, Ross, and Billy—for support, encouragement, and not rolling their eyes (too much) when I announce another book release.

Lastly, a huge, heartfelt thank you to my readers, who have embraced the stories in my Mythmatched universe, and even (*squee* really?) asked for more. You rock! <3